Partners in Crime

PARTNERS iN CRIME

A NOVEL

ALISHA RAI

AVON

An Imprint of HarperCollinsPublishers

P.S.™ is a trademark of HarperCollins Publishers.

PARTNERS IN CRIME. Copyright © 2022 by Alisha Rai. All rights reserved. Printed in the United States of America. No part of this book may be used or reproduced in any manner whatsoever without written permission except in the case of brief quotations embodied in critical articles and reviews. For information, address HarperCollins Publishers, 195 Broadway, New York, NY 10007.

HarperCollins books may be purchased for educational, business, or sales promotional use. For information, please email the Special Markets Department at SPsales@harpercollins.com.

FIRST EDITION

Designed by Diahann Sturge

Prologue illustrations by Chloe Friedlein

Library of Congress Cataloging-in-Publication Data has been applied for.

ISBN 978-0-06-311946-8 (paperback)
ISBN 978-0-06-321273-2 (hardcover library edition)

22 23 24 25 26 LSC 10 9 8 7 6 5 4 3 2 1

For my husband of approximately nine
days (as of the date of publication):
The first thing I asked you was how you felt
about sharing your french fries.
Now I legally own fifty percent of them for life.
Marriage lesson #1: never underestimate
how far I'll go for french fries.
(I love you and I can't wait to see what the future holds for us.)

Partners in Crime

Naveen 34

👊 Lawyer
🏯 Artesia, CA
📍 12 miles away

Signed up so I could delete this thing.

Don't care how tall you are, what you look like, what you do for work, or whether you can make a round roti so long as we click.

Job ✔
Car ✔
Books ✔
You?

Just looking for someone to adopt a dog with sooner rather than later. I'm not getting any younger.

Amira Patel <Mira@gmail.com>
to MatchmakerHema

Dear Hema Auntie,

I understand your frustration with me. I, too, am sorry that none of the people in the last batch suited me.

I know you think I'm being too picky, but as I told you, I know what I want, and none of these men are it. Skydiving? Flying to Paris on a whim? The last one kept going on and on about wanting a *partner in crime*, until I informed him I was looking purely for a partner in legal activities. I cannot have someone who relies that strongly on silly clichés. It's a turnoff.

Looking forward to the next profiles you send over.

Mira

Chapter One

Her matchmaker was going to fire her.

Mira Patel dabbed her napkin at the corner of her lips and placed it neatly next to her empty plate. "Can you please repeat that?"

Her lunch date folded his hands together. "I think we should break up."

She exhaled, long and low, releasing all her breath down to her toes. That's what she'd thought he'd said.

Correction. Her matchmaker was going to *murder* her. "I see."

"I'm so sorry. I talked it over with my mom, and while these past few months have been nice, she just doesn't believe we're compatible." Jay gave her a sheepish look. He was a handsome man, with a shiny shaved head, solid shoulders, and kind eyes. *Physically attractive to me (conventional or not)* had been on her list. There was no grand passion when they touched or anything, but the sex had been satisfactory, with little to no cuddling afterward. Which was fine! Passion wasn't on her list, and neither was cuddling. Actually, she wasn't sure if she knew how to handle either anymore.

She looked out the window at the traffic on Melrose. They'd gotten a good table at one of the best restaurants in Los Angeles. Perfect to see and be seen, though Mira was that rare breed of Angeleno who didn't need to be noticed. "Your mom doesn't think we're compatible," she parroted.

"Right."

"I haven't met your mom yet." It had only been three months, they hadn't gotten to that step. Hema Auntie was a relatively modern kind of matchmaker, and she advised her clients to spend a couple months getting to know one another before bringing parents in. Partner, families, wedding, that was the correct order.

"I've told her about you. As did Hema Auntie, of course, and she has all your information from your biodata. She was concerned from the beginning, but then she ran our star charts. Apparently, Hema Auntie input our information wrong when she had her astrologer look at us."

"An understandable clerical error," she murmured. More like, Hema Auntie was eager to get Mira off her books and she'd fudged the astrology results.

If Mira believed in horoscopes and birth charts, she would have told everyone that hers was doomed from the start. She'd totally made up her birth time. It wasn't like she had a parent she could ask.

A waiter interrupted them to place a plate in front of her, topped with a beautiful frothy white cake. "I took the liberty of ordering dessert for you while you were in the rest-room," Jay murmured.

To make the rejection taste sweeter?

She thanked the waiter, then lightly scraped the raspber-ries off the delicate cake. Berries made her throat itch. "Is this dairy free?"

"It is not, ma'am."

"Oh, sorry, I forgot about your allergy."

Of course he had. She put down her spoon. "Can I ask why your mother was concerned from the beginning?"

Jay grimaced. "I—it's not really important."

"No, I'd love to know." Without too much conceit, she could say she checked the main boxes for most Desi grooms' mothers: attractive without being flashy, well educated, had a good, yet boring job that wouldn't overshadow their son, sensible, respectful. The fact that she was so unassuming and unobjectionable was probably the reason Hema had kept her for a client for as long as she had.

"Well . . . she felt your background was rather mysteri-ous." He hurried to add, "Of course, Hema Auntie wouldn't take on a client who wasn't from a good family."

Unless the client was a family friend of people who had paid her the big bucks twice over already.

Under the table, she curled her hand into a fist. There was that one box she'd never be able to check: *from a good family.* "Not mysterious at all. My parents passed away and I have no siblings. I—"

"Have an aunt who leads a nonprofit focused on educating

young women in underserved areas of the world, so you don't see her very often," Jay finished. "I know. So you've said."

She caught the hint of suspicion in his eyes and clenched her fist tighter. Oops. She'd grown too accustomed to the story. It had become rehearsed, and no one believed you when you got too comfortable. "*Had* an aunt," she said softly. "She passed away last month, remember?"

He had the grace to look uncomfortable. "Apologies. I forgot. You didn't seem that close."

"We were close." Just because they'd talked only a couple times a year didn't mean she hadn't loved and grieved her aunt.

Jay had been out of town that week. She'd cried herself to sleep the first night after she'd gotten the call from some authorities in Mexico. She'd cried again a few days later when they'd shipped her aunt's ashes to her, and again that evening when she'd laid her to rest, all by herself. By the time she'd picked Jay up at LAX, she'd been cried out, and even more grimly determined to focus on her future.

This is how you get thanked for picking a man up at LAX at rush hour a couple months into a relationship. For future reference, that is fiancée/wife behavior only.

"I'm sorry," he repeated.

She wished she could eat a giant bite of this allergy-ridden cake.

"I like you. It's . . . my parents."

"And the only thing that matters is what your family thinks of me?"

He cocked his head, confusion flitting across his face. "I mean, it's very important. You knew that about me."

Yeah. That had been in his profile. What did she want from him, to buck his whole family for her?

Yes.

Mentally, she slapped herself. Thirteen-year-old Mira could dream of a man who did that sort of thing. Thirty-five-year-old Mira understood the value of thinking with your head over your heart.

"I didn't want to waste your time, or mine."

"I understand," she said, and drew her composure tighter around her. No scenes here. "Thank you for informing me."

He placed his napkin on the table. "I can let Hema Auntie know, if you like."

Could she block the woman's calls? No, that wouldn't stop her. Hema would carrier pigeon a pink slip to Mira. "Sure." She straightened. "Can you make sure to tell her it was your idea?" Not that that would matter.

"Oh. Yes." Jay adjusted his tie. "She did let it slip that you've had a number of failed matches over the years. That may have also swayed my parents. My mom doesn't want a picky daughter-in-law."

Damn it, Hema. Clearly her impatience with Mira messing up her perfect track record had come ahead of her business sense.

Mira took a sip of her water. She wasn't about to litigate her failed romantic history with someone who was now a footnote in it. "Sure."

Jay stood. "Goodbye, Mira. Good luck."

"You too."

The waiter came by a couple minutes later and cleared his throat. Mira wondered how many breakups he'd seen. Probably none as bloodless as this one. Mira nodded. "I don't suppose he paid already?"

"Sadly, no, ma'am."

She handed him her credit card and passed the time before she left picking at the smashed remnants of the outrageously expensive cake she'd bought and couldn't eat.

She walked outside and turned her face up to the sky, letting the spring sun caress her face as she waited for her car. The deep ache of failure threatened to embrace her, and she had to consciously beat it back.

The valet brought her car around. She drove around the block, to the public library, and parked in the garage.

Her scream wasn't high-pitched, but a guttural exclamation of frustration. She did it again, and again, until she'd released some of the emotions inside her. Like a bloodletting, but less gross.

One by one, she uncurled her fingers from around the steering wheel, and fished her phone out of the pocket on her skirt. Mira didn't fuck with clothes that didn't have pockets. There was no telling what one might need at any given time, like a lifeline to a friend.

The phone rang. "Come on, come on," she muttered.

Finally, her best friend's pretty, smiling face filled the screen. "Hey, are you having—"

"Jay dumped me."

Christine cocked her head, her blue-black blunt-cut hair brushing her shoulder. She wore a large red and orange cotton nightgown. She and her husband were visiting her extended family in India, but she'd worn those colorful nighties for as long as Mira had known her, since their first night of college, when they'd been matched together as roommates. "That asshole," she said immediately, which made Mira feel better. "Why?"

Because I don't come from a good family. Because no matter how I pretend, your family isn't mine. "It's a moot point."

A throat cleared, and Christine's husband, Ted, moved into the frame. His nose was sunburned and peeling, but he looked happy. "Hi, Mira."

At first glance, they made an odd couple. Christine held herself with confidence that bordered on arrogance, while Ted was meek. Christine looked like she'd stepped off a runway in Paris, tall and angular, with a strong stubborn jaw and gleaming dark-brown skin; Ted was pale and freckled and looked like he'd stepped off the cover of the *Journal of Accountancy* . . . which was, actually, his favorite journal.

"Hi, Ted," she said dutifully. It wasn't that she didn't like Ted, she did. They had a lot in common, and even worked at the same accounting firm. In fact, Christine had met Ted at one of Mira's company parties.

They were both rather awkward people. Talking to each other, with or without Christine there, beyond pleasantries was . . . difficult.

Ted peered at the phone. "Are you okay?"

"Totally okay."

"She's not okay. She got dumped."

"Oh, I'm so sorry to hear that, Mira."

Christine gave her husband a fond glance. "I'm thirsty, honey. Can you please get me some water? And a sandwich."

Ted immediately nodded. "Of course."

Christine waited for a moment, then leaned in close. "He's been shoving water at me every minute since we found out about the pregnancy."

"That's nice," Mira murmured. Why couldn't she have it as easy as Christine? Her friend had met someone, dated him for a year, and now he was hydrating their future child.

"I'm sorry, honey. I know you were tentatively into this guy, at least."

Mira watched a girl skip toward the library, holding her mom's hand. "It's the nature of this game. You can't reject a dozen men and not have one reject you."

"He's clearly a fool," Christine said loyally.

"You think so?"

"The biggest. You are a precious perfect jewel, and he's a slimy slug that got caught in some bubblegum on the floor of a movie theater. I'm sure he was riddled with red flags."

Her lips curved up, her spirits rising, too. "He *was* too rich."

Christine raised an eyebrow. "Oh, no. Not that."

She huffed out a strangled laugh.

"Now I'm glad I never met him. I would have hated him and had to agonize over whether to tell you. Saved us all some agitation."

"Mmm." Christine probably would have hated Jay, but she'd only really liked one of the men Hema had sent Mira's way. Not surprisingly, that had been the only breakup where Christine hadn't unequivocally been on Mira's side. Both because Christine liked the guy, and because Mira's "it's not you, it's me" text after meeting the man's family hadn't been her most mature move.

"What you're going to do is you're going to pull out that spreadsheet of yours and add *NO J NAMES* to your list of requirements. Especially when his name is literally a J. Tell Hema that."

Mira inhaled. "Speaking of, that's kind of why I called you. All I could think about was how upset Hema would be."

Christine leaned back on her bed. The fan turning overhead cast shadows in the dim lights that lit her room in her grandmother's house. "Your first thought after being dumped by a man you were evaluating for marriage was over whether or not you'd disappoint your matchmaker?" Her brow relaxed. "Well, I suppose that's good. It doesn't sound like you're heartbroken."

In order to be heartbroken, the heart had to be engaged, and that wasn't something Mira got close to doing these days. "No. Not heartbroken. Not over Jay. But this may be the last straw for Hema where I'm concerned."

"He turned you down, though!"

And she trusted Jay to admit to that, but it wouldn't make a material difference. "I don't think she'll care. Your family vouched for me with Hema Auntie, so please tell your parents how sorry I am." Christine hadn't needed a matchmaker, but both of her younger sisters had used the infamous older woman's services. Mira had attended their big weddings in Chennai. They'd glowed with happiness and gushed over their diminutive guest of honor, the matchmaker who had paired them with their life mates.

Mira had wanted that. She'd craved it, with every fiber of her being. Not the big fancy wedding, but everything else.

Christine made a dismissive sound. "My parents don't care. And neither do I. We only care about you."

Mira looked away, so she wouldn't have to look into her friend's too-understanding eyes. "When are you coming home again?"

"In two weeks, and we'll go out on a dairy-free ice cream binge."

She blinked rapidly. She must have an eyelash in her eye. "I told you I'm fine."

"And I told you you're not okay."

Mira's gaze drew back to the phone. She gave a low, shaky exhale. "I swear I wasn't in love with him or anything."

"You were in love with the possibility." Her tone was soft. "You've had a rough year, Mira. Go easy on yourself."

Mira bit the inside of her cheek. Christine was one of the few people in her life who knew everything about her, including her past and the recent losses she'd had to deal with. One of those losses hadn't affected her much. The other had.

Her nose twitched.

"Mira? What's wrong?"

She wished she could verbalize at least a fraction of the feelings tumbling inside her. Usually she could temper and bury those emotions, but she was raw today.

I'm sad my aunt died, and guilty over how distant our relationship was.

I'm worried because I'm about to lose one major resource to finding what you have when Hema declares me unmatchable.

I'm tired of going home alone.

Am I a mess?

I really wish that cake I paid $35 for had been dairy-free.

She opened her mouth, but none of that came out, because her phone beeped, signaling another call. Not Hema, thank God. An unknown California caller, but that was common when she had her office number set up to forward during lunch. She was a senior accountant at her firm, and occasionally there were emergencies. "I have to go, I think I'm getting a work call."

Christine nodded. She was in fashion, and very much valued a strong work ethic. "I'll call you in the morning. We're going to go shopping, and I want to buy a few dresses for you."

Mira didn't care about new clothes, but Christine would dress her whether she participated or not, and she wanted to see her friend again. "Sure. Get some rest."

"Love you."

"I love you, too." Mira answered the other line, changing her tone so she sounded less like a single Pringle and more like a certified professional who could be trusted with financial data. "This is Amira Patel. Can I help you?"

There was a pause on the other end, and then a young woman spoke. "I'm looking for Mira Chaudhary?"

Mira stiffened, forgetting all about the footnote she'd just been dumped by and her dismal love life.

Mira Chaudhary.

There was a name she hadn't heard in a while. It was a name that filled her with dread and anxiety and memories she didn't want. "Can I ask who's calling?"

"My name's Aparna, I'm calling from Ambedkar Law."

"And what is this regarding?" Her tone wasn't well modulated now, it was sharp. She often dealt with law firms through her work, but none of them knew the name she'd left behind when she'd fled her family and Nevada at eighteen.

The woman paused, and her tone grew more somber. "This is regarding Rhea Chaudhary's estate. Is this Mira Chaudhary?"

Mira placed the phone on her lap and pressed her hands to her warm cheeks. "Yes," she whispered.

"I apologize for taking so long to reach you, but there was some mix-up, and it took me time to track you down. We're so sorry for your loss."

"Thank you," she replied automatically. "How did you find me?"

Aparna's voice turned wry. "I have excellent investigative skills."

She must. Mira hadn't gone hard underground when she'd left home, but she'd been fairly determined to get away from her dad.

Aparna continued to speak. "We'd like to speak with you about your aunt's estate. I can set up a video conference with her attorney at your convenience."

A video conference where she stared at some man recite her aunt's last wishes through a screen in her echoing apartment?

She squinted at her dashboard. She had a full tank and the rest of this sunny Friday off. "I'm in Los Angeles. Where are you? I can come to your office today, if her attorney has some free time." It might prick her feelings of grief, but dealing with her aunt's estate would be productive, at least.

And it might make her feel like she was doing something for the woman, assuaging some of her guilt. That might be nice.

"Certainly. We'll fit you in if you can come before four.

We're in Artesia." The woman rattled off an address, which Mira input into her phone—Artesia was far by Los Angeles standards, but Mira was no stranger to distance. "Thank you. I'll see you in about an hour."

Before leaving the parking garage, she flipped her mirror down and checked her reflection. Her hair was neatly twisted up and there wasn't a strand out of place. No wrinkles dared to mar her clothes. Her lipstick was still within the lines of her lips, though she'd eaten two courses of internationally acclaimed food.

She closed her eyes for a second. In her mind, she visualized each of her emotions. Sadness, regret, loneliness, fear. They were bundles of throbbing pain wrapped in spikes. Careful of the spikes, she took each one and placed it in a jar, then stuck those jars on a high shelf, securing them in place. When she opened her eyes again, her brain was calm, ready to function. Hopefully, those feelings could stay up there long enough for her to settle her aunt's affairs properly.

Or forever. Forever would be extremely convenient as well.

Chapter Two

I'd like to buy you a house as a wedding present."

His attention finally caught on this otherwise mundane phone call, Naveen Desai rubbed the bridge of his nose and leaned back in his grandfather's chair. Never mind that the old man hadn't sat here in months now. It would always be his grandfather's chair, just as this remained his grandfather's scarred desk, and the sign on the door still said Ravi Ambedkar and Associates.

He fixed his phone where it was propped up on a set of legal books, so he could better see his mother's face. "A house, eh?"

His mother made an agreeable noise. She was backlit by the massive window in her high-rise office, which offered an impressive view of San Francisco. Her hair was loose, the streaks of gray at her temple framing her elegant face. "Yes."

"Not a condo," he clarified. "No shared walls, no HOA."

"A whole house."

"Where?"

"Where what?"

"Where will the house be? We're talking here in Artesia or Hollywood Hills or Malibu . . . ? Location makes a big difference in SoCal."

"Whatever you want."

"Can it have a pool?"

"Of course."

"Four bedrooms might be nice."

"You need some room to grow."

"And are you going to throw in the bride, or do I have to find her myself?"

She pursed her lips. They were painted the same nude shade she'd worn since he was a kid. "You're teasing me, aren't you?"

"A little." He slid over a stack of files. There was always a stack of files. His grandfather was a jack-of-all-trades kind of attorney, so on any given day, Naveen had to wrangle a kid's immigration status, mediate squabbling couples over prenups written on napkins, or dispense precious jewelry to sobbing heirs. It was, at least, way less boring than his former Big Law job at Miller-Lane. And despite the volume way less likely to lead to him becoming a functioning alcoholic.

His mother folded her arms over her chest. Her blunt, perfectly manicured nails tapped on her arm. "Naveen. I have about had it with you."

"I'm sorry, Mom. I'm kind of busy right now. Are hypothetical wedding presents the only reason you called?" He flipped open a folder.

"You're busy doing what? Driving yourself to exhaustion in exchange for being paid in biryani?"

He made a concentrated effort not to look at the mini-fridge in the corner. His grandfather had always had one in here. Naveen had only realized when he'd taken over the practice last year that the fridge was a necessity when you had a number of clients who brought food as payment. "You're the one who's always telling me to eat less takeout. I never have to worry about a home-cooked dinner."

"If you had a wife, you could have home-cooked meals at home."

Smooth, that was his mom. "That's rather sexist, Mom. Don't you want me to have a nice career girl? How's she going to come home from her nine-to-five and cook for us?"

"I'm not saying she would cook. You didn't ever see me cooking for your father, did you? No, but I managed the chef."

His smile was reluctant. While his father was alive, his mom had played the role of dutiful housewife, sitting at home with her Art History degree gathering dust. After his dad had died six years ago, his paternal uncles had quickly realized Shweta had a keen business mind and she'd stepped neatly into her late husband's shoes at the family hotel conglomerate. "I don't need a chef, and I don't need a wife. Don't worry about me."

His mother gave a loud, gusty sigh. "What did you do last weekend, Naveen?"

"I worked. I had three hearings this week."

"And what are you doing this weekend?"

"I'm working."

"And next weekend?"

"I see your point. But I'm fine. I find time for hobbies in between the work." *I just don't want to tell you about those hobbies, because then you'll really get worried about me.* "We're at a busy time right now at the office."

"Oh, I know all about that." Her chin jutted forward. "Your grandfather used to be this busy. The office always came first."

Naveen tried to think of his next words carefully, aware that his mom's relationship with his grandfather was a landmine of unsaid words and resentment. Ravi had been a distant father, and he'd never quite come around on the man his daughter had married. Naveen's grandma had kept the peace between everyone, but after she and his dad died, Ravi and Shweta had gotten entrenched in their bitterness. "I'm not him, and it's not like I have a ton of responsibilities I'm neglecting."

"You're neglecting your future!"

He'd walked right into that. "Relax, Mom."

"How am I supposed to relax? You're hiding in that dismal office, you spend most of your spare time taking care of your grandfather, and you have no marriage prospects on the horizon. What am I supposed to tell my friends when they ask me about you?"

Naveen picked up the will he was supposed to be reading. "Who cares what they think?"

She shook her head, her hair swinging. "You don't care because you don't live here, Naveen. I do."

He paused. His mother lived in a weird bubble, a Bay Area suburb that was populated by rich and powerful South Asian families, including his own aunts and uncles. Naveen's mom was powerful, but the gossips could be vicious. "I'm sorry, Mom," he said quietly. "I understand. You can tell them I'm making my own way in the world as a solo practitioner instead of killing myself to make someone else rich at that big law firm, and that I'm a good grandson who lovingly cares for your father—"

The door to his office was flung open without a knock. "I resent being referred to like I'm some invalid," his grandfather announced, in his big, booming voice.

"I didn't say that," Naveen said calmly.

His mother rolled her eyes, though she couldn't see her dad. "Not now, Baba." His mother's tone was impatient with her dad, but that was nothing new.

"Yes, now, if you're talking about me." Ajoba's wheelchair whirred as he entered the cramped office. The elder man's hair had been carefully combed, and his suit was sharp, though big on his skinny frame. His shoulders were stooped, but Ravi Ambedkar's eyes were nearly as sharp as they had been when he'd hung his shingle out to practice law in this town, almost sixty years prior.

Naveen had always had a connection with his gruff grandfather. It had been Ravi who had coached him into law school, Ravi who had consoled him over his failed engagement, Ravi who had showed up at his doorstep nineteen months ago and bluntly told him that his drinking was out of control, and Ravi who had arranged for his rehab.

So it wasn't a big deal for Naveen to move here to take over his grandfather's office after his Parkinson's diagnosis. The man had saved his life. Naveen could at least try to save the man's legacy.

"Not everything is about you," Shweta said, with exasperation. "I'm concerned for my youngest son, and the fact that he's single and will be alone forever in the middle of nowhere."

Ouch. "This isn't the middle of nowhere. I'm in Los Angeles County, Mom." Reluctantly, Naveen turned the phone so his mother and grandfather could see each other.

Ravi crossed his arms over his chest. "You ready for a bride now, Naveen? I can find you ten girls. Ten girls for every day of the week. You can interview them here."

His grandfather wasn't exaggerating. This office had been one of the first buildings on Pioneer Boulevard, a self-proclaimed Little India, and his grandpa had scratched everyone's back in this community. If any South Asians nearby had marriageable daughters, they'd send them immediately once they found out that Naveen was on the market.

They wouldn't be coming for him, though. They'd barely care who he was, as a person. He'd be Ravi Ambedkar's grandson, as he was Shweta Desai's son up north.

Or Kiran's little brother.

Nope. At the very least, most people knew not to say his brother's name around him anymore.

"He's not hiring a secretary, he's looking for a wife," his mother snapped. "It's quality, not quantity. Son, send me your current headshot and I'll spread the word. You're tall, you will have no problem."

That assurance was more for her than him. His slightly wild past and previous far too scandalous failed engagement did hamstring him a little in the upper-crust fishbowl his mom swam in. "I'm good, thank you for both your offers."

"Hema is eager to assist in any way she can," his mother said.

Naveen sat back, eager to put physical distance between that idea and him. "Um, no. I definitely do not want Hema Auntie's help."

"She has a hundred percent success rate!"

His grandfather guffawed. "That friend of yours has failed twice with Naveen already."

"An eventual hundred percent success rate," his mother corrected herself.

"She never matched Naveen, so it's at least ninety-nine percent."

"She matched Payal." His mother blinked, like she knew she'd uttered a name she wasn't supposed to.

Funny how Payal's name didn't hurt like it used to, though. That was good. Naveen opened his mouth, but no one cared what he had to say.

"How many women is she going to bring to reject Naveen on this round?"

Naveen rolled his eyes up, to stare at the ceiling. He'd developed a thick skin early with his grandfather.

His mom had not. She gasped. "Don't be rude to my son."

"I'm not being rude, I'm being honest. The boy has two failed engagements under his belt already, and he's barely in his midthirties. He needs to get it right this time or people are going to start to wonder if it's him."

"Technically it's one failed engagement," he murmured, though no one was listening to him. He'd allowed his mother's friend and neighbor exactly two chances during a moment of weakness a few years ago, and only because he'd grown up listening to Hema Auntie's glowing success stories. His first match had bolted for reasons he still didn't understand. The second had jilted him.

Neither had made him believe in Hema's hype.

"There are plenty of girls who will overlook Naveen's past once we explain the circumstances."

His grandfather opened his mouth, but Naveen cut him off, certain he was about to say something incendiary. "Actually, good news! I have a date tonight."

As expected, that shut both his elders up. His grandfather blotted his forehead with his ever-present embroidered handkerchief. His hand was shakier than usual, which caused Naveen some concern. "Really?"

"Yes, really," Naveen snapped. "I am quite capable of meeting women on my own."

"Well." Shweta paused. "Tell us about her."

"Not much to tell."

His mom's dark eyes narrowed, and she fiddled with the cuff of her blazer. "How old is she?"

"She's about my age."

"Job?"

"A lawyer as well."

"Local?" his grandfather asked hopefully. "I might know her family."

"Nope."

His mother steepled her hands under her chin. "How did you meet?"

Naveen shrugged. "An app."

"These dating app schmaps are not serious," his grandfather mused. "You're not taking her to one of your escape room things, are you?"

Naveen's ears grew red. He'd mentioned to his grandfather *one time* that he enjoyed escape rooms, and then had to spend an hour explaining what an escape room was. The man couldn't resist using every opportunity to tease him about it. "No."

"What on earth is an escape room?"

"Shweta, listen." Ravi sat forward in his chair. "The boy asks to be locked up in a room."

Shweta's eyebrows flew up, right to her hairline. "Oh no. Jana's son got into something like that." She lowered her voice to a whisper. "It's *perverse*."

He rubbed his temples. "It's not something weird, Mom."

"My friends were right, I should have made sure you had a strong man around after your father died to raise you well."

"Dad died when I was twenty-eight," he said, at the same time as Ravi exclaimed, "He had me!"

"If it's an addiction, we can discuss it, Naveen. You don't need to struggle like you did last time."

Naveen knew that he was incredibly lucky to have family who prioritized and cared about his mental health. He had many a friend whose immigrant parents and grandparents didn't check in with them as often.

Still, they were so clumsy about it. "It's not an addiction, and it's not anything to worry about. It's a game. You use clues to figure out puzzles and eventually how to get out of a locked room. Usually it's themed. Like a scavenger hunt. I went after rehab with a guy I became friends with there, Alan, and we've gone a couple times."

More than a couple times, but they didn't need to know that. There would only be more teasing and worrying.

His mother pressed her hand to her chest. "Oh. Okay. A game."

"He pays good money for this."

Shweta dismissed her father. "He won't have time for such silly hobbies once he's a husband and father. Back to this date."

Right. Your fictional date. "Why are you grilling me like you think I'm lying about her?"

"Because I can tell when you're lying, and I think you are."

Fair, because he was.

Before he could speak, his grandfather jumped to his rescue. "Leave the boy alone, Shweta. Let him have his date."

His mother subsided. "Very well. I will still buy you a house if you get married without my help, you know."

Ajoba rolled his eyes and wheeled his way to the fridge. "You're bribing the boy, now, Shweta? Is that how they do it in your husband's family?"

Naveen tensed. "Ajoba. That's my family, too." He might have issues with individual members of his family nowadays, but he still loved his late father.

His grandfather had the grace to look shamefaced. "Of course, of course. You know what I meant."

Most parents would love their kids to marry wealthy, but Ravi came from more humble beginnings and he'd been suspicious of the Desais from the minute Shweta had eloped with his dad. Not even his daughter's happiness with the man had changed his mind.

And they had been happy. They'd been so nauseatingly in love—well, nauseating for their sons—that it may have given Naveen unrealistic expectations of how marriage worked. Which was probably one of the many reasons he was still single.

"It's a token of love and congratulations, Baba. You wouldn't know about that, I suppose."

Naveen rubbed the back of his neck. "I don't need a house, Mom. I was joking. I'm perfectly happy living in Ajoba's in-law apartment for now." The studio apartment had once been a garage, but it had been converted into an additional dwelling unit, complete with a tiny kitchenette. Which he barely used, thanks to the aforementioned minifridge that Ajoba was rummaging through.

"My grandson doesn't require all the fancy things that you do." Ajoba pulled out a Thums Up soda bottle that the grocer next door had dropped off as part of his thanks for helping with a parking ticket.

His mom, thankfully, ignored the dig. "I just bought your brother a plot of land near our house. It would only be fair."

Her words were deliberately casual, but they landed with the force of a bomb. The only sound in the room was the clock ticking on the wall.

"I don't want anything that Kiran has," Naveen finally said quietly.

"It's been a long time," Ajoba observed.

Naveen rubbed the side of his nose. Here was probably the one thing that his parent and grandparent were united over: reconciling him and Kiran. "Not long enough."

"He misses you," Shweta added.

"He said that?"

"Of course he did."

He shot his mother a wry look. "Now who's the one who's lying?"

His mother's nostrils flared. "I can read between the lines."

Ajoba took a sip of his soda. "He betrayed you. I understand your anger. But he's your brother and always will be."

"I'm tired of having two family group chats, one with you and one with him." His mother raked her fingers through her hair, messing up her blowout. "I need you to speak with him, Naveen. He's reached out to you so many times."

There were two group chats? What good morning forwards was he missing in the other one? "Is that what he told you? That he's reached out to me repeatedly?"

"I know he has. He came to see you in rehab, and you turned him away."

"That was it. That's not many times."

"He always asks about you."

"He calls me to check in on you as well," Ajoba said. "He says he doesn't want to bother you by harassing you over the phone."

"But you can call him. He really wants you to call him." Shweta looked down. "It would break your father's heart to know his sons haven't spoken in two years."

Ouch. Low blow, because he knew she was right.

He'd thought about calling Kiran over the years, but something always stopped him. He simply could not imagine what the conversation would sound like, or what they would say.

And then, there was the anger. The terrible anger that made him feel wild and out of control.

He didn't like to feel those deep wells of emotions. They could lead down dark, dangerous paths, and the last thing he ever wanted to do was fall off the wagon he'd painstakingly climbed atop. "I can't believe either of you. Aren't you two on my side?"

"Of course, my boy," his grandfather said. "I am always on your side. But he is my grandson, too, and he hates how he hurt you."

Naveen rubbed the side of his nose. "He should have thought about that before he did what he did."

A curly-headed woman popped into the room, gamine face curious. "Before who did what?"

"Nothing," Naveen said, grateful for the interruption. He deliberately lightened his tone. *Keep it light, keep it happy.* "Are you here to join this family meeting to harangue me into getting married too, Aparna?"

"Hello, Aparna," his mother said over the phone. He hated how subdued she sounded, but he was too wound up to comfort her right now.

"Hello, Auntie," his cousin said cheerfully. "Nope, not a harangue in sight. I wanted to tell you Ms. Chaudhary is here, and I've put her in the conference room."

Naveen glanced at his watch. "She's early." And he hadn't had a chance to fully look over her file.

"Who is here to see you?" Ajoba demanded.

"The heir to Rhea Chaudhary's estate. Took me a while to track her down. She changed her name, it seems," Aparna filled in. She was his mom's cousin's kid, but he called her cousin as well. She was a few years older than Naveen and also lived next door to their grandfather, though in her own house. She had boy-mom energy, and was, indeed, a single mom to a sweet five-year-old. She was also their resident private investigator, notary, and entire administrative staff.

"Oh." Ajoba narrowed his eyes, and Naveen could tell he was searching the files in his brain and coming up empty. "I . . . I don't recall."

His grandfather hated not remembering anything, and it happened more often now. "It's a small case. You took Rhea on a year or so ago. Looks like you never even met her face-to-face." Naveen had already come on board by then, but his grandfather had still been in the office. It was only when Ravi had started to forget important details that he'd taken a giant step back. His grandpa was proud, but he was also self-aware and didn't want to mess with malpractice. "Anyway, the niece was in the area. She preferred coming in. It'll make things easier."

Shweta shifted. "Very well. I have to get to a meeting. You'll call me tonight to tell me how this date went?"

"If it's not too late."

"Goodbye, Naveen, Aparna." His mom paused. "Baba."

Ajoba inclined his head. "Shweta."

Aparna leaned over the back of his wheelchair. "Would you like me to take you home, Ajoba?"

"I should meet this client. My name's on the door, still." His hand shook when he raised the bottle to his lips to drain it.

He could see the obvious fatigue in his grandpa's eyes. Getting dressed and coming into the office, with his nurse's assistance or not, was becoming more and more arduous for the man. "No, go on home." Naveen slapped the file shut. "This is an easy one, and I'd like some time to get ready for my date after." Luckily, he had plans tomorrow—yes, another escape room with Alan and some new guys—so he'd already intended to stay late at the office today to catch up on work.

Grabbing some dinner at one of the many restaurants down the street and eating his naan and chicken tikka at his desk while he drafted prenups might not be the date his family thought he was out on, but at least it was a peaceful one.

"Fine," Ajoba grumbled. "Stay out late tonight. I remember the first time I met your grandmother, we were up until three A.M., though we had school the next day."

Naveen swallowed, tasting his lie more now. "Let's not get ahead of ourselves."

"You're a good boy, Naveen. I want everything for you." His grandfather opened his mouth, like he wanted to say something else, but then gestured to Aparna to take him home.

Naveen looked down to hide his mixed emotions as his cousin and grandfather left. He had only experienced that sort of helpless fascination with a woman once or twice in his life. Part of him, a big part of him, longed for it now. Another part of him, the part that was clearly winning out, would rather get takeout and draft a prenup.

Don't think about that or your brother. You still have work to do.

He took a minute to finger comb his hair in the mirror on the wall, then walked quickly to their small conference room, trying to speed-read the Chaudhary client's file. Died out of the country; one heir, a niece; only a small envelope of assets to pass on. He fixed an appropriately somber expression on his face, then entered the room. "Ms. Chaudhary, I'm so sorry to keep you waiting, and for your loss—"

He broke off when the woman standing in front of the window turned to face him. She was beautiful, with big dark eyes and a couple of escaped curls that surrounded her sweet round face. Her body was curves on curves, packaged tidily away. She wore a knee-length black skirt that hugged her hips and a pink silk shirt with a frivolous pussy bow tied at the throat. Delicate pearl buttons ran all the way down the front.

Naveen had undone those buttons once, one pearl at a time.

He'd traced her honey-brown skin with his hands, his lips, his tongue. He'd stroked her until she writhed with need under him, her body soft and supple under his. He'd kissed tears of passion away from her cheeks, and nibbled her earlobe to make her smile. It might have been three years ago, and she might have changed, physically—she was curvier, her cheeks rounder, her makeup more discreet, her hair pulled back into a knot instead of ruthlessly straightened and short—but there were some people you didn't forget.

Especially when they made you believe in a happy ending, then shut it down in a single instant.

Her throat worked, her gaze caught on his. "You?" she breathed.

He snapped his file closed. "Amira. Long time no talk." He paused. "Or should I say, text."

Chapter Three

What. The fuck. Was happening.

Was this karma? Or a drawn-out cosmic joke? Had someone in the universe decided today was Mess With Mira Day?

There was no other explanation for why she was coming face-to-face with the very first Hema Auntie–approved match she'd rejected, right on the heels of Hema Auntie's last match rejecting her.

Not just your first match, the first match you brutally dumped. Text-gate.

She'd done a good job of banishing her father's voice from her head, but he whispered now. *The problem is, Mira, you freeze and you hesitate. Your brain always needs to be faster than your body.*

He wasn't wrong. Only a minute had passed since Naveen had entered the room, but it was far too long of a minute. She checked those glass containers where she'd bottled up her emotions, made sure they were secure, and lifted her chin. Running into an ex right now might be bad timing, but she could fake composure and pretend like she belonged. She was good at that. "Naveen. What are you doing here?"

He kicked the door closed behind him, never taking his gaze off her. She catalogued the changes in him as quickly as possible. His body had filled out in the three years since they'd dated, but his face had grown slimmer. His shoulders were broad, his head barely clearing the door. His hair was longer. The soft curls fell over his forehead with boyish charm, a contrast to the rough planes of his face. Threads of silver glinted at his temples.

His hands flexed on his files. He wore a gold ring with a small square black gemstone. It was his father's ring, and his father's Rolex on his wrist. She'd helped him put that Rolex on more than once, after a night together.

They may have only been together for six months, but they'd had a lot of nights together.

She shivered. *Not now. Don't you dare think of those nights now.*

"I work here." He took a step toward her, and she took one back. The room already felt too small.

"You work at Miller-Lane." As a hotshot corporate attorney. He'd been busier and more ambitious than her, and that was saying something. Back then, she'd been determined to make senior status, and he'd been determined to make partner.

"I used to. Now I work here."

"Your name's not on the door."

He raised one thick eyebrow. At some point over the past

few years, he'd taken care of his faint unibrow. She hadn't minded it. It had given his face a brief reprieve from perfection.

"Ravi Ambedkar is my grandfather. This is his office. I'm handling his cases while he's out."

She vaguely recalled him speaking of his grandfather fondly. She hadn't met the man when they'd dated, but that was mostly because she'd usually traveled to see him up in San Francisco. The rest of his family had been up north, in an exclusive gated community. His mother's sprawling house had had two staircases, crystal chandeliers, and a piano nobody played. Talk about too rich.

Mira had sent her now infamous text driving away from that mansion. Good times.

The wheels that had stilled in her brain at the sight of him started to move, clumsy and squeaking. "Wait . . . are you my aunt's . . . attorney?"

"I am, now, I suppose." Naveen checked the file in his hands. "Your aunt became my grandfather's client over a year ago, when he was still active in the practice. He's basically retired now."

Again. What. The fuck. Was happening.

Mira glanced around the small room. It wasn't dirty or dingy, but she'd done enough forensic accounting work that she'd spent time in expensive law firms. This was a solo practice, geared toward the community it served. The waiting area had contained one worn couch and a tired armchair. The elevator was broken, with a sign on it in English,

Hindi, and Urdu, directing her to the stairs. This conference room had one window, and it was up high on the wall, no chance of a view possible.

Rhea would have never gone to a big law firm.

True. Rhea had never been about outward appearances. She'd parlayed what had been a small inheritance from Mira's grandparents into a well-funded nonprofit and lived comfortably off the relatively small salary she'd drawn from it. Meanwhile, Mira's dad, her younger brother, had turned that inheritance into a day at the blackjack tables.

But still, why *this* solo practitioner? What were the odds that of all the attorneys in the world—or even in California— her aunt would choose one Mira knew? "Why would she pick your grandfather?"

"He's been doing estates in this area for fifty years. If she wanted to support a local business, he'd be the first one she'd turn to."

"She wasn't even from here. Why would she care about supporting local businesses?"

He cast her a sideways glance. "Because the city doesn't want to recognize or promote this place as Little India and we've gotten a lot of press for our street dying out? If she cared at all about the culture, she probably wanted to help."

Plausible. Rhea Auntie had run a nonprofit and she'd always been fairly into supporting locals in their own community. This could be another one of those cosmic jokes. But still . . .

There was something her dad had liked to say, about how there were no coincidences.

Mira had told Rhea about Naveen. Her birthday had been the week after the breakup, and she'd been moping harder than she should have been as someone who, covered in head-to-toe stress hives, had sprinted away from the man. Rhea had called, as she always did on her birthday, and Mira had spilled her guts in a very un-Mira-like fashion.

Had she mentioned his name? Maybe his first name. Had she given any other identifying information? Enough for Rhea to track him down and give him her business years later?

For what purpose, to reunite you with your ex from beyond the grave? Absurd. She never even met Naveen when you dated him.

And unlike the rest of your family, she wasn't exactly a master manipulator.

So, what? It was all a coincidence? Fate was real? No way. "And you don't think that's weird?" she persisted.

He paused. "What I do find weird is that we dated for half a year, I introduced you to my family, we discussed marriage, and in all that time, I knew you as Amira Patel. Not Mira Chaudhary."

Ahhhh. In her shock, she'd forgotten the name he'd uttered when he walked into the room.

The silence stretched between them and he took another step. This time she didn't back away. "That's *so* weird, Mira. Isn't it?"

One syllable. She'd deliberately picked an alias that was one syllable off from the name she'd been called for the first eighteen years of her life. A lot of people had naturally shortened Amira to Mira, including Christine, before she'd learned about Mira's past.

So why did it send a shiver down her spine to hear Naveen utter her birth name?

"Patel is my mother's maiden name." True. "I go by that."

"And you go by a different *first* name, as well?"

Mira bit the inside of her cheek. "Yes."

His frown caused deep furrows between his eyebrows. "Huh."

"It's not that big of a deal."

"Isn't it? I'd say it is. I don't have an alias. No one I know does."

Behind her back, she clenched her hand into a fist. "My birth name was too long. Amira sounds more professional to my ears, and it was what my mom wanted to name me. Since she died when I was a baby, I figured I'd go all the way to honor her." She kept her voice and eyes steady.

He studied her for a long moment, then dropped his gaze to the file in his hand. "I see."

She cleared her throat and tried to forget her nagging feeling of something being wrong. She needed all her wits about her. Naveen's eyes were incisive, even more so than she remembered. "Given our past . . ."

"When you say our past, are you referring to the fact that

we've seen each other naked a bunch of times, or is this about the time you ran away from my bed while I was sleeping and texted me that it was over?"

She drew a short inhale through her nose. The repressed annoyance in his words was a tough pill to swallow, but she took it. "Both. Either."

Naveen gave a short, decisive nod. "Fair."

"Is there, perhaps, another attorney here who could handle these details?"

"Unfortunately, no."

That *unfortunately* carried a little too much regret on his part.

He shook his head, and slowly, the shock and annoyance in his face was masked by coolness. "I am sorry about your loss, though. I remember you saying you had only the one aunt. And apologies it took us some time to find you. We have a great investigator, but a name change can slow things down."

Working as long as she had with her father, she'd had access to the best identity forgers in the industry. They'd advised her to go with a completely different new name, but her objective at eighteen hadn't necessarily been hiding, it had been physical and emotional distance.

Hiding had apparently been a by-product, though. "Thank you for your condolences," she said stiffly. "And about the past—"

Naveen's chest expanded and he held up his hand, cutting

her off. "Let's not get into it, okay? You're here for a reason, and I am a professional, and we will get through this and go our separate ways. Deal?"

Get through this wasn't the attitude she wanted men to have about her, but could she blame him?

Not after your behavior. "Deal."

Naveen perused the papers he held. The dark blue blazer and pants he wore were as beautifully tailored and expensive as ever, but there was no tie, which she was grateful for. His ties had always wound up on her bedroom floor.

"It seems your aunt only communicated with my grandfather via phone when she made her will."

Mira nodded. "She mostly worked out of the country."

Naveen cleared his throat and moved to sit down at the small rectangular table. She sank into a seat opposite him. She felt like she'd entered a parallel topsy-turvy dimension, one where it was quite acceptable to sit across from your ex while they read your aunt's will.

You will get through this, as he so nicely put it, and then you will go home and have a nice scream into a pillow.

"Your aunt's estate is pretty simple. Other than a couple of charitable bequests, you are her only designated heir." Naveen shuffled some papers, and then went still. "But . . . I see you have a sister. Funny, I don't remember a sister."

Oh fuck. He didn't remember because she'd never spoken about Sejal.

"In fact"—Naveen ran his finger over his lip—"I distinctly remember you saying you had no siblings."

Whelp.

She folded her fingers together under the table. "We're estranged."

"Deeply, it seems, if you don't even count her as a sibling," Naveen murmured.

He's not your boyfriend or potential husband. His judgment doesn't matter at this point. "We haven't spoken much since she left home when I was fifteen." *Since she abandoned me.*

Naveen sucked his teeth. "I see."

"I don't talk about her to anyone," she couldn't help but say. Christine was the only one who knew about Sejal, and that was only because her older sister had shown up at their dorm when she was a sophomore. It had taken one quick conversation with her to understand Sejal had followed in their father's footsteps. Her sister had been shifty and paranoid, certain someone was after her for something she'd stolen.

Mira hadn't asked her who was chasing her or what was in her battered green duffel, she'd simply told her she could hide there for a few hours, but then she'd have to leave as soon as the danger was past. Sejal had gotten annoyed and left immediately. Good riddance, Mira had thought then.

Rhea Auntie had been their go-between, their way of knowing that the other was alive. She hadn't realized till this minute that with their aunt gone, so, too, was their mediator. "It's complicated."

"Sounds like it."

Mira tamped down the spurt of irritation that threatened

to pierce her calm facade. Naveen had only spoken of Kiran with love and given his brother a hearty hug the one time she'd met him. Kiran had stayed up late with them, telling her all about his younger brother's escapades, with great fondness. What did Naveen know about family betrayal?

"Do you know where she is? Her number?" Naveen persisted.

"No. And no." Rhea had always carefully avoided talking about Sejal or her dad during their biannual phone calls. "I'm sure you find that strange," she couldn't help but add.

An odd look flashed in his eyes. "Not at all. When you do estate matters, you get used to family squabbles."

Is it considered a squabble if your sister jetted at the first opportunity and left you behind even though she knew exactly what you'd go through?

"In any event, since the total sum of the estate is well below California's probate amount, I can dispense with everything now." He handed her a stapled sheaf of papers. "Here is a notarized copy of the will."

"Thank you." She accepted the papers, surprised by how few pages it was. A simple estate indeed. She flipped through them, but it was all boilerplate language. She wasn't sure what she was expecting. A note? Something personal?

She paused on the page detailing Rhea's savings account, which had contained a few thousand dollars at the time of writing. How kind of her aunt, but Mira was comfortable enough. She'd donate the money in her aunt's name.

He handed her a padded envelope. "She also left some things for you in here."

She reached inside the envelope, her fingers brushing against suede. The blue jewelry box was small, and when she opened it the dainty gold jhumkas winked up at her. "I remember these," she said, softly, and felt a pang in her chest. Rhea had often worn jhumka earrings, but these had been Mira's favorite.

Once when Mira had been in the third grade, her aunt had picked her up from school as a surprise the day she came into town. She'd felt so cool getting into Rhea Auntie's sleek red rental car. She'd touched Rhea's earrings when she'd bent over to buckle Mira in and asked if she could wear them. Her aunt had chuckled and told her they were too heavy for her ears. Had Rhea remembered?

She snapped the box closed and put it aside. Then she turned the envelope upside down, and examined the key that fell into the palm of her hand. HAPPY STORAGE the tag proclaimed. She couldn't help her exclamation. "Fuck."

Naveen cleared his throat. "A problem?"

"No. No problem." It was actually a problem, but one that didn't matter, because she wasn't going to deal with it. When she'd left her home at the age of eighteen, she'd made herself two promises: (1) she'd never see her father again, and (2) she'd never go back to Vegas.

She'd kept the first promise until the day he died. She wasn't about to break the second one by returning to her hometown, and that was what this key was coaxing her to do.

She pulled out the last item in the envelope, a folded piece of notebook paper. It said *Mira* on it.

She traced the letters. Her aunt's handwriting. She opened the envelope, trying not to tear the paper in her haste. This was what she'd hoped for. One last communication.

Dear Mira,

If you're reading this, I'm gone. I'm sorry if that was a harsh surprise for you.

I wish we could have kept in more contact, but I understood your desire to get away from everyone and everything that reminded you of your childhood. Please don't feel guilty that we didn't talk very much in recent years! The last thing I want you to do is live your life bogged down by things not said.

I love you so much. There. That's everything I want to say. You didn't have to say it, I knew you loved me.

Your father loved you too. I know you may be rolling your eyes right now, and I know how you felt about him, but he did. He wanted me to give you something. I didn't want to bother you with it before, but I left it for you in the usual place.

I hope you'll split the contents of your inheritance with your sister, if you can find Sejal, but that's on you. If you do speak to her, tell her I love her.

My greatest wish is for you both to be happy and free.

Sincerely,
Rhea

The words were so quintessentially her aunt—nonjudgmental, to the point, loving—that Mira had to choke back the lump that formed in her throat.

They were also, in true Chaudhary fashion, cryptic and coded. While her aunt may not have been in the illegitimate businesses her brother was, she'd been aware of some of what the man was up to. At the very least, it appeared she'd known of one of his hidey holes.

What inheritance?

"That's a storage locker key, I see." Naveen shuffled his notes. "We usually have an inventory for any storage lockers. There's nothing here. Or any receipts or instructions for payment. Where is it? We can see if we can get someone to clean it out for you."

She couldn't explain the significance of this key to Naveen. Not now. So she tucked it into the pocket of her skirt. "Don't worry about it. It doesn't matter. It's like an inside family joke."

Naveen shrugged. "Do you have any questions for me?"

Mira tried to focus on something other than the fact that one ghost from her past was sitting in her pocket and another in front of her. "What about her nonprofit? Is there anything I need to do with respect to her position there?"

"A nonprofit?"

"Yes." Mira couldn't help the pride in her voice. "She helped establish schools in rural areas all over the world."

"That's right. I remember you saying something about that."

That damned rehearsed spiel about her family.

You can revise it now that everyone is gone.

The sharp lance of grief was unexpected. She was usually much better at keeping those pesky emotions on the shelf, but she could be forgiven for the shakiness right now. A lot was going on.

Naveen flipped through the scribbled notes. "I'm unaware of her heading a nonprofit. She did, however, leave a couple thousand dollars to a charity working on research for Crohn's disease."

Her lips flattened. Her father had died of complications related to the disease.

"That is the only charity I see in—Oh wait. There's something here." He paused for a moment. "It looks like she did mention that she was recently retired."

She nodded, like she knew about her aunt retiring, but the woman had said nothing about that on their last call. "Of course," she murmured.

"One second, let me see if there's anything else."

She turned the jewelry box over in her hand while he read, then snapped it open and removed the earrings from the box. Better to put these on now instead of risking losing them.

She placed the post in her earlobe, but then, as always, the tiny gold unscrewed backing immediately slipped out of her hand and fell to the floor. "Damn it," she muttered, and pushed her chair back, scanning the brown carpet. Why did those buggers immediately disappear to the human eye the second they hit the ground?

"You okay?"

"Yeah, just lost the back of my earring."

Naveen pointed right under the table. "Is that it?"

"Where?" She slipped out of the chair and stood. She blinked when Naveen did the same, but knelt on the floor next to the table. "You don't have to do that."

He picked up something microscopic and shook his head. "Nope, only lint."

Awkwardly, she came to her hands and knees as well, unwilling to have him be the only one searching for her earring. "I'm sorry."

"My mom and cousins are always losing these. I swear, the gold is made to be slippery."

His mom and cousins. Not his wife or girlfriend.

Whoa, whoa, whoa. She did not care at all if this man was married twice over by now.

He's not wearing a ring, if he is.

She inspected the carpet like her life depended on it, patting her hands gently over the worn rough fibers.

"Wait, don't move."

"Huh?" She glanced up at him, startled when he crawled closer, and even more startled when he reached toward her face.

She didn't jerk away, though, not even when his thumb barely grazed her chin, even though it sent a shiver down her whole body. He was close enough that she could count every long eyelash, and see the beat of the pulse in his throat, exposed by the open collar of his sharp white shirt. He smelled like her favorite hot winter drink, cinnamon and nutmeg and everything nice.

His long, elegant fingers plucked something off the bow at the neck of her blouse and held it up. "Found it. Right in plain sight the whole time."

Mira took the gold backing from him, and tried to calm the ragged beat of her heart. Holy shit. She had to lick her dry lips. He was so big, and the area under the table was so small . . .

He must have registered the oddly intimate position they were in the same instant she did, because he jerked backward and came to his feet. She scrambled back as well. "Thank you," she muttered.

"No problem," he said, his tone deeper than normal.

Neither of them sat down. Mira quickly finished donning the earrings. She smoothed her skirt, carefully avoiding his gaze. *Do not blush. Do not. Cool thoughts.*

"Uh, any other questions?"

What is wrong with me? Mira shook her head. "No. I'm good."

"Great. Again, my condolences on your aunt." A clear dismissal.

That annoying key was heavy and too big in her pocket. She collected the papers he'd given her, folding the letter reverently and placing it in the envelope. "Thank you."

"Do you need your parking ticket validated?"

"No, the, uh, gate was up so I drove in."

He didn't look surprised by news of the broken garage attached to his office building. "Do you live nearby?"

"Alhambra."

He glanced out the window. "You're going to hit traffic."

"When do you not, in this city?" Yes, yes. They should absolutely talk about traffic. Traffic in L.A., haha, it was always so terrible.

And she could stop thinking of whatever weird feelings had sprung up during that odd moment they'd just shared.

"You should grab food before you head home." He clicked his pen and placed it in his jacket pocket.

Oh no.

Please don't ask, please don't ask, please don't . . .

If he asked her to eat, she'd have to say no. It was awkward enough to have a meal with an ex when he didn't know that she'd lied about who she was for the entirety of their relationship.

Now he knew, if not everything, far too much about her.

But think about how good he smells.

"There's a place that does great biryani like four doors down, and they have Wi-Fi. You could wait out the traffic there."

She released a gush of air, one so strong it made her feel light-headed. Not an ask. Just a polite suggestion from a local, one that any stranger would give another. "Thank you, but I had lunch right before I came here." She was glad she hadn't eaten the cake now, dairy or not, what with all the tumbling her stomach was doing.

He held the door open for her, and she walked past him, trying not to brush up against him. It was a futile attempt at distance though. Her elbow grazed his chest, and they both jumped at the slight tingle of static electricity that jumped between them. Or at least, she'd tell herself it was static.

She hadn't thought about Hema Auntie's imminent dumping for a minute, but now she wondered if it truly was a blessing in disguise. Perhaps a Mr. Right Now phase was something she could look into while she put her search for Mr. Right on hold. Clearly, her body's needs hadn't been attended to, if simply Naveen's tiny touch was setting her afire.

Naveen's touch + the memory of how good it had been between you physically.

They passed an office. It was empty, but she couldn't resist a quick peek inside. There were boxes and files everywhere. Big diplomas and newspaper clippings lined the wall. The print was too far for her to read on the latter, but it wasn't Naveen's name on the former. It also wasn't a place she'd expect him to feel comfortable in, with its big, old-fashioned furniture.

You don't know him enough to know where he'd feel comfortable. You nipped all the possibilities in the bud, remember?

She fixed a determined smile on her face. All Mira had to do was say goodbye to Naveen with utter politeness, then drive home and wait for Christine's time zone to line up so she could tell her about this bizarre encounter. Christine would 100 percent freak out over the coincidence of her ex-boyfriend being her aunt's attorney, and they could squeal together.

There are no coincidences.

She rubbed her forehead. She was quite accustomed to staring at numbers endlessly on a screen for days without so much as an ounce of strain, but the thought of getting back in her car right now had her head pounding.

"Well, Mira, it's been . . . Are you okay? You look warm."

"It's a little hot in here."

"Luckily, it's pretty cool outside."

She had to stifle an inappropriate laugh. She didn't think it was possible for him to say *get out* in a more diplomatic yet clear manner.

It was a far cry from the last time she'd said goodbye to him in person. They'd been at his family's home, and he'd snuck into the guest bedroom to be with her. As dawn had crept into the room, the anxiety tightening her chest had grown and grown until she'd feared she was having a heart attack. She'd pressed a light kiss against his slack, sleeping mouth, then slipped out of his arms and his bed. Hours later, when she sent a text at a gas station midway to Los Angeles, she'd slipped out of his life.

He held his hand out to her now. "Bye, Mira."

Could others brag of two former love interests bidding them adieu on the same day?

There were things she wanted to say, but it was all impossible to verbalize. So she merely nodded. "Goodbye." She grasped his hand and tried not to flinch at the slight shock that reverberated down her arm.

What is wrong with him? Christine had demanded, when Mira relayed the end of hers and Naveen's relationship.

Valid question. He'd been kind, attentive, funny, good in bed, ambitious, and the life of the party whenever they'd gone out. She'd looked ridiculous and demanding when she broke up with him. Hema Auntie had told her as much, too.

She'd given them concrete answers: he was too extroverted, he enjoyed partying more than her, he was a workaholic. Privately, she'd told herself she'd done it because she feared he sought excitement like her father had, and she craved a boring life.

But the real reason was that the tightness in her chest had eased the further she'd driven away from him, and resolved completely the second she'd sent that text.

And a hint of that tightness was back now, along with the buzzing chemistry that ran between them.

She almost turned around to give him one last glance, but the door closed behind her with a resounding thud.

She shook her head. There was no room for regret here. Naveen was a closed road, blocked since she broke it off, but especially barricaded now that he'd scratched the surface of her lies.

Why did you have to pick him as your attorney, Rhea Auntie?

Mira touched her earrings. She'd never know, she supposed.

Mira took the stairs down two at a time. In the lobby, she reached into her pocket and pulled out the storage key. She was going to be generous and assume Rhea hadn't known the full truth of what this key led to.

Her criminal father's safe house.

Well, Mira wasn't about to collect any more family baggage, literal or otherwise.

She walked over to the trash can next to the broken elevator. She held the key above the garbage, then paused. Her fingers caressed the worn metal of the key. Had her aunt touched this key?

It doesn't matter.

Mira tried to force herself to let go of the key, but couldn't quite do it. Instead, she pulled it off the annoyingly cheerful keychain and dropped the HAPPY STORAGE tag into the trash.

She'd throw the key away later, she told herself. Instead of wrestling with her keyring, she tucked the key inside her bra. It was far more secure there than it would be in her skirt's pockets.

The parking garage was quiet and empty, most of the tenants of this office building already gone. Her sensible low heels clipped on the concrete as she walked up to the second floor, as she fished her car keys out of her bag.

Later, she'd wonder how she'd been so foolish.

You should walk to your car with your keys ready. You shouldn't lower your head. All standard stuff taught in self-defense classes at the YMCA, and she'd been raised by a man obsessed with security.

The whisper-soft scrape of a shoe behind her was her first clue that she wasn't alone. Mira started to turn, but someone grabbed her from behind, and a hand slapped over her mouth before she could get more than a squeak out.

No freezing this time. Her instincts took over. She kicked, and her foot hit something soft. The person gave a grunt, and his arms tightened until she feared he might actually crush her. Only then did she still, though her heart was jackhammering, her brain screaming internally, curses that couldn't get past his hand.

"It's her," said her captor. "Definitely the Chaudhary girl."

"Hey!" The low, masculine shout came from far away. The man holding her swung around, which swung her around, and she nearly strangled on her own shock and distress. Naveen?

No, no, no. What was he doing here? Running straight toward a second masked man?

She renewed her struggles, but the man holding her barely seemed to notice, though she tried to use every pointy part of her body. Meanwhile, Naveen was grappling with the other attacker. The masked man feinted left, then punched her ex in the face hard. Naveen spun, his suit jacket flying open, and fell to the ground. The man pulled his foot back and kicked Naveen in the side, and her former boyfriend stilled.

No, no, no!

A tiny prick pinched her neck. She tried to turn her head, but it took less than a minute before it felt like she was moving through molasses. Her brain grew foggy, and so did her vision.

The last thing she saw was Naveen's fingertips twitching. Through the haze of drugs, a shot of relief ran through her. He wasn't dead.

The masked man standing above Naveen pulled out a gun, and her eyes closed, despair running through her.

"Take him with us, too," said her captor.

Not dead yet, anyway.

Chapter Four

Was he dead?

Naveen didn't think he was, but then again, he didn't have much previous experience being dead.

Cold damp air touched his face. Something wet dripped down his neck. He blinked his eyes open and immediately slammed them shut, wincing at the immediate resulting headache. He hadn't really ever had terrible hangovers, despite his excessive drinking in the past, but this felt like one.

He screwed his eyes shut, trying to sort through his most recent memories. No, there had been no alcohol. Amira—correction, Mira—had turned up, as beautiful as the day she'd dumped him.

I don't think this is going to work out. I'd like to break up. Thank you for the memories. Best, Mira.

Dumped him via that terrible text. Thank you for the memories? Who the hell said that? Or signed a text, unless they were grandparents.

He'd tried to hide his dismay about the breakup from his family, but hiding stuff had never been his jam. His mother and Hema Auntie had lectured him about being careful not to get too attached to someone until they were at least engaged. They revised that to married, after his next failed relationship. *Passionate disengagement* Hema Auntie called the courting stage. Something he wasn't good at.

But he'd thought he'd dealt with those emotions a long time ago. When she walked into his office, after the initial shock had worn off, he'd taken quick hold, determined to stay professional and not get lost in her eyes or her secrets.

That had been challenged when he'd plucked that earring off her shirt, he couldn't lie. It had been an automatic impulse to help her look for it, honed through years of helping his earring-wearing relatives search for the screw-on backings. It was only when he'd touched the silk of her shirt that he realized he'd fucked up. Reckless helpful instincts.

The space under that table had shrunk to nothing. All he could see was her big brown eyes, like melted chocolate. Mira was hard to read, but he had always been able to tell the temperature of her mood by her eyes. They darkened in passion, dilated in anger, lightened in joy.

Their last night together, they'd been satisfied, and he'd fallen asleep the same. Until he woke up to an empty bed and that text on his phone.

He hated that he was still angry and confused over her past behavior and current lies. So much so, he'd followed her out of his office. What he'd planned on saying to her, he wasn't sure. Maybe he would have invited her out to get a bite to eat so they could talk properly, so he could ask her what he'd done all those years ago to make her freeze him out. Except he didn't get the chance, because—

Naveen stiffened. The masked men.

That was the last thing he remembered. The pain in his head and face and ribs told him they'd fought.

Not a hangover, then.

His senses came alive in fragments, giving him pieces of a puzzle he had to put together. He raised his heavy eyelids, trying to blink his way into realization. The floor under his ass, the barely there lights that were somehow still too bright for him.

He tried to lift himself up, but his wrists were tied behind him with plastic zip ties. His ankles were bound too.

His breath puffed around the duct tape sealing his mouth shut, warming him despite the chill in the air and the dirty cement floor.

A bare bulb hanging from the ceiling illuminated his dismal surroundings. A small window let in a bit of reddish-purple light from the dying sun. A storeroom of some kind? If it was, it was for a place that had been deserted for some time. The walls were made of paneled wood, decaying and chipped. There were boxes piled high against the walls, but they were either empty or the contents didn't matter, because they were also covered in mold. The door was the most sturdy-looking thing in the room, and the four locks on it were shiny and new.

He rolled to his back and crunched up to a seated position, then scooched back to sit against the wall, the pain making him light-headed. He wasn't a side sleeper for a reason, and his on-fire hip and shoulder were protesting however many hours he'd been in that fetal position.

He didn't need to see the other guy to know that he'd lost this particular fight. The Naveen who had once gotten into bar brawls in college, drunk and short-tempered, was embarrassed for the middle-aged version of him.

A low groan came to his ears, and he stiffened, searching the shadowy areas behind the circle of light cast by the bulb. A lump lay on the floor. The lump moved, and he leaned forward, his breath coming faster. "Mira," he whispered, but the gag rendered him voiceless. It wasn't a question. Who else could it be? He'd clearly interrupted her kidnapping.

She rolled over, partially coming into the light. The shadows under her eyes were dark, her eyeliner smeared. Her long lashes resting on her plump cheeks made her look especially vulnerable. Her hands and feet were bound like his. Other than being unconscious, she didn't look injured, but he was no doctor. His mom had been right all along, he should have gone to med school instead of law school. Brief-writing skills were of no help right now.

He had no idea what had happened or what was going on, but everyone knew being taken to a second location was bad news, no matter why it had happened.

He kept one eye on Mira and twisted his wrists one way, then the other, but the plastic ties only tightened.

His breath came in rough pants as he surveyed the room again, this time searching out a tool to get these bindings off. The rickety table. Perhaps there was a pen or scissors in one of the drawers. Hell, he'd even take a stapler.

He rested his heels on the floor and tried to scoot like a very undignified inchworm. Brace the heels, slide. Brace the heels, slide.

Two feet were all he managed to cover before raised masculine voices from outside the door had him freezing.

"The boss is pissed."

"We did what we were told."

The other man's response was inaudible, but then he spoke louder, closer to the door separating them. "Let's get the information quick, so we can get the fuck out of here."

Naveen slid back to the wall, as the door opened and two men entered the room. No masks this time, but he bet these were the two who had grabbed them.

The first to enter had long black hair tied into a ponytail. He was a little taller than Naveen but far more muscular, built like a tank. His ruddy face looked like he'd taken a few punches over the years, his nose crooked and irregular. A colorful rattlesnake tattoo was visible on the back of the hand that held a big black gun. He wore a black leather overcoat and black jeans, and cut a sinister, hulking figure. This was the one Naveen had fought, given his size and the fresh bruise decorating his eye.

Good. At least Naveen wasn't the only one hurting. Even if he was the one hurting more.

The other man's skin was so pale his blond eyebrows were nearly invisible. The neat tan turtleneck, pressed black pants, and designer coat he was wearing was almost more threatening than the other guy's hired muscle aesthetic.

Naveen tried to calm his racing heart and focus clinically on their bodies and the way they held themselves. He might be able to fight them, but he needed at least one hand free. Or a foot. Anything.

The blond's eyes went to Naveen, and he nearly recoiled at how empty and cold they were. "The guy's awake." His voice was nasally, with a thick Brooklyn accent.

"We're supposed to talk to her first." The other man walked straight to Mira.

Naveen stiffened. He might not know who his ex was anymore, or why she'd lied to him about basic things like her family or name years ago, but he didn't want her hurt. "What do you want? Money? I can give you money. Don't bother her." Only the words came out as muffled.

The dark-haired guy grabbed Mira roughly by her shoulders and brought her to a sitting position, leaning her against the wall next to him. Naveen renewed his twisting against his own bonds, but not subtly enough. The other man shot him a warning glance and placed his hand on the gun holstered on his hip. Naveen stilled, his adrenaline spiking.

Mira shifted and made a face, murmuring something. The one with the gun sighed. He lifted his hand, and Naveen lurched forward, his panic increasing. He tried yelling, but of course it was useless.

But the man didn't shoot her or even hit her. Instead he

pulled a bottle of water out of his big coat pocket and tossed the contents in her face. She sputtered and her eyes flew open. Water droplets scattered as she shook her head, and the men took a step back.

The blond slowly crouched in front of her. He had a scar on his cheek, running from eye to lip. Naveen focused on these details. He understood details. He may not be able to rush these men right now, but he could describe them accurately to the police once they were free.

Once, *not* if.

He must have made a noise, because Mira's gaze darted to him and her eyes widened. He tried to project confidence and reassurance to her, but it was hard when he was tied up like a prize hog at a fair.

She managed to sum up their dire situation far faster than he had, her eyes ricocheting around the room before landing on the two men.

The snake-tattoo guy ripped the duct tape off her mouth. "Hello, Mira."

Naveen stilled, the words penetrating his panic.

They knew her name?

She blinked up at him and moistened her lips. "Who— who are you? How do you know me?"

"We know lots of things about you. You, your family."

"Both of you, actually." Mr. Burberry Coat ran his finger over the floor, then frowned at the dust on his hand. "Though you've been difficult to find, Mira."

"How did you find me, then?"

Burberry gave her a chilling smile. "We didn't. Mr. Desai did it for us. Took us some doing to tap the phone at his office, but as soon as we heard you were on your way down, we decided to meet you there."

His phone lines were tapped? Oddly enough, all he could think was that Aparna would be so livid she'd missed that. She took their security very seriously.

Snakes capped his water bottle and tossed it aside. It came to lay next to Naveen's leg. He eyed it. Could he hone a shiv out of plastic?

"Seems like a lot of trouble to find someone who doesn't want to be found. Why go through that?"

Naveen's first date with Amira—Mira—had been at a bar. He'd been running ten minutes late, and when he walked in, a clumsy drunk guy had been leaning far too close to her, his eyes firmly focused on her breasts.

He'd walked up to hear her rebuff the other man. Her words had been firm and measured, but when she'd turned around, blunt-cut hair swinging, her eyes had been full of fire. It had been a work of art, the way she'd so cleanly put the other man in his place.

Amira had been calm and collected under stress. *Mira* was cold as ice, every inch of her face, eyes included, frozen rock solid. She was speaking to their kidnappers like a queen instead of a captive.

Burberry smiled, and the scar on his face creased. His blue eyes turned to chips of icy murder. "It's about your father. Vassar."

Her father? But her father had died when she was young. She hadn't ever wanted to talk about it, and Naveen hadn't pressed.

"You're a year too late. He's dead."

Naveen made an incredulous noise. He should have pressed, clearly. If the father had died a year ago, then he'd been alive and well when they were dating. *She told you she didn't have a sister either. And a different name. Assume everything you knew about this woman was a lie.*

Was Hema Auntie doing any kind of vetting on her clients these days?

Neither of the villains seemed as surprised as he was to hear her flat announcement. "We know that," Snakes said.

"So why are we here?"

"Vassar took something that belongs to our boss," Burberry growled.

"I don't know your boss," Mira said. "I don't know who you are, and I barely knew my father. In fact, I hadn't spoken with him for years before his death. So whatever he took or you think he stole, I don't have it. You've wasted your time."

Burberry didn't seem to be listening to her. "We want the necklace back, Mira."

Naveen's gaze went to her neck, though her shirt was still buttoned all the way up. What necklace? Mira didn't care for jewelry. The only jewelry she wore today were her aunt's earrings.

"Again, no idea what necklace you're talking about."

Burberry pulled his phone out of his nice coat, tapped something on the screen, and showed it to her. "This necklace."

She peered at the screen, then shook her head. "Pretty. I've never seen it."

Burberry studied her for a long moment. In a swift move, he slapped her.

Naveen jerked forward.

Snakes pulled a knife out of his pocket, flashed it open, and pressed the shiny blade against Naveen's throat, right against his pounding pulse. Naveen tried not to gulp, though the instinct was there. *Remember this. Remember everything about this.*

"Maybe we can jog your memory," Snakes said silkily. He put more pressure on the weapon, and something wet and sticky slid down Naveen's skin.

Mira appeared unimpressed, which was kind of annoying. He was quite impressed by the knife at his throat. "That's not going to do anything, because I have nothing to tell you."

The knife pricked Naveen harder, and he swore. Burberry pulled the duct tape off his mouth, and he inhaled at the swift shot of pain. "What's that, lawyer?"

Naveen ignored the way he said *lawyer*, like it was another word for *cockroach*. He'd heard all the jokes and now wasn't the time to convince anyone he was one of the good guys. "Maybe I can help you."

Burberry clicked his knife shut. Then open. Then shut

again. Naveen tried not to be hypnotized by the intimidating gesture. "You in the business, lawyer?"

He had no idea what the business was, but it didn't sound like one he wanted to be a part of. "I'm in the business of assisting people. Can I see the picture?"

Burberry hesitated for a beat, then showed it to him. He'd grown up with his aunts and mother showing off their jewels, so he understood that this was a pricey piece indeed. It dripped in diamonds, with one major perfectly cut teardrop pendant in the center, and light reflecting off the other six stones surrounding it. "Beautiful," he said, and infused every soothing quality he could into the word. De-escalation might be his only superpower, so he'd use it.

The kidnapper's eyes narrowed. "You know where it is?"

"No. But . . . maybe we could find it for you. If you let us go?" Naveen tried a smile. He had it on good authority that he had an excellent smile.

It didn't seem to have any effect on the men. They turned their attention to Mira, but at the very least, they weren't holding the knife to his throat any longer.

"We heard that you know where your dad hid his shit."

"Where did you hear that from?"

"From your aunt, for one." Burberry pulled a letter out from his pocket. It was the letter her aunt had left for her. "'He wanted me to give you something. I didn't want to bother you with it before, but I left it for you in the usual place,'" he read. "Where's the usual place?"

Mira paused. Naveen was aware that he had a bad track

record when it came to love interests lying to him, so he wasn't the best at sussing falsehoods out, but he immediately knew that Mira was lying when she spoke. "I don't know anything about where my father hid anything. I repeat, I have not spoken to him in years. My . . . lawyer also knows nothing. You have the wrong people. But if you let us go, I'll make it worth your while."

They glanced at each other. Burberry spoke. "Is that right?"

Naveen leaned forward. "She's right. Whatever you're getting paid, I'll double it. You take Venmo? PayPal? Name it."

Snakes sucked his teeth and readjusted his grip on his gun. "You think we accept Venmo?"

"I promise, I'd put the payment on private mode," he tried.

"What my . . . friend . . . is saying is that we're not without resources." Mira paused. "Or people who would miss us."

"Nobody would miss you, Mira," Burberry said gently. "You don't have anyone."

Mira's face went blank, so blank he felt a tug of sympathy for her, despite all her lies and the hot water that her father, her only recently dead father, had landed him in. "That's not true."

"Both of us will be missed," Naveen interjected. "This is a waste of everyone's time. We clearly don't know what you're looking for. Let us go, and we can forget this ever happened."

The man turned back to him. "Our boss is real annoyed we brought you. We probably should have killed you there, made it look like a carjacking gone wrong. We didn't see any cameras in that old garage. It would have worked."

His blood ran cold. There weren't any cameras in that garage.

"But we thought, eh. Family attorneys know more than anyone ever thinks. Once they get over that pesky privilege, they come in handy."

Snakes ominously undid the safety on his gun. "We can kill you and dump you at any time though."

"There's no need for that." Naveen tried to ignore the icy trail of sweat sliding down his back.

Mira shifted. "Look, he wasn't really a family attorney."

"He was your dad's only sibling's lawyer. You don't think she'd tell him something?"

"He never even met her, he only came on—"

Oh no. "I may not have met her, but I am her attorney." He gave Mira a look, which he hoped she could interpret. His grandfather was the attorney who had originally taken her aunt's business. He'd rather die than point gunmen at his family.

The muscle in her jaw clenched. "You're not. You barely knew my aunt. She told you nothing."

"Uh, she definitely told me stuff," he lied. "More than she told any other attorney, that's for sure. Older women, they tend to love me," he weakly finished.

"I don't know why you're lying," Mira said through gritted teeth. "But you don't have to justify your retainer. I've known you for like two minutes, and all you did for my aunt was print up a boilerplate will for her."

"I—"

"Okay, enough." The man came to his feet, his coat falling neatly. "This bickering is annoying. You may want to start racking your memory, the both of you. Our boss'll be here soon."

Shit. Naveen might not be *in the business*, but a boss wasn't good news in video games and it definitely wasn't good news in kidnappings.

The men left the room, and the door locked behind them, each of the four locks turning in succession.

Mira and he were still as their footsteps receded. Naveen caught Mira's eye and tilted his head at the desk. As much as he wanted to grill her about what the fuck was going on, he could get answers later. Finding something to untie them was priority number one. "Could be scissors in there," he mouthed.

She frowned. Her cheek was reddening.

He started with his undignified boot scoot again. The ties on his hands tightened with every movement, until they were cutting into his circulation, but he ignored them.

He had to pause for a second to catch his breath, and that was when he realized she'd twisted and squirmed to her knees, using the dirty wall for leverage.

Well, that was great, but there was the matter of her ties. Perhaps she could hop to the table and—

She leaned against the wall, cocked her butt out, and brought her tied hands down over it behind her. The tie snapped, the noise so loud in the silence that he flinched.

Wait, wait, wait, wait. That couldn't possibly be all it took to remove zip ties?

Not now. Google that later.

With her hands free, she worked through her hair and came up with a bobby pin. She used her teeth to bite off the rounded tip and squirmed until her feet were in front of her.

It took her ten seconds to fiddle with the ties around her ankles, and then she was free of those. "Mira, I mean this with all due respect," he hissed. "But what the fuck is going on?"

"Not now." Her pupils were enlarged, her hair disheveled. Her previously pristine pink shirt was marred with streaks of dust. She crawled over to him. Every scrape and exhale of breath had his adrenaline pulsing.

She stuck the bobby pin in the latch of his ties and jimmied him free as well. His eyes kept straying to the door, on high alert for any noises.

The men had beat him and slapped her. They had weapons. Knives and guns. Naveen might be out of his element, but he definitely didn't trust them to not use those weapons to terrorize them more if they found the two of them out of their bonds.

Naveen rubbed his wrists as he came to his feet. There were pins and needles through his feet and legs, but that was probably not the worst discomfort he could be in tonight, so he'd take it. He tested his ribs, relieved that they felt bruised but were not unbearably painful.

"We have to get out of here, like now. Before they come back."

Naveen glanced around. There was only one door in and out of this place, and it was the one the bad guys had left through.

He patted his pockets, but they were empty, of course. Only the most incompetent of kidnappers would have left them with a way to contact the outside world. "Your phone?"

She checked the pockets of her skirt. "Gone. Keys too." She faltered.

No help coming for them, then. He crept to the door. As quietly as possible, he pressed his ear against the wood. No voices, but that didn't mean they weren't right outside.

"The window?" she whispered.

"You may be able to squeeze through. I can't."

"If you can't, I can't. My hips are wider than yours."

He avoided looking at her hips. He paced to the boxes and riffled through the top ones. Moldy clothes and a broken lamp. From the style of them, they'd been cluttering up this storeroom for forty years.

"What are you looking for?"

"Weapons."

"What are we going to do with weapons?"

"We can't hope for someone to rescue us, and we can't sneak out. That leaves fighting. There's two of them, and two of us." He said it with more confidence than he felt.

He'd already been knocked down by one of those dudes, and Mira's eyes were still dilated from whatever sedative they'd given her. *You're more prepared now. You kickbox sometimes. You've done jiujitsu.*

"What?"

A scrape came from outside, and they froze. "They have guns," Mira hissed, when no one threw open the door.

"Which is why we need weapons." He moved on to the next box and paused when he found a forty dumped in a box full of blankets. It was half full of liquor, and heavy when he lifted it.

"That is ridiculous. We cannot fight guns with a half-empty bottle of moonshine some squatter left behind—"

"And paint." An aerosol can of spray paint lay in the corner. He picked it up, shook it, and tossed it to Mira. He was done discussing this. They didn't have much time before the men discovered they were free. Two men with guns? Maybe when he was twenty, fresh off earning a black belt and filled with bravado and recklessness. Not now that he was thirty-four and plagued with frequent neck pain from a sedentary job. Now he needed the element of surprise. He slowed his breathing and his heart, which was hard when adrenaline was pulsing through his veins. He let his gaze focus on the wooden door he stood behind. As soon as it opened, he'd pounce. "Call for help."

"This won't work," she said.

"We wait until they're both in here, then attack. You spray

them, I'll try to overpower at least one. If we can get our hands on one gun, we can fight our way out of here."

"You're being ridiculous. We cannot do this."

"Do you have a better idea?"

"No."

"And you agree we have to get out of here as soon as possible, especially before this boss shows up?"

She gave a frustrated sound. "Obviously. But these are professionals, not some amateurs."

"I'm not going to sit here and die. You heard them. Call for help."

She bit her lip for a long, pregnant moment. He was about to try to persuade her again, but then she spoke. "Of all the people in the world, I cannot believe I'm stuck here with you."

That took him aback, as well as the fact that she was using her normal voice, but then he caught the way she was readjusting her grip on the can. "Fuck you and fuck that boilerplate will jab," he said. "I'll have you know I give each of my clients my undivided attention."

She tightened her lips. She lifted her voice as well. "A two-bit lawyer like you? My aunt should have gone to a real firm instead of a hack."

Ouch.

Despite the slight sting of her words, and the seriousness of the situation, he couldn't help the spurt of amusement. Two-bit? Mira had a particularly old-fashioned turn of phrase sometimes.

A fist hammered on the door. "Shut the fuck up or I'll duct-tape your mouths again."

Snakes. The bigger guy, the one he'd already grappled with and lost to. He'd be the first one through the door. Naveen shifted his weight from one leg to the other. He nodded at Mira again.

She backed away to the wall and sank to the floor, in the same position she'd been in when they'd left the two of them, and placed the paint can right behind her. "I'll shut up when you get me away from this asshole."

"Asshole? I'm the asshole?" He lifted the jug of moonshine. "Your family is the reason I'm even here."

Her eyebrows lifted, and her voice rose louder. He'd never heard her shout before, and he was mildly annoyed to note it still sounded melodious. "You're nothing more than a cheap lawyer—"

"Did you not hear me?" The locks turned and the door opened. Naveen filled his lungs with air as Snakes sprang into the room. The man had a cowlick, the hair swirling over the crown of his head like a target. He took a step toward Mira and towered over her. Naveen waited a beat for the other man to come in as well, but no one followed, and there were no footsteps.

He caught the instant the man realized Naveen wasn't in the spot he'd left him. He tensed and started to turn.

Mira whipped her hand around, and sprayed a stream of red paint directly into his face. At the same time, Naveen launched forward and slammed the moonshine jug down on their kidnapper's head with all his strength.

Snakes was a sturdy bastard. He stumbled but didn't fall. He turned to Naveen with an incredulous look on his paint covered face, and swiped at the color in his eyes.

Naveen ignored Mira's squeak of alarm. Naveen dropped the bottle and ran for him, tackling him around the mid-section.

They grappled on the floor. Naveen tried to keep his ears pricked for the other guy, but then the kidnapper flipped them so he was on the floor. Even blinded by paint and hit in the head, the man was strong. Naveen struggled, trying to gain the advantage again, but Snakes's hands went around his neck and he pressed his thumbs tight, cutting off his air supply.

Fuck. They were in trouble. Mira had been right. They were no match for professional criminals, even two against one—

A loud thwack split the air, and Snakes's fingers loosened. As Naveen dragged in a much-needed gulp of air, the man slumped to the side, off him.

Mira dropped the broken lamp she'd used to knock the man out, and rushed to the door and peeked outside. "The other guy's not here."

"Close it," he gasped. Naveen pushed the man off him completely and scrambled to his knees, gesturing for Mira to stay back when she came closer.

He gingerly reached into the guy's pants pockets, one eye

on his slack face, and came up with car keys. Finally, a real way out of here. The sigh of relief turned into dismay at the next thing he found.

They both stared at the badge he pulled out. "You've got to be shitting me," he whispered and ran his thumb over the embossed letters. Jason Stuart. Federal Bureau of Investigation. Not a professional criminal. Professional law enforcement.

Fuck. This did not bode well, but they didn't have time to think through all of the ramifications.

The last thing the man carried was a wallet. Naveen added that to the stash in his pocket, then gently eased Agent Stuart's gun out of his holster. The weight of it was heavy and unfamiliar in his palm, but he gripped it tightly and kept his thumb away from the trigger. "Follow me," he said grimly.

She didn't argue with him, for which he was grateful. After ensuring there was no one waiting behind the other side of the door to jump them, they crept through. The front room of this shack was no more extravagant than the back. The space was bare of furniture except for a broken-down table. The windows were poorly boarded up, and glass littered the floor. Here, too, there was a single bulb illuminating the place, hanging above the table. Naveen was frankly impressed the place was wired for electricity.

There was no sight of Stuart's friend, because he was outside, Naveen learned, when they opened the front door a crack. The man had his back to the building, and he stood about a hundred yards away, phone held to his ear.

A hundred yards in the other direction? A black SUV, the Ford insignia matching the one on the keys he'd taken from their resident federal agent. There were no other cars visible. There was nothing else visible, except the sun dying over the mountains in the distance. If a tumbleweed danced over the barren landscape, he wouldn't be surprised.

He closed the door. "Make a run for the car. I'll create a diversion."

"We don't need a diversion." She tapped his hand. "Give me the gun."

"Why?"

"Do you know how to use a gun?"

"No. Do you?"

"Yes."

That was as good of an argument as any for her to be handling the weapon. He passed it over. "Do you have a plan?"

"We're going to threaten him with it and run."

That had been his hypothetical idea, but he balked now that it was coming to fruition. "*We're* going to threaten a man who is probably a federal agent with a gun that is undoubtedly identical to the one on his hip?"

"Do you have a better idea?" she parroted back his own earlier question.

Better? No. He cast his gaze around the nearly empty place. "That bottle of moonshine's still intact. If we can find a lighter, we could make a Molotov cocktail."

She pursed her lips. Her hair was more down than up

now, the curls getting bigger by the minute. "You want us to Molotov cocktail our way out of here."

He gestured. "It would be a distraction, at least."

"This is the desert. One spark could set forty miles ablaze. I don't want to create an ecological disaster."

"Well, that's very responsible and Californian of you."

"I also don't have a lighter."

He took a deep breath. They truly didn't have another quick way out of here. "Fine. Let's go before Stuart wakes up."

She checked the crack in the window boards and nodded at him. She was as soundless as a ghost as she slipped out the door, and he followed. With the man's back to them, he wondered if they might be able to get all the way to the car without any confrontation.

Until he stepped off the rotted porch, and the wood creaked under his foot. He didn't even have time to wince, because the blond whirled around, his camel coat flaring around him, pulling his gun with lightning quick reflexes.

Mira's gun was already up, her hands steady. "Drop your weapon."

The well-dressed guy sneered. "Your dad taught you well, Mira. Where's my partner?"

"In better condition than we were when you brought us here. Now drop it," she repeated, and undid the safety.

"You think I'm worried?"

She tossed her head, the queen of this shack and all she surveyed. "You should be. You can't kill me or your boss will be annoyed. But I can kill you."

His thin lips curled up. "Girl, you have no idea who you're dealing with."

"Neither do you."

"Is that right?"

As far as Naveen could tell, Mira wasn't even blinking. "Go start the car, Naveen."

Normally, Naveen might not be keen on taking orders, but he understood the nuances of this particular, hopefully never to be repeated, situation. He took one step, but Burberry shifted the gun his way. "I can't kill you, but your friend seems pretty useless."

That was both stinging and worrisome. What a conundrum: he may not want these people to think he was involved in this criminal enterprise, but he also couldn't be seen as expendable. "If you think I'm useless, then you really don't know all the things clients tell their attorneys."

Burberry's eyes narrowed, but they swung back to Mira when she took a step toward him.

Naveen took advantage of his inattention to sidle a little closer to the car as Mira spoke. "You have three seconds to put down your gun. One."

Burberry rolled his eyes.

"Two."

The kidnapper took a step.

Naveen expected Mira to say three, but instead a shot rang out, and then another one. All three of them stared at each other in surprise as Burberry staggered back a step, red staining his lush neutral coat at his side and his arm.

He dropped to his knees, his gun falling out of his fingers. "You *bitch*."

Naveen didn't have time to balk at someone getting shot in front of him for the first time ever, though his brain was stuttering. "Run," Mira gasped, and he did exactly that.

Naveen hopped into the SUV and hit the button to start it, throwing it into drive. Mira's smaller figure ran around the hood and hopped in. She hadn't even closed the door when he smashed his foot on the accelerator.

A series of sharp pops behind them almost made him swerve off the road, and he glanced in the mirror to find their weaving kidnapper, his bleeding arm close to his side, his non-dominant hand awkwardly extending the gun as he shot at them and missed.

"Get down," he growled, relieved when Mira complied.

The shots blessedly stopped as Burberry became a tiny figure, then vanished.

It took a good five minutes of silence for Naveen's grip to loosen up on the wheel, and that was about when Mira's head poked up and she returned to her seat. She deposited the gun into the cup holder, then quietly buckled her seat belt and rested her hands in her lap.

"You shot someone." The words were loud in the quiet of the car.

"Yes." Her voice was hoarse, and far away, no longer holding the chill of her composure.

"Have you ever shot someone before?"

"No. Have you?"

"Of course not." Guess she really did know how to use that gun.

Why he should be surprised by that, he didn't know, except he figured it may take his brain more time to square up his mild-mannered accountant ex-girlfriend with the woman who could escape zip ties and shoot a federal agent.

"You're going very fast."

He spared her a glance. "Hopefully a cop will pull me over, then."

Her lips tightened. Fine, she could be annoyed at his tone. He was annoyed at . . . everything. "What the fuck just happened back there?"

"I—I don't know."

"Don't lie to me. They were talking about your father."

"I'm not lying to you. I have not had anything to do with my father for longer than you've known me."

"Guess that's why you told me he was dead when he wasn't."

She lowered her head, her curls hiding her face.

He slapped the steering wheel. "I'm driving, and I don't even know where the fuck we are."

"The loneliest road."

"Very poetic."

"No. I recognize this. It's called the Loneliest Road. We're in Nevada."

He cast her an incredulous look. "Nevada? We're in fucking Nevada?"

"Don't raise your voice to me."

He lowered it to a whisper. "How the fuck did we get to Nevada?"

"Obviously they brought us here."

That meant they'd been out for hours. No other buildings were around them in this desert. The sun wasn't quite gone yet, but it was still dark, no city lights to be seen.

"I think I've driven through here." She shoved her hair out of her face. "Keep going north, and we should hit a hotel and saloon in about ten miles."

A saloon? He hated this Wild West cosplay time warp already. "Great. We can contact the police there."

"The police?"

"Yes. The police." He spared her a glance. "What other alternative is there?"

A beep cut off whatever she was going to say. "What is that?"

She froze, then reached between them and opened the middle console. A radio sat inside, along with another gun. She lifted the radio out gingerly. It beeped again. A voice came over it, a disembodied, computer-modified voice. "Mira. Naveen. I'd like to speak with you."

Chapter Five

Mira ran her thumb over the button of the radio. "What do I do?" That was a question she wasn't accustomed to asking anybody. Then again, she also wasn't used to a lot of things that had happened today.

"Answer me."

The directive didn't come from Naveen, but from the device.

"Might as well pick it up." Naveen accelerated. If she squinted, she could make out the faint line of blood on his neck.

Your family is the reason I'm even here. More specifically, she was the reason he was here. Even though she'd tried to distance herself, she should have known she couldn't escape her past.

What did you steal, Dad?

"Mira?"

Mira shook herself out of her daze and hit the button on the radio. "Yes. Hello." That was far too polite, but she didn't know how else to answer a call.

"You hurt my men," came the deep, distorted voice. "And you stole their car. Not very nice."

She tried to cling to her tattered shreds of bravado and composure. Brazen had been her father's middle name, and, along with zip-tie escaping skills, it was something he'd taught her well. *When in doubt, pretend.* "He's not dead then? Too bad." Her gaze met Naveen's. "Who is this?"

"I'm the one who's been looking for you, Ms. Chaudhary. Where are you?"

He pronounced her name right. "I don't need to tell you that."

Naveen turned the air conditioner off. She swayed toward him, telling herself it was so that he could hear better, and not because she wanted to feel his warmth.

"I think it would be best to have this conversation with you in person."

"I'd rather not."

"We'll find you."

That was ominous. Naveen's hands tightened over the wheel and the needle on the odometer inched up to ninety.

"I have no idea why you're looking for me, or what you think I have. I wasn't involved in my father's business. We don't have anything of yours."

The man gave a disjointed sigh. "Well, see, that's a problem. Because I have something of yours."

Mira reared back when she heard the next voice. It had been so long, yet she could recognize it immediately, even with the radio's static underpinning it. "Mira?"

"Tai?" she whispered, automatically using the title she'd used to use for her sister when she was small.

The world narrowed. It didn't matter how many distant years it had been since she'd last heard Sejal, she would always recognize her.

Growing up, Mira had idolized her older sister. Sejal had frequently been the one who had helped her with her homework, forged their dad's signature on her teacher's notes, and made sure she had food on the table while their parent was off on one of his get rich quick benders. And when her dad had realized that Mira had a particular affinity for numbers, Sejal had been the one to stand between them and talk him down.

That had ended when Sejal had walked out on her eighteenth birthday with a duffel bag. She'd tried to give Mira a hug in their kitchen, but Mira had shrugged her off and choked back tears. They hadn't been tears of sadness, but of anger. An older sister was supposed to protect, not abandon.

Mira's dad had drafted her into his schemes full-time the next week. Only, after a while, she hadn't played getaway driver or lookout like Sejal had. She'd been the scheme.

Her sister's words slurred. "Long time no talk, little sister."

Mira brought the radio closer to her mouth and spoke urgently. "Sejal, what is happening?"

Her voice was dreamy. "I was trying to go straight. That time I saw you, when you were in college. I was going to snitch on this guy who set me up. That's why I was running."

Mira's fingers twitched. She didn't remember all of the

words they'd exchanged that day, only her feelings. The sharp slap of happiness and shock when she'd opened the door to find Sejal there, standing in her dorm hallway. Though she was still angry at being abandoned, part of her had been desperate for Sejal's approval, had hoped that her sister had showed up to express her pride in Mira's accomplishments. Both in attending such a good college and breaking free of their father.

That happiness had turned to anger when Sejal had started talking, her words running far too fast to be anything but shifty. She'd prowled Mira's small dorm room, checking the windows. *I need a place to lay low,* she'd said.

Just like their father, Mira had thought, and the betrayal had hurt.

Like a switch, she shut that yearning for a parental surrogate off. Mindful of Christine sitting on her twin bed, watching with wide eyes, Mira had coldly rebuffed her sister.

And that was that. Whatever fragile thread that had bound them together was broken. Irreparably, Mira had assumed. "You didn't say that."

"I thought I did."

"You didn't." Her voice rose. "I would have helped you. I'm—"

"Dad continues to fuck us over from beyond the grave."

Mira swallowed. "So it seems."

"We had shit luck when it came to parents." Sejal inhaled hard, then spoke fast. "Mira, run, I'll be—"

Her rushed words were cut off with a sinister slap. Mira

jumped, her heart rising in her throat. She may not have spoken to her sister in years, but she didn't want her hurt. "Stop that. Right this minute."

The mystery man came back. "We're taking care of your sister for now, Mira, but we can't guarantee that'll last."

"I have never seen that necklace." Of all the things she'd expected her father to have taken, a wildly expensive piece of jewelry was pretty low on the list. Social Security numbers, a widow's pension, pure cash, sure.

"We were tipped off about Vassar's daughter knowing where my property is. Since the daughter I have doesn't know anything, that must mean you."

Had he hurt Sejal badly to be so certain that she didn't know anything?

"Let's make this easy, Mira. You give me the necklace, and I'll give you back your sister. And I'll ensure your and your boyfriend's continued safety." The stranger paused. "He's a nice boy, this Naveen, from a nice family."

Unlike you. Jay had been quite happy to spell that out for her today. Dear lord, had that only been today?

"His mother's rich. He's had some troubles, so I can't imagine he's the favored child, but I considered ransoming him, you know, to recoup my losses."

Mira swallowed. No, no, no.

Panic had filled her the second she'd woken up in that shack and met Naveen's dazed eyes, and now it bloomed anew. "Leave him and his family out of this. He truly knows nothing."

"Your father's lawyer knows nothing? My man says he gave the opposite impression."

Naveen cleared his throat and finally spoke to the man. "I was Mira's aunt's lawyer. I thought her father was long dead."

"He doesn't know anything," Mira repeated.

"I don't believe you."

"If my dad stole something from you," she said slowly, "then why not go to the police?"

"I like to settle things my way."

No. That was bullshit. There was a reason the man couldn't go to the cops.

Naveen was clearly thinking the same thing. "Or because you'd be walking in with unclean hands."

"I'm not scared of the police. I have eyes and ears in every department in Nevada and California." He paused. "In case you were thinking of heading to a station."

Fuck. Though she'd already guessed as much, with that FBI badge.

"They won't help you. Mira, if you try to get help from anyone, your sister dies. And then we'll get started on Naveen's family. You don't want to risk my anger. Turn around, come back, and we will calmly discuss this."

"Or what?" Naveen asked.

"We'll find you." She'd never thought it possible for a computer-generated voice to sound so ominous. "And then you're going to be very sorry you didn't cooperate."

Naveen took the radio from her hand and drove one-handed. "Call us silly, but we're not going back to a shack in the middle of nowhere to have a nice chat."

"Then I will have to come to you. See you soon, children." The line turned to static.

The silence was pregnant with fear and anxiety. Or maybe that was just her, projecting her fear and anxiety onto him.

"We can't go to the police," she whispered.

"He could be lying."

"We know he has federal agents in his pocket. You think he *doesn't* have corrupt cops on his payroll?" She ran the back of her hand over her dry lips. What she wouldn't give for a nice, cold water right now.

The car beeped, bringing their attention to the dashboard. Naveen cursed. "Low gas."

Because of course they couldn't have been lucky enough to steal a car with a full tank. "If you keep driving, there should be an exit in the next twenty miles. I think." She hoped.

"You grew up here, right? Or was that a lie too?"

She ignored the dig. "In Las Vegas. I don't know this area as well."

They sat in silence for a while as he kept driving. She breathed a sigh of relief when lights emerged on the road in front of them, piercing the darkness like an oasis. Only a couple of buildings, but it looked like a lifeline. Or it would have, if they hadn't just been threatened out of getting help.

She searched the darkness. "I don't see a gas station here. And we have no money."

He took the exit anyway. "It's better to be in a public place than to end up stuck on the side of the road."

Public place was a generous description for the parking lot he turned into. The motel's neon sign flashed VACANCY. Next to the inn was a saloon and a diner. Naveen parked in front of the diner. "Let's go inside," he said quietly. "We need a moment to regroup, and there's safety in numbers."

"The saloon looks busier."

"A shoot-out in a saloon seems a little too on the nose, doesn't it?"

She tried not to shudder. Before leaving the car, she gently tucked the gun she'd fired under the passenger seat.

You fired a gun. You shot someone.

In the bottle, on the shelf, to be dealt with later.

Save for an old man sitting at the counter, the diner was fairly deserted. They grabbed the booth farthest from the door, where they'd be out of view of the wide windows. Mira rubbed her eyes, probably smearing her eye makeup more than it already was.

It didn't matter what she looked like any longer. All of the carefully pressed clothes hanging in her closet, her tidy, contained hair, her perfectly logical job, her well-curated and professional online footprint, her decorated apartment, her 401(k) . . . none of that could rescue her from this situation.

A waitress in a stained garish pink uniform came to their table. Her name-tag said GLADYS. She pointed at Mira's feet in lieu of a greeting. "No shoes, no service." Her voice was gravelly, like she'd smoked a pack a day since infancy.

Dear lord. Mira hadn't even realized that she wasn't wearing shoes. Her sensible low black heels must have gotten kicked off at some point.

Oh, gross. She lifted her feet delicately so they hovered over the floor. If she thought too hard about what she'd walked on since she'd left the shack, she might throw up.

Naveen pointed at the wall above the counter, where the diner's logo was plastered on towels and baseball caps for sale. Mira doubted anyone had bought them in a while. "Can we get a pair of flip-flops?"

"Sure. Large?"

Mira nodded.

Naveen patted his pockets absentmindedly, took out the agent's wallet, and riffled through it. "Do you take credit cards?" Naveen asked.

Mira thought that was an optimistic question to ask of a run-down diner in the middle of the desert, but the waitress shrugged, her styled blue hair holding firm in its helmet cut. "Of course. And Apple Pay, Venmo." She jerked her head toward the back. "We got a crypto ATM, too, if you need that."

This surreal experience took on a new dimension, but she almost welcomed this one, with its gloss of normalcy. "Great," Mira said. "I'll have a tea, please. Whatever kind you have."

"Coffee," Naveen added. "And do you have french fries?"

"Yes."

"Are they good?"

"Eh."

Honest lady.

"I want a plate of them. No, two plates of them. Cover one of them with the fakest cheese you have. Also, I'd like a strawberry milkshake with a scoop of vanilla ice cream."

Mira waited until Gladys left before murmuring, "We probably shouldn't use the credit cards. They can track us."

"Don't worry, there's cash in here. Enough to cover our tab, at least."

He faced her. His lip was cut, and the redness on his cheek foreshadowed a blooming bruise. There was a nick on his throat from when the man had held a knife there, along with some dried blood. His hair was tousled all over the place. His white shirt was streaked with dirt and grime.

Mere hours ago, he'd been comfortable and polished in his worn office with its terrible filing system and single assistant. She'd done this. This was all her fault.

She pulled out a napkin from the dispenser and began rolling it tight. "Do you have any thoughts?"

"Do I have any . . ." He ran his hand down his face, tugging the skin of his cheeks down.

"What?"

"Nothing, you're running this like it's a morning meeting." He folded his arms. "I have many thoughts, none of them very polite. But I suppose, first I'd like an explanation as to what the hell is going on here?"

Mira pressed her hands against the table. She opened her mouth. Paused while the waitress came back with their drinks. Opened her mouth again. "Don't worry about any-thing. This is an elaborate prank I put all my exes through. You win! Now we're going to go back to the hotel, go to the spa, and you're going to have your first ever pedicure."

That was what she wished she could say. What came out was, "I'm not entirely sure."

"Those guys seemed pretty sure about you."

Those guys. One of whom she'd shot. She swallowed the nausea that had threatened to engulf her. *Don't think about the sound of the shot, or the blood. Not now.* "I don't know why. I'm not a part of this."

"What is this, exactly?"

"It's . . . complicated." And she was extremely out of prac-tice in talking about it.

He clasped his hands over his lower face and rested his elbows on the table. They were silent for a few long mo-ments.

The waitress sidled up with heaping plates of limp fries and the rest of Naveen's order, as well as cheap pink plastic flip-flops for Mira. She accepted them and put them on her feet, grateful to have something separating her skin and the floor.

"Can I get you two anything else?" She looked between them and their still-full mugs.

Naveen reached for his abandoned, now undoubtedly cold coffee. "No, thank you."

Gladys gave them a suspicious look, but she popped her gum aggressively and left them alone.

Alone with a thick, pregnant silence. "Mira," Naveen finally said, and his tone was hoarse and raspy. "Please. We both have family at risk here."

Naveen had a wonderful family. She'd met them, liked them, yearned for them.

Mira curled her hands around the barely warm mug. At least it was warmer than her.

The lie had become real to her, words she'd recited so many times that they became her existence. Two parents who were gone, no siblings, distant aunt.

That wasn't reality, though. The reality was that her criminal father had run amok until recently and she had a sister who was currently being held captive and might die unless Mira could come up with some kind of daring rescue. Doing daring things was a personality trait she'd happily abandoned.

His chest expanded. "You look like you're about to faint. Here," he said, and pushed the plain fries toward her. "You eat the ones without cheese on them."

Her lip gave a dangerous wobble before she caught it. He'd remembered.

Did he remember how he used to carry Lactaid for her? He'd surprised her with a packet on their third date, so she could try the cheesecake at the restaurant he'd taken her to. She'd found it more thoughtful than any bouquet of flowers. So thoughtful she'd nearly undressed him in the car heading to his place after.

She wasn't exactly the fainting type, but she picked up a

fry and grimaced as soon as it hit her tongue. Gladys had been right, it was gross.

But it was also a fried potato, so she grabbed another. "My mom died when I was two, that part was true. My dad didn't, as you've learned. He was a conman."

Naveen didn't clutch his collar and gasp, but she supposed he'd already gleaned some of this information over the course of the night. "What kind of conman?"

"He always had different schemes going. When I was young, it was convincing older people to hand over their money with promises of doubling their investment."

"Ponzi schemes."

"Yes. He was good at grifting." When she was little and bored, her dad would hide a quarter under a cup and then move it around rapidly amid other cups. His hands had been fast, and she'd never been able to find that quarter. Had he been of a different time, he probably would have set up shop on a sidewalk. "When I got into my teens, he started targeting casinos."

"Card counting?"

She took another french fry, only to distract from her disquiet. "Sometimes." Did she need to tell him everything?

She mentally pleaded the fifth. "It got to a point where I could no longer sanction what he was doing." It hadn't been a slow realization that her father was wrong. She'd known he was wrong from the time she was young, but he was her only parent, and she'd craved his love and approval no matter how he treated her.

The breaking point had been a slap in the face. Her face. "I didn't speak to him after I left for college and then he died a year ago."

"Was that your choice or his?"

Ouch. Because it hadn't been purely her choice. Her father had probably been as mad at her as she'd been with him. "Mutual."

"So your father was a criminal, and he stole something valuable from another criminal, and now all of our lives are in danger."

"That seems to be the case." Easier to explain than she'd thought.

"You talked about casinos. Could this be Mafia related?"

She shook her head. "No. My dad wouldn't have targeted someone with connections." Though . . . when she was young she'd never really thought he'd put her in physical danger either, and he'd done just that.

His lip curled. "Your sister also became a thief, I'm guessing?"

The way he said it, with a faint hint of disgust, pricked her temper, though that wasn't fair. She felt that same disgust every time she thought of her family and the pain they inflicted on others. The pain she'd once inflicted on others. "I know less about my sister's business. She travels a lot. My aunt would give me updates on where she was. That's how I knew she was alive all this time."

I was trying to go straight.

Mira's guilt skyrocketed. Sejal hadn't sounded like she

was lying. Had she tried to break out of the mold her father had put her in, too? Sejal hadn't had her affinity for numbers, but her dad had used his elder daughter as a prop more than once for his schemes. *Sejal's got brawn, Mira's got brains,* her father would say proudly to his buddies. Like instead of raising daughters he was creating the perfect team to run a heist, which he probably low-key was.

"Was your aunt also a part of this Partridge Family of crime?"

"No." Her answer was swift and sure. "She and my dad never saw eye to eye. Everything I said about her was true. She even helped me get into college and away from my dad when I was a kid."

"I'm glad something wasn't a lie."

She flinched, though she was expecting his disdain. Up until now, he'd been focused on their common enemy. He was justified in being angry at her.

She curled her toes into the cheap rubber soles of her flip-flops.

Mira mentally erected walls around herself, high and strong. They were the same walls that had made it easy for her to walk away from a dozen matches and nearly forget Jay's name the second he rejected her. The same walls she'd used when she'd ended things with Naveen.

She rubbed her ring finger with her thumb. "I can take you to the airport."

He placed his hand on the table. "To the . . . to the airport?"

"Yes." Mira sat up straighter. Silly, a flight would be a problem, with no identification. "Or the bus station. You can go home."

He closed his eyes and appeared to take deep breaths, like he was trying to throttle his temper. Up until now, she hadn't even realized he had a temper. He'd always seemed so fun loving. Though, to be fair, getting kidnapped and threatened with your ex would put anyone in a mood. "I can't leave."

Mira bit the inside of her cheek. "I'll handle this," she repeated. "It's my sister, my responsibility."

"How?"

She faltered. "I—I don't know—"

"You're going to take on the mob?"

"We don't know for sure that this is Mafia business."

"Even if it's not, we know that they're not above kidnapping, assault, or larceny. That's all stuff they did today. They're dangerous. They know who and where my family is. My mom, my grandfather, my cousin, her baby. No, I can't go anywhere. We're in this together until we clear this up."

The *accusation* in that last sentence was loud and clear. Mira dug her toes into the rubber harder.

Naveen stilled. "Jesus. They could hurt my mom or grandfather."

Mira rubbed her hand over her mouth. "They'll have to go to California. It'll take time."

"Unless they have people everywhere, like he said." Naveen pushed back from the table. "I need a phone. Excuse me? Miss? Do you have a pay phone? Or can I use your cell?"

The waitress didn't even stop, just snorted a negative.

Mira fisted her hands. "We could find the necklace."

He turned back to her slowly. "And how do we do that?"

She swallowed. "I might know where it is."

Naveen stared at her for so long a drop of sweat ran along her hairline. She glanced around quickly, then reached into her bra.

To his credit, his gaze didn't drop below her chin.

She pulled out the key she'd tucked up between her breasts. "It's the storage locker key my aunt left me."

"You knew all this time that you had the key to a place where your dad might have hid the thing, and you let them put a knife to my throat?"

She leaned farther over the table, to make sure no one could hear her. "If I'd given them this key, they would have slit your throat."

To her surprise, he blinked, then nodded. "Possible. Yes."

She sat back. "Not possible. Definitely. We were only useful insofar as we could provide them information."

"You sure your aunt didn't get rid of the storage unit?"

"I'm pretty certain it's what she was referencing in her letter. She sold our house, so it's the only place I can think of." When her brother had died, Rhea had asked if Mira would like to go through the man's house to save anything, but Mira had left no trace of herself in that three-bedroom ranch.

By appearances, no one would have known Vassar was anything but a single dad, which was entirely by design.

"It's where your dad kept the things he stole?"

"No, but he didn't really steal things back when I was home. He stole money, or information. The storage unit was mostly for documents he didn't want at the house, and a safe place in case things got too hot."

"Fine. So, we go to this unit, hope it is where he kept his stash, find the necklace, give it back to them."

He made it sound so easy. She hoped it was, but nothing was easy where her dad was concerned.

Naveen signaled the waitress. "First, though, we need another car. They could have GPS on this one."

She hadn't even thought about trackers, though she should have. It wasn't difficult to locate a car.

Gladys came up to the table and placed a check there without them asking for it. Naveen cleared his throat. "Is one of those cars out there yours, ma'am?"

The waitress popped her gum. "What business is it of yours?"

"I'll buy it from you," Naveen said flatly.

Mira didn't know who looked more surprised, her or the waitress. Other than their shiny Ford, both of the cars in the parking lot were at least twenty years old and falling apart. Gladys was probably surprised he wanted to buy anything; Mira was surprised he had any money.

"How much money?" Gladys asked.

Naveen slid his ring off his hand. "You can have this."

Mira lurched forward. That was his father's ring. Naveen had told her that one night when they were lying in bed and she'd traced the gunmetal stone. His voice had been filled with admiration and love and fondness. Normal things that normal people felt for their fathers. "Wait," she interjected, but the other two ignored her.

Gladys picked it up and weighed it in her hand. "Throw in the car you got here in, and I'll give you mine and comp your meal."

"Uh . . ." Naveen looked at her. "Someone might come looking for it. Soon."

She shrugged. "I have boys who can handle that. And take apart that vehicle before they do."

"Can you throw in your phone? Or at least a few phone calls?"

"So whoever's after you can tie us to each other? Haven't you seen *CSI*?" Gladys gave Naveen a pitying look. "Boy, no."

Gladys was an enigma, Mira decided.

"Fine. It's a deal."

The waitress nodded and pocketed the keys to the stolen SUV so fast Mira would have missed it. "I'll go get my CDs out of the car."

Naveen came to his feet a second later.

"What are you doing?"

"We have some . . . CDs we have to remove from our car too."

The guns. "Naveen, your ring. You shouldn't have."

"Don't worry about it. I used it for exactly what it was

intended for." On that cryptic note, he turned away. "Stay here."

She hated the surge of anxiety that ran through her. *Don't you dare get too used to having him around. It definitely will not last.*

She'd been on her own for ages. This was nothing new.

Still, she couldn't resist calling his name. "Naveen?"

He gave her a questioning look over his shoulder.

She swallowed, and allowed one of her walls to drop, if only for the space of one single question rooted in emotion instead of logic. "What if we get to the storage locker, and it's not there?"

He blinked, and his eyes turned to stone. He was angry. Furious. Angrier than she'd ever seen him.

But his words were measured when he spoke, each one deliberate and chilling. "We're finding it. There's no other choice."

Mira watched him walk away. She fiddled with a french fry, then tossed it back on the plate. All she wanted was to suck down that strawberry shake and wallow in a pool of lactose and sugar, but that would be another unfortunate decision in a life where she'd made ever so many of them.

He was right. They'd find it. They had to. It was find that jewelry, or . . .

She tightened her lips. No. The *or* didn't bear thinking about.

Chapter Six

Lights flashed behind Naveen, and he checked the rear-view mirror compulsively. The car behind them turned a few seconds later, leaving the road dark and empty. He returned his gaze to the road and flexed his fingers around the peeling steering wheel. The odometer on this rusted old Camry didn't really go past sixty, so he had to guess how fast he was going. No wonder Gladys had been delighted to trade for it, even if it was for something she had to junk immediately. Thankfully, the car ran, and even more thankfully, had had a full tank.

"You're making me nervous, taking your eyes off the road so much."

He glanced at Mira. She hadn't spoken much during their drive, except to give terse directions. "I'm trying to make sure we weren't followed."

She didn't respond, merely looked out the window. The pussy bow at her throat had gotten unraveled, and it hung limply, a far cry from the jaunty knot it had been when he'd first seen her. There was a streak of dirt on her round calf and on her cheek. Her toes were cute and painted a pink to match her shirt.

Luckily, the pink on her cheek from that slap was fading. He tested his jaw. He wished he could say the same. Tomorrow he was going to have a hell of a mark on his face.

If they made it to tomorrow.

Don't think like that. One step at a time. Look forward, not to the past.

His nose twitched. How was he not supposed to think of his past when a woman he'd once, albeit briefly, thought he'd marry was sitting in the seat next to him?

Oh, he hadn't bought the ring or anything, but they'd both known it was coming. He'd been busy following his family friend's divine plan. Chastely date long-distance, meet the family, get married.

They hadn't been chaste about the dating part, but Hema Auntie didn't need to know that. When Mira had visited him in the Bay for their third date, they'd gone to a nice restaurant on the wharf, then to a bar in Oakland that served the best palomas. Her eyes had been wide and dark in that dive bar. She'd looked out of place with her modest tea-length floral dress, and her straight bob hair, every strand in place.

There had been nothing modest about her in the ride share back to his home. He'd placed his hand on her knee briefly, and she'd stopped him from removing it. Then she'd slid it higher, under the hem of her dress.

They hadn't spoken a word, both of them staring out their respective windows. The back of that car had been hot, though the air conditioning had been full blast. He'd waited for her to stop him as his hand slid up a little farther, and more, until his pinky had flirted with the edge of her panties.

She'd only given a tiny sigh and let her round thighs fall apart.

He'd lived in a ritzy high-rise condo then, all the way at the top, and the elevator had been slow. Slow enough that he'd been able to loosen the tiny fabric-covered buttons that had run from throat to waist and bury his face between her luscious breasts. Thank God no one had been in his hallway, because she'd only clutched the two sides of her top together as they ran to his unit.

Naveen shifted in the uncomfortable bucket seat, trying to shake the memory of what they'd done inside his house.

Time for a distraction. This probably wasn't a great time to ask this, but something had been bugging him since she revealed the truth about her family in that diner. "One question."

"Yes?"

"How on earth did you get Hema Auntie to take you on as a client? I've known that woman since I was born, and she regularly rejects Bollywood royalty. And real royalty. I can't believe she didn't vet your family thoroughly."

She was silent for so long, he wondered if she was going to answer. "My best friend from college, Christine?"

He vaguely recalled the South Indian woman. They'd gone out a few times in L.A. with her. He'd really liked Christine. "I remember."

"Two of her sisters used her services, and her parents are jewelry designers. They're pretty in demand, actually. They vouched for me, so she believed whatever I told her. I'm good enough on paper that she didn't look too closely."

"And she couldn't piss off a wedding vendor." His lips flattened. Hema was nothing if not a businesswoman first. "That makes sense."

"Don't worry, though. As of today, I'm definitely not her client anymore." She picked a piece of lint off her shirt. "So you won't have to tell her everything about me. It would only embarrass Christine, and she already knows."

He shot her a narrow glance. "What happened today, other than this terrible debacle?"

She straightened her dirty skirt. "The last match she found for me called things off at lunch."

"The last . . . wait, are you still using her services?"

"Yes. As of earlier today, at least. You aren't?"

"No. I never wanted to use her in the first place." Matchmaking amongst his parents' circles had always seemed far too insular and full of –isms, the same families sending the same people. He'd never cared what a woman's pedigree was.

But he'd been busy and a little hungry for companionship, so he'd bowed to familial pressure and agreed to let Hema match him. He'd been ecstatic, at first. Mira had been like a breath of fresh air. She'd been different and he'd felt calm in her presence, in a way he hadn't otherwise felt. He supposed he had no idea exactly how different she was.

"You were my first match. About a year after we broke up, I agreed to let her try again, and that also didn't work out." Understatement. "So I quit. How many matches has she found for you?"

"About a dozen."

He drew in a sharp breath before he could stop himself. "A dozen? Over the course of three years? Jesus. You must be exhausted."

"Some of them were just first dates." She paused. "But yes. I am."

Her two last words dripped with weariness, and he believed it. A dozen first dates off an app for casual dating, that was one thing. A dozen matches, where both parties were evaluating for matrimony?

No, thank you. Being with Mira had been oddly easy for him, but he couldn't say the same about Payal.

He had about a million questions about those dozen other men, starting with why they hadn't worked for her either, but he throttled them back. It wasn't his place.

Of all the luck. Why couldn't he get kidnapped with a client he didn't have a fraught romantic history with?

Don't remember how you felt about her or how long it took you to get over her. You had no idea who she was, let alone who you fell for over those six short months.

She was an entirely new person, so he'd treat her like one, at arm's length. He changed the subject. "I need a phone."

"I wish we had one. I haven't had to recall directions in a long time."

"No, to call my family. Maybe there's a pay phone or something somewhere we could stop at." They'd entered a more populated area, and the lights of Las Vegas twinkled in the distance. It was full dark now.

She threaded her fingers together. "We can't stop. They could be chasing us."

"I have to make sure they're okay." His mother was probably still at work, and there was security there.

His grandpa, though . . . his grandfather was all alone. Aparna could go over and stay with him, but what would that do?

"Let's get to the unit first. We're close. We find the necklace, we don't even have to worry about our families anymore. If they know about the unit somehow and get there before us, we lose any leverage that we have."

He hated the thought of not hearing his grandfather's voice for any longer than necessary, but she had a point.

She leaned forward. "Up there. Make a right."

There were few businesses out here: a liquor store, a convenience store, and lots of storage places. The place she directed him to was more run-down than most. HAPPY STORAGE, the sign proclaimed, but there wasn't much happy about it. They drove into the parking lot, which was fairly abandoned.

The units were inside of a large building. She input a code on the door, and they both waited for a pregnant pause. Her sigh followed his when the door beeped and they could enter the facility. Their footsteps echoed creepily on the concrete.

"I hate storage units," she murmured.

"Me too," he admitted. They stopped in front of a unit.

"Ten twenty-four. This is it."

He wasn't a religious man, but he said a prayer when she used the key. It slid into the lock without a hitch, and she lifted the door. The unit was dark and filled with shadows. He groped on the wall inside and found a switch for a light.

He'd half expected the kidnappers to either be waiting for them or to have tossed the place, but that wasn't the surprise he received. "Is this a living room, or a storage unit?"

She wrapped her arms around herself. "I told you, it was kind of a safe space."

There were some traditional markers of a storage unit: boxes were stacked neatly along the walls, and a couple of filing cabinets were in the corner. Other than that, this could have easily been a comfy man cave. A large couch had been pushed up against the concrete wall. Two bookshelves stood on either side, and a chest and ottoman were in front of it. Cases of water were neatly organized under a desk and chair, and a few old jackets hung from a coat rack.

He closed the door behind them. "It looks like no one's been here in a while."

"My aunt must have, at some point, before she died."

"Did she know, about what your dad did?"

Mira lifted a shoulder. Her eyes were shuttered. "I think

so, but no one said it out loud. She had to know, especially by the time I was a teenager."

Why then? But he didn't ask. *Distant.* "Let's stay alert. I'd rather not be knocked out again."

"Nor would I," she murmured.

A puff of air kissed his neck, and he glanced up. "This place is climate controlled."

"It is, yes."

"You wouldn't climate control a place unless you had something to protect." A low hum of excitement ran through him. "Let's look around. There's got to be something here."

"I don't even know what we'd be looking for."

"Ideally, either a diamond necklace or a map with a giant red X on it that says 'diamond necklace found here.'" If only they could be that lucky.

"My father wouldn't be that obvious. He believed in hiding things in plain sight."

"Too bad he didn't believe in not stealing shit." He regretted the words the second he caught sight of her face. Her eyes had grown huge.

While there was no lie in his words, he wasn't trying to browbeat her. "I'm sorry."

She lowered her head. "Why don't you start on that end, and I'll look over here."

He nodded. "Got it." They worked in silence for a few minutes. That silence was one of the things he'd liked about Mira. The day after the first time they'd had sex, they'd gone to a coffee shop and worked—he'd had to work on a brief, and she'd wanted to finish some non-fiction book she'd been reading about space.

It had been one of the more pleasant Sunday afternoons he'd had in a long time. He'd envisioned a long stretch of Sundays like that, filled with quiet, drama-free camaraderie. He'd mourned the loss of those Sundays once they were gone. Though of course, lately, his Sundays had been pretty calm.

He went to the desk, but it was completely empty save for some pens and papers.

"Check for false bottoms on the desk drawers."

He glanced over his shoulder, but Mira was hard at work on her side of the room. As he checked under the drawer, he realized that this wasn't so different from any escape room he had ever done. Except for the much higher stakes.

Wait, okay. He was an escape room master. His face adorned more than one business in Los Angeles for fastest time. He'd channel every single one of those skills now.

His fingers touched paper and he frowned, then he leaned over to pick the thing off the bottom of the drawer, trying not to tear it. "I have something here, I think."

She came to stand next to him as he pulled it off, then straightened. It was a tattered 5 x 7 photo of a family of four, an old JCPenney portrait.

"This is nothing." She took the photo from him, her cold fingers brushing his.

"That's your family?"

"Yes." She dropped the photo onto the desk.

Naveen assumed Mira was the infant in the sailor suit, given what she'd said. The girl next to her must be Sejal, with her bowl haircut and frilly dress. Her mom glowed with life. Her dad was gazing down at them instead of the camera, besotted. "You both look like your mom."

"I know."

"You don't remember her?"

"No. I heard she was nice. And she had a pretty singing voice."

A surge of sympathy ran through him. No matter what she'd lied about, it sucked to lose a parent, especially so young. He studied the portrait, looking for clues as to how this family could have gone astray. "They don't look like criminal masterminds."

She flinched. "They weren't, then," she said sharply. "Obviously, Sejal was a child, and my mom was never involved in any shady stuff. Her death hit my dad hard."

"Hmm."

"What's that supposed to mean?"

"What's what supposed to mean?"

"That judgy *hmm*?"

It had been a judgy noise, but he couldn't help his skepticism. He lifted a shoulder. "Your mother died and he turned into a conman? One person can't flip the switch on someone's morality."

She blinked, and looked away. "You don't get it."

"I do. I mean, I get being affected by a spouse's death. When my dad died, my mother was severely depressed."

Her eyes returned to his face. "I didn't know that."

"Most people don't." He didn't like to dwell on those dark days after his father had died. They'd scared him. He and his brother had lived close enough to visit. Their childhood home, once filled with light and parties and energy, had been silent and closed off. "She didn't eat or sleep or shower. One day, my brother stuck shoes on her feet, put her in the car, and drove her to her therapist's office. She wasn't cured then and there, but she eventually learned to find purpose in her friends and us and work. Legitimate work."

"I'm happy to hear she found something that worked for her. But don't forget that your mother had the privilege of being rich and well respected. She had resources, including you. She started in a different position than my dad did."

He nodded at that. His family was privileged. For one, he was lucky that his mother hadn't been a stranger to therapy. Perhaps Mira's father could have found a more legitimate purpose if he'd been in another situation, with different support.

Damn it. He wasn't trying to empathize with the man who had put him in danger. "That's true," he allowed.

Her nose twitched. "Actually, I'm not here to defend any-one. You're probably right." She shivered.

He took a step toward her, concerned despite himself. "You all right?"

"Yes. Fine," she said tersely. "A little cold."

It was cold in here, and the desert chill wasn't helping. He started to take off his coat, and she shook her head. "I'm okay. I'll just grab this." She put on the beaten-up brown leather jacket hanging on the coatrack. It was oversize on her, so she shoved the arms up. He tried not to notice how cute she looked in the menswear.

She frowned, reached into an inside pocket, and pulled out a silver lighter. He recognized real silver when he saw it, and this was beautifully engraved, with a scrolling C on it. "Your dad was a smoker?" he asked.

"No. I mean, yes, he was when he was young, but he kicked the habit before I was born." She shoved the lighter back into her pocket.

"I could never keep a reminder around like that."

"You smoked?"

"No." The last thing he wanted to do was tell her about his sobriety. Telling people he'd stopped drinking always resulted in one of a few reactions: chagrin or pity or morbid curiosity. He didn't want or need any of that from his ex.

He turned around and busied himself by checking the books on the bookshelf, though he didn't expect to find a diamond necklace behind any of them. For a few minutes, there was silence in the room while they both searched, broken only by a tiny gasp from Mira. "Did you find anything interesting over there?"

Mira cleared her throat. "Not really, no."

SHE WASN'T LYING, she told herself, as she reached into the document box she'd opened. She hadn't found anything pertinent to their quest. But it was something interesting, if only to her.

Compared to the other boxes with meticulously filed documents, this one was empty, save for a tattered brown leather wallet and some childishly scrawled drawings of snowmen and stick people.

The wallet, she recognized as soon as she picked it up. It was probably her imagination that her father's scent, Old Spice, wafted out to greet her.

The wallet held only a beat-up credit card and an expired license. She stared at her father's face for a second, the sound of Naveen behind her fading. Vassar had had the photo re-taken at some point over the last decade, and this was a man she didn't know. His hair had gone completely gray, and he'd gained weight, filling out the slim hollows of his face.

When he'd died, Rhea had called her, her voice clogged with tears. Mira had felt bad. Not because she was also heartbroken, but because she couldn't match her aunt's energy.

"I'm so sorry . . . gastrointestinal . . . complications . . . cremation . . . ceremony . . ."

The words in that conversation weaved in and out of her memory like a bad radio station. She'd tried to comfort her aunt as best she could, conscious that she must be something of a monster, because the only thing she could feel on her dad's death was vague empathy for how her aunt must be feeling at losing a brother.

Rhea had picked up on that. She'd quieted down, her tears fading. "I know you had your problems, but he loved you," she'd said quietly. "He wanted nothing more than to provide for you and your sister."

Bullshit. If he'd wanted to provide for them, he could have actually gone and worked in a bank. But she'd made an agreeable noise, not eager to rehash her less than rosy childhood with a woman who hadn't been around for every minute of it.

Had her dad been a monster? No. Had he ever physically abused her? No. Had he made his love conditional on her ability to financially enrich their family, been neglectful and opportunistic, ready to treat his kids as extensions of himself? Yes.

She smoothed her thumb over his license. There was a touch of a smile on his lips and in his eyes.

She slapped the wallet shut. If this was what losing contact with your kids looked like, then it didn't seem like such a bad life. He looked . . . happy.

Fuck him.

She throttled the surge of feelings. No, no. Better to be cold than hot.

Mira dropped the wallet back into the box and riffled through papers. There was a scrawled *M* on one with a drawing of four stick people on it. She presumed they were supposed to represent their family? Sejal's name, half the letters written backward, was on a drawing of a house, snowman in front.

She traced Sejal's handwriting. She had to stop thinking of how scared and cold and alone her sister must be. Mira wouldn't be able to function if she didn't successfully compartmentalize now.

Why would her dad keep these childhood drawings? For that matter, why would he keep that family photo in the desk? He'd kept so few photos of their mother, so much so that she'd hidden the wedding portrait Rhea had snuck her until she'd left home. She'd been sad later that she'd forgotten it.

Once, after Sejal had left, she'd caught him in his office, staring at the exact photo that lay on the desk now.

Unlike other times, he hadn't tossed it aside, but looked up at her. His eyes had been wet with tears, an open bottle of scotch next to him. *You should have seen me then. I wanted to give her the world after we met. And then after she was gone . . . well, I couldn't seem to get back to where I was. You're like her, Mira. You help me so much.*

And her desire to step into her perfect mom's shoes had made it easy for him to manipulate her into doing whatever he wanted.

Doesn't matter. None of this means anything. Look how happy he was without you.

The lighter was heavy in her pocket, and she reached inside to touch it. She'd asked her father why he always kept the thing around once. He'd explained that he liked the reminder that he'd had the willpower to kick at least one addiction.

She'd understood later that scams were the addiction he couldn't kick.

"Mira. Come here."

She turned to find Naveen kneeling next to the chest in front of the couch. A quilt lay on the floor next to him. He glanced up at her. "These things look personal."

She came to crouch next to him. "Any diamonds?"

"Fingers crossed."

She sifted through the contents of the trunk. *Please let there be priceless jewelry in here.*

She carefully lifted some plastic-wrapped fabric and gently shook it out of its sleeve. Not just fabric, but a blue silk sari, shot with gold thread.

She put it aside and dug into the box, intrigued. She'd never seen this chest before. The box itself was lovely, lined with satin. There were matching heels inside, blue and gold, and a few more saris. A silver tea set and plates were wrapped in bubble wrap. More bangles than she could ever wear. There were also dresses, semi-stitched and studded with crystals, and at the bottom of the chest, a red-and-gold sari.

It was the last things that jogged her memory of the photo she had managed to hide of her parents, getting married in Mumbai right before her dad had brought her mom to America. Her mom had worn this sari for her wedding. "Some of these might be my mom's things." Very carefully, she replaced the items she'd taken out. Everything smelled like mothballs. Her father hadn't taken care of much, but he had taken care of these items.

"Looks like a dowry chest."

"What?"

"An archaic custom, but still practiced in some places, even if having a dowry's not really a thing. My grandparents made one for my cousin. Filled it with items from the time she was born." He shifted. "Most of the stuff either didn't fit or she didn't care for it by the time she was old enough to get married."

"I can't imagine my dad creating a *dowry* chest for us." A panic room, sure, not a collection of items to give her and Sejal when they got married. From what she could remember, he'd never even talked about them having families of their own. He probably couldn't imagine a future where they didn't revolve around him like satellite planets.

"Maybe your mom did it?"

That was possible. She hadn't known her mom or her mom's family well enough to know what she was like or what customs she'd followed. Sejal had claimed to have memories of their mother, and she'd told her stories when she was young, about how much fun she was, how their house had been full of parties and excitement, but Sejal had been only five when their parent died, so her memories were suspect.

She didn't want to think about her mother too much, because then she'd have to think about what Naveen had said. It was handy to blame her dead mother for her dad's subsequent behavior, but he was right, it was also suspicious.

What he'd said about his mom had surprised her. She'd

gotten the impression Shweta had loved her late husband—the woman had photos of him all over the mansion—but she never would have pictured the self-possessed, reserved woman so distraught.

It was odd to think of her and Naveen having something in common with their parents.

"Anyway, no jewelry here, and definitely no diamond necklace."

Naveen turned around to face the couch and lifted the cushions. "I doubt anyone would hide diamonds in a couch, but maybe there's some quarters in here that we can use for a pay phone. Agent Stuart didn't have any change in his wallet."

"If we can find a pay phone. I haven't seen a functional one in ages." She both empathized with and was jealous of Naveen's desire to get in touch with his family. Empathized because she wished more than anything that she could call Christine right now and get a good dose of tough love and kindness. Jealous because her only blood family was being held captive.

The jealousy made her feel small. She liked Naveen's family, and the last thing she wanted was for more innocents to get dragged into her dad's mess.

His stillness caught her attention. "What?" She shut the lid to the chest and twisted.

He reached under the couch cushion and pulled out a nearly obsolete cell phone. "Jackpot." He pressed the button on the side, and to her surprise, it powered on with a chime.

"It kept its charge all this time?"

Naveen turned it around. "It's got an extra battery pack on it."

A low hum of excitement rose in her. "It must be important, then."

"It's password protected. Do you know what his password might be?"

"How would I know my dad's password?"

He looked at her like that was absurd. "I know my mom's passwords for everything. She's been using the same variations for as long as I can remember."

"That's so not secure."

"Trust me, I know. But if she uses a more complicated one, then I get twelve calls a day asking if I remember what it is, and that's not fun either."

Christine had used to bitch about the same thing. This was one of those shared cultural values she couldn't relate to, she supposed. "My dad was good at memorizing long strings of random letters and numbers. I won't be able to get into it."

"Let's try your birthday, or your mom's birthday." Shockingly, he typed without waiting for the numbers.

He still remembers your birthday.

Unimportant. He was as detail oriented as she was. Just because they hadn't been together long enough to celebrate her birthday didn't mean he couldn't remember four digits.

The phone's screen shook in denied access, and he looked at her expectantly. She humored him. "October 24."

He didn't hear the year, because he'd paused in typing. "10/24. That's the number on the locker."

Excitement rose inside her. "Huh. I didn't realize that."

There was a second where she thought they'd cracked it, but the phone merely vibrated again.

"What about your sister's birthday?"

"I promise, it won't be something so simple." She provided it anyway, and of course it didn't work.

"Do you know someone good enough with tech who could get us into this?"

The first person that popped into her head wasn't a viable one. She shoved her too big jacket up her arms. She wasn't still cold, but she didn't want to take it off yet. It gave her an odd sense of comfort, despite it being her father's. "You grew up in the Bay Area. Surely you have a host of hacker friends."

"No one I can talk to without a phone or another way to get their contact information. You don't know anyone?"

She raked her hair back from her face. At some point, she'd have to redo her hair, but the last thing she wanted was the added vulnerability of taking the mass down in front of him to fix it. "I know someone. But it's been a while since I talked to them."

"How long is a while?"

"Since I left this city."

"Do you know how to get in touch with them?" When she hesitated, he pushed. "This is our only clue right now. This could be our map."

"I know where she lived. But it's been years, she could have moved."

"Better than nothing. Let's go."

She did not want to go. She very much wanted to stay here forever. She could survive for a while, there was water in here. Bags of it, not bottles, because plastic could degrade. Her dad hadn't been a full-blown prepper, but he'd always been prepared with a plan B.

Naveen put the phone in his pocket, then picked up the quilt that was folded neatly on the couch and draped it over the chest.

"What are you doing?"

"Trying not to make this too obvious, in case someone comes here after us."

"There's nothing valuable in there." She cocked her head. "But either way, you think draping a quilt over it is going to hide it?"

"It's what I do in my car to hide my laptop. Throw a jacket over it."

She nearly shuddered. She'd seen him do that once first-hand, and it had taken every fiber in her being not to lecture him. A briefcase-size lump in the back seat of a Tesla in San Francisco? It was like a beacon to thieves. "About that, actually."

"I know, I know." He shrugged. "It's for peace of mind more than anything."

Peace of mind. Ha. What was that?

Chapter Seven

Downtown Las Vegas had gotten gentrified in the years since Mira had been there, but the duplex they were standing in front of had not. Mira knocked, and stood back, expecting nothing. It was foolish to think Emi would still be at this address after what, four, five years?

She stuck her hand in the pocket of her dad's jacket and fingered the lighter, oddly comforted by the object, though why, she wasn't sure. Not like her dad had been a comforting figure.

Naveen tensed next to her and she followed his gaze to the boarded-up fifties hotel across the street, its former glory stripped away like the busted neon sign in front of it. A pickup truck sat in the parking lot, and she took a step closer to him. She noticed his hand drop to the pocket of his jacket and she drew a harsh breath in. "Are you carrying the gun?" she whispered. She'd nearly forgotten about the weapon in their possession. The one they'd fired. Correction, the one she had fired.

Don't think about it. Not now.

He didn't even look at her. The driver's side door of the truck opened, and a man stepped out. They both took a deep breath when the older man only drank from a beer bottle and stumbled to the back of the truck.

"Naveen."

He pressed the doorbell again. "Yes, I'm carrying the gun. I've been carrying the gun."

"You don't know how to shoot."

"It's better to have it on us than in the car where it could be used against us."

"Incorrect. Give it to me." She held out her hand.

"But—"

"Which one of us can shoot? You or me?"

His lips flattened, but he handed over the gun. She checked it quickly, relieved to note that the safety was on. It felt warm in her hands, but she knew that was from Naveen's body and not the fact that she'd fired it.

The red blossoming over the man's chest.

Mira closed her mouth and breathed through her nose. "You can't—"

The door opened and Mira froze at the Glock pointed at them. "Drop your gun."

This tall, Rubenesque woman with tear-stained cheeks was not Emi, and she was definitely not playing. Mira carefully squatted and put the gun on the ground, then rose, keeping her hands visible. "We're looking for Emi. We're old friends." That was mightily stretching things, but she'd say anything at the moment to get the woman to lower her weapon.

Not that that was likely, given the annoyance and sadness on the woman's face.

"In that case, fuck off," the woman said bluntly.

"Is she here?"

"Nope."

"We could wait for her," Naveen offered. He gave the woman a smile that was so blinding, Mira had to blink. He'd turned his most charming smile on her before, but it had been a minute.

The woman snorted. "Good fucking luck. I've been waiting for years." She lowered the gun. "Who are you, exactly?"

"I, um, went to high school with her. We need her help."

"She's no help to anyone."

"Nonetheless, we'd love to speak with her. Does she live here?"

"She does, but like I said, she's not here." A malicious look entered her eyes. "I *could* tell you where she is."

"Great," Naveen said, and waited.

Mira cleared her throat. "She wants a bribe."

"I want a bribe," the woman confirmed.

Mira looked at Naveen, who pulled out their FBI agent friend's wallet. He looked inside and grimaced, then pulled out a few bills. The woman took it and snorted. "Eleven bucks?"

"It's literally all we have."

She rolled her eyes and took a step back, still clutching the bills. "Get lost."

"Wait, wait." Mira took a step forward, trying to think. The tears, her animosity toward them, the disdain in her voice. Mira clocked her disheveled hair, her distraught expression. Lovers' spat? Disgruntled partner? "I know she won't want to see us, but it's really important we speak with her."

"Oh, she won't want to see you?" The woman's lips turned up at the corners. She shoved their last eleven dollars in her bra and leaned on the door frame, the gun dangling from her fingers. "She's at the Regal down the street, in room 3202. Tell her Janice fucking hates her and hopes she dies." The aforementioned Janice slammed the door in their faces.

Mira and Naveen looked at each other. Mira scooped up their gun and stashed it safely in her inside coat pocket. "Well, this was a dead end."

Naveen shook his head. "Why? What's the Regal?"

"An older casino down on Fremont. We can't go there."

"Why not?"

"Because she's probably doing something shady."

Naveen followed her down the steps to their ancient car. "You don't know that."

"I know her, and I know that place. She's up to something. Probably gambling, maybe a private game."

"Or maybe she's enjoying a staycation," Naveen suggested.

Mira gave him an incredulous look. "Doubtful."

"Do you know anyone else who could get us into the only lead we have? Someone we can call on right now?"

Ugh. She released a frustrated exhale through her nostrils. "Fine. Let's go. But we're leaving the gun in the car."

The Regal was one of the older casinos downtown, in the area that had originally housed Las Vegas's nightlife, before the Strip existed as it did in its present form. The bones of the building were good, and the bright white lightbulbs on the pathway outside of it gave it an old-world glamour.

That was the best that could be said about it. Inside, the carpet was stained, and the slot machines were ancient. The people playing looked about as exhausted as the decor, but it was a Friday night and there was a big crowd.

Naveen took a good look around. "I don't think I've been here when I visited Vegas."

"You wouldn't have, most likely." She gave a tense smile to the couple who passed them in the hallway, eyeing them curiously. "It's not really a tourist trap."

They walked to the elevator, and she paused. "We're going to need a room card to get upstairs."

He glanced around, then crowded closer. "Put your arm around me."

She stared at him. "What?"

"Your arm." He didn't wait for her to comply, but placed it around his neck. "Pretend you're drunk."

She didn't hear that last part. She couldn't think past the fact that he was plastered against her, touching her in earnest for the first time since she'd crept out of his bed all those years ago.

His shoulders were so broad that they blocked her view of anything around him, and his arm was wrapped around her waist tight, his fingers pressing into her hip.

He'd used to hold her down easily with that hand in bed.

She shuddered. She'd carefully blocked out the memory of how good the sex had been, she'd had to, but all it took was one embrace for it to come rushing back to her.

Physically attractive to me (conventional or not). Yes, he'd checked that box, and then some.

His body, his lips, his *tongue.* He'd used his tongue like a musician playing an instrument. Sex hadn't been merely *satisfactory* with him. It had been so good, it had terrified her.

"Mira," he said, low.

"What?" Why did she sound like she was out of breath?

Without warning, he slumped against her, his eyes rolling shut. She staggered back a step, but righted herself immediately, moving her arm to his waist to better absorb his weight.

A couple walked up to the elevator bank and gave them a cursory glance. She responded with a weak smile. *Oh. Subterfuge.*

The couple pushed the UP button, and she shuffled in, Naveen nearly a dead weight. She collapsed against the back of the elevator. They tapped their key card and pressed 10. "Can you please press 32?"

She said a silent prayer of thanks when the other woman complied. Naveen groaned theatrically.

Her body was trapped between the mirrored wall and his body, and this wasn't the first time she'd been in that position. They'd never been able to wait to get from the entrance to his building to his apartment. That first time, their hands had battled with each other to unbutton her blouse, and he'd licked his way down her neck, right to her cleavage.

She turned her head. He wrapped his arm around her tighter and drew her closer, almost nuzzling her neck. His scent filled her nostrils. Cloves and cinnamon. How did he still smell like winter after hours of being kidnapped and on the run?

Naveen's heart synchronized with hers, each beat pounding through her ears, until she couldn't hear anything but the rush of blood. Mira felt like she was standing outside of her body, watching as she placed her hand on his head. She lightly stroked his hairline, at the nape of his neck.

His weight became less heavy. She turned toward him, his silky hair brushing against her nose. He nuzzled closer, his exhale warm against her neck. His hand at her waist moved, his thumb coming to rest over a pearl button, fingers heavy on her lower stomach.

She took pride in not throwing away her clothes. She'd had this shirt when they dated. He'd liked it, if she remembered right. He'd spent nearly twenty minutes untying and unbuttoning it and kissing the skin that was revealed.

The elevator dinged, the noise like a time-out bell. Naveen

let go first, drawing away as soon as the elevator closed behind the silent couple they'd shared the lift with. She cleared her throat, seeking her equilibrium after that weird minute. "Good idea."

"Thanks." He stepped away and faced forward, so she did the same.

Which was a mistake, because she could see how bizarre she looked in the mirrored doors. While Naveen was only mildly disheveled with his rumpled suit and hair, she'd been through a wind tunnel. Her coat was too big for her, her blouse was wrinkled beyond belief, the bow limp and undone. Her hair was half up and half down, hanging in a scraggly mess around her face.

No wonder the people in the elevator hadn't said anything to them. She looked like they'd taken the "What Happens in Vegas" slogan pretty far.

She quickly undid her hair, combing out the mess with her fingers as best she could.

"Might want to keep one pin in there," Naveen murmured. "In case we need it again."

"You're right." Her words were rusty, which told her she hadn't quite recovered from his touch.

Or the memory of his tongue.

She mentally groaned. *Not now, body! Focus. Remember your sister in mortal danger?*

Thankfully, that reminder worked better than a cold shower.

The elevator opened and they got out. The hallway was

quiet. It was about as run-down up here as it was downstairs.

They stopped in front of the door to room 3202 and Naveen rapped on it. Mira took a giant step all the way back when it opened, and a huge guy filled the doorway. He was bald and had tattoos running from his neck to his wrists, full-color sleeves.

This was not Emi. She'd known her old friend was up to something shady, damn it.

The stranger was bigger than both of them put together, and looked none too friendly. "Yeah?"

"Ah, we're looking for Emi Matsui?" Mira ventured.

The man looked down his nose at them. "No one by that name here." He started to close the door, but Naveen boldly pressed his palm on it. The bouncer looked like he'd be happy to break all their limbs, but he paused.

"We've heard she's here," Naveen said. "We only want to talk to her. We'll be in and out in five minutes."

The bouncer stared at Naveen's hand, then back at them. "You friends of Emi's?"

Naveen looked at Mira. Something wasn't quite right here, but she nodded. "Yes. We're friends."

His lip curled up, revealing a scar bisecting it. "In that case, come on in."

The flash of apprehension Mira felt was immediately confirmed once they were inside, and the man closed the door and shrugged his coat aside, revealing a huge black gun. He rested his hand on it threateningly. "Let's go."

They walked in front of him, and Mira's skin crawled when they got to the living room. It was a big space, and more nicely furnished than she would have guessed it would be from the rest of this hotel, with leather furniture and a giant poker table in the center. There was a balcony that had wide French doors, currently thrown open to let out the cigar smoke. Outside, the lights of old Vegas twinkled and danced.

The room was filled with fewer than a dozen people. Five sat at the poker table, three men and a woman, with another woman dressed in professional dealer garb. Scantily clad people were draped over the rest of the room, either serving food, looking hot, or in one woman's case, playing a harp. The dulcet tones were nearly drowned out by the sound of the concert happening on Fremont nearby.

Crap. This was clearly an illegal poker game. Mira'd been in enough of these rooms with her dad in the past.

She'd *known* Emi was up to something shady.

Mira scanned the suite, holding out a slim hope that Emi would be there, but there wasn't any sign of her. This was bad.

She didn't realize she'd moved closer to Naveen until his pinky brushed against hers, stilling her nervous inching.

A large man dressed in all black at the poker table spoke. "Who is this?"

"Friends of Emi's, they said." The bouncer crowded them from behind, so they took another step forward.

The man in black took a deep drag on his cigar, his thick

gold pinky ring winking at them. His complexion was pale, a dramatic contrast to his slicked-back black hair and bright pink lips. "Interesting. They have her money?"

Mira cleared her throat. "Sorry, I don't know what you're talking about."

"They're probably the ones who helped her, X." One of the other players took a sip of his drink.

"We didn't help anyone with anything," Naveen said, and his carefully modulated tone told Mira that he'd picked up on the bad vibes in the place. His fingers wrapped around hers fully, and this time, she was too distracted to concentrate on his touch, except the comfort it gave her. "And we don't have anyone's money. We heard Emi was here. We thought we could speak with her for a few minutes. If she's not, we can go, no harm done."

X's—she doubted that was his real name—eyes narrowed on them. They were like chips of granite. "Put them in the room with Emi, Ralph. We'll figure out what to do with them after the game. Bad enough she's disrupted us tonight."

"Wait," Mira said, but she was talking to the bouncer's chest, because he'd stepped in front of them.

"Move."

Naveen's chest expanded. "Listen—"

Ralph placed his hand on his gun. "Move."

Mira gulped. She exchanged a glance with Naveen, and he jerked his head. Slowly, she turned, and they were marched off down the hall.

They found another hulking guy standing outside a bedroom. He gave no reaction except for a nod to Ralph.

The bouncer shoved Naveen against the wall, and when he tried to turn around, Ralph placed one meaty hand against Naveen's back. "I gotta pat you both down."

Naveen glared at him over his shoulder, but stood still while the man checked him. It was a perfunctory pat down, but he easily found Vassar's phone in his pocket. "That's not functional," Naveen said quickly when Ralph turned it over in his hand.

The man shrugged. "Don't care. No phones."

"It's barely a phone," Mira managed. "Please, don't take that."

"House rules. If you leave, you can have it back."

That *if* was ominous.

Ralph allowed her to keep her lighter after a matching pat down. He opened the door to the room and shoved them in. It was decorated in seventies porn chic, with a massive king-size bed, gold silk bedding, and red carpet. There was a chandelier and a mirror over the bed, and a fainting couch along the foot of it.

The faucet in the bathroom shut off, and a woman entered the room. Or rather, she strutted into the room.

The last time Mira had seen Emi was right before she'd left for college. Emi had transferred into her high school the middle of their freshman year. Mira had fallen hard, not only for Emi, but for her family. The Matsuis were good, honorable shopkeepers who deeply loved their five daughters, even if they couldn't give them much. Emi had been their wild child, moving quickly from shoplifting makeup to virtual grand larceny in the years Mira had known her.

Introducing the girl to her father surely hadn't helped her come to the straight and narrow. Vassar had spotted her bright, technologically inclined mind immediately. He hadn't drafted her into his team of thieves while Mira was around, but he had encouraged Emi to live up to her full hacking potential.

Any other person might have been shocked to see their high school best friend after more than a decade, but not Emi. Or at least, she didn't bat an eye.

She leaned against the door frame and smiled, her lips slicked with a bloodred stain.

"Well, well, well . . . ," she purred. "Look who's back in town."

"Hi, Emi."

"You haven't changed one bit, Mira."

"Neither have you." Emi was as beautiful as ever. Her svelte body was clad in a sleeveless black leather jumpsuit that must have been hell to put on. It was zipped to mid boob, revealing glowing and blemish-free skin. Her long black hair flirted with the top of her butt.

Emi tapped her finger on her chin. "To what do I owe this honor?"

"They said they were your friends," Ralph said.

"*Friends* is generous," Emi said, and even though Mira had recently thought the exact same thing, it stung a bit.

"X thinks they're the ones helping you."

Emi's laugh was light and musical. "Please. I can get better help than this."

"Helping you do what?" Naveen asked.

Emi lifted a shoulder. "Nothing bad. You know how dramatic these gamblers can get."

Ralph shuffled his feet. His lips turned down, like he was disappointed in Emi. "Emi, X is pissed at you."

"How pissed?" Naveen persisted.

"Pissed enough to lock me up in here with vague threats to kill me if I don't pay them their money back." She shrugged, like it was no big deal, and maybe to her, it wasn't.

Mira massaged her temples. They'd jumped from the frying pan into the fire. "Wait, what?"

"You put cameras in the suite," the bouncer growled. "Had someone feeding you information so you could cheat. We had to move rooms. And you don't have the money to back up what you lost."

Definitely the fire. Or a fire. There were multiple fires, everything was on fire.

Emi pouted. "I needed an advantage. How was little old me supposed to win against your buddies?"

The bouncer didn't look swayed. He took a step forward, and Mira wondered whose side he was on, since he didn't look nearly as intimidating now as he had in the living room. Was he one of Emi's men? Then again, Emi was really good at making people care about her in a short period of time. "You have about an hour, I reckon, before they decide to extract their money from you one way or another. I don't have to remind you how high up we are." Ralph paused. "I mean, if they wanted to toss you over the balcony."

"I think we all understood that threat," Naveen murmured.

"Figure things out, Emi. I'd rather not murder you." On that note, Ralph slammed the door behind himself, making everyone jump. Well, making Mira and Naveen jump. Emi only smiled wider.

"Come in, come in." Emi waved them in like it was her home, and not a bedroom she was being unlawfully detained in. Her gaze critically raked over Naveen. "Who is this?"

That purr was dangerous. "Emi Matsui, this is Naveen. Emi and I went to high school together."

"Is that all we did?" Emi held out her hand to Naveen. "I was Mira's bestest friend in the whole world."

Naveen took her hand. "I was her boyfriend, for a short period of time."

"Look at that. Ex meets ex."

Mira rolled her shoulders. "Emi. What is going on?"

"It's no big deal. I thought I had a good line on skimming some cash off these people. Turns out, my tiny cameras weren't as tiny as I thought they'd be."

"How much," Mira bit off.

"Ten grand?" Emi shrugged. "Don't stress. I have someone at home who has instructions on how to get me out."

"Uh . . . is it Janice?"

For the first time, Emi looked nonplussed at Naveen's question. "Yeah."

Mira puffed up her cheeks. "I don't think she's going to get you out of anything, Emi. She, uh, looked pretty upset when we went by your place."

Emi closed her eyes and let out a long, low sigh. "Fucking hell. I knew she found out about Chelsea, but I assumed she'd calm down and move on. No wonder I was losing; I bet she was feeding me bad info. So hard to fuck good help these days."

Naveen exhaled. "Please tell me that wasn't your only exit strategy. Like, it's not Janice or the window, right?"

"No, no, no, of course not."

"Thank God." Mira looked around, half expecting someone to rappel through the window, or a secret tunnel out of the room. For all her faults, Emi was excellent at not getting caught. The one time she had, Mira had bailed her out. Not that Emi knew about that. "Did you bribe the bouncer or something?"

"Nah, I just met him tonight. You know everyone likes me."

That tracked. "Then what's your plan?"

She sat forward and gave Mira a winning smile. "Hey, Mira."

Oh no.

Before she could speak, Naveen did. "Mira's your plan?"

"Sure is."

"What do you expect Mira to do? We gave the last cash we had to your girlfriend."

Emi's smile brightened, and she didn't take her gaze off Mira. "They're playing poker. Texas Hold'em."

Fuck. She avoided looking at Naveen. "I noticed. I don't play anymore." That wasn't necessarily the truth. She played online sometimes, late at night when no one could see. It helped her sleep, and she was responsible, only trading in small amounts.

"Did you used to play?"

Emi smirked at Naveen. "Oh, you don't know? Your ex was legendary. Mira here could have gone pro easily."

She controlled her flinch. "Emi's exaggerating. I haven't played for high stakes since I left home."

"It's like riding a bike. Rusty you is better than cheating me." Emi nodded at Mira's ears. "Looks like you have some gold on you, Mira. Might be enough for a buy-in."

Mira tucked her hands into her father's jacket pockets and ran her thumbs over the lighter. It was cold to the touch, and she absorbed that ice.

You can't seriously be considering this. Not in front of Naveen.

Wait. Why not in front of Naveen? He wasn't some new guy she was dating. He already knew she'd lied. What did it matter, if he saw her play a fucking card game? Especially if winning the card game could get them a step closer to keeping his family safe?

"No," Mira said.

Naveen nodded. "Exactly. That's absurd. She—"

"Unless you agree to do something for us." She may not

be able to put all the fires out, but this one could be doused fairly quickly.

Naveen gave her a sideways glance. "Mira, no."

Emi regarded him with pity. "Mira, is something wrong with your boyfriend?"

"Ex-boyfriend," he interjected, and Mira avoided the twinge at how quickly he said it. "We are not risking our lives to get a hacker's help. It's not worth it. My buddy, Alan, I think his sister works at Google."

"That'll take time we don't have. Like you said, the phone's the only lead we have, and the only way we'll get it back from Ralph is if we can walk out of here."

"What phone?" Emi asked.

Mira raked her hair back from her face and tied it up in a messy bun, no longer caring what she looked like. "We have a phone from my father, and it's password protected. Ralph took it from us. Can you help us get in?"

"In my sleep." Emi raised her eyebrow. "Uncle Vassar won't give you the password?"

"My dad died a year ago."

"Oh." Emi stilled. "I'm so sorry, Mira."

"Thanks. He had some health issues." The words were bare. It was easier to strip emotion out of them than to analyze what her emotions were over the event.

"Damn. That sucks."

"We weren't close," she felt compelled to say to Emi, like she said to everyone who gave her their condolences. They could save their sympathy for people who deserved it. It made her feel like a fraud.

"You were once."

Mira flinched at those simple words. She'd been hesitant to come here because of the memories she had with Emi, yes, but also because of how those memories intersected with memories of her father. "I don't want to discuss it."

She was glad Emi had never met Sejal, or Rhea, so she wouldn't ask about them. Emi gave a short nod. "Okay. So, yeah. You get me out of my debt, and I will happily open that puppy up for you."

Mira believed her. There was indeed honor among thieves, and it was built on a complicated system of back scratches.

Naveen shook his head. "This is a bad idea."

There had been a time for them to talk, but this wasn't it. Right now, her priority was getting them out, and getting that phone cracked. "I got this." She went to the door and knocked on it sharply. "Hello, Mr. Ralph?"

The door opened, and the bald man's scowling face filled the gap. "Just Ralph. What do you want?"

Mira drew herself up to her full height. A low hum of energy filled her, ready to be channeled somewhere, and she was all out of pillows to scream into. "I'd like to speak to whoever's in charge."

Chapter Eight

Most of Naveen's job was spent analyzing risks, but so was Mira's, so he was quite confused as to why she thought trying to beat card sharks at their own illegal game was a good idea. "Mira, we need to talk," he hissed, while they walked down the hallway again.

She kept her gaze fixed straight ahead, hands shoved into her too-big jacket's pockets. "Don't worry."

"You said you don't play anymore."

"In person? Not since high school. But I play online."

He screwed up his face. "I was president of the chess club in high school, you don't see me risking our lives by entering championships."

"Don't know if I'd brag about your chess creds that loudly, friend," Emi remarked from behind him.

He cast her an exasperated glance over his shoulder. Who *was* this person again? "I am talking to Mira. Mira, we don't have *time* for this." Had she forgotten the federal-agents-slash-kidnappers on their trail?

"Hey. It's okay." She cast him a wide smile, and he was so distracted by it that he nearly tripped over his own feet.

Her smiles were polite affairs, mostly lip tilts. This smile, though. He hadn't seen her smile like that in . . . well, he wasn't sure he'd ever seen her smile like that. It was a reckless smile.

"I can get us out of this. Trust me."

To gamble with their lives, no matter how much experience she might have with the game . . . it was absurd. He was frustrated enough to not mince words on his reply. "How am I supposed to do that?"

Her lashes fluttered. "I know. It's a lot to ask, especially given all my lies. I'm not lying about this, though."

The way she so matter-of-factly owned up to her lies really pierced the bubble of self-righteous anger he'd gathered around himself. It was a tiny piercing, but it was an annoying one, releasing some of his anger like a tea kettle letting out steam.

He opened his mouth, but they were out of time to discuss. He fell silent as they entered the living room again. Ralph cleared his throat. "The lady wishes to pay her friend's debt."

One of the men at the table looked over at them with little interest. He wore suspenders, a bow tie, and black horn-rimmed glasses. "With her body or money? If it's the body, no thanks."

"It's money," Mira said crisply. "But I appreciate your input."

The man in black raised his hand. The other people at the table and in the room quieted. Naveen had clocked him, this mysterious X, as the leader of the group immediately. And the one they needed to watch.

"I'm listening."

Mira cleared her throat. "Let me play. I'll cover Emi's losses out of anything I win."

X snorted. "Why would I let you do that? You probably have a camera or something up your sleeve, like your useless friend."

"I don't. No earpieces, no cameras. No tricks."

X leaned forward, the light falling on his slick hair. There were deep wrinkles around his mouth and forehead, and Naveen was going to guess they weren't from smiling too much. He didn't look like he smiled at all. "Prove it."

"How do you want me to prove it?"

"Take off your shirt."

Like hell he'd let them ogle Mira. They may have their issues, but that wasn't right. "Uh, wait a minute." Naveen stepped forward. "No one is taking their shirt off—"

"It's fine." Mira shrugged off her coat, handed it to Naveen, then loosened the buttons of her shirt with brisk efficiency. She spread her shirt open, revealing a lacy black bra.

He didn't know this bra, exactly, but he did remember her penchant for frothy, peek-a-boo underwear, a far cry from her usually modest clothes.

One glance, and he fixed his gaze firmly on her face. He nearly growled when he realized every other person in the room wasn't averting their eyes.

Not because he was jealous. It was simply common

decency. She wasn't a piece of meat, and he wasn't thinking about the way her sweet curves had pressed up against him in that elevator.

He mentally shook his head. *Not now.*

Shirt still unbuttoned, Mira turned her head this way and that. "See? Nothing. No cameras, no listening devices."

The man with the eyeglasses adjusted them. "I retract what I said about not taking your body."

The lone woman at the table sat back. She was in her fifties and dressed in a sequined black dress that was about a size too small for her, like she'd borrowed it from someone. Her makeup was thick and heavy. Her hair was bleached platinum blond and pulled up high on her head in an updo. "That's not the kind of game I signed up for."

The last man at the table, a skinny Black man, piped up. "Same. I'm here to win everyone's money, and that's it."

Mira buttoned up her shirt, and tucked it in neatly. "I'm happy to let you try."

X tapped his fingers on the table. "You have the buy-in?"

"Not in cash. I have gold." Mira undid her earrings.

"That's not enough."

Mira faltered. Naveen couldn't resist trying to sway the gamblers to an easier way to recoup their losses. "Listen, I can pay back Emi's debt, and we can go on our way. Venmo? Is Venmo good?"

The woman tapped her fingers on her glass. "You think we want you to Venmo us the winnings from an illegal poker game?"

He gritted his teeth. "I'll put it on private mode. Or I can wire transfer it."

"You have twenty-five thousand dollars on you?"

He cast Emi a narrow glance. "You said ten."

For the first time, Emi appeared mildly ashamed. "I may have lost count."

At one time, twenty-five grand would have been pocket change for Naveen, but he didn't work at Miller-Lane anymore, and he was often, as his mom had noted, paid in biryani.

He was rich in family, and his family was rich, however. "I don't have it, but—"

"Who are you, anyway?" X asked.

"I'm her . . ." He exhaled and tilted his head at Mira. "I'm her attorney." Kind of.

"Her attorney," said the woman, with a hearty chuckle. "Hey, Ryder, you know the difference between me and an attorney?"

The Black man raised an eyebrow. "What?"

"I only screw one person at a time."

Naveen rolled his shoulders. He hated to admit it, but that was a good one.

"Looks like you have a nice Rolex there, lawyer. Add that to the earrings, and we can give your client a chance."

Fuck. He cradled the watch protectively. His parents had given the piece to him when he'd passed the bar.

He'd grown up with the knowledge that his family expected their younger son to have some prestigious job where he regularly collected watches that cost five or six figures. But his father had pulled him aside that night at the party they'd thrown for him. They'd both been tipsy, as was usually the case at family parties. *Fancy things can't bring you happiness, son. Wear it, but remember that it's nothing but metal. Metal can be melted down and broken, a good life cannot be.*

He'd clung to those words and the watch when he'd burned out and left his old life behind, using them to remind himself that his father would have valued his mental health over money.

Bartering the ring had been oddly painless. He didn't want to lose this piece of his dad.

Naveen made the mistake of looking down at Mira. Her eyes were huge. *Trust me,* they screamed.

After a long moment, she turned to X. "He's not a part of this."

Wasn't he, though?

It was his life and his family at stake, too. The reasoning he'd given her before for why he couldn't walk away from this endeavor still stood. *It's nothing but metal.*

He undid the watch strap. "Fine," he muttered.

Out of the corner of his eye, he caught Mira's surprise. "I will get it back," she whispered, and the fierceness in her voice convinced him she believed she could. Whether she really would, though, wasn't entirely up to her, was it?

Ralph took their valuables from them and X smiled like the Cheshire Cat. "If everyone's on board, I'm game to have an extra chair filled. We are a man down." X looked around the table and was met with nods or shrugs. "Ralph, pat Ms. . . . what's your name?"

"Amira," she supplied. Her fake name. Funny, how, in the course of a few hours, he'd gotten used to thinking of her as Mira.

"Great. Pat her down more thoroughly. I'm not dealing with any electronics again. You can call me X, and this gentleman is Ryder, and Claudette." He nodded at the bespectacled man, who was still leering at Mira, much to Naveen's annoyance. The man looked like a sweaty, horny weasel dressed like an old-timey bartender. "This is Charles."

"Can't wait for you to lose, Amira." Charles's gaze moved over her like her shirt was still unbuttoned.

"I won't," Naveen's ex-girlfriend remarked, and she took the seat that the silent dealer gestured to.

"We play winner takes all," X said, and his smile was cold. "Hope you can last the next few hours."

"I actually only have an hour," Mira said calmly. "So we'll have to finish by then, tops."

X's laugh was on a huff of air. The others looked equally amused. "Uh, okay. Then the blinds will double every five minutes."

Naveen had only a small inkling of what that meant, but by the smirks of the other players, he had a feeling that it was not a good thing. "Now this is getting interesting," Ryder said softly.

"Fine," Mira agreed. "Let's play."

Naveen's gaze met Mira's and she gave him a single nod.

Ralph prodded him and Emi to go sit on the empty couch behind Mira, next to the harpist, who began playing again, the mellow music filling the room. They wouldn't be able to see Mira's cards from here. "You two can watch," Ralph said, and his tone was almost apologetic, and certainly pitying. "It won't take long for this to be over."

And in the beginning, Naveen believed him. Mira lost steadily, the chips in front of her dwindling. But then, at a certain point, her fortunes reversed, and she started winning back small amounts, a little here, a little there, chipping away at each of the four other player's fortunes. Her bets were conservative even on her best hands, but she was also expressionless and still. The other players had excellent poker faces, but they still had poker faces. This was how Mira *was*—calm, controlled.

"That vein in your forehead is freaking me out. Have some faith in your girl," Emi murmured next to him, sotto voce.

"She's not my girl. And it's not about faith. This is risky."

"And you don't like risks?"

"Not really, not anymore." There had been a time in his life where he'd been all about risks. The risk of working at a big law firm, where every word and action was scrutinized on a daily basis, the risk of not working for his family's company, the risk of meeting and dating someone outside of his own social circles. Then he'd taken one risk too many.

"Sounds boring. Makes sense you're an attorney." Emi rolled her eyes.

He was *not* boring. Or maybe he was, nowadays, tucked away in his grandfather's spare apartment, but that was a good thing.

Your ex was legendary. Mira here could have gone pro easily.

He tried to wave away the nagging discomfort about what Emi had said, but something about it was off, and Naveen did so hate things being off. "Where was Mira playing poker in high school? Were there teen tournaments?"

"Oh, you sweet summer child. Did you think she was playing for Monopoly money before she was legally of age?" Emi smirked. "Her dad had her playing in backroom games with higher stakes than this."

He was naïve, because that had been what he'd assumed. "Against adults?" Naveen had to force himself to speak low, under cover of the music, but his voice wanted to raise on that question.

"Yup. Uncle Vassar would drop Mira off, go get some drinks at the bar, and by the time he was ready to pick her up, she'd be reading a book outside the room. With everyone's money." Emi wrinkled her nose. "I tagged along every now and again. At the time, I thought it was super cool."

Naveen ran the back of his hand over his mouth. "That's not at all cool." That was . . . horrifying. He couldn't imagine leaving his teenager alone in a room with adults like these.

Had Mira been scared? Or had she faced them with the competent calmness she displayed now?

Emi lifted her shoulder. "She had skills he wanted to encourage."

Naveen thought of the careful blankness in Mira's face in her father's storage unit. "Who kept the winnings?"

"You know which questions to ask, lawyer. Her dad kept them."

So it hadn't been encouragement, it had been exploitation.

He placed Mira's jacket next to him. How she was able to wear it, he didn't know. No wonder she hadn't cared much about the dowry chest or anything else her father had left her, and no wonder she'd skipped town as soon as she was legally able to do so.

No wonder she buried everything about her family and didn't tell you about it.

Another piercing of his anger, and this time it was due to compassion.

It got to a point where I could no longer sanction what he was doing.

When Mira had said that in the diner, he'd assumed she'd meant she couldn't tolerate his actions. He didn't know why he hadn't even considered the possibility, until now, that Mira's father might have tried to drag her into his schemes as a child, that she'd left because she could no longer sanction what he was having her do.

Does that change anything where you're concerned?

Yes. He wasn't sure how yet, but he'd figure it out.

"Why wouldn't she tell me about this?" he murmured, almost to himself. If she'd wanted to manipulate him, painting herself as the victim would have done it.

"I don't know. Maybe she didn't want you to pity her. The girl I used to know was pretty proud."

That was possible. The woman he'd used to know had been proud to the point of pain. *You also thought she was scrupulously honest.*

Maybe she hid this one thing, this one major thing, but for good reasons? Everything else could have been true.

Something changed in Emi's demeanor, a twinge of seriousness touching her eyes. "Who ended things, you or her?"

He looked down at Emi. "She did."

Emi didn't seem surprised by that. "Same here." She patted his hand. "It's an elite club. Welcome."

He snorted. "Thanks."

"I can see you're still mad at her about it."

"You don't seem mad at her at all," he countered. It was odd that he felt free to talk to Emi about this, but she did have a very likable quality about her. No wonder she'd befriended Ralph as she had. She reminded him of someone, though he couldn't quite put his finger on who.

Emi regarded the object of their conversation. At the table, Mira shifted. She looked cool and composed, like she was in a forensic audit and not attempting to win their freedom. "I'm mad at her. But I understand her."

"You probably know more about the real her. I only know fragments."

"Ralph, if our guests cannot be quiet, perhaps they need to be placed in the bedroom." X didn't look up from his cards while he spoke.

"We'll be quiet," Naveen said soothingly. Ralph gave them a warning look.

"I bet it really bugs you when someone's messy and all over the place, huh?"

He shot Emi an exasperated look over her still talking given the warning they'd received. The woman really did blow past obvious threats, didn't she? "I don't care if someone's messy." He was messy. "I just like having the whole mess. All the pieces."

Emi gestured at the table. "Watch, then. You'll need this puzzle piece if you want to figure out Mira."

He didn't want to figure out Mira. He had no reason to. They were going to get out of this, and then they'd never see each other again.

Nonetheless, he watched.

He wished he knew more about poker; from what he could tell, the pots and the bets were getting bigger and bigger. Charles was the first to lose all his chips, and he sat back in disgust as X pulled in the last of his fortune. A woman in skimpy lingerie came over from the bar to comfort him, and he looked instantly less sulky.

Ryder was the next one out, and then on the next round Claudette, who growled and tossed back her whiskey when she went bust. The other three players didn't move from the table, though, and Naveen didn't blame them. If he could divorce Mira from this event, he might be excited to watch this showdown, too.

X smiled at Mira over his piles of chips. He had taken the

majority of their opponents' stashes, finishing them, but her smaller wins had proved surprisingly lucrative, especially in later rounds, and they had roughly the same amount of chips in front of them. Actually, Mira might even have a slight edge.

If only they could leave now. Naveen leaned forward, linking his hands together. He wasn't a praying man, but he was praying now.

"Surprised you got this far?" X purred.

The dealer opened a fresh pack of cards. Mira shrugged. "No."

X laughed. There was a flush of color on his pale face. He was loving this. "I promise I'll make this quick, sweetheart. I know you have somewhere to be."

"Thank you." Mira took a quick peek at the cards the dealer placed in front of her. X did the same.

Mira went first. "Call."

X shrugged. "Raise." He tossed in double the chips.

"I'll raise." Mira doubled his bet.

X smiled thinly. "Well, well, well. The lady's getting desperate, I see."

Mira cocked her head. "Do I look desperate to you?"

He chuckled and met her reraise. "Call."

The dealer dealt three cards faceup. Ace of hearts, seven of clubs, three of diamonds.

Naveen wiped his hands on his pant legs. That wasn't a great flop, but maybe Mira could make something out of it. Otherwise, best-case scenario, he'd get another shot at convincing them to let him pay these people back. Worst case, they'd see if the three of them could fly when they got dropped off the balcony.

"Check," Mira said, essentially passing.

X sucked his teeth. "Check."

The dealer revealed the turn. King of spades.

Naveen hoped Mira caught the way X's face subtly relaxed, but her gaze was focused on that single card. Damn it, the man had something in his hand.

"Check," she said, again passing. Was this a strategy?

X tapped one finger on the table, then shoved a stack of chips in. "Raise."

Mira did something she hadn't done before. She peered at the two cards in her hand again. "Raise," she said quietly, doubling his wager.

Ryder shifted in his seat, but he didn't say anything. Everyone in the room was silent, including the harpist.

"Reraise," X said, and shoved another handful of chips into the pot.

Mira studied him, then matched his bet. "Call."

The dealer turned over the last card, and Naveen inhaled. A seven of diamonds. What on earth did Mira have that she was so confident? Or was she bluffing?

A slight movement brought his eyes down to her feet, in those ridiculous pink flip-flops. Her toes were curled tightly.

Naveen's gaze shifted around the room, seeking an exit for that potential worst-case scenario. His heart pounded in his ears.

Mira spoke as soon as it was her turn. "Check."

X's smile grew more confident. He shoved the rest of his chips to the center of the table. "All in."

She let the silence drag out for a second, then matched his bet, leaving her with nothing. "Call."

His chuckle was long and low. "Honey, you really did want to get this over with quickly." X flipped over his cards, and Naveen stood so he could see properly.

A king and an ace.

"Two pair," the dealer intoned, and looked at Mira expectantly.

She flipped her hand over. A seven and a two stared up at all of them.

"Three of a kind," the dealer said, then hesitated for a beat, betraying her first sign of emotion. Trepidation, with a healthy dose of caution. "The lady wins."

Naveen shoved his hand against his mouth, to keep in his shout of exhilaration. His pulse was pounding, and it took all his concentration not to fist-pump and crow in relief. By God, she'd done it.

"Jesus Christ," Emi whispered next to him. For all her confidence in Mira, she seemed as stunned as everyone else in the room.

Ryder let out a low, long laugh. "This chick beat you," he said between chuckles. "With the fucking hammer? A seven and a two."

"Congrats," Claudette remarked. "Well played."

Mira folded her hands in front of her. "Thank you." She

looked at X. "I believe that settles the debt, and then some," Mira said quietly.

"How did you do it?" the man asked. His voice was calm, but there was an edge in it that made Naveen tense.

"I'm not sure what you're asking."

"You count cards?" Charles asked. He lit up a cigar. "I gotta know."

Mira barely spared him a glance. "This is poker, not blackjack. It's impossible to count cards. You must know that."

X straightened his jacket. Ryder interrupted whatever he was going to say. "You have quite the poker face, young lady. Good strategy, but it's the face. You looking for work?"

"Thank you for the offer, but I already have a job." Mira paused. "The money would come in handy, though."

Claudette tossed back her drink. "No recruiting. Pay these kids, X, and let them go."

X looked annoyed, but he capitulated. "Yes, yes. We'll forgive the debt." He reached into his pocket and pulled out her earrings and Naveen's watch, handing them to Mira. "Here. Go on."

She accepted the jewelry, but didn't move. "I won more than this."

Emi came to stand next to her, her avaricious gaze on the pile of chips in front of Mira. "Yeah, she won more than the debt."

"You should be very grateful I'm letting you all leave via the door." X's smile slipped. "Instead of the window."

"We are very grateful," Naveen said hastily. If he could

shove both these women out of here without further threats of defenestration, he'd be thrilled.

Mira shook her head. "Very grateful. But you're running an honorable game here, right?"

"You're calling my honor into question?" The man's glower was chilling.

This was a two-star hotel, not a saloon in the Wild West, but for the life of him, Naveen couldn't tell the difference right now. He took a step forward. "Let's not get hasty. I think what Mira is saying is that things ought to be fair. We were willing to hold up our side. You should hold up yours."

She cast him a surprised glance, though he wasn't sure why. For one, she deserved that cash. Second, they needed it. It probably wouldn't get them out of their diamond necklace jam, but at the very least, it might help them on the remainder of the quest.

Plus, she *deserved* it. She'd played her ass off, and he was . . . proud?

Huh.

The man in black leaned back. There was a tense, pregnant pause, and then he nodded. "You're right, lawyer." He gestured to the woman behind the bar. "Pay them what they're due, minus the debt. And then get out."

"What a night." Claudette came to her feet. "Now, if someone could call me a cab, I have to get back to my hotel."

"State senates don't run by themselves, eh?" Ryder shoved back from the table and smiled cheekily at her.

She cast him and Mira a meaningful glance. "Watch it."

"They'll keep quiet about this night." Ryder gave her his arm.

"We will," Mira said. She gave Naveen an odd glance when he also offered his arm to stand, though she took it.

"Emi. You will not be invited back. I expect you to be discreet anyway." X's gaze settled on Mira. "I hope we play again sometime, little girl."

Mira zipped up her coat and avoided Naveen's gaze. "Perhaps."

Naveen let out a giant breath when the bartender paid them out. It was a hefty stack of bills. At the door, Mira looked up at Ralph, whose longing gaze was on Emi. "Our phone, please."

He nodded and pulled their only lead out, handing it to her. The door shut behind them with finality. Naveen glanced around the empty hallway, then let loose with a quiet whoop and grabbed Mira by the shoulders. "Jesus, did you see that? That was so cool!" He spun her around, then pulled her in for a hug, the adrenaline surging through him finally able to have a release. "He was like, raise. And you were like, I raise you again, *bitch*. And then you won! With a fucking seven and a two." He looked over at Emi, who was leaning against the wall, arms over her chest. "That's hard to do, right?"

"Pretty hard," Emi confirmed.

He squeezed Mira so tight she squeaked. Mira murmured something against his chest, but it was muffled. He was holding her off the floor. He put her down gently and released her. She stumbled back a step and readjusted her shirt. "No big deal."

"No big deal? You didn't just kick ass in there, you handed it to him. I knew you were smart, but that was *cool*."

Mira lowered her lashes and tucked her hair behind her ears. "Oh. Um, thank you."

"Thank *you*. God." He put his hands on his hips. "I shouldn't have doubted you."

"You had reason to."

He did. Or rather, he thought he had. Now he didn't know.

"Do you have a room here, Emi, or are we going back to your place?"

Emi straightened away from the wall, where she'd been watching them like a scientist studying her specimens. He clearly wasn't the only one who liked puzzles. "Of course. Follow me."

Naveen kept pace with Mira as they moved down the long hallway. His arms felt oddly empty. "Really, um, good work."

"Thanks." She reached out to him, and he wondered if she was going to hold his hand. Instead, her fist opened, revealing his watch. "And thank you for this."

"Oh. Yeah. No big deal." He took the watch and fastened it on his wrist.

"It is a big deal. I wish I could get your ring back, too."

He shot a glance ahead of them, but Emi was a few steps away. She was probably listening, but that was okay. "It did its job."

"You said something similar before. What does that mean?"

He paused for a second. The story wasn't one he was particularly proud of, so he'd never shared it with Mira. "When I was about twenty, my friend and I got into a bar fight with some guys over a game of pool. My dad gave me the ring the next week. Told me to pay my debts with it in the future." That was a highly sanitized version, but there was no need to go over his misspent twenties. Not quite wild, but not entirely sedate.

She squinted up at him. "*You* got into a bar fight?"

"Why is that a surprise?" Did she think he was boring, as well?

You want to be boring.

"Sounds messy," Emi tossed over her shoulder. "That's why."

He didn't miss Emi's emphasis on the word *messy*. So he had his own messes, too, and he hadn't revealed all of them to Mira. There was a scale of covering up messy, damn it.

"I never thought you'd be a fighter, is all."

They got to the elevator. The doors opened, and they piled in. He caught Mira's reflection in the door, and thought of how he'd briefly opened his eyes when they'd been in here on the way up.

He'd seen her face in the mirror, then, too. Her lips had been parted, slightly slick, like she was remembering the embraces they'd shared in his old elevator, too.

It was the memory that gave his next words a flirtatious

gloss. "Should have had you with me back then, and it wouldn't have gotten to the fight."

She ducked her head. "I'm not good at pool."

He fiddled with his watch clasp. "Emi said your dad had you playing games like this since you were a kid—"

Mira spoke in a rush, cutting him off. "Emi doesn't always know what she's talking about." He was good at interpreting the looks women gave their friends, and the one Mira shot Emi had *don't say another word* all over it.

Interesting.

Emi nodded. "That's true. I'm a disaster." The elevator dinged. "Come, friends. Let's get into that phone."

Chapter Nine

Mira didn't cry often. In fact, she could remember most of the times she had: when Sejal had left home, when she finally got sick of her father using her, when her aunt had passed away.

Alone in your car, when you decided to end things with Naveen.

That was, actually, the only breakup in recent memory where she had cried.

Mira tilted her face up to the shower. Tears happened so rarely that it wasn't a huge surprise that she didn't cry in Emi's bathroom, even though the pressure building behind her eyes was immense. There was no reason to cry. They were safe, they had emergency funds, Emi would crack the phone for them, and it would hopefully yield that diamond necklace map they were hunting for.

Emi said your dad had you playing games like this since you were a kid.

Bleh. Mira scrubbed at her arms until they turned pink. Emi! She'd known bringing Naveen into the orbit of her old friend was a bad idea, and this was exactly why.

It was one thing for Naveen to see her play poker. Quite another to expose the seedy underbelly of her childhood traumas completely.

I should never have doubted you.

That had been a silly thing to say. He should one hundred percent doubt her.

His trust had thrown her for a loop, though she'd known she could win his watch back. Poker had always come easily to her. Partially it was because it was a game of numbers, and numbers had always been her friends. Mostly because she had, as Ryder had noted, an uncanny ability to hide her emotions.

She didn't hate the game. She'd hated the player, her father, for using her to make himself money. For making her feel like her only worth lay in what she could do, not who she was.

This was the first time she'd played poker and not been low-key terrified. Which made sense, because she had been a kid when she'd played last.

That asshole.

No, no, no. The bottles filled with her emotions rattled, her anger threatening to break free, but she restrained them, breathing deep and even.

She wrapped her arms around herself, using the hug Naveen had given her to ground herself. He'd sounded so proud of her.

Your dad gave you hugs after you won games, too. He was proud, as well. That hug didn't mean anything.

It was the adrenaline. Naveen would cool down soon and remember that she was the one who had lied to him and dragged him into her family mess, and then he'd be distant again. And there'd be zero opportunities for his body to be pressed against hers. Staged or in passion.

Yikes. Definitely, she wasn't thinking about passion with him, or those long-repressed memories were going to come up again. Like the time they'd been swimming together at her hotel, and she'd gone to clean up. He'd knocked on her door, then slipped inside. The shower, and her. His hands had held her hips firmly while his body slid over her—

She realized she was stroking the soap over her breasts and flushed. *The stress is getting to you. Snap out of it. Get back to work.*

Mira shut the shower off. Emi had tossed her some extra clothes before offering her the bathroom. As much as she hated to put on her own underwear again now that she was clean, she did, and then yanked on the stretchy joggers and oversize black T-shirt Emi had given her. Well, oversize on Emi. Regular size on her.

She hesitated before depositing her old clothes in the garbage can. Throwing away anything was hard for her, but these garments were all too soiled and carried too many memories now to keep.

A burst of laughter came from the living room and Mira frowned, worried. She couldn't imagine Naveen and Emi laughing together—both of them had been vaguely wary of each other when they'd met. *What else did you tell him, Emi?*

She picked up her pace. Emi sat at the desk in the corner, hunched over Mira's dad's phone, while Naveen lounged on the couch behind her. "I said I wasn't interested in monogamy, so this is really her fault for—" Emi glanced up, though Mira was soundless. "Oh, hi, Mira. I was telling Naveen about Janice."

"Apparently, Janice thought she could change Emi," Naveen said, thumbing through the hotel magazine on his lap.

"Can you capture the wind, I ask you?" Emi demanded.

Naveen nodded in sympathy. "Rookie move. You gotta take people as you find them."

Mira tensed. What was that supposed to mean?

It means you'll always be what your father made you.

Or his words had nothing to do with her.

"Women, am I right?" Emi sighed.

"I'd rather not answer that, thank you." Naveen tossed the magazine on the table and came to his feet to stretch. Mira tried not to stare at the way his shirt stretched taut over his belly. He relaxed and rested his eyes on her. While he wasn't still bubbling over with the warmth that had taken him over when he'd swung her around the hallway, his gaze wasn't as angry as it had been before. *Don't trust it. It's still the adrenaline.* "Emi's confident she can crack the password."

Right. The password. The reason they were here.

"Ten more minutes, tops," Emi said.

"I'm going to go shower, too, if you don't mind."

"Make yourself at home. *Mi casa es su casa.* Unfortunately, I don't have any extra clothes that'll fit you."

"I don't mind wearing mine." He paused. "Can I use the phone?"

Emi lifted a shoulder. "Yeah. It's on the nightstand. But I'm telling you, man, you gotta kick the screen habit."

"I'll work on it on a less stressful night." As Naveen passed Mira, he reached into his pocket and pulled out the wad of cash from the poker game and handed it to her. "Here, you can hold on to this."

She took it automatically, then looked down at it as he walked away. Mira didn't know what had driven her to push for all the money they were owed, except that she'd been caught up in the moment.

She also didn't know why Naveen had backed her up on it. *Trust me*, she'd told him before the game, and she was truly confused that he had.

She tucked the money into her pocket. "I'm surprised you have everything you need here to do this. Are you sure we don't need to go to your place?"

Emi glanced up from her laptop. Vassar's phone was face up on the desk, plugged in. "All I ever need is my computer."

"You don't want to face Janice."

Emi wiggled her fingers at her. "Bingo. The desk staff here knows me, they always comp me a couple nights when I need it. There's some room service left over from lunch, if you want it."

Mira's mouth watered. Her last full meal, that gourmet lunch with Jay, seemed ages ago now. If she'd known the adventure she was going to go on, she might have eaten that cake, dairy or not.

The tray was pretty sparse: most of an eggplant parmigiana, half a ham sandwich and some chips, but it looked like heaven to Mira. She shoved a handful of chips in her mouth and came back to the couch with the sandwich. "Thank you for the clothes."

"Sorry they're not stylish, but they look better than whatever it was you were wearing before."

"They feel better, at least. We've had a rough night so far." Back in high school, she would have plopped down on the couch and spilled her guts to Emi, but it had been a long time since high school. "Can I borrow some shoes too?"

"What, your hot-pink flip-flops from some rando diner aren't giving you good arch support?"

Emi was even sharper than she'd been as a teenager, it seemed. "It's a long story."

"I bet it is. You going to tell it to me?"

Mira concentrated on polishing her sandwich off. "It's complicated."

"I'm guessing if your dad's involved, it's got to be something wild." It wasn't an insult. Emi sounded almost admiring.

Mira heard the shower in the bathroom go on, which freed her to speak. "My father was nothing if not exciting." Excitement she could do without.

"I remember. I saw him a few times over the years. He told me you two didn't talk much since you left town."

Mira shrugged and ate another bite of her sandwich. That her dad had been more in touch with her ex–best friend than with either of his daughters was extremely on brand for the man.

"I understand you cutting your dad off, of course. He shouldn't have had a literal kid mixed up in his work. That was fucked up."

Mira tried not to go about chasing validation, but she got so little of it when it came to shutting out her family—not even from her aunt—that she absorbed it like a sponge. "You thought he was cool then." It had given Mira instant cred with the wild Emi, that her dad was a conman, their home a den of thieves.

"Because I was young and sick of bagging groceries at my parents' store. Here was your dad, talking about getting rich quick. It was seductive."

Mira swallowed, her sandwich tasting like ashes. "I'm sorry he led you down that path."

Emi shoved her long black hair over her shoulder. "Ah. So it was guilt that bailed me out."

Mira crossed her legs. "Excuse me?"

"What were you up to, say, October, six years ago?"

Mira polished off the last of her sandwich, using the big bites as an excuse not to speak.

That didn't stop Emi. "Because I was locked up, but someone anonymously donated a large sum to my mom to bail me out of jail, with enough left over to pay my legal fees."

Emi looked at her from under her lashes. "I know you told her not to tell me, but she's a terrible liar."

"So it seems." Mira checked over her shoulder. The water was still running. She didn't want Naveen to hear this, and not because she was ashamed. No, she didn't want him to hear this the same way she didn't want anyone to know what organizations she volunteered for or where she donated her money.

Some people, like her late aunt, volunteered out of the goodness of their soul. She did it to cleanse her conscience. "Speaking of, how's your mom?"

"Her cancer came back."

Mira sucked in a breath at the naked pain in Emi's words. "I'm sorry to hear that."

"You knew, though, right? Same way you knew where I lived? And about that time I was in jail?"

Mira shifted. "I . . . I may check in on her social media periodically."

Emi didn't look like she believed Mira, and she shouldn't. Mira did check social media, and then engaged in a little light stalking on Google to keep tabs on the Matsuis. Emi's mom was on her third round of chemo, the store closed last year, two of Emi's sisters lived out of the country, and the other two had deadbeat husbands and no money.

If one knew where to look, information was easy to come by.

"So?"

"So what?"

"Was it guilt? That had you helping us out?"

Mira wiped her hands on her napkin. "I heard about what happened. You're a literal genius, it was a bloodless crime. Your mom needs you and I figured you needed a chance to rehabilitate."

Amusement flashed in Emi's eyes. "Ah. How logical. In case it was guilt, though, you don't have to reform me just because your dad taught me some tricks way back in the day. You know that, right?"

Mira didn't know that. But for her, Emi wouldn't have had a criminal in her life. Maybe she would have grown up to use her brilliant mind for good instead of evil.

Mira had met Emi during English class in ninth grade, and she'd felt a click with her immediately, which didn't happen often for Mira. She'd been a shy, quiet kid, and even quieter after Sejal had left home. Something about Emi's wild, brash personality had called to her, brought her out of her shell.

A couple weeks later, Emi had come home with Mira to work on a school project. Emi had paused in the door to her dad's office and looked over his bulky computers. "Nice setup," she'd commented, and the next thing Mira had known, Emi was poring over the computer manuals with her dad.

After that, Emi had been the one friend of hers whom Vassar had remembered the name of. When she came by, her dad listened carefully to the latest hacking project she was working on, then give her ideas on what to try next or where to look for information.

"He was my father," Mira said. "If I hadn't introduced you . . ."

Emi laughed. "Weirdo. I was hacking school databases to change grades before we even moved to Nevada."

"You . . . what?"

"How do you think we got an A in French? We were so shitty at it. Well, you were shitty at it, and I copied off you."

Mira's mouth dropped open slowly. "Emi . . . you told me participation bumped our grades."

"Yes, and it pained me how gullible you were. Relax, I only tweaked that one of yours. You got into USC on your own merits. Mostly."

Mira groaned. Fuck.

"Anyway, forget I said that. If you want to feel bad about something, feel bad about how you didn't even say bye to me. That sucked."

Mira's eye twitched. She remembered. Her aunt had attended her graduation. Her father had been absent. The Matsuis had invited her out to eat with them, but she'd declined.

She'd come home that day, changed out of her clothes, and packed her bags. Rhea had tried to convince her to stay, told her that her dad was on a *business trip*, instead of holed up in some casino somewhere like Mira knew he was. She'd stood her ground. Finally, Rhea had agreed to help her find a studio in Los Angeles for the summer, until classes started.

She'd felt so free, all alone in her apartment on her own. She'd picked up the phone multiple times, those first couple months, to call Emi, but something had always stopped her. Like her brain couldn't fathom letting even a good part from her past into her life.

Yes, perhaps it had been guilt that had her sending money to Emi's family. "I shouldn't have done that," she managed.

"You're damn right. You should have known better than anyone how much that sort of thing hurts, after Sejal did it to you."

If Mira hadn't been sitting, she would have taken a step back. As it was, she flinched. Emi continued to speak, but it turned into a bunch of babble to her ears.

No. She'd spent all this time mad and betrayed by her sister, and then she'd done the exact same thing? Ghosted Emi, grew distant with her aunt. Anything to forget her childhood and her father, even if it meant excising the ones she'd loved.

It had felt necessary at the time. Had it felt that necessary to Sejal back then, too? Had her sister spent her adulthood racked with guilt for reactive choices she'd made when she was a teenager raised in a dysfunctional home?

Her breath strangled. Her sister had been older than her, yes, but that didn't mean Sejal should have stayed and been miserable for her. And she'd tell her that. If she saw her again.

"Mira? Mira!"

She shook her head, coming out of the fog. "I am so sorry,"

she said, every word dripping in sincerity and anguish. "You're absolutely right. I was terrible to do that to you."

Emi studied her carefully. "While I wish you hadn't ghosted me, my therapist has made me see that that had more to do with you than me." Emi placed her hand over her heart dramatically. "I forgive you."

The tightness in her chest eased, but not all the way. "Thank you. And thank your therapist. She's right. It had nothing to do with you."

Emi gave a decisive nod. "So. Tell me about Naveen?"

No, thank you. "There's not much to tell."

"Was he a one-night stand or something?"

"No!"

"Don't say it like that. People have needs."

Mira tucked her foot up underneath her, and suddenly it was like they were seventeen and in one of their bedrooms again. "I hired a matchmaker and she introduced us. We dated for about six months."

"A human matchmaker?"

"Yes, a human one. What other kind is there?"

Emi spread her hands out. "I don't know, algorithms are pretty advanced."

"This was a woman. She goes by Hema Auntie, and she has a thriving business introducing South Asian singles looking for matrimony."

"She sounds fascinating."

"She has a one hundred percent track record for marriages. Or, ninety-nine percent. Thanks to me." She missed her phone, but she didn't miss the voicemail she probably had from Hema.

"Because you didn't marry Naveen."

"Naveen . . . or the other twelve men she's introduced me to over the last three years."

"Wait, wait, wait. Wait." Emi swiveled around. "Thirteen men you've rejected? My hero."

Mira wrinkled her nose. "Twelve. One rejected me."

"As I said, fascinating." Emi turned back around to the phone. "I'm surprised Naveen knew so little about your skills, if you were evaluating him for matrimony. He was shocked your father had you playing poker as a kid."

"I didn't tell anyone about my dad or my family. Or . . . the stuff I used to do." Mira placed her ripped napkin in her lap. "Did he ask any more questions?"

Emi shot her a look, but it was a gentle one. "No."

Her gaze bounced around the suite. "It doesn't matter. We've been broken up for a long time." And she needed to forget the warmth and gentleness of that hug yesterday.

Nothing. It meant nothing.

Emi hummed. "Whether it's with Naveen, or someone else, for future reference: if you have to hide the parts of you that make you you, it's probably not going to work out."

Hema Auntie would laugh herself silly at that pronouncement. Hiding everything was literally the woman's main advice for finding a husband. "Playing poker doesn't make me me."

"Not poker necessarily. But that part of yourself—the part

that savors the adrenaline rush and craves excitement—is a part of you. It's good to feed that part every now and then."

Emi had seemed exhilarated up in that suite, with danger facing her. She'd loved the theatrics of Mira winning that game and setting them free. Her old friend was enjoying even this, the unpredictability of them entering her life after years with a mysterious phone to crack into.

Aren't you enjoying some of this? Deep down? "I do not like back-room poker games and shooting people and—"

"Whoa, whoa. Who said anything about shooting people?"

Oops. She grit her teeth, pushing back the memory of the hot gun in her hand. "It's not important."

Emi's lips parted. "That sounds very important, but okay. You can not like shooting people, and still enjoy a game, Mira. Unlike poker, life isn't all or nothing."

Wasn't it, though? "You don't know what you're talking about."

"And I think you've been chasing normal for so long you don't even know what it means."

Emi had been one of the few people who could get her worked up enough to shout, and it felt oddly good when her voice raised now. "Why do you even care?"

Emi bent back over the phone, and her hair slid down, hiding her face. "Because I care about *you*, dumbass."

Mira drew back. "Oh."

"Yeah. Despite it all, even though you've done some shitty things, I care about you. If we don't talk for another ten years, and you wander back into my life, I'll care about you. Sometimes you become friends with someone, and you care about them no matter what. Damn it."

"I . . . I care about you, too." She was so unaccustomed to talking about her deepest feelings, that the next words felt like they'd been ripped out of her. "You asked why I bailed you out? It's because I missed you and I cared about you."

"Oh. Cool."

There was a long, awkward silence, broken only by Emi's tapping on the keys of her laptop and the phone screen. They were both bad at talking about their feelings.

Emi cleared her throat. She sat back in her chair and crossed her ankle over her knee. "I'm done, by the way."

For a second, Mira thought she meant done with her, but then she realized Emi was holding up her dad's phone. She came to her feet, trying to focus on the real danger at their door. "What did you find?"

Emi's eyes narrowed. "Something . . . interesting."

Chapter Ten

Naveen wiped his face with a towel and sat in the armchair next to the nightstand in Emi's bedroom, draping his wilted suit jacket across his knees. Her suite wasn't quite as ostentatious as the room they'd come from, but it was still surprisingly large and luxurious, given the run-down vibes of the rest of this hotel.

The plain black landline telephone glowed under the light of the nightstand lamp like a holy artifact. He was thankful for the shower, and the chance to wash off the dried blood stains on his neck, but he was even more thankful for the most wonderful device of all. Finally. A way to check in on his family.

Naveen called his mom first. No answer.

His heartbeat accelerated. She often went to bed early and didn't usually leave her phone on. *It doesn't mean anything. She's fine. She's okay.*

He called his grandpa next, and let out a low sigh when he immediately picked up. "Hello?"

"Ajoba. Hi. How are you? Is everything okay?"

"What? Yes. Everything's fine. Naveen? Why are you calling me from this Nevada number?"

He bit the inside of his cheek. How was he supposed to tell his grandfather about this? In a way that didn't have Ravi immediately calling his buddies in law enforcement?

You can't.

If he trusted any police officers right now, it would be the ones who knew his grandfather.

You trust them with your family's lives?

"Naveen?"

He clenched his jaw. "I lost my phone. I'm using a . . . friend's."

"Ah. So I'm assuming the date is going well, if you're using your friend's phone."

Naveen mentally slapped himself. *Fuck.* The fictional date. His little white lie from hours ago. "Yeah. About that, actually."

"No escape rooms, right?"

Naveen nearly laughed. He glanced around the hotel room. "Perhaps a small one."

Ajoba groaned. "Naveen. You are trying to chase her off, already, eh?"

He knew to expect good-natured ribbing about his silly hobby, but it still stung, as it always did. "An escape room is a perfect first date activity, I'll have you know," he said lightly. "You're forced to work together as a team."

"I suppose being a team is a good way to start something," Ravi allowed. "Very important skill. Take the girl out for a drink, son, like a normal young man."

"Don't worry, we also got dinner." So to speak. "And played poker."

"Oh, she plays poker?" His grandfather's tone changed. The man played a weekly game with his friends, or he did when he was feeling up to it these days. "She good?"

"Really good. She won with a seven and a two." His pleasure in her playing couldn't be repressed. He'd always thought Mira's competency was one of the sexiest things about her, and it had been on full display tonight. Not that he'd been thinking about her sexiness.

His grandfather gave a rough laugh. "That is good. I like her already."

Ravi would have liked Mira, if they'd had a chance to meet before she ended their relationship.

That's right. Remember how she ended things.

"You sound like you're having fun."

Naveen cradled the phone closer to his ear. "I am." Not a lie. For a few minutes upstairs, he'd forgotten their life-or-death issues and genuinely enjoyed himself. "Why are you surprised by that?"

His grandfather hesitated. "I don't agree with your mother a lot, but I do think you've been buried down here for the last year or two. Since you got out of that center."

Naveen rubbed the side of his nose. "I've needed to be buried. I'm healthier now." The thing no one had told him about that work hard/play hard life was that it was also a solid way to burnout. He might work for rice, but he ate well, and didn't need much more.

He adjusted his watch on his wrist. *It's only metal.*

"I do think the break from that fast-paced life you lived before has been good for you." His grandfather's voice grew far away for a second. "You're much healthier than you were, that's for sure. But your brother—"

Naveen reared back. "I don't want to talk about him." The anger he felt toward Mira could be pierced here and there, and it was okay. The steam escaping actually helped him think better.

But Kiran, that was a different matter. That bitterness was more deep-seated.

"I know, I know. I'm sorry if you felt like we ganged up on you earlier. It's just that we love you both. And it's hard to move on with your life when you have something unresolved in it."

"I am moving on with my life."

"You're static, in one place. Your mother is right to worry about your marital status." His grandfather's voice grew husky. "I want you to find someone who will make your life an adventure. How are you going to do that sitting at home?"

Naveen looked out the big window, the glass smudged. They weren't on the Strip, but there was no shortage of sparkling lights to stud the sky. The night had been an adventure, but he could do without the mortal peril and high stakes.

He hated the worry in his grandfather's voice. "I'm on a date, aren't I?" he heard himself saying.

Actually, you are not.

His grandfather chuckled, but it was tinged with a hint of sadness. "Watch out, though, sounds like she's good at bluffing."

Never had anything truer been said. Mira was criminally good at bluffing.

She'd also dumped him once, rather coldly. He wasn't in the market to get hurt again anytime soon. Which was why he needed to not think about how empty his arms felt now that he'd hugged her or how intriguing of a puzzle she was. "I hear you."

"Think about what I said. It's not healthy to carry that much resentment around. Especially for family. You will need your brother someday."

He should know what danger he's in. Tell him something, even if you don't reveal it all. "I'd actually rather talk to you about . . ." He was interrupted by a deep voice in the background and leaned forward. "Ajoba, who is that? The TV?"

"What? Oh no. I have a guest, he was in the kitchen."

Naveen clenched the phone. "It's late, though."

"A little, but you know I'm a night owl. I noticed him sitting outside, and invited him in for a drink. Can't have our local police feel unappreciated." His grandfather's chuckle was a direct contrast to Naveen's growing dread. "You remember Ajay, right? I did work on his father's immigration case. He's on neighborhood patrol. Good boy, he was making us some chai."

Naveen came to his feet, but the cord kept him tethered to the nightstand. God he missed his phone. "I don't think I know Ajay, no."

"Huh?" Ajoba turned away and said something muffled to his visitor, then came back. "Here, Naveen, Ajay wants to speak to you. Ajay, don't bother him with too many legal questions right now, he's on a date. I'll go get the chai, I don't want it to bubble over."

A deep voice got on the phone. "Hey, Naveen."

Naveen swallowed. "Who are you again?"

"Don't worry about it." Ajay's voice changed, and Naveen could tell by the way it hardened that his grandfather had left the room. "You made my boss very mad, Naveen."

Fuck. Naveen was going to guess his boss wasn't solely the city of Artesia. "Listen to me, do not hurt my grandfather."

"Do you think I want to?" The man's voice lowered. "Your grandpa is a local treasure. I jumped to keep watch on him solely so somebody with less scruples wouldn't. But you need to get my boss whatever he's looking for."

Naveen wiped his hand on his pants. His grandfather was a local treasure, but he was also his treasure. "I am trying. I promise."

"He cares about results, not promises."

Naveen would love to put a name to this faceless menace. "Who is he, anyway? Mafia?"

"Worse."

"What's his name?"

"I don't have one. He goes by Cobra."

Naveen rubbed his temples. They were pounding now. "My mom, is she . . . ?"

"As far as I know, the boss hasn't sent someone to her place yet."

That was lukewarm comfort, but he'd take it. "You don't have to do this."

"I do. I have a family to protect, too. Have you told your grandpa anything?"

Naveen grimaced. "No."

"Good. Don't. The boss gave strict orders that there be no leaks."

What was he planning on doing to so-called leaks? "Listen, please, please don't hurt him."

"Get your shit together, man, give him whatever he wants . . ." Ajay's voice changed, became more jovial. "I'll come see you next week. We can talk about the parking ticket. Oh, here's your grandpa." Ajay paused. "I hope you consider what I said. We don't want to bother your grandfather with my problems."

That was a clear warning to keep his mouth shut. "I will. We will get your boss his necklace."

"Great. And I'll keep an eye on your granddad while I'm on patrol tonight."

Naveen didn't know how much he could trust Ajay, but he knew how the community felt about Ravi. He was their grandfather too. He had to trust in Ajay's conscience.

A lot harder to trust in that than it had been to trust in Mira.

There was a shuffle and his grandfather came back on the line.

Was it his imagination, or did the man sound more frail than usual? "Naveen, we're going to have our chai. Stop chatting with us, your date is probably getting mad."

Naveen exhaled. "Uh, yeah. I'll talk to you soon, Ajoba. You know, I tried to call Mom, and she didn't answer? Could you check in on her? After Ajay leaves."

"Why would I do that? You know she goes to bed early."

"Just . . ." He couldn't tell his grandfather. "I felt bad from earlier. I don't want her to think I'm mad at her for bringing Kiran up."

His grandpa harrumphed, but didn't say he wouldn't check in on his daughter. "Go. Have fun. Talk later."

"Yes, sir. I love you," he added.

His grandfather cleared his throat. They didn't say mushy things to each other often, so maybe he was taken aback. "Good boy," he muttered.

Naveen stood there for a moment after they hung up, then dropped the phone back into the receiver. *Fuck.*

He grabbed his jacket and walked to the living room at a fast clip. "They have eyes on my grandfather."

Mira looked up. She was hunched over the desk with Emi. "What?"

"There's a cop at his house. Someone who's in our kidnapper's pockets." He paced across the floor. "He knows my grandpa. I am . . . I'm willing to believe that he doesn't mean to harm him immediately. But we need to get that necklace, stat. Tell me you found something."

Emi spoke, but kept her gaze on her laptop screen. "We found something."

He inhaled, slow and steady, relief flowing through him. "Where's the necklace?"

Mira grimaced. "Well, we don't know if we've found *that*."

"What did you find, then?" He couldn't help that his tone was sharp.

He thought of his grandfather, serving tea to a man with a gun on his hip. Ajay might say he was protecting the man, but if push came to shove and the order was given, would he hurt him?

"There's a file on here." Emi paused for a moment and typed something. Her face was bathed in blue light. "It's a data file, but encrypted well. Hard to force open."

"Impossible to force open?"

Emi scoffed. "Nothing's impossible for me. Might take some time."

Naveen started pacing again. "We don't have a lot of time."

"There's a contact, too. For Sunil Rao."

Mira said the name like it should mean something. "Who is that?"

"We looked him up." Emi scrolled. "Very reclusive and very successful. I know of him. He owns one of the premier strip clubs in the city. They put on a real popular show, tourists love it. No one ever sees him, but the article said he's very hands-on, an eye in the sky."

A strip club. Of course that was their next lead in this tour through Vegas.

Mira straightened. "Sunil Uncle, I used to call him. He was a friend of my father's. I remember him coming to our house when I was young, but eventually he stopped coming by. Even after that, though, my dad talked about Sunil in the context of replicas." She closed her eyes, like she was trying to remember.

"Like, forgeries?" Naveen's voice went up. "You didn't think that was relevant?"

"I said replicas, not forgeries. Knockoffs of Ralph Lauren, not priceless jewelry."

Emi spun around in her chair. "Priceless jewelry? Okay, someone tell me what I'm helping you with, please. You've dragged me into it now."

Naveen thought of his grandfather, ignorant of the danger at his doorstep. "We can't tell you. The person after us doesn't like *leaks*. Or at least, that's what the cop at my grandfather's house said."

Emi snorted. "I can help you better if I know something. Trust me, I can handle myself."

Mira linked her fingers together. "My dad allegedly stole something from someone."

Emi rolled her eyes. "If I know your dad, it wasn't allegedly."

"In any case, they're after me and Naveen now to get it back. And . . . they have Sejal," she finished simply. "She's alive, or she was a few hours ago, but I don't know what'll happen."

Emi steepled her hands under her chin. She didn't look shocked or alarmed, but rather thoughtful. "Kidnapping's a major offense. I wouldn't kidnap someone, unless . . ."

"That sentence should end before unless," Naveen said dryly.

She ignored him. "Unless the item I was retrieving was worth the risk. What did he steal?"

Mira bit her lip. "A diamond necklace worth millions."

Emi leaned back in her chair and gave a long, low whistle. "Can't believe Uncle Vassar dipped his toes into the big-boy pool. Who did he steal it from?"

"That we don't know."

The phone in the room rang, interrupting them. Emi glanced at the phone, back at them, then picked it up. "Hello?" Her gaze shot to them. "Thank you for telling me, Jon. No, absolutely not. Tell them no one's in this room. Stonewall them for as long as possible." She hung up. "There are two men downstairs, trying to bribe the front desk for info about this room. Naveen . . . did you use the landline or my cell phone on the nightstand?"

Jesus *Christ*. How could he have been so ignorant? "The landline. It didn't occur to me . . ." Using someone else's cell phone seemed so terribly intimate.

Emi nodded. "Understandable. I should have clarified." She reached into her drawer and pulled out two packaged phones. Why the girl had a stash of burner phones in a hotel room, Naveen didn't know. "Here, take these."

Mira curled her hands around the phones. "I—What about you?"

"Don't worry about me. I have friends here." Real concern flashed over Emi's face. "I didn't know Sejal well, but she doesn't deserve to be hurt because your dad dropped the ball. Neither do you." She turned to her computer, searched for a couple seconds, then scribbled something on the hotel's notepad. "Here's Sunil's club info. Go there and do your best to sweet-talk your way in to see him. If you don't mind, I'm going to keep your dad's phone. Maybe I can get inside that file. I'll call you if it happens."

"Thank you." Naveen drew close and accepted the paper. His eyes strayed to Vassar's phone, and he froze. "Wait, what's that background?"

"The inkblot? I don't know. Mira said it didn't mean anything to her."

At first glance, the image on the phone's wallpaper didn't look like anything but a blob. But if you turned your head slightly . . . "That's a cobra." He met Mira's eyes. "The cop at my grandfather's, he said he only knew his boss by the name of Cobra."

Mira pressed her lips tight together. "Well. That means some dots are connecting, at least." Mira shrugged on her dad's big jacket, reached into her pocket, and pulled out the wad of cash. She peeled off half of it and placed it on the table. "For your trouble."

Emi fingered the cash. "You're determined not to make us even anytime soon, huh?"

Naveen wondered what that meant, but it wasn't like they had the time to ask. "We need to go." The longer they stayed, the better the chance that their hunters would be here. Was it the same two men? Or different ones?

Emi followed them to the door. On the way, she reached into the closet, pulled out a pair of sneakers, and handed them to Mira, who put them on her feet. "Good luck, guys."

"Thank you." Mira hesitated at the door, then gave Emi a clumsy pat. "I, um . . ."

Emi shrugged. "No, you don't have to say anything more. Talk soon, Mira. Right?"

Mira nodded. "Right."

The elevator took forever to come to their floor, and Naveen paced from one end of the bank to the other until Mira exhaled. "Can you please stop? That's making me nervous."

He stilled and stabbed the DOWN button again. "It was easy enough for us to get to a room floor. They could do the same. We should take the stairs."

She wrapped her arms around herself tight. "We're too high up to take the stairs. The elevator will be faster. They could be coming up the staircase as we speak."

His nostrils flared. "I'm so foolish for using a traceable phone."

"It's not your fault. This isn't exactly your wheelhouse."

The elevator finally opened, and they both breathed out a sigh of relief to find it empty. They stepped inside and Naveen jabbed the button for the lobby, tapping his foot as they began their descent.

After an interminable length of time, the doors opened, and they pushed past the people waiting to pile into the elevator. There were even more crowds now than there had been before they'd gone upstairs. Naveen scanned the floor. Because he was taller, he noticed the pair near the Concierge desk before Mira did. "Three o'clock. Same guys as before." Except now, the blond had his arm in a sling and was holding himself funny, his Burberry coat long gone. His partner's hair looked even greasier from here, and was no longer in a ponytail.

Mira breathed out through her nostrils. "Guess I didn't kill anyone today. That's good."

"Bet you never thought you'd say that." He wrapped his hand around her arm and gently steered them in the opposite direction. "Be casual."

They walked at a brisk clip into the crowds. Naveen dared to glance over his shoulder once, twice. The men hadn't spotted them yet, but they were making their way toward them. If they did run, they'd be spotted immediately.

He nearly stumbled when Mira grabbed hold of his hand and pulled them behind a bank of slot machines. She hopped onto a seat, and tugged him down as well so they were well hidden. "Let them pass," she said quietly. "They're between us and the parking garage."

A waitress shot them a curious look. Naveen fixed a polite smile on his face and held out his hand. "Give me some cash. We have to blend in."

She fumbled a fifty-dollar bill out from her dad's jacket and he stuck it into the machine, his gaze scouring the area around them.

"Sugar pie."

He jerked at the computer-generated feminine voice, and looked up at the machine's logo, three hearts aflame. *Heated Hearts.* "What the hell?"

"The machines are different themes." Unfazed, Mira smashed the spin button without even looking at the display.

"Honey bunch," the machine sighed. They won nothing, and Mira hit the REPEAT BET button immediately.

"Oh, yeah."

Through the gap in the machines, he noticed their kidnappers walk past them and he tensed until the pair passed. Mira hit the button again. And again. And again. A droplet of sweat snaked down Naveen's back as he counted the minutes.

"Ugggggnh," the machine groaned.

"What is this theme," he asked quietly. "Creepy robot porn?"

Mira was stopped from answering when the lights started to swirl around them, and the machine's cries of ecstasy grew louder. A swirl of hearts in the shape of a cyclone took up the screen at the top of the machine. "What the fuck is happening?"

"You unlocked the passion tornado! It's the jackpot wheel."

Naveen looked down at the tiny older woman standing next to him. She didn't even reach his collarbone, and he was seated. "Oh."

"It's loud." Mira came to her feet, her eyes darting around, and her nerves were catching, because he followed her. It was loud, and the attention was the last thing they needed.

"You can have it," Naveen said to the woman.

Mira grabbed his arm. For the second time since they'd been down here, not that he was counting.

"What?" The woman adjusted her thick glasses. "Are you sure?"

"Yup, we have too much money."

"Nice to be you, I guess."

"Come on," Mira tugged at him. He followed her away from the slot machines, toward the parking garage this time.

He dared to glance over his shoulder, and his heart jumped. From a hundred yards away, Stuart's eyes met his and he smacked his buddy. "Fuck," he whispered. "They saw us." He sped up, Mira trotting next to him.

"Let me draw them away. You can keep going. Get the car."

He didn't know why that irritated him, but it did. This was the second or third time now, that she'd suggested they separate. Naveen cast her an incredulous look. "No. We're in this together." He grabbed her hand and walked even faster, dodging tourists and the elderly. He checked behind them again, and noticed the two men keeping pace.

They weren't running, though, or pulling their guns. Of course not, for the same reason they hadn't pursued the necklace through legal means. *No leaks.* They didn't want to call attention to themselves.

An idea bloomed. It wasn't a great idea, but it was all they had. He cast his gaze around until he found his target, then grabbed a frozen daiquiri in a tall plastic cup from where it had been abandoned next to a slot machine. "Follow my lead," he muttered to Mira, then stopped by a woman in a red dinner jacket standing near a craps table. "Ma'am," he said, and gave her his most winning smile. She smiled back. He tilted his head. "You see those two guys behind us? The one in the leather jacket, and the other one with the sling? We saw them acting kind of weird near the high-dollar slots. Like maybe they have something up their sleeves? The machine wouldn't stop paying out for them, but the little lady and I tried the same machines and got nothing. You might want to check them out."

Her eyes moved behind them and hardened. She spoke into her wrist. "Jack, I need backup. Thank you, sir. And what's your name . . . sir? Sir!"

Mira twisted to see what was going on behind them as they power-walked away. "You think that'll work?"

He tossed his drink into the closest trash can. "A casino won't care if people are trying to kill each other, but they'll definitely care if they're being fleeced."

She let out a breath. "You're right. A guard stopped them." She turned around and they sped up toward the parking garage, nearly running by the time they got to their car.

Once the lights of downtown had disappeared and they were on the highway, he stopped checking behind them consistently and marginally relaxed. "I think it worked. At the very least, it delayed them, thank God."

"If nothing else, maybe we'll have a chance to get to Sunil first." Plastic ripped, and he glanced over to find Mira pulling one of the burner phones out of its packaging.

"Bless Emi and Steve Jobs," he said fervently.

"No kidding." Mira turned on the phone. "I'll input the address for the strip club. I hope we can even get to Sunil. If he's that reclusive these days, just talking to him will be the first challenge."

"Fingers crossed." He was doing a lot of that lately.

The GPS directed them for a couple minutes in the silence of the car. "I'm sorry about your grandfather."

He gave her a sideways glance at how well-modulated her tone was. Her hands, though, they were tight fists in her lap. "Thank you. He's a good man."

"He sounds like it."

"I do believe the cop doesn't want to hurt him." He prayed, at least. "He's known my grandfather since he was a child. Ajoba is the reason his father became a citizen."

"I cannot even fathom having roots in a community that deep. My dad never even talked to our neighbors."

He wanted to know what effect that had had on her,

but she hadn't seemed pleased to resurrect her childhood memories. "My mother hated it, growing up. Said it was like living in a fishbowl. I like it, though. Especially tonight, knowing the man watching my grandfather has some feelings for him." He sent another prayer up.

"I'm so sorry."

Her voice broke, and he glanced over. She looked out the window, her profile sharp. Not a single frown marred her face. But those hands were fisted even tighter.

"For what?"

"You said it yourself. My family's the reason you're here."

He hadn't said—oh. He had said that, when they were trying to escape that shack.

"Your grandfather is in danger, and he wouldn't be if it weren't for me. You wouldn't be here if it weren't for me. I wish . . . I wish I'd never come to your office."

Still emotionless, but her hands were so tight he wondered if she was cutting off her own circulation.

He couldn't help himself. With his right hand, he covered hers. She stilled. She didn't draw away, so he didn't either. "Your family's the reason I'm here. Your dad, more specifically."

She tensed, but he continued. "You're not at fault. Or if you are, it's also your aunt's fault for hiring my grandfather. Or my grandfather's fault for taking her on as a client."

"That's extraordinarily fair of you."

His family might say he was *too* fair, especially when he was wronged. "It's common sense." Her hands loosened.

Naveen considered bringing up the bomb Emi had dropped, about her playing poker to line her father's pockets as a child, but he didn't want her to tense up again. "Have you ever played an escape room?" he heard himself saying.

"What? No."

"Do you know what they are?"

"You have to, like, solve clues to get out of a locked room?"

He nodded. "I love them. I started playing a couple years ago. I go almost every weekend, with my friend Alan." And then, because he wanted to see her smile for a change for some unfathomable reason, he added the next words, though he would rather die than reveal this fact to anyone else in his life. "We call ourselves the Who-Dinis."

He glanced over in time to catch the way her lips turned up. Her smile was small, way smaller than that reckless smile in the suite, but it was real.

"Do you get it? It's like Houdini."

"But a pun." Another centimeter to her grin. "Get out."

"Nope. We hold records at multiple locations."

Her smile grew. "Now you're bragging."

He wobbled his head. "A little."

"I don't remember Alan."

That's because I met him in rehab, a good year or so after we broke up. "He's a recent friend, but a great one."

"Escape rooms seem like a very different sort of weekend hobby for you."

He put his signal on and switched lanes. "That's because when you knew me, all I wanted to do was go to a party or a bar when I wasn't working. That was my outlet then. This is my outlet now."

"Sounds very wholesome."

"I like it because it forces you to play as a team." He shot her a glance. "Consider this an escape room, Mira. We're partners. We have to play as a team."

Her smile faded. "Hmm."

"That means we collaborate on any plans going forward. We trust each other, and believe that we have each other's best interest. And no more splitting up, no more even floating the idea of splitting up. Got it? We're going to get through this but only if we can work together."

Her fists loosened, and she flipped her hand, so they were palm to palm. He didn't budge, though driving one-handed was awkward for him. "You said that earlier. And what if we can't get through it? There's a real possibility that this is a wild goose chase."

His grandfather's words came back to him. *You might need him someday.* His eye twitched. No, he couldn't go running to his big brother.

Even if your lives depend on it?

He bit the inside of his cheek. "I may have a resource we can tap. But I need to think about it some more."

They were silent for a while. Finally, she tightened her hand on his. "Okay. Let's be a team."

Chapter Eleven

If Mira could hold Naveen's hand forever, she would be okay with that, which was surprising. Holding hands was not something she'd ever cared very much for. They hadn't held hands all that much while dating. It was nowhere on her spreadsheet for a desirable mate.

He's not in the running as your mate.

Except as a teammate. Which was unique, because she wasn't sure if she'd ever been a part of an official team. At work, they often made noises about being a team player and handed out free fleeces with logos on them, but she preferred to audit alone. Or rather, everyone assumed she liked to audit alone, because that was what she'd always done, so they didn't hassle her.

We're going to get through this.

It had sounded different when he said it this time. Less grudging, more certain and optimistic. Unless he was faking, and she didn't think he was, the depth of his fairness and maturity was shocking.

Don't get your hopes up. Her life motto, really.

Lights flashed over them from the passing cars and billboards as they narrowed in to their destination. Las Vegas traffic wasn't like L.A. traffic. Things were far apart in the desert, but it was moderately easier to get to them.

They pulled up in front of the big building. He parked, and withdrew his hand from hers. It was only then did she realize that he'd been keeping her warm.

He peered out at the strip club. They weren't far from the Strip, and the lights and noise spilled over onto this street. The building itself was huge, with multiple stories. Music blared from within.

"Magnificent Mike's," he murmured. "Interesting name."

"Emi didn't tell me what it was called."

"I'm guessing this place is for men strippers?"

Mira checked her phone and scrolled through the Yelp listing. "Uh, looks like it's a mix. Each floor is different."

"How inclusive."

Judging by the variety of customers in line, the place was inclusive, and as Emi had noted, extraordinarily popular. The crowd wrapped around the parking lot. More than one person gave them dirty looks as they passed by. They finally reached the bouncer, who gave them a cursory glance. "Staff entrance is in the back."

Naveen took a step forward. "We're here to see the owner."

"No one sees the owner." The bouncer looked them over

again and gave a delicate sniff. "And if you're a guest, no one gets in here in sweats, ma'am."

"These are joggers, not sweats," Mira muttered, as Naveen pulled her away. There was a difference.

"We don't have time to argue with him."

She grimaced, certain of what he was thinking. "We're going to pretend to be staff, aren't we?"

"You know it."

They went around the building, and got there as a young woman got out of her car in the back parking lot. Naveen pressed his hand to her back, and she tried not to notice the heat of his body between the layers of her shirt and jacket. They slowed, walking behind the woman as she trotted to the back door, too engrossed in her phone to notice them. She keyed in a code and slipped inside the building. Naveen took extralong steps, and caught the door before it could close.

"Do we just . . . ?" Mira asked.

"We walk in and pretend we belong. Hope you're good at improvising."

I am not.

They walked inside to find a white sterile hallway that looked like it could belong in any soul-sucking office building. Clearly, management didn't see fit to put money into ambiance for employees. Out of the corner of her eye, she clocked the camera in the corner, moving and adjusting. As casually as possible, she ducked her head, hoping that her loose hair would hide her features.

She caught the back of the woman they'd followed in

turning a corner, and she nudged Naveen with her elbow. "That way."

They were a few feet past the door, when a voice rang out behind them. "You two. Stop."

Her heart in her throat, Mira and Naveen turned slowly in unison to find a harried-looking older woman holding a clipboard. A dark halo of flyaways surrounded her head, her blush two spots of bright red, spotlights on her olive complexion. She frowned at them. "It's about time."

"Yes. It is about time," Naveen said slowly.

"Roshan and Jyoti, yes?"

The woman was butchering the pronunciation, but Mira was only concerned with the possibility of being immediately tossed out on their asses.

"Yes." Naveen took a step forward. "That's exactly who we are."

Oh dear.

Since she was trying to be a team player, though, Mira gave a weak smile.

The woman looked them over, taking in Naveen's stained blue suit and Mira's wild hair and oversize leather jacket. "You don't look like the photos the agency sent over."

Mira cleared her throat. "They're, ah, filtered."

There was a pregnant pause where Mira held her breath, and then the woman shook her head. "Figures. You don't exactly have the right vibe, but hopefully we can fix that with wardrobe. Come with me, both of you. I'm Glenda, I'm in charge of talent."

What were the odds that another South Asian couple was scheduled to show up tonight and the person in charge couldn't tell South Asians apart? This was kismet.

Naveen exhaled, which told Mira she wasn't the only one holding their breath. "Sounds good." They started following Glenda down the hall. "Any chance we'll get to see the owner tonight? We'd love to meet him."

Glenda rolled her eyes. They were an intense green shade that Mira was pretty sure could come only from contacts. "Yeah, well, so does everyone. Mr. Rao and the rest of the top floor is served by a very select group of vetted employees, not newbies. If that's a problem, you can leave."

She sounded legitimately stern about this, and Mira wasn't sure what to say.

"Of course, no problem," Naveen said, and his gaze met Mira's.

He let Glenda get ahead of them and spoke to Mira in Hindi, which he'd never done before. "Let's wear whatever she tells us to wear, try to blend in, and then make our way to the top floor somehow. That's where we'll find him."

Or at least, that's what she thought he'd said. Even if her dad had been interested in teaching her about their culture, he'd come to the United States when he was a teenager desperate to assimilate, and they'd spoken only English at home. Her main source for most of her Indian knowledge, Christine, spoke Tamil. Mira had, however, taken Hindi as a language in college and watched plenty of Bollywood films, and though she wasn't entirely fluent like Naveen, she could pick out enough words to get the gist. "What if the people we're pretending to be show up," she asked, clumsily.

She knew it was clumsy by the way he frowned and listened carefully, but she was relieved he didn't mock her or laugh. "Don't worry about that now."

Silly man. Didn't he know she was a professional worrywart?

Still, there was something quite comforting about having a literal shared language with Naveen, even if he was better at it than she was. Like they really were a team.

They nearly walked into Glenda when she stopped. "Men's dressing room." She eyed Naveen up and down. "You're not as jacked as our other bartenders, but some people like that tall and lean look. Anyway, step in here and change into your costume, it's on the hanger behind the door. Brad will be by shortly to show you where to go."

"Bartender. Great." Naveen gave one last look to Mira, and stepped inside the room, closing the door gently behind him.

"You, follow me."

As they walked, Mira's ears were pricked with awareness for someone to creep up behind and tackle her as an imposter, but all she heard was the steady bass pump of music coming from what she assumed was the bar.

Glenda led her to another room. It was empty in there, a bunch of stools lined up in front of lighted mirrors, clothes hanging off everything.

Mira balked at the scrap of fabric Glenda handed her. "I can't wear that."

Glenda scowled and checked the handful of dental floss. "You're right."

Mira breathed a small sigh of relief.

It was abruptly curtailed when Glenda turned away, rummaged on a rack, and came back with another identically tiny bunch of fabric and strings. "You definitely need a larger size. I've told that agency a million times to not lie about the girls' sizes, but do they listen? No."

Mira took the outfit, if it could be called that, generously. *No, I mean I cannot wear this, because I am an accountant. Not in a sexy euphemism kind of way, in the Internal Revenue Code kind of way.*

A thought struck Mira. This was a strip club. Was she expected to perform? "Ah, what exactly is in my job description?"

Glenda screwed up her face. "You don't know?"

"No, of course I know. They, uh, didn't tell me what I'd be wearing."

"I thought you worked here before."

Fuck. She tried for the most vacant smile. "I work in lots of places, they all blur together."

"This is what all the waitresses wear. Am I going to have to put you through training all over again?"

The waitresses were expected to serve in thongs? Well, of course they were. This was Vegas.

But she could handle being a waitress, thong or not. Kind of. Maybe? "Um, no. No need for training."

Glenda shoved Mira to the curtained-off dressing room. "Then hurry up! I have other shit to do, I don't have time to babysit you."

"Um, right." Mira opened and closed the curtain. Oh no. What had she gotten them into? What had she gotten Naveen into?

Just hurry up, change, and you can meet Sunil. Get through this.

She undressed and put the outfit on. It took some doing, since the bottom half of it was like a complicated cat's cradle of string and judiciously arranged fabric triangles. Once it was on, she avoided looking in the mirror. She wasn't uncomfortable with her body, but the bustier and tiny panties were more daring than her most daring underwear.

What did the bartenders wear here?

Do not think of Naveen in tiny panties right now.

She carefully folded all her clothes. Her father's lighter fell out of his jacket and she scooped it up, and tucked it into her bustier. Not like she had pockets, and she felt an odd compulsion to keep the damn thing on her. She added their bundle of cash to her top as an afterthought. Good thing she had space to hold things in there.

She donned the stilettos Glenda had given her and emerged from behind the curtain to find Glenda standing there, checking her phone. She looked up at Mira and nodded. "Not bad. You're a different type from most of the girls, which might work well for you tonight. For future gigs, though, you might have to lose ten pounds."

"You can say that to someone you're hiring as a waitress?" Mira asked, skeptical.

Glenda smirked. "You're all models, sweetheart. We can dictate your appearance. Now, chop, chop, do your hair and makeup." Glenda took in her empty hands. "I assume you brought your cosmetics with you?"

Mira finger combed her hair. "No. Sorry."

Glenda's sigh came from her toes, and she used a key to jerk open a drawer, from which she pulled a sealed red lipstick, eyeliner, and new brush. "This will come from your paycheck."

Mira whispered a silent apology to the absent Jyoti who she was impersonating, and took the items. Her hair had grown curly and wild during their adventure, so she only brushed it to make it bigger, then slicked the lipstick and eyeliner on, drawing it much heavier than she usually did.

She squinted at herself in the mirror when she was done. Whoa. Who was she?

Mira took pride in her appearance, but she was honest enough to realize that she wasn't exactly sexy, and she never tried to cultivate sexy anyway. She was cute, she was quietly attractive, she was presentable: all the things that looked good on her wife resume.

She felt sexy right now, though.

"Good. Let's get you out there with the others."

Mira had never been to a strip club, but this one was more like lush club. Or perhaps the set for some HBO show. Half a dozen waitresses dressed like her milled around, some chatting with men at the bar, others draped over the plush burgundy booths and chairs where patrons were sitting. The massive stage had multiple poles, and seriously athletic and talented women gyrated on them in various states of dress and undress. The bar was gorgeous black granite, underlit with neon lighting.

And Naveen was not behind that bar. "Um, where is my, um . . . the guy I came with?"

"Your boyfriend is on the second floor. It's ladies' night up there. Don't worry, you'll work both floors. But don't waste time chatting with him, or you won't be making any tips tonight and it's unlikely you'll get to come back. Now go on. You can go to the bar to get your assigned section." With that, Glenda turned and left.

Mira glanced around her, some of her confidence in her sexiness leeching away as shadowy men observed her.

She didn't have time to be self-conscious, though, and she definitely didn't have time to figure out which section was hers. Pray she didn't need to be here long enough to even have a section.

Second floor, second floor . . .

The elevator was off a hallway, discreet enough. She pressed 2, and smiled tightly at the tipsy men who got on the elevator with her. She could feel their gazes on her butt when the door opened and she got off.

The vibe on the second floor was similar to the first, except up here, the majority, but not all, of the patrons were women, and the strippers were men. Mira stopped as the curtain on one of the stages parted and a jacked firefighter came out.

He danced down the stage, losing his clothes with a smile on his face. His suspenders cut across his washboard abs, and his pants were definitely not flame retardant, given how they tore away. Once he was down to just a G-string, he suggestively peeled it lower and lower as the customers tucked dollar bills into them.

Holy shit.

Oh no. Was *bartender* code for *stripper*? Was Naveen currently in the back, waiting to go onstage?

A waitress passing by bumped into her. "Hey, are you new?"

Mira nodded, wary. "Yes."

"Heads-up, you gotta work instead of ogle. They got cameras all over this place, and the owner is always watching. He'll sic Glenda on you if you look like you're not busy." She gave Mira a conspiratorial wink. "A friendly tip."

The owner. "Have you ever had to meet the, um, owner?"

"Nope. He's kind of a hermit. Hope you don't, either. I've heard he's really mean." The woman hesitated, like she'd said too much, and cast a worried glance above them, at the various cameras. "But also fair," she said, louder.

Mira gave her a weak smile and scanned the room again.

Where was Naveen? Had Sunil already made him as an interloper? Or had he left, deeming this far too much for him?

She wouldn't blame him if he had stormed out of here. After all, who would . . .

We have to play as a team.

No. He wouldn't have left. She had to believe in him a little. "Thanks for the heads-up. Where's the bar on this floor?"

The girl pointed, and Mira made her way through the crush of screaming and hollering customers. One good thing was that if their kidnappers did chase them here, the two men would stick out like sore thumbs.

It was when she was about five feet away from the bar that a gaggle of women in BACHELORETTE sashes swanned off and she caught sight of Naveen. All of the air vanished from her lungs.

Holy mama.

He was wearing tight leather pants that fastened below his belly button, and a bow tie around his neck. And literally, that was it. No shirt. Nothing.

Unlike the other bartenders and the strippers, he didn't have a perfect six-pack, but the man didn't need it. He was muscular without being showy, and somehow, the sexiness of his lean brown belly with its slight curve was better than all of the defined stomachs in the world.

He took the stack of glasses from one of the other bartenders and his forearms flexed. God, those forearms. *Remember those forearms?*

She'd traced them with her fingers and her tongue. Once he'd pushed his shirtsleeves up in front of her, and she'd nearly attacked him.

Naveen nodded at the other man and turned to place the glasses behind him. His torso stretched and moved. The lust hit her out of nowhere, desire pooling low in her belly.

Her eyes met his, and her breath strangled, because he was looking right at her, looking through her, and that self-consciousness she hadn't had time for downstairs came rushing back to her.

She was essentially wearing lingerie, but she may as well have been wearing nothing. He'd seen her in nothing, after all.

Heat trailed down her body, setting every place his gaze touched on fire. She walked toward him like she was hypnotized, unable to help herself.

Think about his nerdy love of escape rooms, or his Who-Dinis team name.

Except she'd always found nerdiness and niche interests adorable, damn it, so that wasn't going to help. If anything, one of her complaints to Hema about him years ago was that he was far too cool for her. If he'd had anything he'd geeked out about then, other than the law, he'd hidden it well.

He shot a look at the two bartenders next to him, then made his way down the bar, tilting his head to indicate that she should follow him. She came and met him at a relatively quiet spot. "Hey," she said, her words breathy and impossible to modulate, pitched above the pounding music.

"Hey." He gave her another once-over. "Ah, you look nice."

"Thank you. So—so do you."

"Thanks." He leaned in closer. "That . . . that looks like the lingerie you wore for my birthday."

Another burst of heat. They'd been together for only one special occasion, his birthday. She'd worn a teddy. Then he'd peeled it off her. "That was way more revealing than this."

"Was it?" he murmured. "I don't—" He straightened as another bartender came by. "I'll get that water for you."

She ran her fingers over her throat. Good. She was parched.

Naveen filled a tall glass with ice and water and slid it over the counter. "Here you go."

She took it and took a hefty gulp, and then another one. A little water dribbled out of her mouth, and she was embarrassed. Until she lowered the glass and realized Naveen wasn't embarrassed at all, but staring at her breasts, mounded over the top of the bustier.

He picked up a napkin off the bar and gestured. She nodded, breath caught, as he dabbed the droplets off her chest. The napkin dampened, and she could feel every single callus on the pads of his fingers as they moved over her curves. "I think it's dry," she said, her voice hoarse.

He withdrew his hand and his gaze met hers. "Fair warning, if you turn around at some point, I will probably look at your ass," he said, and his guttural words made her shiver.

She licked her lower lip. "Me too," she confessed, barely above a whisper. She'd always liked his butt. It was nice and round and perky.

And in leather? Well, he might have to mop up her drool.

"Get a room, new guy," said the annoyed bartender passing behind him.

Naveen looked down and away. "Sorry, Brad is the worst."

"I would beg to differ, Glenda is the actual worst."

Naveen crossed his arms over his chest, and his biceps seemed to grow two sizes bigger. "Brad pinched my belly—without asking first, by the way—and told me I had to lose weight."

Do not stare at the lovely brown expanse of his belly. "You don't, and neither do I, though Glenda told me the same. I'm certainly not surprised at the rampant body dysmorphia in the modeling industry. In what world is this a large?" She gestured at her breasts, overflowing the bustier. "The clothing manufacturers have a lot to answer for."

He cleared his throat. "Yes. Um. Do you want something else to drink? For real?"

"No, thanks."

"Good, because it's been a while since I've handled any alcohol."

She took another sip of her water. "You don't drink anymore?"

"Nope. Been officially sober for almost two years."

She raised an eyebrow, distracted from her lust for a moment. Naveen had definitely been an enthusiastic social drinker when they were together, both around his family and when they went out on dates. "Oh. I didn't know—"

"So how do we get to see this Sunil? Keep working our way up the floors of this building?"

She subsided. Okay, so he didn't want to talk about his sobriety. She should understand, since there were things about her past she didn't want to talk about.

But she was still curious. "I don't think I'm a good enough waitress, or you're a good enough bartender for us to get to the top floor."

"Fair enough. So how do we talk to him?"

"The owner's always watching," she murmured. "Is there a pen and paper behind the bar?"

He looked around and grabbed a menu and a pen.

"Oh, they have pretty good deals on mozzarella fries." She flipped the menu over.

"None for you. Remember that time you had fried ravioli without taking your pill?"

She bent her head, so he wouldn't see her flush. Yeah, she remembered, and she'd hoped he'd forget. No one wanted their few months old boyfriend to see them hunched over with nausea. She scribbled a few words down, and handed it to him.

"I'm Vassar's daughter. We need to talk." Naveen nodded. "Short, to the point. But how are we going to get this to him?"

Mira nodded at the camera above the bar. "He might come to us."

Understanding dawned in Naveen's eyes. "The eye in the

sky." He turned and held the note up as far as he could, so the camera could see it.

And Mira got to make good on her promise, and check out his butt. She wished she had that menu back so she could fan herself. It was like two perfect globes, encased in black shiny fabric. There were twin dimples at the small of his back, right above where the waistband of his pants started. She could spend hours tracing those little indents.

"Someone's looking at this."

She tore her gaze away guiltily, and then realized he was talking about the camera, and not her ogling. The light above it blinked a slow, steady red, and the pupil inside the camera grew large, then small again.

Naveen lowered the note. "Well, we're either about to get our wish or get kicked out of here for gross incompetence and impersonation."

"If it's the latter, is there any high-proof alcohol back there? I can smuggle it out of here. I have a lighter, after all, next time we need a Molotov cocktail, I'll be ready."

He chuckled. "You know how to make a homemade bomb?"

"Yup." She took a sip of her drink. "It was my second grade science fair project."

"What?"

"*Which Alcohol Will Burn Fastest?* My teacher called my dad in that day. She was surprised to learn it was his idea." She cringed in remembered mortification for her young self. "Then he dated her for a month, dumped her, and I had to deal with a very bitter teacher for the rest of the year."

His eyes narrowed. "Wow."

"Sejal—" She faltered, then caught herself. "Sejal made sure she helped me with science fair projects after that. The next year I made a regular old volcano and got a solid A minus." Sejal had been in middle school, but she'd skipped her morning period to help Mira carry the volcano into her cafeteria.

"Sounds like a good big sister."

Guilt stung her. Sejal had been a better parent to her than her own, and it was Mira who was wrong to have expected her sister to sacrifice like she was actually her parent.

You'll tell her that, when you see her. Don't worry.

She cleared her throat, unsure what had made her share that anecdote. "Anyway, yes. I can probably make a simple explosive device."

"Let's hold on that." He tapped his fingers on the bar. They were nice fingers, long and elegant. "Still thirsty?"

"Yes," she admitted. In more ways than one.

He pulled out two fresh glasses. He filled them both with ginger ale, then added an umbrella and cherry on top. "Here's a drink I've gotten to know well."

They tapped glasses, but she only took a sip, more interested in the way his throat moved when he swallowed.

He put the glass down and leaned over the bar. "Did you get a good look?" he asked, quietly. "When I turned around, that is."

This time, she couldn't hide the fire in her cheeks. So she hadn't fooled him.

He picked the cherry out of his drink, and popped it in his mouth. "I'll get my turn later," he said, and she wrapped her hands tighter around her sweating glass.

She didn't get to answer, not that she had anything witty to say. Two guards appeared next to them. "Ma'am. Sir. We need you to come with us," the larger one said, and the relief at his next words nearly made her light-headed. "Mr. Rao would like to speak with you immediately." He cleared his throat and handed her a large jacket. "He'd also like for you to put this on, please, ma'am. He said he'd rather not see his niece dressed like this."

Chapter Twelve

Sunil Rao wasn't what Naveen was expecting. He was small and rotund, dressed in a garish velvet red-and-gold smoking jacket. His round cheeks split with dimples when he smiled. He also had an eye patch, like a very jolly pirate.

He waved them into his expansive office on the top floor. His office was as luxurious as his jacket, decorated in hot pink and black, with a huge desk with a throne-like gold chair in the corner. The wall behind the desk was made up entirely of security monitors that showed every single angle of the club.

Sunil dismissed the security guards who had escorted them up. "My God, Mira. Is this Mira? I would have never recognized you." Sunil beamed at them and came around the desk. He grabbed Mira's hands and brought them to his lips. The oversize suit jacket they'd given her nearly covered her hands. "I haven't seen you since you were a baby. This big." He looked at Naveen curiously. "And this is . . . ?"

She adjusted the jacket. It wasn't the most full-coverage

garment, but at least it mostly hid her bustier and broke the worst of the spell she'd cast over Naveen.

It did mean, sadly, that he hadn't gotten to see the back of her.

What are you doing, flirting with your ex while in mortal danger? Truly, he had no idea, and he didn't think he'd been consciously flirting. He'd seen her, touched her, and opened his mouth.

He'd known he was going to be in trouble even before she'd wandered close to the bar, when he saw what all the waitresses were wearing—or rather, not wearing. Still, the force of his attraction had hit him like a swift kick in the gut, letting out all the air he'd been holding, thanks to fucking Brad and his unnecessary comments. His whole plan of cautiously trusting her for this specific circumstance had gone out the whole damn window.

Being a team does not mean ogling your teammate's ass. Or informing them of said ogling.

Mira gestured to him. "This is Naveen."

Naveen nodded. He was used to dealing with honorary uncles, but not ones who also owned a lucrative strip club. "Hello, sir."

Sunil squinted at him. "You're not a cop, right? You have a cop air about you. As soon as you two snuck in, I thought, this man may be a cop."

Mira took a step forward. "You saw us come in?"

"Of course." Sunil gestured to the bank of television screens. "I see everything. I didn't know who you were, but

Glenda seemed to recognize you. It was only when I started to see you wander aimlessly, Mira, that I took a closer look." Sunil's lips thinned. "I will have to give Glenda some training on being able to tell people apart, I see. But! Back to my original question, son."

"I'm not a cop. But I am a lawyer," Naveen offered.

Sunil shuddered. "That might be worse. But a good thing to have as a boyfriend. Well done. A nice, handsome-looking boy." Before either of them could correct him, Sunil continued. "It's good to see you, Mira. Or meet you, I suppose, as an adult for the first time. I just feel like I know you, from your father."

"Is that right?" she murmured.

"Yes. He used to talk about you all the time. Come in, have a seat." He gestured to the hot pink suede couch and sat in the giant leather armchair across from it.

Mira perched gingerly on the very edge of the sofa. "We need your help, Sunil."

Naveen dropped down next to her. The couch was too cushiony, and he tried not to slide against Mira.

"Please, call me Sunil Uncle." His skin was leathery and tough, like he spent far too many hours baking in the Nevada sun. A thick handle-bar mustache drooped over his upper lip. It was the kind of mustache at least four of Naveen's uncles were proud of. "What kind of help?"

"There are some people after us. They say my dad stole something from them."

Sunil's sigh was long and low. "Fuck."

Mira drew back slightly, and Naveen echoed her. It didn't sound like Sunil was surprised at all, which did not give him any kind of good feeling.

Naveen shifted, ready to grab Mira and bolt, half-dressed or not. "They kidnapped us," he emphasized.

"They're holding my sister hostage and have threatened Naveen's family."

A range of emotions flickered over his face. "Ah, no. I hoped they wouldn't go that far."

Naveen tried not to growl. "Sounds like you know these people."

"I don't know them intimately." The man sat forward on the chair and flipped up his eye patch. A large purple bruise decorated his eye. "A couple of men jumped me when I was on my way to my car last week. Kept asking me about the necklace. Luckily, my security team came quickly and they ran. I've been very cautious since, not that I go out very much."

The way he said *the necklace* and not *a necklace* had Naveen narrowing his eyes. "You do know about the jewels he allegedly stole."

"Not allegedly. He stole them." Sunil released a deep sigh and stood. He went to the bar cart in the corner. "I need a drink. You want a drink?"

"I'm good," Mira answered Sunil, and he echoed her. He had seen more alcohol tonight than he had in years. His grandfather had removed everything from his home, even beer, and the friends he hung out with the most nowadays, other than Aparna and her kid, were fellow former addicts from rehab or group therapy. They obviously avoided bars and clubs.

He was a little surprised he wasn't more tempted. Two years ago, he would have *needed* that drink too, but not in a remotely healthy way, and he would have taken the buzz happily to forget about whatever negative emotions he held. He'd had to consciously learn how to be uncomfortable with his own feelings, and he was grateful to see that some of his work might be paying off.

It had also been easier than he'd thought, telling Mira about his sobriety. It had slipped into the conversation pretty naturally.

Her uncle poured his scotch. "Vassar was one of my best friends, the Porthos to my Athos. I knew about all his jobs." Sunil came back to his seat. "He told me he was going to get his biggest score ever. So big I told him not to do it."

Mira tucked the suit jacket around her. "It was out of his league."

"Oh, I don't think the necklace itself was out of his league. Jewelry gains its value here, you know." Sunil tapped his chest. "Which means that rich people will pay top dollar to stuff it in their safe and never tell anyone that it exists. He could have used that necklace as a bargaining chip if he ever got caught. Or he could sell it for a neat retirement fund."

Naveen preferred a different kind of diversified portfolio, but to each his own.

"Who he wanted to steal it from, now that was the out of his league part." Sunil took a shot of the scotch.

Naveen leaned forward. Finally, a name. "And who was that?"

"Cobra."

So not a name, but the same alias, uttered in that awestricken way. "Who is this Cobra?"

"A bogeyman, or so I thought." Sunil turned his glass this way and that, watching the liquid move. "You know Vassar and I met in America as adults, but we both grew up near each other in Mumbai. Both of us had heard whispers back then of a criminal named Cobra. His gang was widespread. They robbed, murdered, scammed, demanded protection money. Cobra's identity was more protected than any state secret."

No different from any mafia. "That was in India, though."

"Yes. He went off the grid decades ago, and everyone assumed he was dead. But then he popped up here, in America. Running the same game, but on a bigger scale, thanks to the internet." Sunil took a sip of his drink, like he was washing out his mouth.

Mira shifted. "He must be very old now, though."

"Perhaps. Or someone has picked up the Cobra name and his network. Either way, they've established themselves. I would not cross Cobra, and I told Vassar the same. Cobra's more powerful than God."

Mira pressed her palms on her thighs. "So why does

someone that powerful care about the loss of one small piece of jewelry?"

"Because they also have the ego of God," Naveen guessed. "They're probably pissed. And after your dad died, they probably didn't know where to go next."

Sunil wrinkled his nose. "It is also not a small necklace. It's worth upward of ten million dollars."

Naveen's eyebrows shot up. "Jesus."

"Yes. If your dad hadn't died, he would have been able to have an extremely comfortable retirement." Sunil resettled his shoulders, and suddenly looked very old and small in his oversize chair. "That was a hard call to get. Your aunt never liked me, anyway, so it wasn't like she spent much time comforting me."

Mira narrowed her gaze on her uncle. "Were you one of Dad's friends she always complained about? One of the ones who always flirted with her? Because in that case, I can imagine her not liking you much."

Sunil drew back, affronted. "I wouldn't have flirted with her when her brother wasn't even cold yet. I observe a solid mourning period for hitting on women. Speaking of which, has she said anything about me recently?"

Mira's hands disappeared into the sleeves of her jacket. "I'm sorry, I thought you knew. She passed away."

Sunil's eyebrows shot up. "Rhea? No!" True sorrow crossed his face. "That's heartbreaking. She was a firecracker. It's not every woman who can resist me. Apologies, Mira."

"Thank you."

Naveen rubbed his jaw, something bothering him. "You said you hoped they wouldn't come after Mira. You thought they might?"

Sunil sucked his teeth. "I was hacked a few weeks ago. Fired my whole IT team over that. I had emails from your dad in there. I assume that was why they came to me."

"What does that have to do with me?"

Sunil picked up his phone and typed, then turned the screen around so they could see. "Your dad sent this to me before he died, from India."

Naveen read over Mira's shoulder.

Sunil,

No complications with the transaction, but in the hospital.

If you see my daughters, tell them I'm sorry. I don't blame Mira or Sejal for leaving home. I was a shitty father. Hope they do better. Left them something, they'll know where it is.

Talked to Rhea, she says Mira might get married soon. I wish I could make it to her wedding. Feels like something's missing.

Thanks for everything. Talk soon. Vassar

Naveen cast a look at Mira. Mira calmly tapped the FOR-WARD button and sent the letter to herself without asking for permission. "So that's why they think Sejal or I know where this thing is. Sunil Uncle, you should have warned us."

Her words were calm and without inflection, which in anyone else would have been good. With Mira, it was worrisome. She wasn't unaffected, reading this final note from her dad, she couldn't possibly be, but she was really good at pretending indifference.

As a recent recruit to the Feel Your Feelings Club, he knew that level of bottling up couldn't be healthy.

Sunil grimaced. "I didn't even know your number, Mira. Or I would have surely at least sent this note on to you. I wouldn't keep his apology from you."

"It's not an apology. I don't know what this is, but the man I knew would have never apologized. This is some kind of code that I don't know how to crack. Another scheme."

"No, no." Sunil's forehead creased in distress. "I disagreed many times with Vassar over how he raised you and Sejal. That was the main reason I stopped coming around your house. Well, that and my own anxiety. But the man clearly loved you. Your mother's death affected him too much."

"You knew him when my mother was alive?"

"Well, no. I met him after. He spoke of her often, though. How she kept him focused and grounded, and without her he was nobody. How badly he wanted to be somebody again."

"He never spoke of her to me. He wouldn't even let us keep photos of her."

"That wasn't right, and I told him that. I know your relationship was strained, but he was like a little brother to me."

Sunil's face softened. "Last time I talked to Rhea, she said he started planning for your wedding from the moment you were born. He loved you."

Mira turned her face away. Naveen wondered if she was thinking of that chest in her father's storage unit that seemingly corroborated what Sunil was saying. "He loved money," she said flatly. "I was a convenience for him, and when I stopped being useful, he was happy for me to leave."

Every protective hackle inside of Naveen rose. The defensive wall he'd built around his heart the second her secrets had started to unravel chipped even more. Every clue he got as to her childhood made him even more certain that she'd lied to him, not out of malice or because she was intrinsically dishonest, but because she was desperately trying to forget.

Naveen's hand went to her lower back. She didn't shrug him away, so he left it there. "The thing is, Mira doesn't know where the necklace is, and Sejal doesn't seem to either. So whatever Vassar is talking about here, it's not that."

"Of course. I didn't say Cobra was correct in assuming Vassar was referencing the necklace, merely that this might be what pointed him to the girls." Sunil gave a dramatic sigh. "If my security team hadn't been so quick, I would have told Cobra's minions that I know exactly where those diamonds are."

Mira inhaled. Every time she thought this night couldn't contain any more twists and turns, it went topsy-turvy anew. "What?"

Naveen tensed, but he didn't remove his hand from her lower back. She was grateful for that. At some point, she wouldn't have his support anymore, but she'd enjoy it while she did. "Where is it?"

Sunil sneered. "Vassar sold it to a businessman by the name of Steve Wyatt. He has interests all over Vegas and the world."

Mira regarded her uncle. It was growing easier to look at Sunil head-on, but it still stung. He reminded her so much of her dad and the life she'd left behind.

I wish I could make it to her wedding.

Her first reaction had been annoyance that her father had looked forward to her wedding more than he had her college graduation. Why should her getting married be a greater event than that?

And then for a brief, ridiculous moment, the sentimental part of her had softened to mush, imagining a fantasy universe where her father sat with her in the Mandap. She'd been focused on finding a groom for years, but she hadn't dared to think far enough to a wedding. What a delightful life it would have been, to not worry about who would be with her at the altar.

Later, she'd access her emails on the burner phone and stare at her dad's words. Not because she wanted to burn his apology into her eyeballs, but because she knew they must mean something else.

He loved you. First Rhea, now Sunil. Bullshit, he'd loved her.

Naveen's thumb rubbed against her spine. "So Vassar

stole this necklace from Cobra and sold it to someone else, and Cobra thinks he kept it? Why would he think that?"

"No idea, except Wyatt's no stranger to stolen goods. You don't parade them around. It wasn't like either of them advertised the sale."

For the first time, Mira saw a sliver of sunlight in this interminably dark night. "So we can tell this Cobra that this Wyatt guy bought the necklace, and they can duke it out, rich people style."

Sunil eyed her with some pity. "Dear, do you think you can call Cobra up and tell him such a thing, and he will believe you and release your sister?"

She thought of that merciless computer-generated voice she'd spoken to as they'd raced away from the place they'd been held. No accent, no identifiable qualities, no pity.

Sunil sat back and crossed his ankle over his knee. "Lucky for you, I know where Wyatt keeps it and can tell you exactly how to get to it." He gestured at his wall of monitors. "I helped him design his security. We used to be friends."

Naveen narrowed his eyes. "Why aren't you friends anymore?"

"Vassar was really the glue that kept us together. With him gone . . ." Sunil shrugged. "That's how some friendships work, sadly."

"Are you saying that you think Naveen and I should waltz into a rich man's house and just take a diamond necklace worth millions of dollars?" Mira shook her head, confusion vibrating through her. "Sorry, I missed the part where we look like professional cat burglars."

Sunil pointed his finger at her. "You've managed to escape from and evade one of the most scary underworld characters in recent history. This'll be a piece of cake in comparison. I have blueprints, diagrams, alarm schematics."

Mira looked at Naveen. He should have looked absurd, sitting in that chair in his too-tight pants and his bow tie, but his commanding nature made even that ridiculous costume work. This could have been a boardroom instead of her honorary uncle's strip club office.

You're biased, due to his belly and forearms.

Probably. "Naveen? Don't you want to say something?" He would be the voice of reason, like he'd been during that poker game. He'd say no, they weren't going to break into some millionaire's mansion and steal—

"Yeah, let's do it."

The room went silent for a beat, but the silence was broken by Sunil's peal of laughter. "The man has some huge steel balls on him."

Mira wasn't going to laugh, but she concurred.

"My balls are normal," Naveen said bluntly. "But if it means protecting mine and Mira's family, I'm game."

Oh no. Naveen had lost it. "Yeah, I choose life, thanks."

Sunil hummed, tapped something on his phone, and turned it around to show them. "Wyatt's having a party tonight. A benefit, for heart disease. It would be easy for you two to sneak in."

She skimmed the article. *Drink and mingle with one of Las Vegas's most eligible bachelors!* "It's late."

"Not for this city," Sunil scoffed. "I can even get you on the guest list with a call or two."

"Where does he live?" Naveen took the phone from her and scanned the piece.

"In Billionaire's Row."

Only the richest of the rich in Vegas lived in the enclave, which boasted not even a dozen mansions on expansive grounds. Mira pulled her suit jacket tighter around her. "We definitely won't look like we belong there. Even in the clothes we were wearing when we walked in here. I don't even have makeup."

"One thing strip clubs are rich in is makeup, with or without glitter. We also have costumes here." Sunil took his phone back. "I can email you the information I have. I'll go see what I can scrounge up in the way of disguises for you." He got up from his seat and left the room.

Naveen removed his hand from her back and turned to face her. "We have to do this, Mira."

"It's not a good idea."

"Sunil seems to think it is."

"Sunil's best friend was a criminal, so I don't think his judgment is the best." She shook her head. "This is extremely rash, and neither of us is a rash person."

"Aren't we? Seems like we both have hidden, rashy depths."

That sounded disgusting.

"This isn't the time to play it safe. We are so close to this necklace, I can almost taste it. Can't you?"

"We can speak with Cobra—"

"It'll take us longer to convince a crime lord that we're telling them the truth, and that's not a hundred percent. We get this necklace, we physically hand it over? It's done."

"And you don't mind stealing from someone?"

"Stealing from someone who knowingly bought a stolen necklace?" Naveen raised a shoulder. "It's a shade of gray I'm comfortable living in. Come on, Mira, we can do this."

"Have you always had this huge amount of unearned confidence?"

"Yes. It comes with being a man. I want this to be over, Mira. So we can move on with our lives."

Her breath caught. Move on with their lives alone, was what he meant. Not together.

What is wrong with you! Are you in high school?

She tried to shove all her emotions to the side, but that was almost impossible. They grew out of her heart like a venomous vine, sneaking out to her brain and taking it over. "If we get caught, we're dead."

"Objective number one: not dying." He gave a faint smile, but it faded. "I meant what I said about us being a team, though. If you're not on board, we can figure something else out."

Was she on board?

She closed her eyes for a second, clearing out the messiest parts of her feelings and thinking. No matter which way she looked at it, she could see the validity of the points Naveen was making. "Fine." She looked at him. "Let's do this."

Sunil entered the room at a faster clip than he'd left it, a guard close at his heels. She and Naveen rose to their feet. He tossed Naveen a duffel. Naveen caught it one-handed, which made an unidentifiable thrill run through Mira. "You two need to get out of here, now. Go with Bob here."

His sudden urgency made her heart stutter. "Did something happen?"

He strode to the monitors and pressed something on his phone. Mira took a step back as the screens all narrowed in on one area. Naveen steadied her with his hand on her shoulder. "Fuck."

She concurred. There was Agent Stuart, prowling through the first floor, looking over the crowds.

"We have a facial recognition software. This was the same man who attacked me."

"He's one of the ones who kidnapped us." Mira pushed her hair back. "There might be another one close behind him, with his arm in a sling." Her stomach pitched. While she was glad she didn't have a death on her conscience, her horror over shooting someone might never fade.

"We'll look for anyone else. They either assumed you would come here, or they traced your vehicle."

Perhaps someone had seen them drive away from the casino. Fuck.

Sunil nodded at the bag. "The keys to one of my cars is in

there. Take it in good health. There's some clothes and wigs and stuff, things you might find useful. You, uh, you two need cash?"

Something about the paternal concern in Sunil's voice made her ache. "No. We're good on money."

"Gun?"

Their gun was in Gladys's rust bucket parked outside. "It's in our car outside."

"I'll take care of that." Sunil opened his bottom drawer and pulled out a handgun. "You know how to use it?"

Mira nodded and accepted it. Her dad had taken her and Sejal to ranges out in the desert as soon as they were able to hold a gun. She hadn't exactly been the best student, but they needed some form of protection. "Thank you."

Sunil surprised Mira by hugging her tightly before they left the office, and she held him for a beat longer than necessary. If she closed her eyes, she could pretend that he smelled like Old Spice, and that it was her dad who was hugging her. Like it was that alternate reality.

And Sunil cemented that fantasy by leaving her first. No wonder he and her father had been friends. "One more thing: you need to create better working conditions for your employees," Mira said hoarsely.

Sunil raised an eyebrow. "I pay them well."

"I've worked with enough corporations to tell you that constant surveillance is a sign of poor management. Also, Glenda is the worst."

"Brad's not great either," Naveen chimed in, and touched his perfectly lovely belly. "Rampant body shaming going on in this place."

Sunil raised his eyebrows. "Um, I will take that under advisement. Mira . . ." he started, but then seemed to change his mind. "Go. We will detain this man. Good luck."

As they followed Sunil's silent guard down the back stairs, Naveen held out his hand. Another surprise. She put her hand in his, and he squeezed lightly, his fingers big enough to completely cover hers. He moved closer, so his naked arm brushed against her. "Go team."

Warmth spread through her. "Yes, sir. Let's go not die."

Chapter Thirteen

Naveen had never changed into a suit in a car, and he really wished his first time wasn't in the admittedly sexy, but far too small, red Mustang convertible they'd borrowed from Sunil.

They'd found a fast-food restaurant and pulled into the parking lot behind the building to don their party wear. Naveen paced away from the vehicle while Mira changed. The windows were tinted, but she'd turned her back while he'd dressed, so he did the same.

To occupy his hands and mind, he made a call. His grandfather's voice was groggy when he picked up. "Hello?"

"Ajoba." Naveen closed his eyes. "You're awake."

"Barely, boy. I took my melatonin. Why are you calling?"

"Um. I wanted you to know that I'm going to be out later."

His grandfather had a smile on his face, Naveen could tell. "Good. Have fun. Don't bother me unless you need a ride home."

His grandfather would probably always treat him like he

was a teenager. It had been maddening in his twenties, but was comforting now. "Has Ajay left?"

"Ajay?" His grandfather sounded confused. "Yes, of course. He had to go back to patrol."

Naveen feared that patrol meant the man was simply sitting outside his grandfather's house, but there was nothing he could do about that right now. "Okay. Good. Make sure the alarm is on."

"It is. I spoke with your mother, by the way. She was short with me, I'll have you know. But she's fine. She was going to bed."

Naveen exhaled, relief seeping into his bones. Thank God.

"Now, stop calling us, or this girl will think you have some issues." His grandfather hung up.

Naveen almost dialed his mom next, but he didn't want to wake her, so he texted. *Hey, it's Naveen, lost my phone, so using this one. Please call whenever you can.*

A flash of movement caught his eye, and he swiveled his head to the car. He could see Mira's shadow in the back seat. She twisted, and shimmied, and he immediately faced forward again.

Last thing he needed to do was get turned on by her shadow.

Naveen looked down at the phone and ran his thumb over the screen. *Feels like something's missing.*

That had been the most poignant part of Mira's dad's email. Whether he meant it or not, Naveen had felt the words.

There was one person he hadn't checked on yet in his

family, and that made him feel both ashamed and guilty. He might not have talked to his elder brother in two years, but that was no reason not to ensure his safety.

You don't have to make up with him to check in on him. Naveen hesitated, then he punched in another number. It rang and rang, and finally went to voicemail. "Hello, this is Kiran Desai. I'm not available to take your call."

Naveen hung up. He didn't know if he was glad the man hadn't answered. On the one hand, uncomfortable conversation avoided. On the other hand, was he not answering because he was asleep, or because Cobra had him?

There's no reason for Cobra to mess with Kiran when he already has more vulnerable members of your family in his grasp.

He pocketed the phone and walked back to the car. His borrowed shoes were too tight and heavy.

He gently knocked on the window. "We should get going, if you're ready." Instead of rolling the window down, Mira opened her door and stepped out.

He nearly swallowed his tongue, and momentarily forgot his inner turmoil. She was wearing a silver sequined dress, which shimmered in the streetlight with vibrant energy. It was floor length, but when she moved from sitting to standing, her thigh emerged, round and supple.

He shifted. The last thing he needed was to get aroused as they walked into a dangerous, rash situation. "Wow."

She clutched the bodice to her chest. "I'm not accustomed to wearing formal clothes."

"Well, it works for you." Wait, did that sound like he

was complaining about her usual wardrobe? "That is, everything works on you. You always look good." He shut his mouth before he continued babbling. It was true, Mira always looked attractive, but she was a bombshell in this. The neckline dipped low, and her round breasts rose over it, shoved up and out by the snug material. The fabric was shiny and metallic, like someone had taken her body and dipped it in liquid silver. Her heels were ice pick thin, and she didn't look entirely comfortable on them, but he hoped they weren't causing her too much pain. Her lipstick was a dark berry, and her eyes and the tops of her cheekbones glittered with a rose gold glow. Sunil had even given her jewelry; silver bangles adorned each wrist.

"Thanks. Uh, so do you."

He twitched his suit jacket aside. It wasn't too different from what he'd worn before he'd been forced to change into leather pants and a bow tie. Sunil had told him this was one of their *Bachelorette* fantasy costumes, whatever that meant. In monochromatic blue, he hoped he could pass for Sin City cool. "Thanks. Are you ready?"

She turned around, flipping her hair to one shoulder. "Can you zip me up?" Her back was long and bare, her black bra a stripe across the honey-brown expanse of her skin.

Oh man.

He'd wanted to see her from behind in her waitress outfit, but this was nearly as good. No thong visible, but nearly as intimate.

He grasped the zipper pull. When it got midway, he had to hold the fabric taut to finish it. His knuckles brushed her flesh as he dragged it up and he didn't think he imagined the shiver that ran through her.

She slipped back into the car. He went around the hood, shaking his head to clear it of his pesky attraction. *Get your head back in the game. This was your idea, now follow through.*

They drove to the address Sunil had emailed to them, cruising down massive tree-lined streets. They followed a Bentley past a large set of open gold gates. That was good; it meant they weren't so late as to be noticeable.

"You looked at the blueprints?" Mira asked. Her body had grown more tense with every minute.

"I did." He'd been blessed with a fairly decent spatial memory. He patted his jacket pocket. "Got 'em on the phone, too, no worries."

"Wyatt's probably increased his security for the party," she fretted.

"Then we walk in and walk right back out. It's not like he's going to pull a gun on us during a gathering, Mira." He hoped he sounded much more confident than he was. It was true, he didn't think anyone would pull a gun on their guests during a party, but then again, he hadn't dealt with anyone as rich as this. Wyatt was Illuminati rich, and maybe they had ritual sacrifices at their charity events and no one batted an eye.

He stopped at the valet and got out of their car. Mira

rested her hand on his arm as they walked up the steps behind the svelte blond couple who had exited the Bentley. Naveen's date's body was tense and tight, and he squeezed her hand in silent comfort. "Relax," he murmured.

"I don't know how I'm supposed to do that."

"Imagine everyone naked." *I've already done that with you.*

"I always found that advice suspect. Got anything else?"

He tossed his glib advice aside and considered her question seriously. As an adult, people considered him an extrovert, and he could be one, but he'd also been a scrawny nerdy kid who no one wanted to play with or date. He'd learned to navigate social situations with a drink in his hand. Doing it without was much harder, not that he'd had many opportunities in the last couple years.

You've been hiding.

Yes. He had. And now he couldn't. But that was okay, because he had all the tools to do this inside of him. "Fake it. Pretend like you belong, even if you feel like you don't."

She averted her gaze. "Fake it. I'm good at that." He wasn't sure if those words were a reminder for him or her.

Mira lifted her chin and lengthened her stride. Naveen's confidence lasted only until they were facing a smiling Black woman in a red couture dress at the door, wearing a headset and holding an iPad. A heavyset man stood behind her. The guy was visibly security, and visibly bored with the gig.

Naveen was over bouncers. Did every place in Vegas have someone lurking outside it, ready to shove people out?

"Welcome, what's your name?"

"Amira Patel," Mira said, so authoritatively, even he believed her.

The woman scrolled. And scrolled.

A trickle of sweat worked its way down Naveen's neck. Mira had emailed Sunil her alias in response to the blueprints he'd sent, but had the guy managed to get them on the list? The last thing Naveen liked to do was impose himself, a result of having parents who had been just rich enough that they didn't mind imposing themselves anywhere. His cheeks were ready to light up at their being caught sneaking into a fancy party.

Think about your family. And Mira. Fake whatever you need to fake.

He firmed his lips and watched the woman. She paused, and her nail tapped the screen. "Here we go. Thank you so much for coming, and for your generous contribution." She pulled wristbands out of her pocket. They weren't the paper ones you might get at a festival, but gold-plated bracelets. Or possibly not plated, but actual gold.

Illuminati. Nonetheless, Naveen allowed the woman to click the bracelet around his wrist, and Mira did the same. He paid semi-attention as she directed them to enjoy the party.

He breathed a sigh of relief when they passed the bouncer and entered the courtyard of the home. The mansion was built around a huge green space, and that was where the event was taking place. A string quartet played on a dais in the middle of the estate. Tuxedoed servers passed by with champagne and appetizers. "First hurdle down," he murmured to Mira. "Should we get a drink?" People always paid less attention to a person with a drink in their hand.

"Might as well."

Mira tugged at her dress as they moved through the crowd. She was dressed no differently than other women here, and many of the men wore clothes similar to Naveen's. They fit in physically, at the very least. As unobtrusively as possible, his gaze climbed the four-story structure all around them, trying to line up the windows with the blueprint in his mind.

If only his grandmother were still around. She'd taught architecture. She would have been able to figure out the diagrams and would have had a blast on this caper.

They stopped at the bar. He got a ginger ale. Mira ordered a Coke. He wondered if she felt odd ordering alcohol after he'd told her about his sobriety. "I don't mind if you drink around me, by the way." Aparna occasionally had a drink in his presence, and it hadn't tempted him.

"I need to keep a clear head." Her gaze scanned the courtyard. "So you haven't drank in a while?"

"Nope. Not since I went to rehab."

Her eyebrows lifted. "Oh. What was rehab like?"

"It was actually nice. Quiet. Calm. I'd been working around the clock at the firm then, so it was kind of like my first vacation in years. Once I left, I went into a twelve-step program." He'd taken some helpful tools from Alcoholics

Anonymous, though he preferred to talk to a therapist individually.

She sipped her soda as they drifted away from the bar to a less crowded spot. Though he didn't normally like telling people about his sobriety, Mira was unusually easy to talk to and he was happy to keep her distracted. She didn't look tense, but her knuckles were white. "I don't remember you drinking much when we were together."

"Because I was a highly functioning alcoholic. I also stepped up my drinking more after we broke up."

Mira drew back. "Because of me?"

He stopped under a tree. He had been bummed Mira had broken up with him, but he'd faced rejection and disappointment before. "No. It would have happened with or without you. It was me. I was under a lot of stress." The higher that pressure got, the better the alcohol had tasted. He took a big gulp of his ginger ale, savoring the sweet bubbles as they quenched some of his thirst. "Alcohol was a big part of my firm culture. My family's too. It was a quick slide for me from social lubricant to something I needed to function, what I used to treat anything bad I was feeling."

"What made you quit?"

"A few things went wrong all at once. I lost three big clients, my fiancée left me, and, well, I drank too much one night at a bar, drove home, and got a DUI." He could say the words easier now, but they hadn't exactly been easy experiences. "My grandpa came and gave me a wake-up call, but I was already thinking that the best thing to do was to get rid of one of the things actively making me miserable. I just didn't know how to do it. Rehab helped a lot with that."

She had stilled, and he wondered if she was thinking about the DUI. "I got pulled over before I got into an accident or anything," he hurried to assure her. "No one was hurt. Trust me, I know exactly how wrong I was for getting behind the wheel." Explaining it to his mother, and the state bar, and a judge had been the most humbling and mortifying experiences of his life. He could only thank God he hadn't injured someone.

"Good," she murmured. "Did you say fiancée?"

He tried to remember if he'd told her that he'd been engaged after their relationship. "Yes. I told you Hema Auntie introduced me to someone else after you."

A line appeared between Mira's eyebrows. She seemed almost disturbed? "You didn't tell me you were engaged to her."

He'd felt so much pressure to get the second relationship right, that he'd proposed before either of them were ready. If he could not talk about Payal, though, that would be fine. "It was a short engagement."

Mira opened her mouth, but before she could respond, the sound of metal hitting glass filled the air. They turned their attention to the stage in the center, where the quartet had paused in its playing to make way for a tall man.

Naveen knew from pictures on the internet that this was Steve Wyatt. He looked exactly like he did there, tall and imposing, with a solidly muscular bulk around his middle.

His nose was crooked, like it had been broken a few times, and his ears were big. Despite the cost of it, his suit was vaguely ill fitting, as if he'd run out of the tailor's before he was finished.

Some rich men looked soft. Wyatt looked like he got in a boxing ring regularly to get his face rearranged for fun.

All smiles, revealing one gold tooth, Wyatt clinked the metal tines of his fork against his champagne glass. Once the crowd had quieted, he stretched his arms wide. "Friends, thank you so much for coming." He spoke into a microphone, but Naveen didn't think the man needed it, his voice was so booming.

Mira moved, and Naveen looked down at her. He wondered if she'd consciously placed her body between him and their mark.

It was cute, either way.

Wyatt cleared his throat. "As you all know, my family has long suffered from heart disease. I'm happy to do anything I can to help with awareness and raising funds. To that end, I hope you've all seen the silent auction items, they're fantastic. I know you're wondering, where's Steve's contribution? What, is this house not enough? You all are eating and drinking me into the poorhouse." There was a polite laugh, and Wyatt waved it away. "No, no, I know. So, here's my contribution." He waved at someone, and they brought a covered item out. He whipped the covering off, revealing a large painting underneath.

Naveen didn't know art, but even he could spot a Picasso

when he saw it. The gasp that echoed through the crowd would have tipped him off either way.

Wyatt introduced the painting, then smiled. "We are starting the bidding at five hundred thousand dollars. Do I have five hundred thousand?"

"A million!" Came a shout from the crowd.

"Two million!"

Wyatt lifted his hand. "Do I have three million?"

Mira stopped a server who was walking by, his neck craned to watch the spectacle of millionaires and billionaires blowing their money like it was candy. "Excuse me, where's the restroom?"

"Oh, it's inside, to the left. If that one's full, there's two more, down the hall, before you reach the kitchen."

She gave Naveen a look, and he waited a beat, then followed her. Smart, to infiltrate the house while their host and the crowd were too busy to notice.

He caught up with her and grabbed her hand when she walked right past the bathroom, and tried not to notice how natural the move felt. "This way," he murmured.

"I thought the stairs were near the kitchen?" she asked.

"They are, but staff will be crawling around the kitchen like ants. There's a servants' elevator. We'll take that up." He walked as confidently as possible down the hall, even when a waiter turned the corner and walked right toward them. The man didn't give them a second glance, though they'd blown past the restroom. *Fake it.*

They made it to the elevator. It was an old-timey one, with a metal door that had to be manually closed. "This is probably a bad time to tell you that I'm a little claustrophobic," Mira said.

Naveen would have assumed she was joking, but for the way her eyes shifted around the space. If it was possible, he would have said they could take another route, but it wasn't possible. He closed the door behind them and pressed 3. Then he drew his arm around her and pulled her to his side. "Close your eyes," he commanded her.

She rested her head against his shoulder and did that, and though he should have been watching the elevator climb, he couldn't take his gaze off her sweet, round face. He'd never noticed how stubborn her chin was, or how fine her eyebrows were. Though she wasn't frail, she felt small next to him. He wanted to pick her up and shove her inside his coat to protect her.

What are you thinking, buddy.

He wasn't sure. He tried to reach for any of that anger that had protected him, but she'd poked so many holes in it, all of the steam had escaped, to be replaced by hunger.

The lurch of the elevator stopping shook him out of his daze. "We're here."

She blinked her eyes and pulled away, leaving his entire side cold and bereft. "Oh."

Naveen cleared his throat and opened the elevator door. The floor was deserted when he peeked his head out.

He didn't need to check the blueprints on his phone—they were burned into his brain, along with the location of the security cameras—and he thanked his photographic memory for that. He kept an eye out for any security protocol that hadn't been in the dossier Sunil had sent them, but there was nothing new.

Until they nearly turned a corner and almost ran smack into a guard. He grabbed Mira and pulled her back. "There's someone standing in front of the library door," he whispered to her.

"Can you take him?"

He gave her an incredulous look. "What?"

"You've taken down an FBI agent."

"I was hyped up on adrenaline."

"Well, can you get hyped up on adrenaline again?"

"Making a Molotov cocktail would be less risky." He peeked around the corner again. This man was much bigger than Stuart, and he looked more competent too.

A click came from behind him, and he turned to find Mira holding her father's silver lighter, the lid flipped open. "I was kidding."

Her big eyes looked up at him. She handed it to him. "You're taller. Hold it up to the smoke detector."

He nearly kissed her. Of course. They should have thought about setting off the fire alarm ages ago. It would get everyone out of the house, temporarily.

He pushed the lighter gently away. "There's a better way."

He jogged back the way they had come and found a fire alarm box on the wall. It was odd to see one in a private residence, but this place was huge, and Wyatt did house valuables. He opened the lid and yanked. The sound was low at first, but gained steam as it echoed through the upstairs.

He came back to Mira, who was peeking around the corner. He joined her and watched as the guard spoke into his wrist, then shook his head and left his post. As soon as he was out of eyesight, Naveen nodded at Mira.

The doorknob turned under Mira's hand. They entered quickly and Mira closed the door behind them. She used her phone flashlight to illuminate the place.

Bookshelves lined the walls and big cushy chairs and couches dominated the room. It was a place he'd love to include in his mental blueprint for his own future home, except he didn't have millions to blow. "We did it," he said. They'd done it easily.

Too easily.

"There's no way he keeps his precious treasures in this room, with no security, no lock, and no alarms," Mira said quietly, echoing his thoughts. She found a lamp and turned it on. The delicate glow bathed the leathery books and shelves. "Sunil must have been mistaken."

"There could be a secret room here." He pulled out his phone and examined the blueprints again. Then he looked up at the ceiling. It was popcorn in here, which was odd, given the sleek modern finishes of the rest of the home.

Also odd was that the blueprint showed three stories, but he'd counted four outside. His grandmother would be very proud of him for noticing that. "Look for an attic entrance in the ceiling," he whispered.

"Naveen?"

"I bet there's a seam somewhere."

"Naveen."

He looked away from his ceiling perusal to find her frozen in front of a bookshelf. "What?"

"Maybe this guy is cocky enough to leave his treasures out in the open."

He came to stand next to her. There, between the shelves, was a small glass box with the diamond necklace that they'd spent their entire night risking their lives for. "Holy shit," he whispered.

The fire alarm stopped, but his phone ring took its place. The vibration in his hand shocked them both. He spun away and answered it, not realizing until he did that it was a video call. "Naveen, I woke up to a missed text from you, I was worried—" His mom stopped. "Was that . . . that wasn't Amira that was just behind you?"

Fuck. He looked over his shoulder at Mira, who stood frozen after having taken two giant steps out of frame of his camera. "Uh. Yes."

"Interesting." His mom drew the word out. "Very interesting."

"Mom, we'll talk about this later."

"We most certainly will." His mom's eyebrows were

pushed so high, they'd nearly disappeared under her hair. "I didn't know you were still in contact with her."

"Yeah, it's a recent thing."

She lowered her voice. "She was your first match from Hema."

"I know, Mom."

"I liked her very much."

He grimaced. His mother had loved Mira. "I know. Mom, don't worry about it, I'll call you later, I wanted to make sure you were fine."

"Where are you? What's that fake necklace behind you? It's so gaudy. Wait, are you in a jewelry store? Is there one open late?" Her voice rose. "Naveen, why are you texting from a Nevada number, are you buying your ex-girlfriend a fake diamond ring in Las Vegas and getting married in some tacky ceremony?"

"No, no—"

"Wait," Mira whispered. "Did she say fake?"

"Of course I said fake, I can spot good jewelry ten miles away," his mother said loudly. "Just like I can spot a real Vermeer, like the one next to it. Though that's odd, I thought that one was stolen years ago, I must be rusty on my art history. Amira, if my son is buying you diamonds, please make sure they're real. I can't be embarrassed like that."

He pinched the bridge of his nose. "Mom, I'm going to call you back."

"Wait!"

He paused. "Yes?"

Anxiousness drew his mom's face tight. "I know what this is. My sweetie, it's okay."

Mom, stop calling me your sweetie in front of Mira. "What's okay?"

"I know why you reached out to me. Your grandfather said you called him, too. Now I see you in Las Vegas with your ex and lying about a date. You found out, didn't you? Your brother didn't purposefully keep the baby a secret—"

"Wait, wait. Baby?" He took a few steps away from Mira without even thinking about it. "Kiran had a baby?"

She stopped, like she realized she'd said too much. "Payal's six months along. I thought you knew. Oh no."

He puffed out his cheeks. "I did not know." He wasn't sure exactly what he thought about this, beyond shock, but he was abruptly reminded of where they were when he shifted, the floorboard creaking. Right. They were in the process of stealing jewelry from an extremely rich man.

Fake jewelry? No. Impossible. "I have to go, Mom. We can talk about this later."

She nodded meekly. "Please call me back. If not tonight, then first thing tomorrow."

"I will." He shook his head to recover from the curve ball she'd thrown him. "Make sure your alarm's on. You're okay, right?"

"Not with fake diamonds for your new girl. I demand you have the wedding I dreamed of for you, Naveen! Not some Elvis dancing schmancing one."

"There's no wedding," he said, mildly desperate. "Goodbye Mom." He hung up, both thrilled she was fine and horrified by the whole conversation.

He turned to Mira. She was watching him with detached interest. "Your brother is having a baby?"

"It seems that way."

"Congratulations. Is Payal his wife?"

"Yes. His wife." Naveen shifted his weight from one foot to another. "My ex-fiancée."

Loud footsteps cut off any response she might have made. They froze for a second, then Mira reached behind her and unzipped her dress. The fabric sagged on her front, and he barely had a chance to process that before she launched herself into his arms.

Oh. Yes, he was on board with this plan.

This had the added advantage of his getting to kiss her, though he wouldn't focus on the kissing, not when they had their lives on the line.

He wouldn't focus on it . . . much.

Her lips softened against his, and parted slightly. He flicked his tongue out, collected her sighs. She tasted like spearmint.

Adrenaline and fear pulsed together with lust, turning into a heady cocktail that zapped his brain cells. Her breasts were soft and heavy against his chest. He placed one hand on her hip and pulled her close, his other hand drifting down her back, pausing briefly to skate over the clasp of her bra. Her skin was so soft and warm. He rested his fingers just below the small of her back, his knuckles pushing the fabric down. If he flexed his fingers slightly, he could finally get that good look he'd wanted before. Or, at least, a good feel.

That didn't happen, though, because the next sound that pierced his hunger was a throat clearing. And it didn't come from either of them.

Chapter Fourteen

Mira considered herself a woman who always had her wits about her, but not when she kissed Naveen.

At some point, she'd stop being shocked by how good he was at the art of lip-locking, but that point wasn't during this kiss. His hands were heavy and hot on her hips and back, and they molded to her body. He used to love her butt. She hoped he still did.

That too-perfect mouth moved over hers, ready to find out every single one of her secrets. How could she have been ready to settle into a passion-less marriage?

Because a passion like this could sweep you away, and that's really terrifying.

When he yanked his lips away, she nearly groaned and dragged him back. Then she heard the sound behind them.

Oh, right. They were in the middle of a heist. See, the passion was a problem. It made her forget everything.

Mira whirled around, holding her dress to her chest. The two men standing there stared pointedly above hers and Naveen's heads. They looked like twins, both bald with shiny heads, in dark suits. "You're not supposed to be up here," one of the men growled.

"Oh, um. I'm sorry. I didn't hear anyone. Oh gosh. So sorry," she babbled, and her dismay wasn't an act, even if she'd intended the kiss to be.

She reached behind her awkwardly to zip up her dress, but Naveen was already there. He quickly did up the closure. He placed his hands on her shoulders, subtly moved her aside and came to stand in front of her. "Gentlemen, apologies."

"You're not supposed to be up here," the man repeated again.

Naveen adjusted his jacket. "My fiancée and I were merely looking for a private spot."

"The first floor is for guests."

"We weren't aware." Naveen gave them a smile. Neither of them reciprocated. "Hey, we're sorry. The alarm was going off, and it was quieter in here, is all. We'll get out of your hair." Naveen took a step, and the two men moved as one to block him, folding their arms over their chests.

They looked like an impenetrable wall of muscle. "Our boss would like to speak with you first."

Oh no. Oh no, oh no. The boss had to be Wyatt. How had the man found out about them so quickly?

Because they'd been right, and it had been too easy for them to get in here. Either this had been a trap, or they'd tripped some alarm. Fuck.

To his credit, Naveen didn't look bothered at all. "There's

no need for him to be called away from the party." His hand tightened on hers, belying his cool facade. "If you don't mind, we'll leave."

"We mind." One of the men moved his suit jacket, revealing a gun. A big, scary gun.

Mira froze. How many times could they be threatened with a gun today?

"Come on, guys," Naveen said easily. She'd learned that soothing kindergarten-teacher voice was his de-escalataion tactic, the one he used to try to get everyone to do what he wanted. It hadn't worked amazingly well tonight, but she was willing to let him try. "We got engaged yesterday, and we wanted some time together. You understand how it is, right?"

Why had she left their gun in the car? They should have brought it with them, even if she would have had to get creative with where she stashed it. Her dress wasn't exactly meant to hold a weapon. There were no pockets, which was maddening. She'd had to hide the lighter and her phone in her bra.

"Our boss is very curious about anyone who seeks privacy in certain areas of his home." The man walked to the wall and pressed against it. The section swung open, revealing another room.

The man motioned. "This way."

As cool as a secret hidden room was, Mira didn't believe that going inside one could ever lead to a positive thing. Especially if guns were involved. "I'd love to speak with him," she said weakly. "But I'm sure he's enjoying the party. We'll go down and say hi." She took a step backward and walked right into a brick wall.

Slowly, she tilted her head back. A third bald man had appeared behind her, and he raised an almost invisible eyebrow. Was being hairless a prerequisite of working for Wyatt? "On second thought, we'll go with you," she finished.

The wall behind her grunted and jerked his head toward the secret door. Mira slowly started to walk, and Naveen followed, after a brief hesitation.

They entered the door to find a small office, dimly lit by a lamp on a huge wooden desk. Two leather chairs faced the desk. There were more bookshelves in here. She was sure part of Naveen's brain was cataloging the impressive library and stuffing it into the recesses of his book-loving brain.

Did his fiancée love books, too?

She shushed the catty voice inside her. Why did it bother her at all that Naveen had gotten engaged to the next woman Hema had brought along? It shouldn't. Not after Mira had been the one to end things.

And it was his ex-fiancée. There were a million questions she'd wanted to ask about that, including what the hell had happened with his brother, but they'd been interrupted. She wasn't sure it was her place, even if they hadn't been.

"Sit," one of the goons growled.

"Gentlemen, I fear you're taking this a bit too seriously. We have apologized—" The guy with the gun opened his suit jacket again, and Naveen shut his mouth. He gave Mira a glance, but she was similarly at a loss.

Mira lowered herself into a chair, her mind racing a million miles an hour. She had anticipated this as a worst-case scenario, of course. Her anxiety allowed her to do nothing else.

Unfortunately, she hadn't had time to formulate a real plan for what they would do if they were confronted by the man they were stealing stolen jewels from.

She held her breath, until her head grew light. What were they going to do?

Before she could spiral fully into panic, a light touch brushed her hand. She looked at Naveen in the chair next to her. He gave her a slight shake of his head, and that was all she needed to take a deep breath. One-by-one, she relaxed her fingers.

He leaned over and murmured into her ear. "Sunil knows where we are. We'll get through this, don't worry."

Don't worry. Ha. Worrying over all the worst possibilities was how she'd made it this far in life. Anxiety was her one and only superpower.

We'll get through this.

In the beginning when he'd said that tonight, it had been resentful, then it had been a promise. This time, and she didn't think it was her imagination, the emphasis was hard on that first word. For most of her life, it had been *I*.

We had been what she'd sought with her whole foray into

finding a husband, what she'd been chasing for the better part of the last three years.

No wonder she'd chased it so hard. It was heady, this sense of us against the world. They were a unit. Partners.

It's only for tonight, and out of necessity. Do not get comfortable.

She settled for pressing her palm to Naveen's and letting his larger fingers close over hers. The guards hadn't searched the two of them yet. They still had their phones. Naveen could fake appendicitis. She could . . . something-something related to her period? That had used to work when she was a kid in gym.

Before she could respond, the door behind them opened and closed. Mira didn't stiffen—no need to make them look guiltier—but she couldn't help but internally sweat when the owner of the house rounded the desk and braced his hands on it, smiling benignly down at them. She didn't trust that smile one little bit.

Naveen was muscular like a runner. Steve Wyatt was muscular like a wrestler. His tux was high quality, but Mira didn't find that surprising. He had the money for a gold-encrusted suit.

"Hello, there," he said to them, and the soft tone coming out of his broad face surprised her. "I understand you two wandered into an off-limits area of my home."

Mira blinked at the greeting. Was it . . . was it possible that the man wasn't furious about that? Or was this like a creepy silent rage kind of calm?

The same thing seemed to occur to Naveen. He cleared his throat. "We do apologize, sir. My fiancée and I got engaged yesterday, and we were looking for privacy." He winked at the man, and if Mira wasn't in a pickle, she might be annoyed at the boys-will-be-boys smirk.

"Oh, engaged." Wyatt dragged the word out and sank into the seat behind the desk. The wood was a three-foot-wide expanse between them. "Congratulations. Amira Patel, right? Thank you for your generous contribution to the cause tonight."

Mira blinked. Perhaps, for the first time tonight, Naveen was going to talk them out of something. "Yes. That's my name."

"I looked you up," Wyatt continued. "You're from L.A., right? An accountant. Hefty donation you made on an accountant's salary."

Shit.

"I do well." She crossed her legs.

"It's funny, you don't seem to have much of a history in philanthropic circles."

"We do our philanthropy quietly," Mira added, as regally as possible. That wasn't a lie. She wouldn't be caught dead telling everyone who or what she donated to.

"What's your name, again?" Wyatt asked Naveen. "The list said 'and guest.'"

Fuck. They'd been so focused on getting in, they hadn't created an elaborate enough cover story for them.

In her mind, she imagined her father tsking and shaking

his head. *Amateur move, Mira. You should have been more prepared. Prepare for the worst, hope for the best.*

"Kiran," Naveen supplied.

Wyatt's smile slipped. "I can tell you're both lying. FYI, I don't care for people casing my home, let alone when I'm hosting a charity event. Taking out trash at a time like this is inconvenient as far as my public image goes."

Mira drew herself up, trying to look as dignified as possible. "We certainly weren't casing."

"No?"

"No. In fact, if the bathroom hadn't been occupied, we would have stayed on the first floor and we wouldn't be in this situation. Perhaps you should work on having more restrooms for your guests."

A glimmer of amusement lit Wyatt's eyes. "Are you saying this is my fault? Because I don't have kissing booths on the first floor?"

She folded her arms over her chest. It was a losing argument, of course, but she had no choice but to go down with this ship. *Fake it.* She was good at that, playing the cold bitch until people were unnerved. "Yes."

"Uh-huh." He nodded at his bodyguards. "I have to return to my party. Hold them here. We'll question them after and figure out what to do with them."

Oh no.

The clock on the mantel chimed on the hour, as if to remind them of their rapidly dwindling time.

Naveen shifted. "I don't think you want to do that, sir."

Wyatt leaned back and adjusted his cuffs. "Why not?"

"People know we're here. They'll call the police when we vanish all night, and I don't think you want the police to know what kind of art you have in here. I saw at least three paintings back in that room that I bet have fairly questionable provenance. That Vermeer, for example, is stolen property."

Something flashed in Wyatt's eyes, something dark. Mira tensed. "What do you know about my art?"

"We know a good chunk of it's not from legitimate sources." Mira wiped her sweaty palms on her thighs. "Like the necklace."

Wyatt paused, then glanced at the bodyguards, standing at attention. He nodded at them, and they left.

When the three of them were alone, he linked his hands over the desk. Wyatt's smile was calm. "Uncertain origins make things fun, in the collector world, you know?"

That wasn't how the law worked, but Mira wasn't about to explain how theft made all future sales of a piece void. They had bigger fish to fry.

"Who are you two, exactly?"

Mira willed herself to be calm, pulse even. "My name's Mira Chaudhary, and this is my friend, Naveen Desai."

Wyatt stiffened. "Wait a fucking minute. I thought you looked familiar." His eyes narrowed. "You're Vassar's kid."

"Guilty."

"Son of a bitch." He drew himself up, somehow making himself look even bigger. "That snake? You're coming in here to, what? Rip me off like your dad and his buddy did?"

Naveen leaned forward. "Listen, her dad took the necklace he sold you from someone named Cobra."

"Yeah, I know that." He waved his hands impatiently. "I didn't care where Vassar got it from. He cheated me. The diamonds in there are fake, the asshole switched them out."

Mira inhaled. "What?"

Wyatt pushed back from the desk. "Stay here." He left the room through the secret entrance.

Mira looked at Naveen. "Your mom needs to work for a jeweler, if she can spot a fake in a second over a video call."

"No kidding."

Wyatt returned and tossed the diamond necklace to Naveen, who caught it in midair. Again, his fast reflexes impressed her.

He held out his hand, the twinkly gems glinting there. "If these are fake, why do you keep it in a fancy box in your office then? Next to real art?"

Wyatt sneered. "To remind myself that no one can be trusted."

That was dark.

Isn't that what your dad taught you too? You don't keep a fake diamond necklace on hand to remind you of that, but you do keep all your wounds inside you.

No, she wasn't that bitter. She trusted . . . two? Two people.

Naveen rolled the necklace in his hand. The stones caught

the light like real diamonds. Mira would never have known the difference, but she didn't exactly handle precious stones on a regular basis. "Well, where are the real gems?"

"That's a really good fucking question. Do you know how much money I paid for these? Millions. Vassar assured me I was getting a deal." Wyatt rubbed his hand over his jaw. "I believed him."

Mira knew very well the hurt and disillusionment in Wyatt's tone. She'd felt it for most of her life. "Cobra's after us," she said hoarsely. "Sunil told us you had the necklace, that we could steal it from you and give it back to the original owner."

"Sunil . . . son of a bitch." Wyatt leaned back and turned his computer on. It was angled so they could see.

With a few keystrokes, he made a phone call. Sunil picked up immediately, his face filling the screen. "Oh, hello, old friend—"

"Don't you fucking 'old friend' me, you jackass. You want to explain these two?" Wyatt pointed the camera at them.

Mira gave a weak wave. Sunil sighed. "Damn, I should have known they couldn't pull this off."

What now?

"What the hell were you thinking? Sending Nancy Drew and a Hardy Boy to steal my shit in the middle of a charity gala?"

Mira wasn't expecting the other man to sneer. "I was thinking you were a dick and needed to be taken down a peg or two."

"Well, joke's on you, I've been expecting you to pull a stunt like this since you helped Vassar sell me a fake necklace."

"I didn't! If it's fake, that wasn't my doing." Sunil pouted. "And you should have known that. I was one of your best friends."

What was it Sunil had said? That Vassar had been the Porthos to his Athos?

The Three Musketeers. She had a feeling she was in the home of Aramis. "Gentlemen," she said softly. They stopped their bickering and looked at her. "It seems my father cheated you, Mr. Wyatt."

"Vassar wouldn't do that," Sunil began, but Mira raised her hand.

"He one hundred percent would, and pretending otherwise is just enabling a dead man. He cheated, he lied, he stole, and he didn't care who he hurt, whether you were family or lifelong friends."

"People change, Mira. He wasn't the man you knew."

"Sometimes people change for the worse. See? His own daughter knew he was a cheat." Wyatt sat back. "You took his side over mine, Sunil."

"Because you called me a cheat as well, and I didn't appreciate that!"

Wyatt braced his hands on the table and glared at the monitor. "I was not. You assumed I was calling you a cheat. And then I did assume you were a cheat."

"So because of your own pride, you tanked a good friendship."

"Because of your pride, you tanked a good friendship."

"Seems like you're both very prideful," Naveen said quietly. "And hurt. And in that hurt, Sunil, you sent the two of us over purely to fuck with your old friend. I don't appreciate being used like that." He bit off each word, his voice rising. He flexed his fingers, and she realized that she'd dug her nails tight into his skin.

She loosened her grip immediately, though Naveen's anger mirrored her own. "He's right, Sunil. You knew the necklace was a fake. You deliberately didn't tell us, even though you knew we were running for our lives. For my sister's life."

"That's not true," Sunil protested. "I assumed Wyatt must be lying, since he wouldn't let me examine the necklace. Also, I am trying to help you! I'm holding one of your kidnappers for you, and have my men on the lookout for any associates. I wouldn't do that unless I cared."

"What's this about kidnappers? And your sister?" Wyatt asked sharply.

"Cobra's got Vassar's elder daughter," Sunil said quietly. "They're holding her for ransom."

"Oof. That sucks."

"That's all you can say?" Sunil sneered. "See, Mira? I'm helping you out much more than your other uncle."

"I'm not anyone's uncle."

"If you were her father's friend, you're an uncle. That's how we work." Sunil leaned forward to glower into the camera. His eye patch made him appear less threatening.

"Right now, I'm not happy with either of you. Neither of you are my uncles," Mira said.

"Look, my anger at Vassar and Sunil aside, I feel for you. But there's not much I can do," Wyatt said.

Naveen placed the necklace on the desk. "Don't you want to get to the bottom of what happened? We could work together. Perhaps we can use the art in your possession to lure her sister's captors out—"

Wyatt lifted his hand, palm out, to stop Naveen's desperate plea. "I believe in charity, but that's a little more than writing a check. I bought that necklace as a one-and-done transaction. I've already lost millions on this."

Mira stared hard at the painting behind Wyatt's head. The swirls of paint all came together. She was falling into them, and into a vat of despair. Instead of the old man on the canvas, all she could see was her sister. Or what she imagined her sister looked like now, an older version of the woman who had come to visit her in college.

We had shit luck when it came to parents.

When she'd been in kindergarten, all Mira had wanted to do was join the Girl Scouts. Their father had been uninterested, and their aunt had been out of town, so Sejal had gone with her to Brownie initiation day.

While Mira had recited the oath, she'd checked behind her to find Sejal beaming, eyes bright under her bowl haircut. Afterward, Sejal had wrapped her chubby arms around her neck and squeezed her tight.

"Mira?"

She shook her head and looked at Naveen. "Yes?"

"Are you okay?" Sunil asked, his tone gentle.

"Yes. Of course." Mira pleated her dress between her fingers. "My sister is in the hands of a notorious crime lord, Naveen's grandfather is currently being watched by one of Cobra's minions, the two of us have spent our night sprinting through this city trying to find this necklace, and right when we thought we had it right in reach, you tell us it's fake and there's nothing we can do." She nodded rapidly. "Yes, I'm fine. Why wouldn't I be fine?"

"I understand your issues, and I will . . ." Wyatt hesitated. "I was going to say think of you, but that seems cruel."

Sunil gave a long, low sigh. "Wyatt."

"No. I'm not doing anything."

"I was Vassar's friend forever, and you—"

"I was his sister's friend first," Wyatt said, surprising Mira.

"But you were our friend for the last ten years. We have an obligation. Vassar did love his daughters."

Mira tried not to let her eye twitch at that ridiculous statement.

"I don't have any kind of obligation to anyone, after he cheated me." Wyatt crossed his arms over his barrel chest. "I'm not getting involved in blatantly illegal shit. The last thing I need is attention from Uncle Sam. I already give the man enough."

Mira was sure his tax bracket was near or at zero, like every rich person she audited, but fine.

Sunil sighed. "I will help you two as much as I can. I can go question the man I'm holding, see if he has any more info."

She was still pissed at Sunil for sending them here, and for his obvious huge blind spot where Vassar was concerned, but he sounded genuine, so she nodded.

Wyatt leaned forward. "You do that. We're finished, old man." He turned the computer off when Sunil started sputtering. Wyatt's smile to them was sympathetic, but firm. "I hope you make it, I'm really rooting for you."

That was a dismissal if she'd ever heard one. Naveen rose to his feet first, still holding her hand, and tugged her up. They turned away, but stopped when Wyatt said, "Wait!"

The man nodded at the necklace. "Take that worthless necklace. I didn't suspect it to be a fake until I had it in my possession. You can try a bait and switch like Vassar did with me."

That sounded like a terrible idea, but Naveen scooped up the necklace. "Thanks, I guess."

"Do you really think Sunil helped my dad cheat you?" Did they need to distrust Sunil?

Wyatt paused. "I don't know. It's hard to separate the two of them now, in my mind, you know? I suppose I shouldn't believe they're both the same, but it's hard not to."

Mira nodded. Wasn't that exactly what she'd done with Sejal? Presumed guilt by association? Even though her sister had been trying to do the right thing. "If you care at all about this relationship, you may want to give it some more thought. Determine if you're reacting because you're a generally distrustful person, or because he's given you a reason to be distrustful." Why she cared, she wasn't sure. It wasn't like she was feeling kindly to either of her father's friends right now.

In fact, she wasn't feeling anything. She was encased in ice, every bottle on her mental shelf completely frigid. Perhaps that was why she was speaking. So she wouldn't break into a million pieces.

Wyatt nodded slowly. "Now, did you valet your car? Allow me to walk you out."

Chapter Fifteen

When Naveen was young and on road trips with his family, his father had insisted on staying at roadside motels. His dad had said he'd wanted to keep them *grounded*, but Naveen had suspected it was partially market research. The family company owned more than one humble franchise. Generally the motels they'd chosen had been clean and safe.

The particular inn Mira and him had wound up at was at least one of those things, relatively clean. It was off the highway, with burned-out parking lot lights and a tired lobby. But the sleepy clerk had taken cash and hadn't looked at their faces, so that was a win.

Mira had protested when he'd said they had to rest, but he'd persuaded her. He was bone-deep exhausted, bogged down with the weight of their survival, and he didn't see how she was doing better.

Naveen pulled into the spot in front of their room and collected the Walmart plastic bags in the passenger seat. Neither of them had spoken about renting two rooms. He didn't want to be far away from Mira.

The sound of the shower met his ears when he walked in. "It's me," he called out, lest she'd heard the door open.

Naveen placed the plastic bags on the table as the shower turned off. He sat on the edge of the bed and toed his shoes off. He also hadn't thought to ask for a room with two beds. Mira hadn't seemed to mind, but he'd sleep in the chair if need be.

Mira emerged in a towel, her hair in wet tangles around her face. Steam billowed out around her. She'd scrubbed all her makeup off, and her face was shiny and clean without it. The towel was too small, and gaped when she walked toward him, revealing a slice of soft thigh each time.

He averted his eyes and gestured to the bags. "There was a Walmart around the corner that was still open, so I got us some food and drinks, as well as some necessities."

She poked through the bags. "You remembered my underwear size?"

His cheeks threatened to grow warm. He'd been on autopilot, and had thought nothing of tossing a pack into the cart. "Well enough. I tried looking for bras for you—"

"Regular stores don't really carry my size." She sat down on the edge of the bed next to him, holding the panties he'd bought. Her delicate shoulders were only a few inches from him. If he turned and pressed her down to the bed, she would go. And so would that towel.

Naveen sprang to his feet and picked up the pack of cheap boxer briefs and a toothbrush. "I'll go shower."

He turned the knob on the shower from hot to cold before

he got in. The frigid droplets weren't his favorite thing, but they did help cool his body.

He put his new underwear on and debated donning more clothes, but found himself apathetic to the thought of dressing.

Mira hadn't moved except to scoot back against the headboard and stretch her legs out. The necklace lay on the nightstand next to her, winking in the light of the cheap lamp. As beautiful as her naked legs were, her drawn face killed whatever lust the shower hadn't.

He came to sit next to her on the bed and folded his hands over his belly. "Are you okay?" It was a foolish question, given how not okay they were, but they needed to start the conversation somewhere. Mira had been distant and quiet since they'd left the Wyatt estate.

"No," she said, quite clearly.

He nodded. "Understandable."

"My dad double-conned a con." Her throat worked. "Stole the necklace, ripped out the valuable part, sold it to Wyatt, who trusted him, probably sold the diamonds to someone else."

"Yeah." He'd come to the same conclusion.

"We have no leads on the real diamonds. And Cobra isn't going to be happy with only the setting."

"No."

She dropped her head into her hands. "I don't know what to do. I can't leave my sister. I can't go to law enforcement."

He dared to stroke her hair. It was rough and wet under his hands, but as he combed through the strands, they sprang apart to form curls. She'd never worn it curly when they were dating, only straight. The only time he'd seen it like this was when she was just showered, or on the nights when she worked coconut oil through the strands. He'd wanted to massage that oil into her head for her, but hadn't gotten the chance. "There's another option."

"What's that?"

"We give Cobra cash."

Her laugh was dry. "I'm sorry, do you have tens of millions of dollars lying around? Because I sure as hell don't."

"The necklace is appraised for that much. It was probably stolen to begin with and it's not like a stolen necklace can be sold at Sotheby's."

"Right, so it'll bring in much more with black market art collectors and criminals like Wyatt. I don't have that kind of money."

"I have a family member who does," he said simply. "Not tens of millions, no, but a few million. If we can convince Cobra we don't have the real jewels, and this is the best deal they're going to get . . . they may be amenable."

She stilled. "I can't let you do that."

"Why not?"

"Why not?" She stared at him. "Naveen . . . you think your mother's just going to give you that kind of fortune without batting an eye?"

"It wouldn't be my mom. Most of her money is tied up in equity. It would take too long to liquidate it." He swallowed. "I would . . . I would call my brother."

"Your brother?"

"Yes."

Mira bit her lip. "It doesn't sound like you're close with Kiran any longer."

That was an extremely diplomatic way of putting their relationship. "Well, that happens when a man runs away with his brother's bride."

She winced. "Understandable."

He could hear the curiosity in the single word, though he knew she'd never ask. "You want to know what happened?"

"If you want to tell me."

He adjusted the limp pillow behind his back. "It's not a long story. About a year after we broke up, Hema Auntie introduced me to Payal. She was nice and kind, and she had a lot of the same qualities I liked about—" *You.* He cut himself off. No need to be completely vulnerable with Mira. "We got engaged quickly. And then about a week before the wedding, she called a family meeting with my family and hers. She and my brother told us that they were in love, and they'd run away to Vegas and gotten married." He winced, remembering how his mother and her mother had exploded. He'd sat there stunned, staring at his brother. Kiran hadn't looked at him. He'd only had eyes for Payal.

Mira drew back. "Oh no. I'm so sorry."

He cracked his neck. "Yeah, it was pretty embarrassing.

Everyone knew, of course. Her family runs in the same social circles as ours did. My brother's into real estate, he's
fairly wealthy outside of the family business. Two high profile people."

"I'm sorry. You must have loved her a great deal and felt
betrayed by both of them."

He scratched his neck. His heart hadn't been broken by
Payal. It had been broken by his brother. "I don't think I
loved her. Honestly, part of me was glad she ended things, if
she didn't care for me like that. Saved us both a painful and
ugly divorce."

"Then it's your brother you're mad at. Like I was mad at
Sejal."

"You're not anymore?"

"No. I've been thinking lately that my resentment toward
Sejal was partially because she was older and I was used to
her caring for me and shielding me. Like, she was supposed
to sacrifice her happiness for mine. But that's not very fair,
is it?"

He opened his mouth, but paused. Huh.

Had he expected Kiran to sacrifice his own happiness
for him?

Sounds like you're both prideful. And hurting. His own words
to Sunil and Wyatt came back to him. "You're very good at
perspective, did you know that?"

Her breasts rose and fell. The knot in her towel was pre-
carious. "With other people, maybe."

"My brother's been trying to talk to me, hash things out.

Now that I know that Payal is pregnant, I'm guessing that's why."

"If he wants to reach out, might be worth hearing him out. But you can't talk to him just to ask him for money."

Naveen raised an eyebrow. "I don't see why not."

"For one, it's a lot of money. Second, he'll ask who it's for, and then you'll have to tell him it's for me, and then . . . and then everyone will know about me."

"Who is everyone?"

She gave a long sigh. "I don't know. Everyone. And then they'll all know I'm not someone who *came from a good family*." She said the words almost brokenly, and the despondence in them hurt his heart. "That's what I got dumped for yesterday. You know, it's part of the criteria for a good wife."

What an asshole her ex was. "I'm sorry," he murmured. "For the record, I don't care and I never cared about your family or where you came from. You didn't have to hide it."

Her lips curled in disgust. "I didn't want anyone to think I was like my dad."

"Because of the poker, right? I don't care about that." On the contrary, her prowess was really fucking cool.

She was silent for so long he wondered if she wasn't going to explain, but then she spoke. "I was a smart teenager."

"I don't doubt that." He could imagine Mira as a sharp kid.

"No, like, really smart. I was my dad's partner. He liked to finesse casinos back in the day."

"Card counting?"

She shook her head. "Too unreliable, though I was good. He was an early adopter of technology. Lasers."

"What?"

"He found out that some people in Tokyo were using lasers to predict the velocity of the ball on roulette wheels. He had to discreetly use the laser to calculate the ball's speed, and then it would automatically feed into the computer and he'd get a signal on where to place his bets. It wasn't a perfect system, but he'd win about eighty percent of the time."

"Where did you come in?"

"I held the laser, in case he got caught." Her shoulder hunched. "He got me a fake ID, and I looked older than I was."

"That was wrong of him." How could anyone drag their child, their teenager, into such dangerous activities? His parents hadn't been perfect, but they'd never endangered him.

"I was happy to do it. I enjoyed it."

"You were a child. You didn't know what you were doing."

"I know." Her gaze grew distant, her pupils dilating, like she was seeing something far away and scary.

Naveen held out his hand. He didn't know what had put that upset look on her face, but he'd like to get rid of it. "Tell me."

She hesitated, then scooted closer to him, clutching the thin towel to her chest.

It wasn't close enough. He pulled her onto his lap and she

rested her head against his bare chest. He stroked her hair again, letting the curls twine around his fingers. As good as she felt, all soft and round on his lap, he was too concerned for her to be distracted by her nudity.

"That's not the worst thing I've done."

THE LAST THING she wanted to do was reveal herself down to her nitty-grittiest, but she'd come too far now. Best for Naveen to know exactly what she'd hidden all these years. In fact she felt like she had to tell him, like she had to lance this boil. He said he didn't care where she'd come from, what she'd done?

He didn't know. Once he knew, he'd bolt.

"We were on the Strip one night, working. These Russian men cornered us. They'd figured out that we were running the same scam as them, on their turf." They'd been huge, those guys, and they'd towered over her slender, shorter father.

Mira could still feel the sweat on her neck as they'd forced them into an elevator. Her father had been calm. "They took us to their room. It was on the eighteenth floor." The suite had been glamorous to her young eyes, the view spectacular.

"What happened?" Naveen's voice seemed to come from far away, like they were underwater.

"They kept us there for a long time. Hours in the living room, while they talked amongst themselves. I didn't know what they were saying. They offered me an orange soda."

She still couldn't stand the smell or taste of orange soda. "They got into an argument and one of them pulled a gun. He pointed it at us. I was so terrified. My dad rushed him, and they tussled, and the gun went off." She licked her dry lips. Until the day she died, she'd remember the sight of the blood soaking the man's white suit as he fell to the ground. "The guy got shot, and my dad hustled me out while the others were panicking. We went to the storage unit and waited there."

His warm hand stroked up and down her back, rubbing her thin rough towel against her skin. She welcomed the touch. "Waited for what?"

"The police, or his friends, I don't know. Some reprisal. But there was nothing on the police scanner about it. I have no idea if that man survived or if I watched my dad kill someone." As much as she liked how Naveen's arms felt around her, she was far too restless. She scooted off him and stood, tucking her towel in closer. Perhaps she should feel shy about being around him in a towel, but he'd seen all of her already. What did it matter?

Mira went to the bathroom to get a glass of water. She came back, chugging it. Not that anything would rid her mouth of the bad taste, but she could try.

Naveen sat in the same position, his hands folded neatly over his lap. His thighs were bigger than they used to be. The man hadn't skipped leg day in the years since they'd been together.

Someone had rejected him? How?

You rejected him.

She pushed that aside. She was different.

"I can't imagine how much shock you were in. I could tell you were shaken when you shot our kidnapper. That must have triggered some bad memories for you."

"Especially because I was aiming at his feet." She took a sip of her lukewarm water. "I should probably tell you, I may know in theory how to use a gun, but I'm a terrible shot."

He raised an eyebrow. "Noted."

"But yes, I was in shock. It was a bloodless game to me, until that night. After it, I couldn't sleep, I couldn't eat. It bothered me that it had happened, and it bothered me even more that my dad didn't seem to care that it had happened. The next week he came to me all excited because he had some new scheme." She tightened her grip around the glass. "I told him I didn't want to do it anymore. He was so mad at me. I graduated the next week, and I left."

"And you never came back."

"No. And he never apologized. He never tried to bridge that distance." The grief rose, its edge as sharp as a serrated blade. No wonder she'd felt nothing when he'd died. Her grief was like a heavy coat she'd never shed, always on her. "He didn't care. Or if he did care, if he did love me, like Sunil and Rhea claim, he didn't show it, and that fucking sucks." She drained the glass, and with one smooth move, threw it against the plain beige wall. It shattered, and fell to the stained carpet.

She stared at it in surprise, like someone else had thrown it. Her hands shook. Her body, too.

Another glass appeared in front of her. "Break this, too."

"What?"

Naveen pushed it at her. "Break it."

She took the glass from him, then threw it, as well. Each shard on the ground was like the shard of one of her mental bottles, her emotions leaking out of her. Her breath came fast, and her hands fisted at her side, but Naveen held her hands, loosening them. "It's okay to feel mad." He pressed his lips to her cheeks, and that was when she realized she was crying. He kissed each tear away. "He was wrong."

"I enjoyed it though," she tried to explain. "I thought it was fun. The poker games where I fleeced his friends, cheating casinos."

"There's nothing wrong with loving the thrill of adventure, but there is something wrong with endangering someone who is under your protection, and that's what he did. It's okay to be visibly furious over that." His gaze was so understanding and kind, and she fell into it. "He may have been a great friend to Sunil, and a good brother to Rhea. But he was a shitty father to you. You can grieve the father he wasn't, and miss the parts of him you loved, and hate how he took advantage of you. All of those feelings are valid, Mira."

She shook her head, not because she didn't believe him, but because the thought of anyone actually seeing her emotions was terrifying.

She shook her hands free of his grip. He started to step back, but she grabbed his head, rose up on her tiptoes, and kissed him.

It was a clumsy kiss, but it gentled almost immediately. His tongue came out to flirt with hers, and that was when need and longing ran through her. She wrapped her arms around his neck and deepened the kiss.

He responded for a hot, wet second, then pulled away. "Wait," he murmured.

"Why?" She made her way over to his ear and worried the lobe between her teeth. When he didn't respond, she licked him. "Naveen?"

"Huh?"

Mira had to smile. "Why wait?"

"Oh. Right." He placed his hands on her shoulders and pressed her away. His snug gray boxer briefs outlined the curve of his erection. She missed his leather pants, but these were nice, too. "You're vulnerable."

"I am?" She leaned closer and pressed a kiss on his nipple. He shuddered. "Yes. So we should wait?"

He said it like a question, so she took it as one. "No, I don't think there's any need to wait," she said. "I'd like you to fuck me now."

He blinked at her polite request. "Oh, uh."

"Can you do that?" She trailed her fingers up his bare arm, over the surprisingly large curve of his biceps. "Can you fuck me, Naveen?"

"Yeah. We can do that." He tugged at her towel, easily

loosening the knot. It slipped down her body. She'd stayed naked after her shower out of exhaustion, but now she was extremely glad she had, if only to give him easier access.

"I have missed these," he murmured, and lifted her heavy breasts. With the tip of his nail, he teased one nipple. How did he remember she preferred light touches to rough ones? Had he tucked that information away in his massive brain?

That's not the only thing that's massive . . .

Heh.

She slid away and ran her hands down his long torso and perfect chest, until she got to the waistband of his new underwear. She tucked her fingers under it, and touched the velvety soft head of his penis. He groaned. "If you touch me, I'm going to go off."

"That's fine with me." She sank to her knees and pushed the fabric down at the same time, and he stepped out of it. His erection was thick and weighty, and she took a second to admire it and trace the vein that traveled down its length. His hand fisted it and she lowered her head to taste what he offered.

His groan came from his very toes when she sucked him in. She got more comfortable between his legs and rested her hands on his hips, letting her thumbs fall into the dips that framed his groin. His fingers tunneled through her damp hair, guiding her where he wanted her to go.

Mira didn't think she was great at this particular skill, but he'd never seemed to care about her experience level. Judging from the sounds he made, at least that hadn't changed.

He tugged harder on her hair on a down stroke and she gave a muffled yelp. He released her immediately. "I'm so sorry."

She came up for air and licked him, gazing up at him from under her lashes. "I don't mind a little hair pulling, actually."

His nostrils flared. "Oh yeah?"

Mira formed an O with her finger and thumb and slid it up and down his slick cock. She tightened her grip, until his eyes rolled back, and then sucked the very tip quick and hard. "Yeah," she breathed on him.

He gave a moan and pulled her up and away. She'd never thought of herself as a small girl, but he made her feel delicate.

His kiss this time was wild and open-mouthed. He walked her backward to the bed. The room spun as he twirled her around and pushed her down to the mattress, her legs hanging off the bed. She rose up on her elbows, but he kept her pinned with a hand between her shoulder blades. "Finally," he breathed, and ran his other palm over her buttocks. "I've been dying to see this."

She almost rose and demanded he turn around, but she wanted something else more than the chance to gaze at his butt. "We don't have any protection," she said, and he squeezed a cheek.

"Already ahead of you. Got some at the store." He left her for a second, then came back. There was a rip of cardboard and foil, and then the rest of the box landed on the bed, in her line of vision.

He really had gone power shopping for all their essentials.

She wanted to make a joke about optimism, but his thick thigh came between hers, forcing her legs open.

The tip of his penis slid inside her, barely an inch or so. "Good?"

"Yes." She rocked back on him, managing to take another inch. It wasn't nearly enough. "Please."

"Shh, shh, shh," he crooned, and stroked her ass. "Be a good girl, and let me give it to you."

Mira shuddered, her body growing slicker. She pressed back again and was rewarded with a slap on her butt. "Harder," she whimpered. "And call me a good girl again."

She could tell he was smiling when he responded. He lowered his body over hers, until his heat covered her, inside and out. "You're such a good girl, Mira," he said, directly into her ear. His breath tickled the sensitive skin, causing goose bumps to break out over her arms. "You're going to listen to me, aren't you?"

She tried to move, but couldn't. His hips had her pinned. She nodded. "Please, fuck—" She nearly swallowed her tongue as he seated himself all the way. "Me," she moaned.

Lawyer in the streets, criminal *in the sheets.*

He echoed her cry of pleasure, and then his hips picked up speed, pistoning back and forth. The rough linens abraded her nipples as he did exactly as she'd pleaded and fucked her. He moved his grip to her hips, using it to serve her body up to his again and again. Her fingers and toes curled as the pleasure built, the tension growing tighter and tighter, until it released in a sharp burst.

The pillows muffled her cries as she came. He lowered his body, his sweat layering over hers. He thrust deep one last time. His groan was rough and long as his body spasmed over hers in pleasure.

He caught his weight on his arms, and their breath filled the silence in the room. Her body felt like liquefied bone and flesh.

She murmured when he pulled out of her, but she had the presence of mind to raise up on wobbly arms. "Steady there," he cautioned.

"Be right back," she muttered, and staggered to the bathroom.

Once she'd done her business and washed her hands, she came back out to find Naveen reclining on the bed. His body was long and sinewy, and so pretty. Fuck that Brad guy at Sunil's club, honestly. This man was perfect in every way.

He lifted the comforter and she clambered in with him. She nestled on top of him and rested her head in the hollow of his throat like she belonged there.

"I really need to know something," he said softly.

She looked up at him from under her lashes. "Yes?"

"Were you satisfied with that level of fucking?"

Her laugh was startled out of her, and though it wasn't

even that funny, it turned into a peal of chuckles. He joined her in a second. She didn't know what they were laughing at; the joy of being alive, perhaps.

When their giggles subsided, Mira nuzzled in deeper. This warmth and security was a problem. She couldn't rely on it, and she knew that, but she waved the concern away in her hazy brain.

"Mira."

There were questions in his voice, ones she wasn't prepared to entertain or answer. "Can we talk tomorrow? Can we please just rest, for a few hours?"

He paused. "Yes." He pulled her close and she snuggled in, her lids growing heavy. Tomorrow, she'd deal with the fallout from this decision and figure out what they were going to do about everything. Tonight, she'd sleep, with her body and mind exhausted, and her arms full.

Chapter Sixteen

Mira was a morning person, and apparently the skill of waking at dawn carried over whether or not she was on the run for her life. Her eyes popped open, and she stared at the ceiling, tiny fingers of brighter blue breaking through the motel room's dingy curtains.

She turned her head and looked at Naveen. His lashes were long, resting against his cheeks. His full lips were slightly parted, his breath puffing against her arm.

Her heartbeat accelerated, but oddly, her chest wasn't tight with panic, like the last time she'd woken up with Naveen. She was gentle as she extracted herself from his arms. Mira was a bit sweaty from the all-night cuddle session, but she didn't mind all that much.

You're in big trouble.

Mira crept across the carpet and picked up the debris she'd made of the glasses the night before. She still had no idea what had come over her, smashing the damn things, but there was no denying that it had made her feel great.

Better than her car screams. Like a catharsis for all the pent-up feelings she didn't normally get to express to anyone.

And then Naveen had told her those feelings were okay. That she was right.

She carefully tossed the glass in the trash can, making sure no shards were left in the carpet. She didn't want someone else to have to clean up her mess. Though the glasses had clearly been from the dollar store, she pulled a twenty from their stash of cash and went and placed it on the vanity as reimbursement.

After she got dressed, she stood for a moment, wondering what to do. She wished she could call Christine for her wisdom, but she didn't have her friend's number memorized. She could email her, but the last thing she wanted to do was freak her best friend out when she was oceans away. As it was, Christine had probably grown a little worried when Mira didn't answer her call last night for clothes-shopping.

Her phone vibrated on the nightstand where she'd placed it the night before, and she jumped. She grabbed it, wondering if she'd somehow summoned Christine. The *No Caller ID* on the screen made her heart seize up.

It's probably not the bad guys.

Mira glanced at Naveen, who was sleeping soundly. She escaped to the bathroom. "Hello?" she half whispered.

"Mira, it's me."

She lifted an eyebrow at the terse words. "Emi?"

"Yeah. How are you hanging?"

There wasn't time to tell Emi everything that had happened since they'd left her presence. Mira dropped the toilet seat lid and sat. "Still alive. What's up?"

"Listen, I've been playing with this phone you gave me all night. I think I've figured this file out." Her words came fast and rushed, and Mira wondered if she was hyped up on something, or if it was the rush of solving a puzzle.

"What is it?"

"It's a data file. A wallet file, to be exact."

"What's a wallet file?"

There was the sound of clicking on the other end of the phone. "Someone more fluent in cryptocurrency can answer this better than I, but it's basically a text file that contains two keys: a public address that anyone can use to see how much is in the wallet, and then a private key that lets the owner access those funds. I can see the public address. I can't hack this to see the private. There's too many possibilities. Basically, I need a passcode to get to the passcode. Does that make sense?"

"Huh. From what little I know of crypto, yes."

"I looked up the public address to see if there was any coins parked there." Emi cleared her throat. "Mira, there's, like, over five hundred million dollars, by rough conversion."

Mira nearly dropped the phone. "Five hundred *million*?"

"Yeah. Like, half a billion dollars' worth of crypto. And listen up, I searched through some places that I know these particular geeks like to gather, and this wallet is super-duper old. It is lore. This data file has been floating around for a while, and occasionally it gets sold to someone trying to crack it."

"So my dad probably collected it." That fit. Her dad had been the ultimate treasure hunter. "That doesn't mean he knows the passcode."

"Oh." Emi sounded mildly deflated. "Right. Just seems weird, right? Why keep this one thing on this phone? Like it's important?"

"What's your theory?"

"That the real treasure isn't some diamond necklace, but a fortune in crypto, ha."

If her dad had gotten access to that money, if they could get access to it, then they could buy off Cobra. Naveen wouldn't have to go beg his brother for the money.

The joy she felt at that thought was undeniable. Kiran was the easy way out, and the part of her that was her father's child wanted to take someone else's money and run. But also . . . it wasn't her money. And she had no idea how she'd pay off such a huge sum. Or how beholden she'd feel to Naveen because of it.

She rose to her feet, still thinking. "Let me call you back, Emi."

"Fine, but I'm going to keep trying to figure out how the hell to crack this."

"Go for it." Mira hung up and left the bathroom. She turned the phone around in her hands, thinking, and paced to the table where Naveen had left the bags from last night.

She picked up the silver lighter. She didn't know why she'd kept it around. Part of her missed the leather jacket she'd had to abandon at Sunil's. She did grieve, for the relationship she hadn't had with her only parent. As Naveen had said, that was normal.

It was odd that she'd needed someone else to tell her it was normal to feel. If they got out of this, she'd definitely be looking into therapy.

She flipped open the lighter and tried to light it, but the flint only sparked. Out of fuel, probably.

Last time I talked to Rhea, she said he started planning for your wedding from the moment you were born.

Wish I could go to her wedding.

Weird. Really, really bizarre that her distant, uncaring father had found a way to mention her hypothetical wedding to two different people in two different ways. Especially when she could have sworn the man had no interest in his daughters.

People change.

Her eyes narrowed on the sparking flint. Not her dad. He'd been cheating Wyatt, his own friend, at the very end of his life.

Wedding.

She struck the flint again.

Wedding.

She nearly gasped, but clapped her hand over her mouth. Of course. How could she have been so foolish?

Naveen was still fast asleep, but she could go to the storage unit and come back before he woke up. See if her hunch was real before dragging him across the city again.

Silently, she put on her shoes, and grabbed the keys and some cash. Her hand was on the doorknob when a hoarse voice growled behind her, "Leaving already?"

NAVEEN HAD BEEN in the midst of a most glorious dream, lying on a beach with Mira, when something nudged him awake.

He was glad for that, because he opened his eyes to find Mira at the door, fully dressed in the black sweatpants and T-shirt he'd bought at Walmart, car keys in hand.

She froze when he spoke and turned to face him. "I was—"

"You were what? Bolting?" He swung his legs over the bed, and grabbed the boxer briefs he'd eagerly taken off last night. "What the fuck, Mira?"

"Listen—"

"No, you listen. You want to panic because we had sex and it was really fucking amazing, go for it. But this isn't the before times, where you could run away while I'm sleeping. Panic, but panic in the same room as me, and then actually talk to me." He hadn't expected to wake up to cuddles and snuggles, given their urgent situation, but this was too much.

"I wasn't running away. And I wasn't panicking." She paused. "Much. I thought of something, and wanted to go to the storage unit and see if I was right."

That should have appeased him, and it did on one factor, but then another concern bloomed. "Without me?"

She spread her hands wide, like she was frustrated now. "You were sleeping!"

"I don't care. Remember when we agreed we were in this together?" His tone was sharp, but he couldn't help it.

She frowned at him. "I know that—"

"But you were going to go out there and put yourself in danger anyway. That's not playing like a team."

She pursed her lips, then went to the grocery bags. She pulled out some sealed Twinkies, and tossed them at him. He caught them against his chest. "What's this?"

"I take your point, and you're right. I wasn't thinking like a team, but in my defense, I'm used to being on my own, and I truly did think I was doing you a favor, letting you sleep. Your tone is getting a little pissy with me, and I assume you're hangry. You always did wake up ravenous."

He opened his mouth, then closed it again, her steady acknowledgment of her misstep taking the wind out of his sails again. "I am hungry."

"I said hangry, not hungry."

"I know what you said." He opened the Twinkie. "Tell me why you were going to the storage unit?"

She told him about the phone call with Emi while he ate and got dressed.

"Interesting," he said, after she was done. "But—"

"And the other thing is . . . it's weird that my dad said he was looking forward to my wedding in that email he sent Sunil."

He paused and softened. "Mira . . ."

"No, no, no." She nodded, her hair bouncing. She'd slept on it wet the night before. It was frizzy, creating a halo around her round face. "People might change, but not my dad. He wasn't the type of guy to change. He was always himself. And who he was only cared about me as far as my usefulness went, and I simply can't believe he had a late-in-life epiphany, despite what he said to my aunt or Sunil. No, I was thinking, what could possibly be the connection to my wedding . . ."

The realization hit him as she spoke. "The chest? With the wedding clothes? You think the gems are in there?"

"Or the passcode to that crypto fortune. Or anything valuable." She drummed her fingers over her lips.

"Or clothes," Naveen said gently. "Mira, he could have just saved that file on his phone."

"Trust me, this makes sense. At the very least, it wouldn't hurt to go back to the storage unit and double-check. We have no other place to go from here."

He studied her drawn face. There was an edge of desperation in her tone that worried him, but he could hardly blame her. These were desperate times. "Okay. Let's go see. But if we don't find anything . . . we have to talk about calling my brother."

"If I'm right, we'll have more money to bargain with than your family could ever come up with."

He shook his head. "Why are you so against tapping my family?"

"I'll never be able to repay them."

"You won't have to repay them."

"I'll feel like I will. I'm your ex. I can't take their money."

"What if you weren't my ex?"

The silence stretched between them. "What?" she finally asked.

He hadn't thought this through completely, but as he said the words, they sounded right. "Mira, we have similar values and aspirations. I'd like to . . . maybe we could consider getting back together after all this is over?" If he sounded stilted, it was because he was trying his best to not freak her out.

She stiffened, which told him he hadn't done a great job. "I don't think this is a good time to have this conversation. And even if we did get back together, I especially wouldn't want to take money from your brother. I'd feel indebted to you."

He drew away, physically, but also emotionally. "Well, please, the last thing I'd want is for you to feel like you were stuck with me. Consider the money a ransom for my family, and not yours. How's that?" *This is unfair. You are still reacting to thinking she was running away again.*

Logically, he knew that, but he couldn't get his knee-jerk pain to subside, nor could he bring himself to tell her the truth.

I'm hurt. "You know what, why don't we talk about this later? Let's go check out your hunch."

She nodded, but her eyes were wary, which he hated. He grabbed their stuff and followed her out the door. The sun was just starting to rise, painting the concrete with a crimson glow. It wasn't until they were in the Mustang that he noticed the police car parked at the far end of the parking lot. The windows were tinted, and they were far away, but Naveen could see that there was a figure inside the driver's seat.

And he was looking straight at them. As he watched, the guy picked up his radio.

Naveen backed the car out, his brain switching away from their relationship troubles back to their regular troubles. "You got everything important out of that hotel room, right?"

"Yes, of course."

"Good. Because I don't think we'll be able to come back."

She followed his gaze to the cop car and stiffened. "Oh no. Do you think . . ."

"Put your seat belt on."

The cop pulled out behind them, and Naveen flexed his fingers on the wheel. "Fuck," he muttered. He made a sharp left, then a right, and the car stayed with them.

He turned again, keeping his eye on the rearview mirror. Exactly seven beats behind them, the police car turned as well.

Naveen breathed deep. "Your belt's on?"

"Yes."

"Good. Hold on." He accelerated fast, and tried not to notice the tiny yelp Mira gave. He went faster and faster, then did a quick left, and got on the freeway.

The police car kept pace with them easily, as he dodged and switched lanes. Mira looked over her shoulder, nearly vibrating with tension. "Why isn't he pulling us over?"

"He probably has instructions to either follow us or herd us into a more private area."

Mira pulled her phone out and dialed. Emi's face popped up on the screen. She looked like she hadn't slept much either. "We need help," Mira said, and quickly recounted the car following them.

Emi's voice was brisk in response. "On it. Hang on. Let me track your phone, see where you're at."

"She can track us?" he asked Mira, but she shushed him.

"Okay, I see you. Naveen, can you hear me? Follow my exact directions."

"Sure."

"Try to get in the far right lane. There's an exit that usually gets semi-backed up with a two street split. You're going to fake this guy out. You'll have to move fast."

"The faster we get rid of him the better." He switched lanes, and the cop followed.

He put his signal on for the exit, and the officer did the same. Naveen almost took the first exit, then switched quickly at the last minute, driving over the divider. Mira gave a strangled squeak. The cop had no choice but to go straight, not without causing an accident.

"Go left at the stop sign."

Naveen drove fast even though the immediate danger was past. "They know our car now," he said grimly. "And that it's registered to Sunil. Where are you directing us?"

"Nirvana."

Mira let go of the handle at the top of the door. "That's a hotel on the Strip."

"Yeah, I holed up here last night, just in case. There's plenty of people. Come here and we'll figure out next steps."

Mira hung up on her friend and looked at Naveen. His heart was still beating like a jackhammer.

"Where did you learn to drive like that?"

He was embarrassed to say. "One of my cousins was really into cars. He liked to street race when we were young."

"Like *The Fast and the Furious*?"

Naveen rubbed the side of his nose. Telling anyone that he'd run around the city in his late teens and early twenties with too-privileged fools wasn't his idea of a good time. That it was Mira, after they'd already had a squabble this morning, was even less fun. "With less Vin Diesel, and way more luck that we didn't die."

"Interesting." Mira settled back into her seat. "I wouldn't have thought you were a fast car kind of guy."

"I'm not. I'm an electric car kind of guy." Now. "But I

know how to maneuver, I guess. It's like riding a bike. Like playing poker is for you." He shrugged, uncomfortable. "It's not that big of a deal."

She rechecked the safety of her belt. "Give me some more warning next time you do any evasive moves, thanks. Big deal or not."

Chapter Seventeen

Naveen was thankful that Emi had rented such a large suite. The better to pace it, from one corner of the living room to the other. Sometimes his pacing overlapped with Mira's.

"So how much was that again, trapped in this data file?" Sunil asked politely on-screen. Emi had graciously allowed them to use her tablet to set up a video conference with the man. He looked far more well rested than any of them and was hoovering a fruit plate.

Mira stopped. "It's not trapped in the data file. It's in a digital wallet. And it's not money, it's cryptocurrency that has a rough dollar conversion rate."

Sunil nodded and stuffed a piece of pineapple in his mouth, talking around it. "And how much in dollars?"

Emi gave Mira's honorary uncle a glance. As far as Naveen could tell, she hadn't budged from the position they'd left her in the night before in front of a computer, though she'd swapped one hotel out for another one. Her hair was mussed, sticking straight up, like she'd run her hands through it a thousand times. Her makeup had either worn off or been smeared to create dark shadows under her eyes. "Almost six hundred million dollars, at the moment. But it's only on paper," Emi said flatly. She leaned closer to the computer and typed furiously.

"What do you mean on paper?" Naveen asked. "It's a functional currency."

"Do you know how the blockchain works?"

"Not really. Explain it to us."

Emi swiveled around. "Refreshing, explaining crypto to a man for once. Okay, the blockchain is public: every transaction is recorded and visible. That's how I know how much is held at this address. Since it was such a large amount that sat dormant for so many years, it caught the attention of hackers. Because crypto is decentralized, there's no password recovery service. Without one, the money is untouchable." She grimaced. "We don't know who the original owner is, so it's not like we can even beat anyone with a wrench for this passcode."

Mira pivoted. "I'm sorry?"

"It's an old saying," Sunil announced, and ate a strawberry. "People think something is so well password protected, but really, the thief just has to beat someone with a five-dollar wrench to get the passcode. I already tried threatening your friend Stuart with worse, but he's not talking, so I doubt he's got the information."

Mira rubbed her eyes. The shadows under them were pronounced. Not for the first time, Naveen regretted adding to her stress earlier, but it wasn't like he could bring that up now, with Emi and Sunil watching. "So this could also be a dead end."

"Your father never did anything without purpose," Sunil said firmly. "If that file was on that phone, it's because it meant something. When we can get the money, we exchange it for Sejal." Sunil buffed his nails. "I've done a million ransom drops. They're going to propose you meet somewhere enclosed, like a house or a warehouse. We want an open space, in public. Since we have the more valuable item, we can negotiate easier."

Naveen straightened. "That's her sister, man."

Sunil had the grace to look embarrassed. "I'm sorry, Mira. Of course, you're right. But we do have *so much* money."

"If I can get the passcode," Emi reminded them, with some exasperation. "Again, it's theoretical."

Naveen passed Mira. He felt stiff around her now, and he hated it, after the breakthrough he'd thought they'd had the night before.

He was such a fool. A prideful, too eager fool. *Passionate detachment*, he was clearly not good at. One night with Mira, and he was ready to jump right back into a relationship with her.

It was smart she'd pumped the breaks. Even if it didn't feel good right now.

Mira flopped on the couch. She shoved her hands in her pockets and worried something there. "We can't access the storage unit because this Cobra has eyes everywhere, we don't know whether Sejal is alive, and we don't actually have access to anything that isn't already public knowledge. Doesn't seem like we're doing very well here."

Naveen's phone rang and he pulled it out of his pocket. His ears grew warm at the number there. "It's my brother," he said quietly to Mira. "Do I ask him or not?"

She bit her lip. Her chest rose and fell. "Yeah."

He knew that admission cost her. It was about to cost him, too, though in a different kind of pride.

If you get the money, and you do date, won't you always feel like she's doing it out of an obligation?

Yeah. He hadn't thought of it until she'd brought it up, but he was a lawyer. He understood conflicts of interest. Which was why they wouldn't be able to be together, if he got this money.

It was going to cost him pride and her. And that was okay, because at least it would mean this nightmare would be over and the people he cared about would be safe. Including Mira.

He answered and went into the bedroom for a small degree of privacy. He didn't want everyone to hear him lay his soul totally bare. "Kiran."

"Naveen. Hi. I didn't know whose number this was when you called yesterday, but Mom left me a message to call you back. It was kind of a confusing message and, well . . ." Kiran trailed off. "Ah, did you really get married to your ex in Vegas with a fake diamond?"

"Not quite."

"But . . . you're in Vegas?"

"Yeah." He rubbed his hand over his jaw. His beard was coming in strong. He'd kill for a razor, but that was something else that would have to wait. "Where are you?"

"In Paris. Payal—" he faltered. "Ah, we wanted to go shopping. I'm sorry I missed your call. I'm . . . I'm surprised to hear from you."

"I know."

"But happy," Kiran continued, rushing to speak. "Very happy to hear from you. Is everything okay?"

Naveen sat on the edge of the bed. "Yes, everything's fine." He gave a half laugh. "Actually, scratch that. It's not at all fine."

Kiran quieted. "What can I do to help?"

"I need money, and I can't quite tell you why."

"It's yours," his brother said, and Naveen immediately knew what Mira meant by not wanting to feel like she owed someone.

"It's a lot."

"How much?"

"Millions. As much as you can spare."

A slight hesitation, but his brother agreed. "Done. I'll have to see what I have, but I can liquidate."

Naveen swallowed. "Don't give it to me because you ran away with my fiancée," Naveen said quietly.

There was a squeak of a chair, and Naveen imagined his brother leaning back and crossing his legs over his desk. That had been how he'd always taken phone calls back in the day, at least. "I didn't mean for that to happen. It was a mistake. We couldn't help how we felt for each other, and well . . . she said she didn't feel that way for you."

"I know now that I didn't feel that way for her." *You may be what I said I wanted, but you're not what I need*, Payal had told him earnestly during that god-awful family meeting, and that had made sense to him. He'd felt kind of the same way, that he'd caved to family pressure and agreed simply because it was the right time, and she was somewhat similar to Mira. Quiet, reserved, kind.

But she hadn't been Mira, and he couldn't be angry at her for being herself.

His anger at Kiran had lasted a lot longer, though. They had been best friends as well as brothers. "It was a shitty situation."

"I know."

"And then . . . I didn't know what to say to you afterward."

"Same. I felt so damn guilty. I hate how society treats us, especially her. We feel like pariahs, like we're a huge source of shame."

Naveen frowned. "No, I'm the pariah. Everyone pities me for being jilted. They know about my rehab and blame me for not making Payal happy."

His brother scoffed. "No. I'm the black sheep."

"I'm the black sheep."

Kiran paused. "Well, this is a pickle."

Naveen raked his hands through his hair. "Maybe we

could both admit that we're objects of shame, but also, who gives a fuck." Running for your life could really give you some perspective. It was like someone had put glasses on him after a lifetime of myopia, and he could actually see the things that were really important. He'd thought he didn't care what people thought, like his mother did, except he had, a little.

"I would love to not give a fuck," Kiran said.

Naveen tapped his fingers on his knee. "You're happy?"

"Very. I love Payal more than my own breath, even if I hate how we met."

His next question was a surprise to him. "How did you know you loved Payal?"

Kiran paused. "Well. Um. I don't know, Naveen. It's not something I can fully describe. It's just . . . this knowing."

Mira chose that moment to enter the room and it was like all the oxygen got sucked back into his lungs. His eyes refocused on every little thing about her, the faint elevens between her eyes, the way she fidgeted with her hands and feet when she was nervous, like she was fidgeting with whatever was in her pocket right now. "I need you to do me another favor," he said to his brother.

"What's mine is yours."

"I need you to send security to Mom and Ajoba and Aparna. Someone you trust, someone incorruptible. No cops, private security. And for yourself too."

Kiran's voice changed. "Is something wrong, Naveen?"

"Yes."

"You're with Amira. Does this have something to do with her?"

His brother hadn't become this successful by not being sharp as a tack. Naveen watched Mira fidget some more, and wished he could take her unease away. Soon. "I'll tell you later." If he got the chance, that is. Grim, perhaps, to think they wouldn't make it out, but given all the twists and turns of the night, they might not.

"Okay."

"And one more thing." He rubbed the back of his neck. "Coffee. When you get back in the country."

He could tell his brother was smiling. "Coffee."

"Yes. So I can congratulate you on my new niece or nephew."

"Mom let it slip, huh? Nephew."

"Nephew." He started to smile, despite the situation. It felt good, to have something pure in this shitty time. "Wow. Cool."

"I miss you, brother. I'll look forward to coffee with you." Kiran cleared his throat. "Now, stay on the line for a second. Let me see how much I can get you."

Naveen placed the phone on mute and looked at Mira. How had he ever thought her expression was unreadable? It was perfectly, terribly obvious.

Before he could speak, she did. "Did you resolve things with him?"

"Yes." Kind of. "It feels like a weight is off me, to be honest."

"I'm happy for you. I hope I get to settle things with Sejal, soon, too."

Naveen sobered. "He's going to give us the money."

She pressed her lips together but didn't protest. "Okay."

"I know you don't like that but it means we can move on with our lives, you know?"

"I know. It's fine. You're right, this is the best thing we can do. That's what I came in here to tell you. I'm sorry, if I hurt you earlier."

"You didn't hurt me." *Yes, you did.*

"I did."

Mentally, he sighed. "It's not a big deal."

"I don't think you understand. I'm not used to relying on anyone. My dad saw relationships as transactions. I . . . I didn't want to introduce that element here."

He bit the inside of his cheek. That made perfect, painful sense. "I see. You're correct. Which is why, I was thinking, we should table any talk about a romantic relationship, given my brother's involvement."

She stilled. "Oh."

"Keep it simple."

"Right. Right. Fine. Good."

He cast a meaningful glance at her coat pocket, where she was currently strangling something. "You're upset. Your tell is pretty obvious."

She sighed. "I have a tell?"

"Only to me." *Stop flirting with her.*

Mira pulled out her father's silver lighter. "I don't even know why I'm still carrying this around, to be honest. Habit, I guess. He always did."

He softened. He knew why she still carried it. The lighter was, other than the stuff in the unit, the last thing she had of her father. "You don't need a reason."

"It's foolish," she whispered, like she hadn't heard him. She drew her arm back, and he almost expected her to fling it at the wall. Instead, she tossed it neatly into the silver garbage receptacle in the corner.

Naveen knew he didn't imagine the weird rattle the object gave when metal hit metal.

His gaze met Mira's. She'd heard it, too.

He walked over and picked the lighter up. "This thing is kind of big, for a lighter." He shook it, and the rattle came again.

"There can't be anything in there. It sparks when you try to light it."

He didn't know much about lighters, but he couldn't imagine it was that hard to get a working flint and spark on a dummy device. "Check anyway."

Mira rummaged in the desk and found a letter opener. He handed the lighter back to her. "You open it."

Her fingers fumbled, but she finally wedged the blade under the bottom panel. A few twists later, it popped off.

Over half a dozen diamonds fell out. Including one pear-shaped gem that perfectly fit the necklace they'd taken from Wyatt.

"Holy shit," she whispered. "I've had a fortune in my pocket. And my bra."

"When your dad said you would know . . . ," Naveen said slowly.

"She'll know what's missing," Mira quoted. "It was weird that he left this lighter behind in the unit instead of taking it with him. But he couldn't have possibly known that we wouldn't toss this. Why . . . ?"

"I don't know." He had zero idea how Mira's father's brain worked at this point.

"Naveen?" His brother came back on the line. "I have good news for you on how much we can liquidate."

Naveen unmuted the phone. The way his brother said *we* warmed him, but they no longer needed to borrow that cash.

That means there's no reason you and Mira can't date.

He could think about that later. "Scratch that, Kiran, we're good."

"You sure?"

"Yeah. I think we hit a jackpot here."

THE FIRST THING Naveen insisted on doing, after showing Emi and Sunil the diamonds, was calling his mother. Shweta had been able to clock the fakes from a state away, so Mira hoped she could authenticate as well.

She held her breath from the bed while the woman perused the gems over the video call.

"Yes, those are real," Shweta said, finally, as Naveen scanned the camera over the diamonds. He'd spread them out over the desk in the bedroom, like it was a jewelry shop.

Naveen flipped the camera back on himself. Mira tried to make herself smaller, though she'd already made sure she was firmly out of the frame this time. "You're sure?"

"Yes, of course. Nice ones, too. I would say D, maybe even E grade, very very slightly occluded."

"I have no idea what that means. They're valuable?"

"They're gorgeous." Shweta cleared her throat. "One of these is for Amira, my dear?"

"Mom."

"Simply asking. I heard from your brother that you two talked. See? I told you, once you settle things from your past, you can move forward. Now you're buying a ring for that sweet girl."

Sweet girl?

Mira pressed her hands over her cheeks. She'd liked Shweta and she'd thought Shweta liked her, but the woman had seemed more reserved when they'd met years ago.

"Did Kiran say anything else to you?"

"Only that he wanted to send a security guard over. Some issue with a business rival of his. Silly, but I'll humor him."

Naveen didn't have a poker face at all, but Mira felt his relief. "Great."

"I'm so happy you and Kiran are speaking, my dear."

"And now, you and Ajoba need to talk," Naveen said.

"You both want me and Kiran to get along, and you two fight like cats and dogs."

"That is different."

"That is pride. On both your parts. Figure out a way to swallow it, and talk to each other without sniping for once." His voice grew husky. "Life is short, and you two love each other. Try, please."

Mira couldn't see his mother's face from here, but she might be swayed to talk to her dad too if Naveen spoke to her in that tone. If the man was still alive.

"Amira has an interesting effect on you, son. It's not a bad one." Shweta snorted. "Fine. I'll talk to your grandfather."

He glanced at Mira. "She goes by Mira, now, actually."

Mira scratched the side of her nose. Was he telling his mom that because he thought she'd be in his life later?

Your worry about the reason you can't date is gone now. What does that mean?

Something that they didn't have time to worry about right now.

Naveen said goodbye, then looked at Mira. "You heard her. These are the real deal."

"Let's roll."

Once they had the diamonds confirmed, the plan naturally unfurled. Mira rented another suite under her real name. The penthouse was all that was available, and while it was a bit of a pain paying in all cash from what was left of Mira's poker winnings, Sunil was able to call and use his influence on someone in management to take their payment. Once Emi had the place bugged, Naveen went to the vending machine and swiped one of the credit cards from Agent Stuart's wallet.

The call came about twenty minutes later on the penthouse's room phone, and they all froze. Mira picked it up. Emi reached over and turned on the recording device plugged into it. "Hello, friends," came the technologically manipulated voice. "How's your Vegas trip going?"

Mira's throat felt almost too full to speak, like it was blocked with fear and anxiety.

Naveen seemed to sense that she needed a second, and he spoke for her. "Not well. We've been pretty busy."

The man tsked. "You should take the time to enjoy our lovely city, Mr. Desai. Is Ms. Chaudhary there?"

Mira cleared her throat and leaned over Emi. "Hello."

"I wanted to see if you've been productive."

"We have your diamonds, yes." *Please let Sejal be okay. Please let this be easy.*

A low laugh interrupted her desperate mental pleas. "I knew you'd come up with it, Mira. You just needed a little motivation. Where was it?"

"In a hiding place. In plain sight." Her father's favorite trick.

"Your dad was such a smart guy. Shame what happened to him. Now we can swap."

Mira licked her lips. She'd watched enough police dramas to know what she needed to do next. "I want to know that Sejal is still alive, before we talk any further about an exchange."

"Oh, of course." There was a slight pause, and then her sister's sluggish voice came on.

"Mira?"

Mira closed her eyes. Relief, guilt, and affection ran through her. "Sejal." She had to clear her throat. "Don't worry, honey. We're coming."

"Told you not to do anything."

"We have what Cobra's looking for."

"No. Don't give it to her, Mira, it's—"

The creepy modified voice came back. "That's enough of that. You two can catch up on things when you're reunited, eh?"

Emi gestured at her, and Mira nodded. "I want to do the exchange somewhere public. The casino floor would work."

The kidnapper gave a disembodied laugh. "Like hell."

She'd never had a problem being cool and emotionless at work, and she tried to channel that attitude now. "Do you want your jewels or not?"

"Do you want your sister or not?"

Mira clenched her teeth. Damn it. Because no matter what Sunil said, the diamonds were worthless to her, when it came to the safety of her only living family. And Naveen's family. "What do you propose?"

"Given that we're ten minutes away from you, I'd say we can come right up and do it in your room."

This was a 2200-square-foot penthouse, but she already

felt claustrophobic at the thought of being enclosed in here with people with guns. "I don't think that's such a—"

"You don't have much of a choice."

Mira narrowed her eyes at the phone. The order sounded so smug and controlling, and she was very much over being controlled. She might value Sejal's life over these diamonds, but that didn't mean this person did. "No, you don't have much of a choice. We can do it in this room, but no weapons. If you bring a single gun or knife in here, I'll throw your jewels over the balcony."

The voice grew amused. "Very well. Do I need to explain in graphic detail what'll happen if you have the police or anyone else with you?"

"No," Naveen said quietly. "We're clear."

"Excellent. Leave the door open and sit on the couch." He hung up.

Mira looked at Emi, but she shook her head. "Traced to a burner."

She hadn't expected there to be any trail, but she couldn't help the disappointment. Knowing Cobra's identity prior to their meeting would have given them a leg up. "Thought as much. Well. What now?"

"Now we wait." Emi stood. "Excuse me. I'm going to double-check the audio."

Naveen got to his feet and shook out his arms. "I'll stretch."

She paused. "Stretch?"

"I'm not about to throw my back out trying to tackle someone again."

Her smile was small. Mira walked Emi to the door and paused there for a moment. "Thank you for helping us."

"I told you. I owe you."

And you care about me. "I think we're pretty even after this."

Emi leaned against the door frame. "I talked to my mom last night. Mentioned I saw you. She said she was proud of us. Two accountants."

Mira almost choked. "Your mom thinks you're an accountant?"

"Nobody asks questions when you say you're an accountant." Emi fiddled with the strings of her hoodie. She'd swapped her leather for comfortable cotton at some point during the night. "She said we'd come so far from high school. And I realized, I hadn't. Like, you had. But not me. If helping you is my good deed for the year, I don't mind."

"I've come far professionally. Not personally." She thought of Naveen, and all the men in the past. Perfectly good men, whom she'd bolted from.

"We won't even get into my personal life. At least you're trying."

"Am I?" She shook her head. "I say I'm looking for stability, then chase off perfectly stable men."

"Maybe because you think they'll see the parts of you that are 'unstable.' You reject them before they can reject you."

Mira drew in a deep, shaky breath. Not a groundbreaking note, but a real one, from a real friend.

We should table any talk of a romantic relationship. Naveen had only been repeating what she'd said. It shouldn't have hurt her, but it did. Because it was easier to leave than be left. "Yeah."

"Been there. Done that. Naveen seems cool, though."

"He is, but, you know, it would be far too complicated." Would it? Even now, with her original reason for why it couldn't work, because of his brother's money, gone?

Emi's lips twisted. "Can I pass on some advice my mom gave me that I didn't listen to? Whatever action you're taking, take it toward something you want instead of running away from something you don't. You might get better results."

Where had that advice been when she'd started her matrimonial quest? "Your mom remains cool."

"She does."

Mira hated to pressure Emi, but she did have some contacts in tech. "If you're interested, ever, in moving toward something positive, I could try to help you get a lucrative job. I know a few people in the industry who would certainly at least give you an interview. You'd have to figure out other ways to feed your need for excitement, but you'd get good benefits, and it would help you with your mom."

"I do like the sound of that. I need the money."

"If there was a real way to access that crypto . . ." Mira shrugged at Emi's surprised look. "I'm aware it's misbegotten, but if you could crack it, and give your mom enough to live comfortably, I'd be game."

"Little Miss Black-and-White is seeing shades of gray? I'm stunned," Emi said.

"I can evolve. And so can you."

"You're determined to make sure we're never actually even, huh?"

"No. We're even. So anything we do for each other after this, or if we keep in touch, it can be purely because we want to. Not because we're obligated to or as part of a transaction." She couldn't hide the hope in her voice.

Emi pursed her lips, then nodded. "Deal." Her friend's manner turned more brisk. "Okay, go crush this. Remember, I'll be listening below, even if you can't hear me."

"Where is Sunil?" She'd thought for sure he would have listened in on Cobra's call, but the tablet Emi carried had been dark.

"I don't know. He was in my ear before Cobra called, said he got a message from someone and needed to answer it." Emi shrugged. "He'll call back and listen, too, remotely, in case they make me. I like that guy. Anyway, you're good?"

Mira inhaled, then exhaled. "Yes. Good. We're moving toward something."

Emi wiggled her fingers. "In this one isolated case, literally running away is okay, too. Especially if they do bring those guns."

Chapter Eighteen

Can you stop tapping?" Mira asked Naveen.

He flattened his hand on his thigh. "Sorry."

"It's okay."

The pause was pregnant between them. "What is taking these people so long? It's been longer than ten minutes."

"Parking on the Strip." Mira adjusted the tea kettle on the coffee table in front of them. The fully serviced kitchen in the suite had had a beautiful silver set, and she'd needed to keep busy. "Everything's farther than it appears."

"I'm going to guess that a notorious crime boss is not going to navigate a parking garage and walk through a casino lobby with their kidnap victim like a regular Joe. No, something's up." Naveen's face was tight and pinched, and her own teeth ached for how hard he must be grinding his.

"I'm sure it's fine," she said, as calm as she could possibly be when her heartbeat was pounding in her own ears.

"Yeah, you're right. This'll be over before we know it." He fixed the pen in his shirt pocket. "Are you okay?"

"Nope." She held her hand out, and it was rock steady. "Working on my tell, though. No fidgeting."

He smiled. "I told you, I doubt anyone else can see it. Soon, I'll introduce you to my grandpa, and you can try your poker face out on him."

She readjusted her spot on the couch. Did that mean he was now anticipating her being in his life? "I'm going to meet your grandfather?"

"Of course." Naveen's eyes darkened. "I mean. If you want to."

Did she want to? "I thought we agreed we weren't going to try for anything more."

"The reason for that no longer exists."

She opened her mouth, then closed it again. "Doesn't it?" Didn't some reason exist?

He turned to face her completely. "What are you saying?"

"I'm saying, we should talk about this later, when we're not exhausted."

The muscle in his jaw jumped. "I won't change my mind later. I want us to try again."

"Why?"

"Why do I want to date you?"

"Yes. You proposed getting back together with me because it made sense." Her feelings were no longer in bottles, and they oozed around inside her, getting on everything. "I look good on paper, which I know I'm a hypocrite for complaining about, because I had a whole fucking spreadsheet for my ideal mate, but being wanted for my surface qualities isn't enough for me anymore. You may never love me. And then where will I be?"

It was only when the room grew completely silent that she realized how cringey she'd sounded, bleating her fears out. She rubbed her fingers under her nose. "I mean, uh—"

"Mira," he said, at the same time.

"No." She shook her head. "Stop talking. You don't have to answer that."

What did she want him to do, get down on his knees like this was a movie? Tell her that his heart beat only for her?

She swallowed the lump in her throat. She was not so foolish.

"Mira—"

She opened her mouth, but the door clicked open. She faced forward. "They're here."

And Emi was listening to this soap opera. She inhaled, then exhaled and looked at Naveen.

He gave her a subtle nod. "I have your back."

Warmth spread through her, replacing the icy parts. In this, at least, she knew he did. "And I have yours." Mira tried to regulate her breathing and the beat of her heart. "I think I'm going to throw up," she admitted. Another moment of foolish neediness.

Naveen rested his palm on Mira's neck and rubbed it. "It's okay."

Soft footsteps came down the hallway.

Burberry walked into the room, arm still in a sling, gun

in his other hand. He sneered. There was a new bruise on his face, and Mira wondered if his boss had given it to him on account of his letting them get away.

"Your friend's holding my partner," he said in greeting.

Sunil. The man had done something right. "I don't know anything about that," Mira lied.

Burberry's smile was terrifying. His nearly invisible eyebrows drew together. "I'm sure you don't." He prowled around the room, checking everything, even the cabinets and under the TV.

Emi, I hope you hid those bugs well.

Naveen held out his hand, and Mira put hers in it. All she wanted was to be out of here. Soon. With her sister.

"It's clear," the agent said low, into his phone. He left the room, and came back a second later.

Mira forgot about her own safety and stood when he yanked his bound captive in.

Mira hadn't seen Sejal in years, but she'd never seen her big sister like this. Sejal had always had a large frame, and she'd filled out in the past decade, her shoulders broad, her muscles impressive and standing out in her tank top. The shirt had torn, revealing even more muscles, her abs a perfect six-pack.

None of Sejal's brawn could take away from how poorly she'd been treated. There was blood in her short hair. Her face was badly bruised, one eye nearly swollen shut. They'd tied her hands behind her back, and a dirty gag had been shoved into her mouth.

Mira covered her mouth to hold in her cry of dismay. Sejal staggered as the man pushed her to her knees. "Sejal," she said quietly, then louder, to be heard across the distance between them. "Are you okay?"

Her sister barely raised her head. She swayed, held upright only by Burberry's hand on her shoulder. Either they'd beaten her so badly she was concussed, or they'd drugged her sister to bring her here.

Mira's anger roared to life, and it stiffened her spine, trumping her fear. She rose to her feet. "What did you do to my sister?"

Out of the corner of her eye, she clocked Naveen giving her a warning look, but she ignored it.

"She's fine, Mira," came a soft, dulcet tone. "I wouldn't hurt either of my babies."

Mira finally looked past her sister, and her knees grew watery. She was barely aware of Naveen guiding her back to the couch. "What the fuck," she whispered.

The South Asian woman who had entered was in her fifties, svelte and beautiful. Her hair was thick and tumbled to her shoulders. She had a hint of an Indian accent, but it had morphed after years in America. She sounded nothing like the digitally modified voice that had been on the phone. Her red suit hugged her figure and highlighted her brown skin and dark hair. She was no taller than Mira, even in her thin stiletto heels.

"Mom?"

Naveen didn't react, which meant he'd already put things

together. To be fair, her mom hadn't visibly aged much since that old family photo they'd found in the storage unit.

Her mother gave Mira a sweet smile. "Hello, my dear. It's been so long. Look at you. You're as beautiful as your sister." She stopped next to Sejal and dared to pat her on the head, like she was a puppy. Sejal sluggishly jerked her head away. Mira was happy to see at least that much fight in her. "Don't worry, Mira. The drugs'll wear off soon. She's not permanently damaged."

"You . . . you're Cobra?"

Her mom gave a lilting laugh, and Naveen's hand tightened on hers. She looked at him, but he hadn't taken his gaze off her mom. Mira thought she had a poker face, but his was utterly blank.

"What a silly nickname that is," her mom said. "I hate it." She surveyed the tea in front of them. "How nice of you. I could use some tea. What do you have?"

"Darjeeling," Mira answered.

"That will do. Pour it."

Mira responded automatically to the directive. "I'd love to know what's going on here."

Her mother—her mother!—accepted the teacup and took a sip. "Well, obviously, my dear, I'm not dead."

"I see that." She sat back on the couch and tried not to look at her sister. If she looked at Sejal, she wouldn't be able to think.

We had shit luck when it came to parents.

Don't listen to her.

Sejal had been trying to warn her. Not that Mira would have ever conceived that this would be where their adventure led to. "Can we back up more? Who are you, exactly? How are you Cobra?" Her mother would have been a child when Cobra was active.

"I'm not Cobra. At least, not the original one. Cobra was my father. Vassar worked for him occasionally." Her face softened, like she wasn't a monster. "We did love each other back then. When my father died and things got a little warm for me, Vassar told me to come to America. We would be married, it would be the perfect cover. And then, of course, he told me kids would be an even better cover, and that he would take care of you and your sister so I wouldn't have to." Her lips twisted angrily. "I didn't realize until it was too late that he was trying to keep me trapped with him. Silly man."

Your mother is alive and she never wanted you.

Mira had been a cover before, for her father. This shouldn't hurt. *Stop hurting.*

She was so tired, but she mentally pulled out a fresh empty bottle, and put those feelings away. "Can I ask why we thought you were dead?"

Their mother took a sip of tea, her pinky up. "Your father said you might feel abandoned if you knew I left you all."

It didn't take a child psychologist to puzzle that out, but Mira was still surprised her father had been that sensitive.

"Apparently his sister insisted he tell you I was dead instead of gone. What was her name? Rena? Rekha? She was always sticking her nose where it didn't belong."

"Rhea," Mira said faintly. Okay, it made more sense that Rhea Auntie had proposed this solution.

"Yes, Rhea."

"Why did you leave?"

"Mummy had a business to run, dear." Her mother cocked her head. "Speaking of which, let's get to the business at hand, eh?"

So that was that. The entire unpacking of her mother's faked death.

Not that there was much to unpack. Her mom was a sociopathic criminal who had never wanted her, and her father had done the bare minimum to make her and Sejal feel like not total pawns.

Normal family stuff.

"I'm glad you two decided to be sensible and came alone."

"Of course we did," Naveen said finally. "We did everything you asked."

Burberry came back from investigating the suite. "I found and neutralized four listening devices and cameras." He tossed the electronics on the table.

Her mother raised her thin eyebrows. "Not everything, I suppose."

Mira ran her tongue over her teeth. She hoped Emi had planted at least one more device somewhere. "Can you blame me? I am your daughter."

There was a tense silence, and then her mother gave a tinkling laugh. It pinged something in the recesses of Mira's memories. Had she heard that laugh, when she was a baby?

"I guess you are. More than your elder sister. She couldn't evade me at all."

Sejal gave a piteous groan from behind her gag. Mira's gaze flickered to her, then back to the rattlesnake in their midst. *Put your feelings on the shelf. This is what you're good at. Come on.*

"What a strong boy you are. My name's Rushali, by the way."

Naveen placed his hands on his thighs. "Hello, ma'am."

"So polite and handsome. Photos didn't do you justice! Do you know how hard it was to find anyone in your home-town to go keep an eye on your grandfather? I still can't even say that the man I sent wouldn't rather die than touch a hair on his precious head. I can only dream of that sort of loyalty. Now." Rushali clapped her hands together. "Where is my necklace?"

Mira reached under the couch cushion and pulled out the lighter.

Her mom balked at it, but accepted it. "What the hell is this?"

"The diamonds."

Her smile was hard and vicious. "Your father always did have the worst sense of humor." She opened the lighter, dumped the diamonds into her hand, and snapped her fingers. Burberry supplied a jeweler's loupe.

Rushali took a few tense minutes examining the stones, then she put them in her pocket. She closed the loupe and came to her feet. "Kill them all but make it look like an accident."

"Whoa, whoa, whoa," Naveen said, drowning out Mira's immediate dismayed cry. "What is the problem?"

Rushali turned, and her face was carved in granite. Mira had never seen anyone so cold. Sociopathic criminal indeed, if her mom was fine with murdering her two daughters. "Listen, I don't want to kill you. I didn't even want to hurt you. You can blame your father for dragging you into this. First he comes to me out of nowhere, telling me about some lost treasure, then he steals it from me after I do all the hard work to track it down? And then he had the nerve to go die before I could find him."

"Those are real stones. We had someone look at them." No way Shweta had let them down.

"Oh, those are gorgeous stones, and I will consider them my parting gift. Those are not the stones from the necklace. I want my necklace, and nothing else." She dismissed them. "This has cost me enough time. Mark?"

Burberry took a step forward and pulled out his gun.

Mira's brain went into overdrive. "Wait. If you don't want the necklace for the diamonds . . . it's something in the necklace? Maybe a password? To a crypto wallet?"

The woman turned to face her, and Mira caught the slight tremble at the corner of her mouth.

Her tell. Bingo.

"I have it," Naveen said softly. "The necklace is in the bedroom." He pointed in the direction of it. "We thought . . . well, clearly we were mistaken."

"Mark. Go get it."

Burberry walked away, and Rushali glared at them. "If you're fucking with me . . ."

"We're not," Naveen said quickly. "Promise. Vassar sold it to someone, and we got it from them. It's the password, right?"

"Yes, of course. Why would I be chasing pennies when I could be taking a fortune? The passcode is engraved inside the stones."

Like certificate numbers were, inside real diamonds.

Naveen scowled. "What is your plan here exactly? Take that password to access a fortune that half the dark web and every kid sitting in their basement with a computer is after? That law enforcement is probably keeping an eye on?"

Rushali smirked. "My boy, you could not imagine the amount of power and skills I have at my disposal. Those coins will disappear, and I will be a ghost."

"Hmph." Naveen folded his arms over his chest. "I don't know. Doesn't seem like you thought this through."

Mira had known Naveen could talk, but what the hell was he trying to pull right now? He wasn't even being diplomatic like usual.

A shadow detached from the wall near the kitchen. Oh. So that was what Naveen was doing.

Mira did her best not to tense. She didn't want to blow

anything now, if Emi had managed to make her way up here to save them.

"*You* don't think I've thought things through?" Rushali dismissed them and turned slightly away. The shadow froze. "Please, the day I take advice from a two-bit alcoholic attorney is the day I retire."

"Don't call him that." Mira pulled her mother's attention back to her. "He's a good person."

"You dumped him—he can't be that good."

"I dumped him precisely because I feared he was too good. And I've lived my life terrified I'd be like my dad and fuck up good things. But I'm nothing like him. And I'm nothing like you."

The shadow came closer, and Sejal made a muffled noise. Her eyes rolled back in her head, and she slumped to the ground.

Out of the corner of her eye, she noticed Naveen unclasp his watch. Why, she wasn't sure, until he dropped it to the ground. "Oops," he said, and bent, giving her a meaningful look as he did so.

The lost earring back he'd helped her search for in his office.

"What the hell are you doing, get up," Rushali snarled.

Mira ducked as well, and Naveen grabbed her arm, yanking her down and shoving the big coffee table so it formed a barrier, the tea service crashing to the floor.

Mira braced for gunshots, but instead a loud *thwack* filled the air. What the hell?

They both peered over the table.

It was Rushali who had crumpled to the ground, and that was enough to trigger Mira's flight, on her sister's behalf, not her own. She ran toward Sejal, unaware of everything, even Naveen's warning shout. She got to Sejal just as a silenced gunshot split the air, and she used her body to shield her sister. She half expected a fiery pain to hit her, but nothing came, except another smacking sound. Something warm surrounded her, and she realized it was Naveen, creating a cocoon around them both.

She looked up when the room was quiet. Her mom lay on the floor, groaning.

Good. "Sejal." She lightly tapped her sister's unbruised cheek. Her long lashes fluttered open.

"Mira," she drawled. Confusion and panic set in. "No. Mira, you can't know—"

"It's okay . . ." Mira swiped at her cheeks. "I think it's over."

Sejal thrust her face toward hers. "No. It's not."

The plush carpet cushioned the sound of footsteps. She and Naveen looked up, and Sejal twisted in her arms. A figure stood above them.

Mira's lips parted. "Rhea Auntie?"

Chapter Nineteen

Hello, dear." Her not-so-deceased aunt stood in the suite, her face flushed, her chest moving fast.

Because she wasn't dead.

Rhea was dressed stylishly, her round and plush figure in a trendy top and jeans with low boots. Her jewelry was understated, her hair a sharply angled bob. Her most alarming accessory was the giant frying pan in her hands.

Again, she was alive.

Rhea Auntie kicked away the gun Rushali had dropped. Mira barely had time to process that before her aunt casually punched her ex–sister-in-law in the face. Rushali slumped, fully unconscious.

"What the hell is happening?" Naveen asked quietly. His body was a spring of coiled tension behind Mira. She didn't blame him. This was beyond anything she could have planned for.

"This is my Aunt Rhea," Mira said slowly.

"The Rhea Auntie whose will I read."

"Correct."

"The one who is dead."

"I thought so," Mira said. "But I—I guess she's not dead."

Rhea gave them a sympathetic smile, like she was well aware she'd thrown them all for a loop. "I'm not. Hello, Naveen. Nice to finally meet you in person. Sorry it had to be this way."

Naveen looked between them. "I don't know what's happening. Is anyone who is supposed to be dead, actually dead?"

"Their father is." Rhea crouched next to Sejal.

Her aunt smelled like her favorite perfume, Gucci Bloom, and the notes of jasmine were cloying. "I bought a bottle of your perfume after you died. How could you do this?" Her grief and anger rose up inside her. "How could you make me hurt like that?" She was yelling, and she didn't care. Naveen's arm came around her, giving her something solid to brace herself against as she raged. If she had a glass, she'd throw it.

Sejal spoke, her words slow and slurred. Definitely drugged. "Oooh. You made Mira mad. Good girl, let it out."

"I would love to," Mira said grimly, and Naveen tightened his grip on her.

Naveen raised his hand. "Should we call the cops? Or tell Emi?"

"I spoke with Emi downstairs. Lovely girl." Rhea leaned toward Naveen and spoke into the pen in his pocket. "Hello, Emi. See? Everything is fine."

Define, fine.

"Don't worry, children, this will all get cleaned up." Rhea gave a low whistle, and a man in black appeared in the hallway. Naveen tensed, but Rhea didn't look at all concerned. "This is my associate. Harold, you've taken care of my ex–sister-in-law's man?"

The man's lip lifted in a sneer. "Certainly."

"Excellent. Tie this one up and place her in the bedroom so the authorities can reach them both easily when they come."

"Yes, ma'am."

Rhea shook her head as Harold easily picked Rushali up. "What a day, what a day."

"What will happen to Cobra?" Mira couldn't bring herself to call that woman her mother.

"Don't worry. She's done a lot of things in a lot of places. I doubt she'll make bail, and if she does, she won't be coming back to bother you." Rhea's smile was hard. "I'll make sure she knows the consequences of something so foolish."

That was something. "I grieved for you," Mira repeated, but she didn't have the energy to yell again.

Sejal coughed. "You grieved for a liar."

Rhea tsked. From her jacket, she pulled out a small pouch and briskly took out some first aid items. "I do regret that, believe me. The last thing I wanted was to hurt either of you. I faked my death because Sal was after me. I had no idea what your father had embroiled all of us in by poking Cobra. I had nothing to do with this, like I had nothing to do with him trying to domesticate your mother." She scoffed. "I told your father not to marry her, but did my brother ever listen to me? At least you two came of it, so it wasn't a loss."

"Who's Sal?" Mira asked. This cast was growing by the minute.

"Oh, an old gentleman friend from whom I stole some precious heirlooms and accidentally learned about his terrorist plot." Rhea lifted a shoulder, like that was a perfectly normal thing. She carefully dabbed some antiseptic on Sejal's cut face. Mira's sister hissed and tried to jerk away. Rhea kept her firmly in place. "I became a witness for the prosecution, and he was spectacularly mad."

"I am so confused."

Sejal tried to jerk her head away again, to no avail. "There's nothing to be confused about. Our aunt never ran a charity. She was as much of a crook as our father was."

Their aunt regarded Sejal patiently. "Sejal found out about my real career a few months ago. She hasn't taken the news well. But to be fair, Sejal, I was quite charitable. I stole only from people who deserved it, and I gave quite a bit of it away."

"It would be great if we could start from the beginning," Naveen said, in his most lawyerly of voices. "I am also quite confused, given that I read your will yesterday."

Rhea sat back. "Mira, did your dad leave any actual cigarettes around or just his lighter?"

Mira frowned. "You don't smoke."

"Not anymore. You think Vassar was the only one with

that habit? Took me a lot longer to kick it than it took him, I'll tell you that."

"Rhea Auntie."

"Okay. Okay. Short version: I was a jewel thief. I snitched on another thief, Sal. He got mad, I faked my death. Turns out, your father left us all a mess, his silly ex dragged you two in, and here we are."

"If you've been in federal protection, how did you know we were in trouble?"

"I put an alarm on the storage unit. It tripped when you went in there, Mira. I was surprised you'd come to Vegas so soon after getting the keys, so I checked in on you. Your tracker was erratic, so I had Harold follow you. He was the one who figured out something was amiss."

"My tracker?"

Rhea nodded at the jhumka earrings Mira wore. "I wasn't trying to track you for nefarious purposes, of course, I only wanted to make sure Sal didn't come after you. I'd kept my distance as much as I could over the years, but it wouldn't have been impossible for him to find you."

So she hadn't been solely responsible for the minimum contact between her and her aunt. Mira shed another layer of her guilt, even while her incredulous anger grew.

"Once I realized who was chasing you, I did my best to ditch my federal protection detail as quickly as I could and make my way back here. All of these diamonds and passwords and whatnot, it's absolutely ridiculous. I called Wyatt once I was in town, and after he got over his shock, he was happy to tell me everything and put me in touch with Sunil. To be honest, I was kind of hoping you wouldn't have to see me. The last thing I wanted to do was hurt and confuse you even more." Rhea took a deep breath and finished cleaning up Sejal's various injuries. She patted her gently. "There, I think that explains everything on my end."

There was a long silence for a moment, and then Mira bowed her head. Naveen came to his feet. "I'm going to let you three talk. I'll, uh, go downstairs and see if Emi needs any help. Just one thing?"

"Yes, dear?" Rhea folded her hands over her plump belly.

"Did you know that Mira and I had dated when you contracted my grandfather to do your will?"

Rhea beamed at him. "Yes. Of course I did. I could tell Mira was sad when she broke up with you, and I wanted to give you a second chance. Call me an old romantic. Did it work?"

Naveen squeezed Mira's shoulder. "I think that's our business."

"What a considerate man," Rhea said approvingly as Naveen walked away. She sat cross-legged. "I'm glad I got to meet him, Mira."

There was so much to process, Mira didn't know how to wrap her brain around it all. "I don't know what to say."

Rhea's smile faded. "I'm not surprised your father did this, but I wish he hadn't. That was our dynamic for our whole life, I'm afraid. Me hoping he'd make different decisions for your sakes. I suppose that's why I kept up the facade about my job for so long. I wanted you to have at least one good role model."

Sejal hauled herself to a seated position. The drug was wearing off, Mira hoped that meant. "You genuinely didn't know he was on a job that would net him hundreds of millions of dollars?"

Rhea shook her head. "I understand your skepticism, but no. I did not. Vassar only told me he was working on something big before he died. Had I known it was with her, I would have cut ties with him right there."

"You would have cut him off?" Color her cynical, but Mira didn't think there was anything that would get Rhea to not protect and defend her little brother.

"Yes. I am well aware of the risks of biting off more than you can chew. I did it far too often." She rested her hands in her lap. "There comes a time in your life where you realize that money isn't nearly so important as people. I know I reached it when I walked into our local FBI field office to turn witness. I'm sure your father reached it when he realized he'd risked his life and gotten in bed with someone dangerous enough to hurt his daughters. I bet, if he'd been alive, he would have protected both of you."

Mira may not have seen Sejal in a long time, but the glance they exchanged was as familiar as her own arm.

Rhea noticed their skepticism. "You don't believe me? He left those diamonds in a place you could find."

"Those diamonds don't even access the crypto fortune." Sejal hooked her arm over her knee. "He didn't care about us."

Rhea set her lips. They were painted a deep maroon in her signature shade, Clinique Black Honey. "He loved you both. He was looking forward to your weddings."

Mira snorted. She believed that part of her father's email hadn't been a clue, now, but it was still ridiculous. "That's possible, but showing up to a wedding isn't what makes a person a good parent."

"Also what if we never get married?" Sejal said impatiently.

"Then you'd still have gifts from him. That's why he created a dowry chest for—"

The light went on above Mira's head. There was too much familiarity in Rhea's voice when she talked about that chest. "Aha."

"What?"

"You put that chest with all those clothes in the storage unit for us, didn't you?"

Rhea opened her mouth, then closed it again.

"Don't lie," Mira warned. "I'll be able to tell."

The sheen of tears in her aunt's eyes surprised Mira. "Yes. I did."

"I know he was your little brother, Rhea Auntie, but you don't have to protect him forever." Mira looked directly at Sejal. "You have a right to live your own life and be happy and not feel any guilt over that."

Sejal raised one thick eyebrow, but didn't speak.

Rhea sniffled. "You both have trouble with relationships because you think you come from bad people. Maybe I do defend him too much, but I loved you so much and wanted you to feel loved by your father."

Oh, fuck. How could she be mad when her aunt put it that way?

Rhea dashed her tears away, then checked her phone. "Harold says the cops have a ten-minute ETA."

"Well, that's my cue." Sejal struggled to her feet. She was even bigger and taller than Mira remembered, but that didn't mean she was invincible.

"You're leaving?" Mira asked, and rose as well.

"Yeah. Cops and I don't play well together." She surprised Mira with a hug. Mira nearly stumbled back a step, but she returned and savored it. It was quick and fleeting, gone before she could truly appreciate it. "Thanks," Sejal whispered into her ear.

"Wait," Mira said, desperate to get out the words she'd been holding in for years. "I'm sorry I didn't help you all those years ago when you came to my dorm. I should have."

"Makes sense why you didn't." Sejal pressed her lips tight together. "I'm sorry, too. About leaving you when we were kids. I had to get out."

"I understand."

"No, I mean, Dad made me get out. He kicked me out."

Mira frowned. She remembered Sejal and her dad fighting the night before Sejal left, but all their fights had been loud and explosive. "I . . . I didn't know that."

Sejal looked down. "I'm sorry I left you with him."

"What should you have done, taken a minor with you?

You were my sister, not my mom." She cast a glance over her shoulder, at the room where their biological mother lay unconscious. "Though you were a better mom to me than she would have been, no doubt."

Sejal wiped the back of her hand over her forehead. A bit of blood came off, but she seemed uncaring of it. "Be well, Mira."

Naveen came back into the room, just as Sejal walked out. Her sister only gave him a terse nod and left.

Rhea sighed. "That young woman is full of anger."

"Can you blame her?"

"No." Rhea dusted off her jeans as she rose. "You both need to leave as well. I don't want you tied to this."

Mira licked her lips. "My name is on this hotel room."

"No, it's not. Sunil saw to that. And we'll wipe everything down. You two were never here. Go on, go to that storage unit and clean it out. In case it comes across law enforcement's notice, I'd rather you'd have already claimed what you want. And I hope you take that chest I painstakingly put together for you. If you see Sejal again, share it with her. The items in it are . . . some good things, from me to you. Nothing shady or misbegotten about them, okay?"

Mira nodded. She wasn't sure she'd entirely processed her aunt also being a criminal. Again, she made a mental note to look up a therapist. "Okay."

Rhea's eyes glinted. "I'm sorry, Mira. For your childhood, for your father, for everything." Rhea tucked Mira's hair behind her ear. "Be happy, dear." She rested her cheek against hers.

Someone coughed, and Mira raised her head to find Emi at the door. "The cops are on their way, Harold's got the recordings from this reunion if you need them. I'm bouncing before it gets hot."

"Thank you for everything," Mira replied. "I can't repay you."

"No repayment necessary." Her friend's avaricious gaze landed on the diamonds. "So, uh, the passcode for the crypto are on the fake diamonds, eh? Genius."

"It is," Rhea said. "But the feds will be able to see if anyone touches that money." She walked over to where the lighter had fallen, picked it up, and tapped out two diamonds. "No one will miss a couple of these, though. Here."

Emi glanced at Mira like this was a trick, but Mira nodded. No black and white, right or wrong here. "Take it. She's right. Be careful."

Her friend's forehead relaxed and she snatched up the diamonds. "Cool. This will help a lot. And I'll be in touch for that job, Mira." Emi disappeared.

Rhea pulled away. She gave Naveen a misty smile, and grabbed his hand to squeeze it. "Look out for this girl for me, will you? I know she seems like a tough cookie, but she has a gooey center to her."

That was an embarrassing description, but Naveen gave a solemn nod. "I'm aware. Thanks for your help here."

"What else is a favorite auntie good for, if not knocking some skulls together?"

"Will I ever see you again?" Mira asked, and brushed wetness away from her cheek.

Rhea blinked rapidly. "I don't think so, dear. Generally speaking, when the government fakes your death, you stay dead. One way or another."

Mira breathed deep. Naveen's arm came around her shoulder, and she welcomed the touch. "Oh."

"But I'll keep an eye on you, or rather, I'll have Harold tell me if anything goes awry." She tapped Mira's earrings, and they swayed. "Wear this and think of me. Think of the people who love you. Never doubt that you're entirely lovable, yes?"

That was a tall order, since she'd spent her whole life doubting that. She'd spent years trying to craft herself into a person who was worthy of love, and it had meant hiding most of her.

"Have a good, long life. Possibly with this handsome fellow over here, eh?" Rhea raised her shoulders, ignoring Mira's blush. "I've always thought, in another life, I would make an excellent matchmaker."

Chapter Twenty

Naveen and Mira switched hotels, but stayed on the Strip. The guy at the front desk gave them some odd looks. Probably because they were shell-shocked and dusty. Not only were they running on little sleep, they'd taken Rhea's advice and gone to her dad's storage unit first.

After the diamonds in the lighter, Naveen hadn't trusted that anything was what it looked like, and they'd torn everything in the unit apart. They'd loaded up what they could in the small Mustang, including the chest.

After they got their hotel room key, they made their way to the elevator. It was early in the day, and the casino floor wasn't crowded yet. They got into the elevator alone.

Naveen looked at Mira across the way. She was kind of a mess, yes, but so was he, and she'd never looked more beautiful to him. "Mira," he started, but she was in his arms before he could finish.

He collapsed back against the wall, and tunneled his hand through her tangled hair as she kissed him, long drugging kisses that made his body tighten with need. The plastic bag he held with their toiletries banged against her legs, but she didn't seem to mind. Instead, she bit his lips, sucking them into her mouth.

The ding of the elevator pulled him out of his daze. She grabbed his hand and led him out.

In the hotel room, though lust was strumming through him, Naveen dropped his bag on the floor and did up all the locks on the door, then checked them thrice. This was a nice place, and the danger was ostensibly past, but they'd been kidnapped from his own parking garage, so he was wary of everything now.

He turned back to her and nearly swallowed his tongue. She'd stripped her shirt off and was backing away. He grabbed a couple of condoms and followed her.

She laughed when he reached her and pulled her in close, and he nearly groaned in pleasure, both at the sound, and at her body pressed tight against him. As pretty as her lacy bra was, Naveen preferred it gone. The fabric sagged when he unsnapped it. He tossed the thing aside and cradled her bare breasts.

Mira's nipples were tight and hard, and he bent his head and licked each one. Her fingers tunneled through his hair as he pressed the flesh together and buried his face between them, like he'd wanted to for forever. "So pretty," he murmured against one brown peak.

He walked backward with her and gently guided her to sit in the chair facing the window. The view inside was better than anything the hotel could provide.

The sun played over her, burnishing her golden-brown skin. She was warm and precious and alive. They were both alive.

He wanted this experience to be one that was indelibly stamped in her memory forever, just like the picture of her, legs spread, brown nipples tight and wet from his mouth, stomach muscles clenched, would be stamped in his.

Forget the practicalities of life. He shrugged off their families and the weight of expectations as he sank to his knees. He kissed away the minutiae of worrying about their lives as he slid his lips down her stomach. Here it was only her and him, and their bodies.

His hands slid up her legs and fondled her round thighs. She gave a little squeak when he tightened his grip and pulled her further down the chair.

"You like this?" He pressed hot, wet kisses up her inner thigh.

Her yes was almost inaudible, but he heard it. He stripped off her joggers, lowered his head and nuzzled her, right over her panties. Her surprisingly muscular thighs clenched on either side of his head.

He shifted away only to pull her panties down. When they were hanging over an ankle, he returned to his position. Her gasps told him how and where to move; where to hold longer, where to suck, where to nibble. Her fingers tightened in his hair and he welcomed the pain.

She took her pleasure in sighs and breaths, not screams. Her body grew tighter, more tense, until he felt the telltale signs of her release against his tongue. He drew away from her and swiped the back of his hand over his mouth, then pressed a kiss on her thigh.

She ran her finger over his cheek. "That was nice, but I need more."

So did he. He drew her to her feet. His lips sipped at hers, and she wrapped her arms around his neck.

They had a cushy mattress for once, and he was going to take advantage of it, damn it. He pulled her close and she wrapped her legs around his waist, clinging to him like a monkey. He grasped her butt with both hands and walked over to the bed, coming down on top of her.

They wrestled his clothes off, the various pieces getting tossed off to land somewhere in the room. He ran his hand up her torso and luxuriated in the dips and valleys of her body. Naveen bent his head and licked her nipples, taking her gasps as encouragement.

Her short nails dug into his shoulders. "Condom," she moaned.

"I wouldn't mind some more foreplay." Or a chance to take another peek at her ass. He carefully licked the tip of her breast, enjoying the way the brown flesh puckered.

"Don't need it. Do you?"

"Needs are different from wants." He licked the skin again. "I don't need it, but I'll always want it."

Her nails turned harder, more insistent. "I want you, inside of me. Now."

His body hardened more, almost to the point of pain. "As you wish."

He grabbed a condom and donned it in record time. When he slid inside her, they both groaned. He braced his weight on his arms and lowered his forehead to hers. They stared into each other's eyes as he rocked back and forth.

Naveen pulled almost all the way out, then slid back in, luxuriating in the wet glide. He couldn't hold off for long, especially with her rising cries and the way she clutched his skin. He lowered his lips to her ear. "You're so tight and wet," he growled. The praise made her whimper, and he licked her lobe. "You take me so perfectly, don't you?"

"Yes."

"Me, and only me. You looked so pretty in that chair. I could stay on my knees for you forever. Would you like that?"

"Yes." Her body shuddered around him, and he lost it, driving inside her one last time.

As their sweat settled on their bodies, he rolled off her and stared at the ceiling. "It gets better every time."

She gave a breathless laugh. "No kidding."

He pulled her closer, so she could nestle her head on his shoulder. That spot was made for her. They were silent for a while, until he finally spoke. "You okay?"

Her face was relaxed, but contemplative. "Not really."

"What's up?"

"Seems weird to think my aunt's not dead anymore, but still gone to me. Should I mourn her? Should I not?"

"I'm not sure. A very weird position to be in, yes," Naveen agreed. And to think, he'd thought his family was complicated.

"And Sejal. I know we didn't have a relationship like you and your brother, but I thought we'd at least get to exchange numbers or something."

"Yeah." He took her hand. "I'm sorry, Mira." He could tell she didn't want solutions, just listening, and he was happy to give it to her.

"It's been a really wild night."

"That it has." He'd already called his family, and everyone was okay. Kiran was sending a plane for them tomorrow. He'd be glad to get out of Vegas soon.

"I wonder what my dad had planned to do with that money," she mused.

"I think he genuinely left those diamonds for you and your sister."

"And the crypto fortune? He had the passcode in his hands and handed it to Wyatt instead of accessing it. That's weird."

"Or he's a better friend to Wyatt than Wyatt thought." Naveen shrugged. "Maybe your dad just wanted to see if he could get one over on your mom for once." It pained him to think of six hundred million dollars—poof!—lost to the United States government, but better it be in official hands than criminal ones. "I'm sorry your mom turned out to be someone else," he said quietly. The disillusionment in her gaze had been hard to watch, so living it must have been brutal for her.

"Me too." She stirred. "All this time, I thought . . . my dad was the evil one, but my mom and aunt, at least, were good. People with morals and ethics. Someone I could look up to, and feel a connection with." She shook her head. "And that was all a lie."

"I don't think it was a total lie. I mean, yeah, your mom is a mess. But your aunt? She might do crime too, but she saved us. And it sounds like she tried to be as good of a person as she could be with the resources at her disposal." He'd liked Rhea Auntie, despite her deception. She'd reminded him of a couple of his aunts with their fiery personalities and fierce protectiveness.

Could he imagine any of his proper aunts dirtying their hands to steal gems or turn state's witness? No. But he could definitely imagine them smacking someone with a frying pan upside the head if they felt their precious children or nieces and nephews were in danger.

Also, Rhea had purposefully brought Mira and him together again, and that was wonderful.

Mira hasn't agreed to date you yet. In fact, that conversation was decidedly tabled. Stuff she said during sex doesn't count.

"I suppose so."

They sat in silence for a few minutes, and he wondered how to bring up their relationship. He opened his mouth, but all that came out was, "Hang on. Let me go to the bathroom." *Coward.*

When he came back, he found her using one of the brand-new phones they'd bought on their way from the storage unit to replace the ones the kidnappers had taken from them. He hadn't set his up yet, but he believed he might kiss it when he finally did. God, he missed his phone.

The odd expression on her face stopped him. "Is everything okay?"

"Yeah, listening to my messages. A few from Christine, and then this one." She hit the speaker button and a familiar voice blared out.

"Hello, Amira. Unfortunately, as I warned you, I can no longer represent you." Hema Auntie spoke briskly, but that's how she did everything. Naveen imagined her in her lavish home in the Bay Area, sitting at her ornate wooden desk imported from India, dark hair pulled back in a bun, Cartier reading glasses perched on her nose. Hema was both ancient and ageless, her skin smooth but her eyes full of wisdom. And annoyance. "I hope you won't argue with my decision. I have two families flying in from Edison tonight, and I don't have time to hash this out. I have run out of matches for you. You are getting older, and you are only getting more difficult. I have my metrics to consider. Perhaps you could try one of those apps. Goodbye, and good luck."

"Guess I can take *of marriageable age* off my own spreadsheet, since I'm such an old crone," Mira muttered, and tossed the phone onto the nightstand.

He got back into bed with her and braced himself. "It doesn't matter. You won't need Hema anymore. You have me."

She drew the sheets over her and he mourned the loss of the view. It was good, though, because he could focus on her words. "You know why I ended things before with you, right?"

"I was too extroverted for you." Hema had shared that as part of his debriefing.

"That's what I told Hema. You were too ambitious and extroverted. You worked too much. I didn't want those qualities in a mate because I was scared that meant you might be like my father, craving too much."

He nodded again. While it hurt to hear her talk about why she'd left him so matter-of-factly, he appreciated what she was saying. "I don't think you were wrong. I wasn't settled back then, and I definitely wasn't comfortable with myself yet. That was probably why I sought out someone who could make me feel balanced."

"I see the work you did, in you. But also, all those reasons were kind of bullshit. Because the real reason I ended it was because I was scared and I ran."

He nodded.

"You could at least pretend to be surprised by that reveal," she said dryly. "I worked hard all these years, trying to rationalize it."

"Oh my God. I cannot believe it."

She huffed out a laugh, and he savored it. "I ran from uncomfortable things once upon a time, too. I ran right into a bottle so I could dull what I was feeling. Why did you run?"

"I was scared. Of so many things. Like, what if my entire family is just genetically predisposed toward being bad people?"

"That's bullshit." He lifted her hand and flipped it over. With one finger, he traced the vein in her forearm, right to her wrist, where her steady pulse reassured him. "Blood pumps through your veins, same as mine. Your family may have given you DNA, but who you are is up to you."

Her eyes turned glassy, and a single tear squeezed out. Knowing how little she cried, the tiny tear moved him. "What if I'm not a good person? And one day you see all my messiness, all my ugliest parts, and you hate me? And then you leave, and I'm heartbroken?"

He considered that. "That's a risk, yes. One that everyone in a relationship has to deal with."

She sniffed. "Of course."

"What you said before, though, about thinking I won't love you, that's bullshit. All that stuff about us being compatible, I was only trying to appeal to your pragmatism. I was nearly in love with you when you left, and I'm almost all the way there now."

"You are?"

"Yeah. If it helps, I've already seen some messy parts of you, and all it did was allow me to understand you better. Like the puzzle pieces fit together better now than they ever did." He took her hand in his, linking their fingers together. "And you've seen more of the messy parts of me. I hope they haven't scared you off."

"Not at all. I feel the same. Like I know you better now than I ever did before."

He kissed her knuckles, and got under the covers with

her, adjusting the sheets so they were cocooned in high thread count. "When that gun was on you, I realized that my feelings already ran deeper for you than I could have imagined. I can't stand the thought of losing you." The fear he'd felt then had been bone-deep. He didn't think he'd ever known fear like that, and he hoped he never would. "That's my main request, Mira, if we get back together. No more bolting in the middle of the night if you get scared again, or cryptic texts. You can talk to me." He'd had to deal with two rough rejections in a row. No more, please.

"I absolutely understand. I'll never do that again." Her eyes were very big as she looked up at him. "Emi said that it's better to run toward something you want than it is to run away from something you don't."

"Emi is an extremely smart friend and we should listen to her."

Her smile was faint. "I didn't think I was a romantic, but I very badly want to try with you again. And if I start to get cold feet . . ."

He tucked her feet between his thighs, and winced at her icy appendages. "You always have cold feet, but I'll warm them up."

They kissed for a long time, and he pulled back to whisper. "I don't care about your past. Just your future."

She brought his head down to hers and kissed him. "Same," she murmured against his lips. "Okay. We'll try. As a team."

"As a team."

Chapter Twenty-One

One Year Later

I thought we were a fucking team."

Naveen ran the back of his hand over his brow. The room wasn't too warm, but sweat had dripped down his back, making his shirt stick to his skin. "We are."

"Then help me."

"I am helping you!" He held up the books he was perusing from the shelf above the jail cell's sink. "I'm searching for clues."

Mira sighed dramatically. She reserved her poker face for poker these days. Around him, she was quite emotive. "We're never going to get out of here. The clock is running out."

"We got this."

Mira blew a curl out of her eyes and rattled the bars of the cell. "You created this room, Naveen. Tell me the combination to this lock before I beat you with a wrench."

Naveen clicked his tongue. He'd discovered that Mira

was both fiercely competitive and quickly frustrated with escape rooms, which was why they didn't do the activity very much with other people. It was hard to explain to his friends that his girlfriend's loving threat to beat him with a wrench was an inside joke left over from the time they'd had to run for their lives in Las Vegas. "I'm only an investor. I don't create the escape rooms."

"Bull. You and Alan have stayed up late for the last six months working on plans for Who-Dinis. There's no way you don't know how to get out of here."

That was true. When his friend Alan had come to him with the idea of taking over an existing escape room business a few months ago, Naveen had been hesitant. Until Mira had asked if he was hesitant because he didn't want to do it, or because people might tease him for it.

Once he'd realized that it was the latter, he'd decided to go for it, pooling his savings with Alan to buy the place. Investing in this business had been his second biggest joy this past year, notwithstanding his blossoming relationship with Mira. Though he was still only a silent partner, Who-Dinis was his. He wasn't Ravi Ambedkar's grandson or Shweta Desai's child here. He was himself.

Mira bent over and double checked the numbers on the loose tile on the floor. He tilted his head, admiring the way her jeans clung to her ass.

"Are you checking out my butt or finding the combination?"

He jumped and cast a guilty glance at the eye in the sky,

mindful that they were being watched. "I can do both," he muttered, and riffled through the pages of the book.

The problem was, she was so beautiful and so distracting. Even when she was frustrated, her cheeks glowed with a light those days that told him she was happy and satisfied. He took pride in knowing that he was a part of that happiness.

They'd gone on so many adventures. Up and down the coast of California, to New York, to New Orleans, to Vancouver, and Europe next year. His desire to show her all his favorite things trumped his desire to hide out. He trusted himself to venture further and keep the balance and peace he'd worked so hard to find within himself over the last few years. In the process, their partnership had grown rock solid. As solid as a diamond.

Of course, they'd had challenges, too. Mira was still dealing with PTSD and nightmares around shooting Burberry, though she was working it out in therapy, amongst other issues. His grandfather wasn't doing very well lately. Mira had sold her tidy condo so they could purchase a home large enough for both of them near Ravi, in Artesia.

And of course, there was her family.

It had been radio silence from Sejal and Rhea, which he knew hurt Mira. Her mother, on the other hand, had not been silent, at least in the press. When she'd gotten arrested, the police had uncovered a web of crime spanning continents and decades. Media coverage had been intense.

Rushali had already sold her life story to Netflix. Mira

and Naveen were running bets on which Bollywood actress would play her.

Ironically, the arrest of his former wife had made Mira's father into something of a posthumous legend. From what he knew of the man, Naveen thought Vassar might have preferred that to living out his life as a billionaire.

All of the attention meant that he and Mira did have to deal with some extra scrutiny that neither of them really wanted. It was one of the topics they covered in their couples counseling sessions.

"Naveen." Mira rattled the bars again. "Come on."

"If you want a clue, you know you only have to ask."

She shot him a narrow look and ran her thumb over the lock. "Are you being patronizing?"

"Not at all." He welcomed her open displays of annoyance, though. Anything that told him she felt comfortable enough with him to show him her emotions. "Okay, fine. If you lay down on the cot and—"

"Never mind." She showed him the open lock in her palm. "Got it."

He groaned, though he was secretly delighted. "Mira, that's cheating."

"What's cheating?"

"Hacking the lock."

"Then get locks I won't be able to break into." She held the lock up to the camera in the corner and swung it back and forth. "Hear that Alan? All I had to do was listen to the chambers click."

"Okay, okay. What's next?"

She opened the jail cell door. It was a standard prison setup. Players had to get out of the cell and figure out where the key was hidden in the warden's office.

He watched her prowl the place, delighted by her analytical mind. Even if he didn't have ulterior motives, he'd have Mira test each room they created before opening it to the public.

They found Morse code on the back of a tray, which led to a pay phone, which led to a maze game, which led to lasers, which opened a locker. Inside, was a wooden crate filled with glass bottles.

Her eyes brightened. "The truth is at the bottom of every bottle," she quoted from the torn newspaper they'd found stuffed in the pay phone.

She took the bottles and ran to the corner where a stuffed dummy dressed in a police officer's uniform sat behind a desk. A slight snoring emanated from him. There was no way to get inside the booth he sat in, but there was a red button on the wall.

"The prison guard will wake up in six minutes," Alan intoned over the speaker. "You don't have much time."

Mira picked up her first bottle and threw it at the button. The glass shattered and she jumped. "Oh God, I didn't think it would do that."

"It's stunt glass, don't worry," Naveen assured her, then handed her the next bottle. "I thought this part would be therapeutic for players."

"Ha." She shared a smile with him, despite the clock ticking. "Smart." She threw another bottle, then another, and finally hit the button on the fourth try. A click sounded, and a hollow brick slid out of the wall. She whooped. "Is this the key?" She looked inside, and froze.

Naveen reached past her and picked up the blue velvet box. "Kind of." He dropped to his knee, and grasped her hand. "Mira—"

"Is this for real?"

He chuckled. "Will you let me talk? I've rehearsed this speech."

"Sorry, yes."

He took a deep breath. Shockingly, he was not that nervous at all. "Mira, you're the best person I know. I love everything about you, and I want to build a life and family with you."

She nodded. A single tear streaked its way down her face. "Yes. I mean, I love you too."

"I check all the boxes on your spreadsheet?"

Her sob ended in a laugh. "I threw that spreadsheet out long ago. You're perfect for me in reality. Not only on paper."

"So will you marry me?"

"Yes." The large wall behind them slid aside, and Mira laughed. "Would the door have opened if I'd said no?"

"I guess we'll never know."

Their family and friends crowded into the room. His mother was the first to reach them, but she ignored him to sweep Mira into a hug. He didn't mind. Shweta and Mira had become good friends: Mira needed to be mothered, and Shweta loved mothering. It was a relief to have his mom's support, especially given all the press about Mira's family. He'd initially feared Shweta wouldn't be able to defy the gossips in her social circle, but he was happy to have been proven wrong.

His grandfather pulled Mira away next. "My turn," he said.

Shweta rolled her eyes, but there was less annoyance and more affection in her gaze these days when she looked at her father. They hadn't totally buried the hatchet, but father and daughter were definitely kinder to one another than they had been before.

Naveen and Mira hadn't shared all the details of what they'd gone through that time in Vegas with everyone, but he supposed what they had shared had bonded his mom and grandfather together in horror, at least.

Kiran clapped him on the back, Payal at his side. "Proud of you, brother."

Payal murmured her congratulations as well. They'd had dinner together, him and Mira, Payal and Kiran, not long after their adventure. Things had been stilted at first but Payal was a born hostess, and he credited her with smoothing out the awkwardness. It wasn't long before he and Kiran had been getting together on their own, and talking on the phone. His brother had even lent his considerable business advice to the escape room venture.

Alan came by next, and handed him a glass of sparkling grape juice. He was a slender Black man, who had once played professional golf, and had a considerably sweet smile. "Well done, partner." He dropped his voice. "How the hell did she break into that lock? I got the most expensive one."

"She's exceptional," he admitted. He found Mira in the crowd, showing off her new ring to Christine and Ted and Christine's parents.

Mira made her way back to him eventually, and he put his arm around her, locking her close to his side. "Happy?"

"Yeah. How long were you carrying that ring around?"

"We don't need to talk about it." She didn't need to know he'd created this whole escape room mostly for this purpose.

"Can't possibly be as long as I've carried this one around." She reached into her pocket, and stuck something on his finger.

He withdrew his hand to look at it. He sucked in a quick, sharp breath. At first glance, he thought the ring might be a perfect replica, but then he saw the tiny chip in the gold, from a biking accident he'd had in his twenties. "My dad's ring."

"Yup. Pray we never need you to use it again."

It might be only metal, but he was so happy to have the familiar weight back on his hand. "How did you do this?"

Her eyes were full of secrets, ones he'd happily spend years exploring. "Let's just say, Gladys runs a hard bargain."

Seven Months Later

Mira woke up early. She lay in her bed and watched the light and shadows shift on the ceiling. Today was a special day.

She lifted her hand and gazed at her ring finger. Her mehndi stain had come out a deep dark red, and the design went all the way up her arm. A delicate wedding band would join the engagement ring there today.

She got up from the bed, careful not to wake up Naveen, who was lightly snoring next to her. They were in their new shared house in L.A., so she had to navigate around the boxes on the floor.

She moved down the hallway, some instinct telling her where to go. The scrape in her living room had her lifting an eyebrow. Had she felt any danger, she might have gone and woken up Naveen, but she pressed forward.

The living room looked like a wedding had exploded in it, with silks and fabric all over the place, and that was because it had. Shweta had wanted to do a full week of festivities, but Mira and Naveen had managed to negotiate her down to two events, a Mehndi/Sangeet party and the ceremony/reception. The party had run late into last night. They'd come home around two in the morning from the downtown L.A. rooftop they'd rented, and barely had the energy to peel off their clothes before collapsing into bed.

The mess didn't surprise her, but Sejal standing right in the middle of it all did.

Her sister looked up from the chest. "Oh. Hi."

"Hello." Mira leaned against the door frame. "You look better than the last time I saw you."

Sejal tossed her head. Her short hair was freshly buzzed on one side. A hoop studded her nostril. Her skin was clear and glowing, emphasized by the black leather pants and vest she wore. It must be for aesthetics; Mira couldn't imagine that that much tight fabric would help with mobility. "Thanks. You too."

Mira studied the big duffel Sejal had obviously been stuffing with the contents of the chest. "What are you doing?"

"It's my stuff," Sejal said defensively. "I'm only taking what's due."

Mira nodded. Despite her complicated feelings about her dad, she couldn't help but be happy that Rhea had left her so many beautiful items. She'd figured, at the very least, she could follow her aunt's wishes and honor her only decent parental figure by wearing some of them during her wedding. "I'm not saying you shouldn't take half. Everything I want to use for my wedding is already hung up, anyway. I meant to give you what was left, if I ever saw you again."

"Well, good," Sejal muttered, and continued hauling the items into the bag.

Mira came farther into the room, moving slow, like one might around a skittish animal. "You left before we could talk."

"I didn't want to talk to the cops."

"I wasn't talking about in Vegas. I was talking about yesterday, at the Mehndi."

Sejal licked her lips. She crossed her arms under her chest. She'd been working out. Her biceps were even more defined now. "I don't know what you're talking about."

Mira scoffed. "Just because I went straight doesn't mean I don't remember what Dad taught us. You're not so good at skulking."

"I am fantastic at skulking, I'll have you know."

"Ehhhh." Mira wiggled her hand. "You're a medium-level skulker at best. Why didn't you come say hi?" Her heart had swelled when she'd realized who the shadow at the back of the crowd was, but before she could corner her sister, she'd left.

Sejal snorted and put her hands on her hips. "You don't want me there. Bad enough that our mom made national news. I'm sure there were more than a few people on your man's side who wanted to cancel you over that alone."

Yes, Naveen's mother had naturally had some concerns, especially since Mira had reclaimed her birth name, but she'd rallied a lot faster than they had expected, especially after Naveen had firmly told her Mira's past didn't matter to him. Mira couldn't pinpoint the exact moment that she'd fallen in love with her fiancé, but she'd definitely fallen a little more in love with him right then.

Some others in his extended family hadn't been quite as willing to forgive. When Mira had gotten anxious about that, he'd only shrugged and said it was a great way to narrow their guest list.

He hadn't been wrong. Planning a smaller wedding had been a blessing, and way less stressful.

Mira spoke as calmly and evenly as possible. "If you're embroiled in anything shady, I can help you."

"Aw, Mira. My cute little sister. Always looking out."

"We should look out for each other now. Like we couldn't when we were young. You have to stop running sometime." If Sejal gave her the chance, she'd tell her all about the beauty of not running.

Something flickered over Sejal's face. "It's too late for that."

"Listen, would you like to stay for some chai? Naveen will be up soon. I don't drink it, but he always makes a pot, first thing."

For a second, she wondered if Sejal would accept, but then she zipped up the bag with an air of finality and slung it over her shoulder. "Nah. I hadn't realized what our aunt had left you until I saw you yesterday. That's the only reason I'm here."

That was a lie. Sejal would have skulked properly if she didn't want to see Mira for real. Mira hesitated, then said the words she knew would irritate her sister. "I had no idea you had so much sentimentality. Creeping in to take Rhea Auntie's stuff."

Sejal's lip quirked. Her lack of annoyance should have warned Mira.

She dropped her duffel and went to the dress Mira had

laid out on the couch, the one she'd worn to her Mehndi last night. Mira blinked, and there was a knife in her sister's fist. She took a step back, but Sejal wasn't using the knife for bodily harm. Oh no, it was the dress she was attacking.

Sejal carefully pried a crystal off. She threw it up in the air and caught it, then tossed it to Mira.

Mira turned the blue stone over in her hand. The light hit it, shooting rays of sapphire all over the living room.

Oh shit. It wasn't a plastic gem. It wasn't even a semi-precious stone.

Mira surveyed the dresses with dismay. How was she to know that she was parading around in a veritable fortune in precious gems?

Mira, I very much like these clothes. I see you're finally dressing with the stature befitting a Desai. Be careful, perhaps tone it down for a while, though, given the unfortunate situation with your parents. No need for anyone to wonder where this all came from.

Oh, for crying out . . . she nearly palmed her face. No wonder Shweta had been so complimentary of her aunt's lehenga.

Red and blue and green and clear stones decorated the clothes. Now that she knew what to look for, Mira could immediately tell that they weren't simply decorative textiles, but carefully sewn-in jewels.

"Are you fucking kidding me," she muttered, and she wasn't sure if she was muttering it at her family or the universe in general.

"Rhea Auntie specialized in gems in her heyday. I guess she wanted to make sure you and I were taken care of."

I hope you'll split the contents of your inheritance with your sister, if you can find Sejal, but that's on you.

Her aunt's letter. *That's on you.* The jewels were literally on her. No wonder Rhea had been so insistent that Mira go and get the trunk out of the storage unit before cops found the place. It hadn't been for purely sentimental reasons. "What the hell am I supposed to do with these?"

"Spend them. We deserve something for all the bullshit we've had to put up with." Sejal grabbed her bag again and went to the window and swung her leg through it. Her smirk was as annoying as it had been when they were children. "Knowing you, though, I'm sure you'll help a lot of people once you pawn your half."

Mira refocused on her sister. "I love you."

Sejal froze for a split second. "Come on, now."

"I do. I love you very much, and I hope one day I'll see you again. Soon."

Her sister's throat worked. When she spoke again, it sounded sincere, more sincere than any other words she'd uttered today. "Congratulations, sister. On your wedding, but on life too." She looked over Mira's shoulder, and her face hardened. "If you hurt her, I'll rip each of your teeth out through your ears."

Naveen came to stand next to Mira. "Noted," he said calmly.

With that threat against Mira's bridegroom, Sejal slipped away into the early morning light.

"She could have used the front door," Naveen remarked. Warmth surrounded her as Naveen wrapped her in a sweet embrace. Mira's deepest, most fervent wish was that they never ever be in a life-or-death situation ever again, but yes, it was nice to know that if they were, Naveen was a cool, smart head to have by her side.

Naveen hugged her tighter. She'd discovered that he was a bit of a cuddle bug, and it was actually pretty okay with her. "What did your sister want?"

"Her share of the stuff from the chest." She lifted her shoulders. "We're millionaires."

Naveen sighed, and his reply was tinged with humor. "Where's the password this time?"

"No password. I'm serious." She jerked her chin at the clothes. "My aunt sewed jewels into the clothes. An inheritance for me and Sejal."

He was silent for a minute as he surveyed the fabric all over the room. "Okay. Well, we'll figure this out. Emi's mom, for one, could use the help, yeah?"

Warmth bloomed inside her at his steady, calm confidence and kindness. She couldn't wait to face all of the wild external conflicts they might come across with his unflappable intelligence at her side. "I thought Sejal might have come to see me, but she was here for the money, of course. We're the only family either of us has now, but she doesn't even want me."

"She may not know how to express herself. Either way, you have me." His big hands settled over her belly. "We'll make our own family."

She placed her hands over his. It was still their little secret, this bean inside her, and she hoped she could keep it that way for as long as possible. She'd had to switch to elastic waists lately, and Ted had definitely clocked how tired she was at work, but the symptoms were otherwise pretty manageable. "I know."

"Sejal will come home someday, when she's ready. You can't rush this sort of thing."

"You're right." Mira looked over her shoulder. His hair was sticking straight up, and his eyes were bleary from sleep. He looked utterly beautiful.

Mira had never thought she'd be so gaga over a guy, but here she was. Totally smitten. And, she was happy to note, he was just as smitten. They'd seen so much of each other, both good and bad, and it was all perfect.

"I love you."

"I love you, too."

Their love carried her through the day—through makeup and hair, and the clucking of her soon-to-be in-laws, through the Hindu wedding ceremony around a fire and the Western ceremony they'd opted to have with Christine presiding as their officiant.

It carried her through various Desais looking down their noses at her, and her mother-in-law and brother-in-law and sister-in-law rescuing her from their clutches with smiles and love. It carried her through her grandfather-in-law and Sunil and Wyatt arguing over politics, and Emi disappearing with one of Naveen's cousins, only for both of them to reappear with smudged makeup and messy hair. It carried her through her heel breaking, and Christine literally giving her the shoes off her own feet.

It carried her through running into Hema Auntie, who had opted to wear a silver pantsuit to their wedding. She squealed when she saw them both, her henna-red hair loose and flowing around her shoulders. "Oh my God, what a great success story you two are for me."

They looked at each other. "For you?" Naveen asked.

"Yes, of course. Nothing can beat a human algorithm." She smiled in a superior manner at the people walking by.

"Mmm, I don't think so." Naveen cocked his head. "I believe you fired Mira before we met, yeah?"

Mira tapped her finger on her chin. "Yes, I distinctly remember that voicemail."

Hema sputtered. "I—I introduced you years ago! You were each other's first match. I can't help that you decided to go your separate ways."

Mira made a soothing noise. "That's a valid point, Hema Auntie."

"We will certainly take it under consideration when we write our Yelp review," Naveen added, and guided Mira away.

"Yelp!" Hema nearly shouted. "What is that?"

"That was mean," she said to her new husband.

"Not as mean as she was to you," he said cheerfully. "Come on, we have to go be in love." Naveen guided her away, and Mira allowed it, still thrilled at the word.

It was a good, strong emotion, turning the culmination of months of stressful planning into a dream. So much so, she nearly rubbed her eyes when she saw the dark shadow at the back of the hotel ballroom.

Not again, she thought, and started walking toward the person. Familiarity tugged at the edges of her consciousness, especially as she got closer.

It was when she was fifteen feet away that she realized that this shadow was far too small to be her sister.

Her breath shortened, especially when the shadow slipped out the door soundlessly, ducking behind a larger couple. By the time Mira made it to the hallway, there was no one there.

She looked one way, then the other. She took a few steps and raised her hand to her throat. Then she stooped and picked up the single, half-smoked cigarette that was on the carpeted floor.

"Mira?"

She jumped, but didn't drop the cigarette. "Yes." She stood.

Naveen came toward her, brows knitted together. "Is something wrong?"

"I thought . . ." She looked down the hallway again, then back to the cigarette.

"Someone smoking in here?"

She touched the stick. It had lipstick smudged on one end of it, a deep plum. "Does that look like Clinique's Black Honey to you?"

Naveen slowly took the cigarette from her and examined it. "I have no idea what that means."

"It was on the floor." She took it back, feeling vaguely protective. Though her instincts were telling her to toss the cigarette, she shoved it into the pocket that she'd sewn on to her lehenga.

She tossed her head and put the mysterious wedding crasher out of her mind. For the moment, at least. "Come on. Your mom's had four drinks, minimum."

As expected, that distracted Naveen immediately. "Did you tell the bartender to water hers down?"

"Yes."

"Because last night, she kept going on about the aphrodisiac properties of mehndi after the first three drinks."

"Let's go check on her anyway."

Naveen surprised her by pulling her close as they walked into the ballroom. "One second." To her surprise, he dropped to his knees and patted his thigh. "Put your foot here. Your dress is stuck."

She glanced around the empty hallway, then did as he asked, flushing when he flipped the skirt up. Though they were married, and he'd seen much more, he certainly didn't touch her like this in front of his family.

He gently untangled the caught thread from the silver anklet, the payal, that his mother had gifted her. When he was done, he pressed a kiss on her calf and gave it a quick squeeze. "I love you very much," he said.

"And I, you."

He released her and rose to his feet, offering her his arm. "Let's go be a boring married couple."

As far as she could tell, there was nothing boring about their lives, not to her. Which was why she refused to look over her shoulder, at the empty—or not-so-empty—hallway behind her.

She was only looking forward from here on out.

About the author

About the book

Insights,
Interviews
& More...

Meet Alisha Rai

Elizabeth Burgi

ALISHA RAI pens award-winning contemporary romances. Her novels have been featured on the Indie Next and the LibraryReads lists, and have been named best books of the year by the *Washington Post;* NPR; New York Public Library; Amazon; *Entertainment Weekly; Reader's Digest; Kirkus; O, the Oprah Magazine;* and *Cosmopolitan.* When she's not writing, Alisha is traveling or tweeting.

To find out more about her books or to sign up for her newsletter, visit www.alisharai.com.

A Letter from the Author

Dear Reader,

I don't know if anyone understands how many stars have to align for a book to appear. If I trace the origins of *Partners in Crime*, for example:

I had to move to Los Angeles on a whim, swipe right on a guy who loves poker, have a lot of unexpected time to binge everything on Netflix, go to Vegas with my pandemic boyfriend out of a desperate need for a getaway, spend hours on a road trip brainstorming, and convince multiple smart people to sign off on an idea that I pitched as "like, if *Indian Matchmaking* and *Date Night* had a baby, but set in Las Vegas?" Oh, and then I had to write it.

No one is more amazed than me that all of that resulted in the book you're holding.

I consider this novel my love letter to two places that were integral to my own romance. Artesia is our home away from home, where I first took my then-boyfriend to introduce him to our food when I was isolated from my family, and where he found my engagement ring a year later. Las Vegas is our reliable and regular escape, and the site of half of my elaborate two-step marriage proposal (what good love story doesn't include ▶

A Letter from the Author *(continued)*

Gordon Ramsay? But that's a tale for another time).

It seemed fitting that the only date our Vegas wedding venue had open was around the release date of this book. Truly, the stars aligned.

Thank you so much for reading *Partners in Crime*. I hope it felt like an escape or home, whichever one of those you might need right now.

All my love,
Alisha ∾

Reading Group Guide

1. Do you understand why Mira broke up with Naveen the first time they dated?

2. Mira dumped Naveen via text. What's the harshest way, in your opinion, to break up with someone?

3. What do you like most about Naveen's relationship with his family?

4. Can you empathize with why Mira felt as though she had to hide her past from suitors?

5. Why does Mira continue to pay a matchmaker when she's usually the one who ends up rejecting her matches? Is it understandable pickiness, or something more?

6. Do you think Naveen is right to be so angry with his brother? With Mira?

7. Have you ever been to Vegas? What's your favorite memory of the city?

8. Which scene surprised you the most? ▶

Reading Group Guide *(continued)*

9. Mira and Naveen were initially matched by a matchmaker. Is that any different from using a dating app?

10. What do you think is next for Mira and Naveen? ❧

MORE FROM ALISHA RAI

FIRST COMES LIKE

"With twists and turns right out of a Bollywood drama . . . [a]nother win from this rising romance star."

— *Booklist*

GIRL GONE VIRAL

"*Girl Gone Viral* is a fun, sexy rom-com that's impossible to resist."

— PopSugar

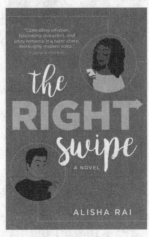

THE RIGHT SWIPE

"Alisha Rai delivers compelling emotion, fascinating characters, and edgy romance in a razor-sharp, thoroughly modern voice that readers will adore. I sure did!"

— Jayne Ann Krentz

HURTS TO LOVE YOU

"True to Rai's style, family secrets and surprises add complexity to this strong story about how wealth and privilege can do as much to destroy happiness as to facilitate it."

— *Publishers Weekly*

WRONG TO NEED YOU

"Rai has crafted a series as deliciously soapy as a CW drama . . . some of the best romance writing of the year here."

— *Entertainment Weekly*

HATE TO WANT YOU

"Alisha Rai blends emotional characters with passionate sensuality in some of the best examples of erotic romance available."

— Sarah MacLean for *The Washington Post*